About the author

Blair Wylie is a retired Canadian oil and gas engineer and manager. He worked for thirty-five years in a number of interesting places, including the Arctic, Western Siberia, the North Sea, Newfoundland, and Trinidad and Tobago. In his second career as a writer, he prefers to stay in the plausible world with respect to science, and character studies. His stories place everyday people in awkward, if not outright terrifying, situations, then have them discover hidden strengths while they rescue themselves. He hopes readers will come away feeling better about themselves, and about the future in general.

THE PERILS OF ISOLATION

A TRILOGY

Blair Wylie

THE PERILS OF ISOLATION

A Trilogy

Vanguard Press

VANGUARD PAPERBACK

A CIP catalogue record for this title is
available from the British Library.

ISBN 978 1 784654 90 0

*Vanguard Press is an imprint of
Pegasus Elliot MacKenzie Publishers Ltd.*
www.pegasuspublishers.com

First Published in 2018

**Vanguard Press
Sheraton House Castle Park
Cambridge England**

Printed & Bound in Great Britain

Mic Muk Mac

1

Greg Naughton woke up at three-thirty in the morning. His head was throbbing, and he needed a drink of water very badly. He also urgently needed to pee.

'First things first, though,' he said to himself. 'Where the hell am I? Oh yea, I'm on the couch in Johnny Carson's living room.'

Incredibly, that started to make sense.

They had finished their last beer at one-thirty in the morning. Greg had been sleeping fully clothed, and he was sweaty.

He was a skinny, twenty-year old guy, with bushy, long blond hair. It was very warm and humid in the old, crappy, one-bedroom, upstairs apartment. The fourth of September in southern Ontario was still basically summertime, and his friend Johnny could not afford an air conditioner.

Greg looked at his watch to confirm the time using the weak light coming from a faraway streetlight through the only window in the small living room. Then he remembered the little alarm clock he had placed on the floor beside the couch, and he turned the alarm off. He noted without surprise that it would have gone off in only a minute or two. Greg seemed to have his own biological clock.

He got up to go to the bathroom. As he went by the closed bedroom door, he banged hard on it, and yelled, "Johnny, it's time to get up!"

He was not surprised when everything was still quiet and dark when he came out of the bathroom.

He went over to the rusty tap in the small, darkened kitchen and poured himself a tall glass of water. After downing the whole glass of lukewarm water without stopping, he poured himself another glass to sip on. Then he banged on the bedroom door again and yelled, "Come on, Johnny, we've got to go!"

There was still no sound from within the room, so Greg opened the door and turned the light on. "Get up, you pecker-head," he growled. "It's three-thirty, and Goolee's waiting."

Johnny covered his eyes with the back of his right arm, and mumbled, "Give me another half hour."

"No way, Jose," said Greg. "Goolee told us he would leave without us if we weren't there by four o'clock. And the last beer was your idea, remember? Now let's *move!*"

"It seemed like a good idea at the time," grumbled Johnny. He got up and put on his pants, tried unsuccessfully to smooth his curly red hair then stumbled to the bathroom.

"It always seems like a *great* idea at the time!" yelled Greg after Johnny had closed the bathroom door. Shouting made his head hurt even more, and he instantly regretted doing it.

It had been a typical Friday night, starting at the local Royal Canadian Legion in their home town of Hounslow, Ontario. Hounslow was a small, conservative, semi-rural place, with two thousand people. It was located southwest of the city of London, at a crossing of two-lane highways. It had evolved into a bedroom community, basically becoming a suburb of the city.

It was 1976, and Pierre Trudeau was the elected prime minister of Canada, and ex-Vice President Gerald Ford was the president of the United States, standing in for the disgraced Richard Nixon.

Greg was glad he had insisted Johnny pack his bag the night before when they got back to Johnny's apartment. Greg knew the only way his best friend was going to be ready on time was to get him to do that, and to stay overnight so that he could wake him up early in the morning. Johnny was *definitely* not a 'morning person'. The truly incredible thing was that Johnny worked nights, stocking shelves in a supermarket. Greg had no idea how Johnny managed to keep his job. But he figured he must be good at it.

When Johnny had put on his shirt, and downed two tall glasses of water, they were ready to go. Physically fit twenty-year-old males could put up with an amazing amount of physical abuse.

After Johnny pulled the door to the outside shut, Greg asked, "Aren't you going to lock it?"

"The lock's broken," said Johnny. "And there's nothing worth stealing in there anyway."

They went down the outside stairs then walked down the gravel lane to Greg's old Volkswagen Beetle. They could hear a loud orchestra of crickets everywhere around them. It was all very quiet otherwise, and it was too early and warm for dew.

The apartment where Johnny lived was on top of an old garage behind a massive, brick, Victorian-era, two-storey house that was owned and occupied by a kind, little old lady. Overhanging the lane were one hundred-year-old maple and oak trees, still fully in green leaf, and dripping water on their heads.

They had driven home in a thunderstorm, and there were still mucky puddles in the lane. The back seat of the small, dilapidated and rusty car was completely filled with their duffle bags, sleeping bags and fishing gear. They had stowed the stuff there the night before.

"The floor's still wet, and so is the seat!" said Johnny with disgust as he reluctantly climbed into the front passenger seat. The windows were completely fogged on the inside. They rolled the door windows down, and Greg wiped the inside of the windshield with an old rag. The vents in the floor were rusted in the open position, and water had gushed in the night before during the short drive to Johnny's place.

"That's not the only thing wrong with this two hundred dollar 'sports car'," warned Greg. "I hope your landlady and your neighbours have a sense of humour."

Johnny started laughing when Greg started the car and revved the engine. It was as loud as a stock car.

"What's wrong with it again?" yelled Johnny.

"It's got an air-cooled engine!" yelled Greg in return. "The heat exchanger for interior heat rusted off, and so has the exhaust manifold now! I couldn't afford to fix it, and with no back pressure, I bet I get another five whopping horsepower, too! It's amazing how *peppy* this Bug is with sixty-five horsepower!"

Greg backed the old car on to the main street of the previously silent town in a cloud of blue smoke. They both couldn't help laughing as they drove along. With the windows down in the car they could just barely hear the angry backyard dogs barking in protest over the racket they were making.

Goolee lived with his widowed mother on the outskirts of Hounslow, but it was still only a short drive away. As they pulled up to his house, they could see Goolee about to pull a tarp over his small fibreglass powerboat. It was on an old trailer hooked up to his equally old Chevy pickup truck. Gurdy and Scotty were helping him with the tarp. Scotty's small Toyota Corolla SR5 car was parked at the entrance to the driveway. Greg's only option for now was to park his car on the road in front of Goolee's house.

"It's only Johnny and The Professor," said Gurdy when he saw Greg and Johnny walking up the paved driveway. Then he quipped, "Hell, I thought it was *Richard Petty* coming up the road." Gurdy was a somewhat short but muscular nineteen year old young man, with light brown hair. He was about to enlist in the navy.

"At least you got here before Dick and Wally," said Goolee, eying Greg and Johnny carefully to confirm they were fairly sober. They looked okay, so he said, "Better go back and get your stuff, you guys. We'll put it all in the boat before we put the tarp on." Goolee was a stocky and powerfully built young man. He lifted weights and drove a truck for a local lumber dealer.

As they hoisted their bags into the boat, Goolee asked, "How are you getting away with driving that shit box of yours, Mr. Professor?"

"Well, actually, it has to go into the shop when I get back," said Greg. "My old man needed to borrow it Thursday night, and a lady OPP officer stopped him here in town. When he said it was owned by his 'poor university student son', and wasn't his, the cop just said, 'Well, fix it for him, and stop being so cheap!' So, that's what he's going to do!" They all laughed with Greg.

Goolee bent down to look at the right wheel on the trailer. "With all the food, gear and the beer stowed in the boat, and in the truck, we're over-loaded," he said with concern. "But I greased up the bearings on the trailer, and the tyres are good. We should get there all right. And we'll be a lot lighter coming home."

Just then, a jacked-up Ford Galaxy sedan with extra-wide rear tyres and puffing dual-exhausts pulled up in front of the house with a deep growl. The driver parked it in front of Greg's car. "That's Dick and Wally," said Goolee. Then he added, "I'll go and get Mac now. Geez, this could be interesting. What a pain in the arse."

Goolee walked across the front lawn to the house next door on the right side of his mother's house. He waved at Dick and Wally as they were walking up the driveway to where the others were standing. Dick was a tall, dark-haired athletic guy who just started working as a letter carrier for the post office. He played centre for a 'Junior C' hockey team. Wally was a bit shorter, with short blond hair, and he was also athletic. Wally was a farmer's son and pitched for the town's Junior Men's fast-pitch softball team. Most of the others in the fishing group played for the team as well, but mostly just for a laugh. Wally was engaged and had started studying drafting in college.

Everyone had a nickname. Some names were obvious choices. With his last name, Doug Carson just had to become 'Johnny' Carson. William Gould was 'Goolee', and Angus Sinclair was 'Scotty' after the Star Trek character. Angus could do a very good imitation of an old Scot, inspired by the way his grandfather talked. Helmut Gurtman had become 'Gurdy'. His friends knew he *hated* his real first name and would call him 'Helmut' when they really wanted to piss him off. Gregor Naughton was called 'The Professor', after the Gilligan's Island character, as he sometimes went well off on tangents, and talked about scientific things most people didn't know anything about. He was also a bit more conservative than his friends. They called Richard Laurier 'Dick', and Jeff Walters 'Wally'.

The young men shared some coffee that Wally had brought with him in a thermos bottle. When Goolee came back up the driveway, walking beside him were Michael 'Mac' McDuffie and Mac's father, James. Goolee was carrying Mac's sleeping bag, while his father was carrying Mac's large duffle bag. Mac was carrying a cheap fishing rod and a small tackle box.

Everyone said formally, "Good morning, Mister McDuffie."

"Good morning, lads!" said James with a broad smile. He was a friendly-looking, dark-haired man of average size, but with huge triceps like the cartoon character Popeye. He had worked on cars all of his life. He added happily, "The missus and I are *sure glad* you're doing this for Michael! We *know* you'll take really good care of him.

"Now, Michael, you do exactly what your friends tell you to do, and if you give them any trouble, they'll bring you straight back here. And I'll have to make it up to them somehow." Mr. McDuffie then shook everyone's hand using both of his large hands, squeezing really hard, and then he walked back down the driveway, while waving back at them a couple of times.

Mac had been a tall, handsome guy with brown, curly hair. But he had a nasty scar on his forehead now, and he walked with a limp. He had once been a smart teenager with a passion for science-fiction, and girls. But he also had a passion for excessive drinking, dope smoking, arguing and fighting; and for driving way too fast while totally intoxicated. He had caused a head-on collision eight months before. The driver in the other car had thankfully only come away with a broken leg and a broken collarbone.

But Mac's extensive injuries had included severe head trauma. He had been in a coma for a month. He had only started talking a few months before, and his recovery was going slowly. He was now behaving like a ten-year-old boy for the most part.

Mac's father, James, was a high school auto-mechanics teacher. He had re-built an Audi Fox for his son, Mac. It was a high-performance car that had been in at least one previous accident. When Mac finally 'totalled' the Audi, and nearly 'totalled himself', James had felt guilty as hell.

James had known his neighbours, the Goulds, since William was a toddler. James, and his wife, Alice, were overjoyed when Goolee and his friends agreed to take Mac along with them on what had become an annual fishing trip to Lake Nipissing. 'The doctors say this will be the best therapy for him, William,' James had told Goolee. Then he explained, 'Putting him in a situation with his old friends away from us might help bring back the old Michael, they say.'

When James McDuffie was out of earshot, Goolee looked at his friends and said, "Okay, let's throw Mac's stuff in the back of the truck and get started. It's a *long way* to Parry's Landing, and we have to be there by eleven o'clock because the camp boat will leave the dock right at noon.

"The Professor will come with me, in the truck." Greg was the most experienced driver in the group other than Goolee. Then Goolee added, "Scotty will take Mac and the 'Hurdy Gurdy Man' along with him and follow us. So that means Johnny and Dick will go with Wally in his 'dragster' and follow Scotty. We'll all stop for gas in Barrie, and for breakfast in Huntsville. We can switch around a few times if we want to smell different beer farts." Everyone but Mac laughed at that. Mac just stood there looking very confused, and a bit scared.

"I want to go with Goowie in the twuck," said Mac with a lisp.

"That's not going to happen, Mac," said Goolee forcefully. "It's got a floor-mounted stick shift, and there's no room for you."

Mac looked like he was going to cry. Then he whined, "I want to go in the twuck."

"No, you're either going in Scotty's car, or not at all," said Goolee firmly. When Mac hesitated, Goolee said, "Give me his stuff, I'm taking him home."

"Okay, I'll go with Scotty," said Mac with a pout. Everyone was sadly and silently shocked again by what had happened to their friend.

While Scotty and Gurdy got Mac sorted out in the back seat of Scotty's small but mechanically sound two-door car, Greg parked his thundering, dilapidated Beetle at the edge of Goolee's driveway. He left enough space for Goolee's mother to get past it with her car during the week they would be away.

Then Greg hopped in the passenger side of Goolee's truck, and they started down the road with the boat in tow, and the others closely following behind.

They had managed to get away by four o'clock.

2

Greg was gradually feeling better. He had sipped on two more cups of coffee, this time out of Goolee's thermos bottle. They were just passing Kitchener on Highway 401, and dawn was just minutes away. It was going to be a hot, humid, sunny day, but they didn't need to roll their windows down quite yet.

"How are the others doing behind us?" asked Greg.

"They keep passing each other, probably for something to do," replied Goolee while looking in the rear-view mirror. Then he added with a laugh, "Kids, you can't take them anywhere!"

"So, what's the deal this year with a cabin, Goolee?" asked Greg.

"Same as last year," replied Goolee happily. Then he explained, "We'll have the big 'deluxe' cabin with three bedrooms and two fold-away cots in the living area. I figured the newcomers, Mac and Wally, can have the cots.

"Yesterday I talked to grumpy old Neil, the camp owner, on his radio-telephone. He's got two of the four older and smaller cabins rented out this weekend. We'll have the *whole* camp to ourselves when those people leave on Tuesday." Goolee was working the steering wheel a lot, and continually looking in the rear-view mirror.

"Is something going on with the truck, or the trailer?" asked Greg with concern.

"The steering wheel has a lot of slop in it," replied Goolee. Then he added, "You have to let the truck start wandering a bit before making a correction. And when you do make a correction, the trailer with all of its weight takes a lurch. I'll get us past Toronto, and then you can see for yourself."

"Oh, boy, I can't wait," said Greg, with a grin. "Sure you don't want Mac for company?"

Goolee looked over at Greg for a second. Then he said grimly, "I'm really sorry about this. I can't believe I got talked into it. I took pity on Mac's mother and father I guess. It's been really hard on them, and they clearly need a break. He's like a bad little kid now, you know, a brat."

Greg waited a minute, and then he asked, "So, is Mac going to court soon?"

"You won't believe this one," said Goolee while shaking his head. Then he explained, "The cops decided not to charge him with anything, I guess because of his serious injuries. And the guy he injured won't press charges. Mac's father made him an offer to pay his additional medical expenses and buy him a better car than insurance would provide, and the guy accepted!"

"It's an *amazing* time we live in, Goolee," said Greg, also shaking his head. Then he said, "The drinking age went down from twenty-one to eighteen in 1971. There's booze in the high schools, and dope and harder drugs, too. The cops and our parents must be really frustrated with the system, and maybe they've even given up to some degree. Hell, I shouldn't be driving myself some nights. I know it, but it seems I'm always the only one with a licence and a car. And the damn thing is, with all of my practice, I'm actually good at it."

"You *are* good at it, I've noticed," said Goolee. Then he added, "You drive slower and smoother when you've been drinking, and that's the *opposite* of most people. And the cops are watching out for young hotshot guys in 'muscle cars', not long-haired hippies in Volkswagen Beetles."

"Well, I'm not proud of myself, Goolee," said Greg. Then he admitted, "I think I've mostly just been lucky, and I'm going to stop before my luck runs out." They both starting thinking about the bad experiences some of their friends had been through, including Mac.

"Back to Mac, the very worst time to be in his car was when he had a few drinks, and Golden Earring's 'Radar Love' came on the radio," said Greg. Then he added, "For some reason, that song *meant* something to him. He would crank the volume right up, and floor it. Hell, he was doing well over one hundred and sixty kilometres an hour on Highway Two one day with me and Johnny after we went golfing near Delaware, and he wouldn't slow down to just 'regular speeding' until the song was over!"

"I heard that about Mac," said Goolee. "I just *refused* to ride with him." Then he laughed, and added, "Well, I did end up with him once. I drove out to Wally's farm near Glanworth, and I got pretty loaded. I figured correctly that I better not drive, but then I foolishly hopped in with Mac. He immediately got us lost in the trees on the farm looking for a 'short cut'. We were on a really narrow, muddy trail, and we came up to these two big trees in the pitch-black dark. I could *see* there was *no way* the trees were far enough apart to get through them with the car, and I told Mac that.

"But you know Mac, he would argue about *anything*, and do his utmost to prove you wrong. He wedged his Audi in so tight we got completely stuck and couldn't open any doors! We had to crawl out a window. We spent the night in Wally's barn, and I drove us home in the morning. Mac went back with his father the next day. They had to ask permission to cut a tree down to free up the car." Goolee laughed again, and Greg joined him.

"You might not have heard this one about Mac," said Greg. Then he explained, "You were heading up to Nipissing to fish with your brother last year when we went to a fastball game on a Friday night on one of the reserves. I forget which one. We had a great time and joked around a lot as usual with the Indian guys during the game. I remember, though, that Wally almost pitched a perfect game, and had all of his 'best stuff', spinning the ball off his thigh, and he had a great knuckle ball.

"Anyway, the Indian guys, and the reserve cop who was watching the game, were all cool with the scene, and knew we were all going to leave as always in a convoy right after the game. Mac had come along with us as our only spectator. We didn't find out that Mac hadn't come back with us until we were sitting in the Army-Navy back in Hounslow having a beer.

"Incredibly, he decided to go on the reserve to play poker and got drunk. He was *stupid* enough to win and get in a bit of a scrap. He took off in his car down a gravel road, but a group of guys came up behind him, and threw an unopened beer bottle through the rear window of his car. It exploded inside!

"Mac stopped the car somehow and kept it on the road. They hauled Mac out of his car and roughed him up a little, but not too bad. Then they threw his glasses into the woods on one side of the road, and his keys went into the woods on the other side.

"They left him there by himself. The reserve cop picked Mac up, and threw him in jail for, 'trespassing on the reserve'. His poor old man had to bail him out and get his car out of hock! They used some spare keys to get his car home. Mac's older sister had to drive one of the cars because Mac had no glasses."

"I haven't heard that one before, but there are others like it," said Goolee with a grim smile. Then he added, "And then there's Gurdy. He didn't exactly get off to a fine start."

Gurdy had his licence taken away at the start of the previous summer. He and his brothers had been at the family cottage up in Kincardine. They went out for a 'crop tour' in their father's car with a case of beer. Gurdy's younger brother, Kurt, was sitting behind Gurdy, and decided it would be somehow funny to reach around with his hands and cover Gurdy's eyes while he was driving.

Gurdy had swerved off the road and taken out a telephone pole with a transformer on it. The little resort village had no power over a holiday weekend, and Gurdy was charged with drunk driving and spent a night in jail. His father bailed him out, and eventually paid to replace the telephone pole and the transformer. To their credit, Gurdy's brothers owned up to what happened. But none of them was allowed to drive the *new* family car.

"I guess there's also Scotty," said Greg. Then he speculated, "He must be awfully close now to losing his licence on demerit points."

Scotty had just got another speeding ticket. The winter before, he had been charged with careless driving. He was an excellent goal tender, and he had been drinking beer in the dressing room after a 'Junior D' hockey game in Belmont. On the way home, he thought the car ahead of him was being driven by a friend on his team. He raced up behind the car a few times, slamming on the brakes each time just in time to avoid a rear-end collision. Then the blue and red lights went on in the back window of the car ahead. It was an unmarked police car, and the OPP officer was far from impressed with his story.

"I just can't even think about drinking and driving," said Goolee. Then he explained, "My livelihood depends upon being able to drive. But I've done my share of stupid things too, while sober but maybe a bit hung-over. I once almost tried to take a three-and-a-half metre high truck through a three-metre high tunnel. The cops had to stop traffic to let me back up down a busy road. I got a big ticket for 'obstructing traffic'."

"No other generation has been through this, Goolee," said Greg seriously. Then he added, "You and I had our driver's licence at sixteen. There's no picture on the licence, and pubs accept it as proof of age. So, a lot of young people are borrowing licences and getting into bars and taverns underage, which means some sixteen and seventeen-year-old teenagers are in bars. I always get asked for proof of age and get suspicious looks whenever I show them my licence. But I still get served." Greg looked more like eighteen, not twenty. Goolee looked his age of twenty.

Greg and Goolee sat quietly for a few minutes. Then Goolee tried a few radio stations. "Sounds like *both* kinds of music this morning on the old 'squawk box', country *and* western," he said with a chuckle, then turned off the radio. Both young men were into rock.

"You went up earlier this summer, didn't you?" asked Greg.

"Yep, I took Jenny up with me first week of July, and we stayed with my brother Bob and his wife," said Goolee. Then he added, "They just built a cabin on Lake Nipissing, about five kilometres from Camp Mic Muk. We'll pass it on the way in, but they're not there now." Jenny was Goolee's girlfriend. They had been going out for about a year. Everyone liked Jenny; she was an energetic and athletic blond-haired farm girl with a great sense of humour, and the same common sense as Goolee.

"What was the fishing like?" asked Greg.

"The pickerel fishing was really good, when we could get out on the lake," said Goolee. "It was *rougher than hell* half of the time. I almost got sick once, and that hasn't happened to me since when I was a kid. I used to get car sick even, so I must be susceptible or something. It's usually a lot less stormy this time of year. But the fishing might not be as good now. There's a lot of rod pressure in the summer."

"While you were fishing, I was learning how to install telephones and the new telephone jacks," said Greg. Then he smiled and added, "But I made some really good money this summer, and with free room and board from my parents, I should have enough 'dough' to get through another year at Western. That means I can get you in the student side for free again if you want to see another football game?"

"Count on that!" said Goolee loudly. Then he yelled, "Hard on, you Mustangs!" After a deliberate pause he added, "I don't get that cheer at all. It must be a *lot* more difficult to play with a 'hard on'." After a laugh at his own joke, he asked, "What was your first year of engineering like?"

"Humiliating," replied Greg, with a frown. Then he confessed, "I went from 'As' in Grade Thirteen to 'Bs' and 'Cs' and even a few 'Ds'. But I got through it. It's supposed to get easier, if you make it to fourth year. Half the first year class won't be coming back though." He paused for a second, then he laughed and said, "The professors actually *encourage* engineers to do pranks, maybe to let off some steam and keep our sanity.

"Johnny helped me with one. There's this three-panel wall sculpture hanging outside a side door to the old engineering building. There's a human female breast on the first or left-side panel, then this 'blob' that looks a bit like a brain on the middle panel, and then a blank panel on the right. I think the artist was trying to represent the human life-cycle in brutal terms, you know, birth, life and death?

"Anyway, I made a big ugly nose out of paper mache stretched over chicken wire, with plywood for backing, and a hanger made of flat, thin wood. I painted it really carefully all the same green-grey colour as the sculpture. Then at the end of March, just before the start of a night shift, Johnny helped me sneak up to the sculpture and hang the nose on the empty panel.

"On my way to classes the next day, I saw it was still up there. The Dean was standing in front of it, smiling and looking at it while smoking his pipe. I think that means he approved. That was better than getting an 'A' for something!"

Goolee laughed with Greg. "So, when do you start back at school?" he asked.

"A week from this Monday," replied Greg. Then he added, "Geez, Goolee, I just installed my last telephone yesterday. I've got to pack a *whole* summer vacation into one freaking week!"

"Well, you've got some friends to help you do that," said Goolee with a big grin. Then he laughed and said, "We'll have a few 'yuk-yuks' at Mic Muk, don't you worry about that."

3

The three vehicles cruised in tandem through Toronto ahead of the morning traffic, making the turn on to Highway 400 to go north. They stopped for gas, and switched the drivers around, just past Barrie. They were then on Highway 11, which went on to become the Trans-Canada Highway at North Bay, just after their turn-off point to go west to their final destination, Parry's Landing.

The whole trip would cover a little over four hundred and eighty kilometres, but they would average only about eighty kilometres per hour. Goolee did not want to push the wheel bearings on his rusty old trailer too hard.

They got to Huntsville just before nine o'clock and pulled into a diner for breakfast. Everyone was stretching and yawning as they climbed out of the vehicles. Greg was glad his 'hitch' at the wheel was over. Fighting the truck all the way from Barrie had been gruelling work.

Goolee hung back to go into the restaurant last with Scotty, his best friend. "How did you get on with Mac?" he asked Scotty quietly just outside the door.

"Man, what a pain in the ass he is," replied Scotty with disgust after letting the door close behind their friends. "He must have asked, 'Are we there yet?' a dozen times. And he's got a bag of cookies with him he doesn't want us to know about for some reason. We hear the 'rustle, rustle' sound as he's fishing in the bag for another one, and when we look back at him, he closes his mouth and stops chewing, with crumbs hanging from his lips!"

"Then, do you want me to take him for a while?" asked Goolee. Then he added, "The Professor gave me a good break at the wheel."

"No, that's all right, we're almost there anyway," replied Scotty, shaking his head. "Come on, let's get something to eat." Then they went inside and joined the others.

The restaurant was packed. An elderly, friendly waitress sat them together at a long table that was still being cleared by a teenage boy. "Sorry, guys, this is probably our busiest weekend up here," said the waitress cheerfully. Then she added, "But it shouldn't take more than a minute, and I'll come back with your menus, and some coffee."

When they had ordered some breakfast, and were drinking their coffee, Goolee said, "We're making really good time guys. It's all downhill from here."

"So, how long will the boat trip take?" asked Wally. As one of the newcomers, he was a bit apprehensive.

"Old Neil's got an old, steel hulled cabin cruiser he calls the 'Lady Mic'," replied Goolee. Then he laughed and said, "He probably should have called it the 'Lady Muk'. It draws a lot of water, and he's got it stuck in the East River a couple of times close to Parry's Landing, where he docks to pick up paying guests like us. The old hulk only makes about ten kilometres per hour, and the trip to Camp Mic Muk is about thirty kilometres. So, on a calm day like we'll probably have, it'll take about three hours. I'll do it in about half that time in my boat. I'll go on ahead with Mac, and get the cabin organised."

Goolee stopped talking while their orders were placed in front of them. Most of the young men had selected bacon and eggs. Mac had just wanted chocolate milk, but Goolee had ordered him a full breakfast.

After a few minutes of serious eating, Wally asked, "So, what's with the name 'Mic Muk'?"

Goolee laughed and said, "I asked Neil about that once. His last name is McManaman, and he wanted something that sounded a bit like that. Apparently 'Mac Man' sounded too much like 'Pac Man'; or 'McMahon', as in Ed McMahon, you know, the side-kick of the real Johnny Carson on TV, not our Johnny. Old Neil doesn't like Ed McMahon for some reason.

"And he didn't want to use 'Mic Mac', because that's a name of an Indian tribe, and he didn't want to piss-off the Dokis people who have a reserve nearby on the French River. So, somehow he figured 'Mic Muk' was the way to go. That doesn't make a lot of sense, does it?"

"Well, he had to name it something, I guess," said Johnny, who was sitting beside Goolee. "I bet alcohol was involved when he decided on the name, though."

"So, what will be the sleeping arrangements?" asked Wally.

"Mac and you are the rookies, so you'll get the cots by the eating table. The rest of us get to use double beds in the three bedrooms." He stopped to put his arm around Johnny. "Surprise, surprise, I get to sleep with my best buddy Johnny Carson, golllllleee, Shazam!" He said it in a voice like Gomer Pyle USMC, the comic character on TV.

"Get your arm off me, you silly bugger!" yelled Johnny with a laugh while pulling away. Then he said, "I'm just glad I've got a zipper on my sleeping bag that only opens from the inside!"

Then they all laughed with Johnny. The people at the next table had overheard Goolee in his high-pitched drawl, and they were laughing too.

"How about the food, and how much do we owe for the cabin?" asked Wally.

"Forty dollars each for the food to me," replied Goolee. Then he explained, "We have to take in our own food, and we're going to eat well since I picked it all out. And eighty dollars each for the cabin, which includes two cedar-strip boats with twenty-horse motors for the week.

"I'll need it all in cash, please, because that's what Neil wants. So, it'll be a pretty cheap holiday. We'll have to pay for the gas we use, which won't be very much. And you've already bought your beer, which is in my boat, and the booze you stuffed into your bags."

Every man checked his wallet to confirm he had enough money. Goolee said, "We'll settle up at the end, don't worry about that now guys."

"So, we're only allowed one case of beer each?" asked Gurdy with disgust.

"Yep, old Neil wasn't very impressed with us last year, I guess," said Goolee. Then he shook his head, and added, "He said he got *complaints* from the people who rode in on the boat with us. Something about us corrupting their young children with our vices."

"Well, I hope they're old enough now to find out what weed smells like," said Gurdy with a look of protest on his face. Gurdy always brought a bag of marijuana on the trip, and passed a joint to anyone who wanted a toke.

"No worries about that, unless you light up on the boat, which would be really stupid," said Goolee. "The deluxe cabin is at the far edge of the camp. And I'm sure old Neil will have the other guests close to his house this year, at the other end of the camp. He knows us, *oh so well*."

4

They arrived in the village of Powassan just after ten thirty in the morning. It was time to exit Highway 11 and travel west. The turn-off place was easy to remember; there was an Ontario Provincial Police, or 'OPP', station at the corner.

They made their left turn on to a narrower, two lane, scarified road. There were a few potholes, so Goolee had to slow right down to protect the old trailer from damage. When he was relaxed again at the wheel, Greg asked, "Do you remember, Goolee, when you picked me up at that 'cop shop' two years ago? My mother had dropped me off there, and then she went back to the cottage she had rented with my dad in Parry Sound."

Goolee laughed at the memory, and said, "Yea, a cop almost arrested you for vagrancy."

"Actually, he said I was 'defacing a public property' with my long-haired hippy appearance, and I needed to get my 'patched-up, blue jeaned arse' out of sight of *his* highway," said Greg with a laugh. Then he added, "But then he actually helped me carry my bags, behind the building."

"*Damned hippies*, served you right!" laughed Goolee.

The drive along the narrow, winding road through the countryside was slow but very pleasant. It was a warm, sunny day, so they rolled the windows down in the truck. The small farms along the road had stone and split-rail fences. The countryside was rustic and picturesque.

When they got to Parry's Landing, they saw that the big camp boat, the Lady Mic, was tied up at the dock. Two other groups of people were loading their stuff on to the boat. There was no sign of Neil anywhere, but that was to be expected. He would be in town, shopping.

Goolee and Greg didn't recognise the other people. They appeared to be two married couples with their children.

Goolee stopped the truck near the camp boat, and he and Greg got out. Then Goolee said, "Let's unload the truck and the stuff in my boat right here. And then we'll launch the boat down at the ramp."

Goolee waved and smiled at the other people. "How are you folks doing today?" he called to them while taking the ropes off the tarp on his boat.

"Just fine, how are you?" one of the men yelled in return, while struggling with an armful of canned carbonated sweet drinks. All the adults in the other group were smiling and laughing, and they looked like nice people. Then Greg and Goolee saw some canned beer going aboard, and that looked hopeful for defusing a potential conflict with Neil. There would be greater strength in numbers now.

"How can you not feel *great* at the start of a vacation, and on a fine, sunny day like this one?" asked Goolee, and the strangers all nodded and smiled back at him.

Wally and Scotty then pulled up in their cars, and parked close to the camp boat as well. Everyone got out and started unloading baggage. Then they worked a 'bucket brigade' to load it all on to the big, old boat. The two, presumably married, men they just met stepped in to help, and it took very little time to complete the loading. Goolee remembered how Neil liked to stow stuff, and he mostly just supervised what the others were doing. Then Goolee went back to his truck, and backed it up to launch his boat at the ramp nearby.

Goolee made it look easy. When the trailer wheels were just into the water, Scotty stepped out along the tongue of the trailer, released the bow-latch and grabbed the bow-line. He threw the cheap nylon rope over to Greg who was standing on the small wharf, and then Scotty jumped down off the tongue on the trailer. Then Goolee backed the trailer up until the boat was afloat. Greg tied the bow-line off on a cleat on the wharf. He then reached down with a boat hook to grab the stern-line, and tied it off as well. They were in business.

"Follow me up the road with the two cars, and I'll show you where to park!" yelled Goolee through the open window of his truck. He then pulled the empty trailer up the ramp, and went up the gravel road out of sight, with water streaming off the old, rusty, trailer the whole way.

About fifteen minutes later, Goolee, Scotty and Wally were walking back down the gravel road to the dock with Neil alongside. They were all carrying bags of groceries. Neil was a fit-looking man in his early fifties. He was a little below average height, with short, curly-grey hair, and a tanned face. Neil greeted everyone with a handshake and a smile. He even shook the children's hands. He looked to be in a really good mood.

Neil was in an even *better* mood when he saw that everything had been stowed in the boat the way he liked to do it himself.

He must have seen the cases of beer, but he said nothing.

"Climb aboard everyone, and we'll get underway!" said Neil cheerily as he started the old diesel engine in the boat. Greg noted they were getting away a bit early at eleven thirty.

"I have my own boat again this year, Neil!" called Goolee from the wharf using his hands as a megaphone. Then he motioned for Mac to step down into the boat, and said, "Come on, Mac, let's get going ourselves." Mac had spent the whole time while they were getting ready throwing stones into the water from the dock.

It took a few minutes for Neil to manoeuvre the big old boat away from the dock and turn around in the bend of the slow-moving, muddy river. Goolee was still trying to start the old thirty-horsepower, two-stroke outboard motor on his boat when the Lady Mic moved out of sight around the bend in the river.

It was about two kilometres from Parry's Landing on the East River to East Bay. There were a lot of fallen down willow trees extending well away from the river banks, making the navigable channel very narrow in places. The other vacationers and their kids enjoyed seeing turtles sliding into the water as they were passing, and they saw a couple of Blue Herons stalking small fish in the shallows. The banks looked a bit like a mangrove swamp. The underbrush was thick, right down to the water.

"Where are you folks from?" asked Greg with a smile. Everyone had gathered in the open area under a steel canopy at the back of the Lady Mic. It was too hot down in the cabin. Johnny had already started playing around and laughing with the kids. If there was ever a man destined to be married with children, it was Johnny. He loved kids, and he was good with them.

"Toronto," said one of the men. He seemed happy to see someone else was entertaining the children now. So he added, "Hi, I'm Steve, and this is my wife, Penny." Everyone started shaking hands all around. The adults were all in their thirties. Steve was dark-haired and a bit overweight, and Penny was a cheerful looking red-haired woman. They were wearing sweat pants, and matching tee-shirts from Disneyland.

The other lady said, "And I'm Janet, and this is my husband, Philip. These are our children, Margaret and Christopher. Margaret is ten, and Christopher is eight." Janet was a short brunette, and Philip was tall and skinny with a bald head. They were dressed in expensive-looking European hiking clothes. Phillip looked a bit suspicious of the long-haired young men.

"And these little rascals are Jake and Max, our two boys," said Penny. Then she added, "Jake is eleven, and Max is nine." She grabbed the two boys as they were running around, and got them to shake hands with all the young men.

"Have you been up here before?" asked Gurdy.

"No, it's the first time for all of us," replied Penny. Then she added hopefully, "We've heard it's a really great place though."

"You'll really like it, I'm sure, and so will your kids," said Greg. Then he added, "There's a nice sand beach. They don't have showers, so you actually have to jump in the lake to keep clean. But the water will be warm when it's sunny. The cabins are a bit basic, with old wood-burning stoves inside, and cold water piped in by gravity from a tank above a well. The water is okay to drink, but it's got iron in it. And you have to use an outhouse. But there's an old refrigerator in each place, and a communal freezer for the fish you decide to keep."

"Well, the kids really liked camping, and that sounds like a step up from that," said Janet. Then she added, "We brought a camping stove to cook with, and a lot of our camping gear, probably too much just for a long weekend."

"You'll make out just great," said Dick with a smile.

"It's a long trip in, isn't it?" asked Philip. He looked to be finally relaxing a bit around the young men.

Greg looked at Neil who was seated at the wheel. They were passing out through channel markers into the bay. Neil probably heard the question too, but was concentrating on his duties as skipper. So Greg decided it was okay to say, "It'll be about three hours, probably. The bay looks calm, and that's a good thing."

"The brochure said a boat and motor comes with each cabin," said Steve, who looked a bit worried. Then he confessed, "I've only operated a boat once. And Philip and Janet have never even been in a small boat. Are they tricky to operate?"

"Just tell Neil your situation," replied Greg with a cavalier tone. He looked at Neil, but he didn't engage, so Greg added, "He'll give you some coaching, I'm sure. But you should probably only go out when it's calm, and stay fairly close to the camp. You'll still get lots of fish.

"The boats are made locally, on the north shore of Lake Nipissing. They're a bit like wooden canoes with varnished oak frames and cedar strips, and with painted, canvas-covered bottoms. They're really strong, but they're also a bit rounded on the bottom, and a bit narrow for their length. They roll pretty badly when they're not pointed right into big waves.

"And there's not much freeboard at the stern, so if you're going in the direction of big waves, you have to adjust your speed to 'surf' down the front of a wave. Otherwise, you can take on green water if a wave breaks over the back." He could see the married adults were now looking really agitated, so he added, "But you won't have to worry about *any* of that if you only go out in nice weather. The waves come up really fast on the lake in a storm, and they're closely spaced together because it's shallow in places. So, if you see storm clouds, just head for home, and you'll be okay."

They were out of East Bay and out on the lake when they finally caught sight of Goolee's boat coming up behind them. "That motor on his boat *did* look a bit suspect," said Wally.

"He'll be fighting that beast all week," said Gurdy, shaking his head.

When Goolee passed them with a relaxed wave of his hand, they could see Mac sitting at the back of the boat with his arms crossed. He looked to be sulking in silence.

It was a pleasant journey, but it was starting to get a bit boring by the time they were getting closer to the camp. There were just a few cabins here and there along the southern shore of Lake Nipissing. The road ended at Parry's Landing, so everyone had to get to his or her summer cabin by boat.

There were a lot of small boats to be seen at the start of their journey, usually closer to shore where most people were fishing. The cabins became fewer and farther apart the further along the shoreline they travelled. There was very little wind, and the fumes from the old diesel engine were annoying at times.

"That's Cross Point," said Greg to Steve, while pointing. Then he added, "It's a pretty good fishing spot. There's a rock shoal extending well out from it. You can see the wooden cross on the shore. It might actually be a grave, but it's a pretty useful landmark."

About twenty minutes later, Greg told the newcomers, "The camp is just around the next point. The start of the French River is straight ahead, about five kilometres."

The camp was in a bay protected by headlands on either side. The cabins were spaced out along the broad beach within the bay. As they were going into the bay, they could see wooden docks on piles on the left side, and a big boathouse on a rock outcropping where Neil hoisted the Lady Mic out of the water every winter. Neil's house was about thirty paces away from the boathouse. Neil's wife, Jill, was waiting for them with a big old Labrador retriever. She was standing on the biggest dock beside a gas pump. She caught the lines tossed over to her by Neil and tied off the boat. When Neil had turned the big inboard engine off, Jill said with a smile to everyone, "Welcome to Camp Mic Muk!" Jill was in her early fifties as well. She was blonde, fit and good-looking, and could have passed for forty.

Neil stepped over to the dock from the high gunwale, kissed Jill on the cheek, turned back to face his paying guests and said, "I'll go get the tractor and the wagon now. If you folks could offload your gear and carry it up beside the boathouse, it would really help us get you settled quickly into your cabins."

5

The young men walked right behind the wagon that was packed with their baggage. It was being pulled by an old tractor along the sandy trail under the pine trees beside the beach.

When they reached their 'deluxe cabin' at the very end of the trail, they saw Goolee come out of the cabin door. He helped them unload the wagon. Then Neil rode off on the tractor with the empty, dilapidated, handmade wagon bouncing along behind. Neil gave them a friendly wave of his hand, and they yelled back to him, "Thanks, Neil!"

Goolee had taken a cooler with him in his boat, and had left some sandwich materials out for them inside the cabin, and some stubby bottles of cold beer. After stowing their food and gear in the big cabin, they all took a seat on the shady wooden deck beside the cabin, and enjoyed a sandwich and a beer. There were a few deer flies buzzing around, but the mosquitoes were not too bad.

"Jill says the fishing has been really slow," Goolee mumbled through a mouthful of another sandwich. Then he swallowed, and added, "I think we should take it easy for a while, and maybe get a nap, then go out a bit later to troll around a bit. If it really is slow, I think we should head down the French River tomorrow, and check out a few spots for bass." Everyone thought that was a good idea, so Goolee added, "I pulled some steaks out of the cooler for dinner, and we can barbecue those and bake a few potatoes in the wood stove, and maybe have some salad on the side."

"Sounds great, but hey, where's Mac?" asked Gurdy while looking around. None of them had noticed Mac was missing.

"He's in the next cabin, lying down I think," said Goolee with disgust. Then he said, "I checked with Jill, and she said we can make use of the other cabin for free since it's the end of their season, and business is so slow now. I think Mac plans to sleep there.

"He's being a complete jerk. He started whining when I couldn't get the motor started. It went further downhill from there. I almost smacked him once."

After lunch, Greg watched the others head to places to lie down. He could never sleep in the daytime. So he decided to set up their naphtha-fuelled camp stove inside the cabin. Then he put a pot on the stove to make some percolated coffee. It was too warm inside the cabin to start up the wood stove, even with all the screen windows open. But they would need the stove later for warmth at night, and on cold rainy days.

Greg then went outside and started splitting wood. Johnny and Gurdy found they couldn't sleep either, so they all took turns with the axe. They stashed the split logs under the cabin to keep them dry. They also made some skinny 'splits' for kindling, and put them all in a box to take inside the cabin. Scotty was up when they had finished, and they all enjoyed a mug of coffee on the deck together.

"I've been thinking about this all year," said Johnny with a big grin. Then he added, "You just can't beat this place for a vacation." Gurdy, Scotty and The Professor were in total agreement.

They were all out on the water just after five o'clock in the afternoon. They put on treble-hooked spoons and artificial minnows, and trolled around the next bay almost as far as the start of the French River. Johnny and Dick always fished with Greg in a cedar-strip boat, but never wanted to be the driver.

So, Greg got pretty good over the years at adjusting the speed of the boat to avoid snags when they made turns and the lures sank closer to the weedy bottom. The group always held their own with the others in the overall fish count. Johnny hooked a small pike, but it kicked itself off at the side of the boat. Dick hooked and retained two nice smallmouth bass using a worm-harness.

Scotty usually fished with Goolee, but Goolee's boat was just big enough for two, and Goolee had to 'baby-sit' Mac on this trip. So Scotty went with Gurdy and Wally in another cedar-strip boat. They quickly hooked and released a four pound pike. They also hooked and retained three nice 'walleye', a great eating fish they preferred to call a 'pickerel'.

So, the fishing actually was not too bad. When the sun was setting, Goolee cruised up to each boat and yelled, "Screw this, let's go drinking!" Goolee and Mac had been 'skunked'. The others then knew for sure they would be going down the French River the next day.

At the dock, Greg said, "Look, everyone give me their fish, and I'll clean them down at the point." It was a camp rule that all fish had to be cleaned well away from the cabins to keep the bears and racoons away.

"I'll go get a lantern and a few beers and help The Professor," said Johnny. Greg knew he meant 'watch', not 'help', but he was not about to refuse the company. It was dark and lonely down at the point, with a long walk through the woods to get there and back again.

"Great, we'll get some dinner on the go," said Goolee.

When Greg and Johnny got back to the brightly lit-up cabin, it was completely dark outside. Gurdy was on the deck, and he was just putting the steaks on the charcoal barbecue. He only had the murky light coming through a greasy window to see by. Then Gurdy said, "We decided to boil the potatoes on our own stove. It's still too warm inside to light the wood stove, and boiling the spuds will be faster than baking them."

"Sounds good," said Johnny putting the lantern on the railing of the deck to provide more light. "I'll go get us a few beers. This is yet *another* job that requires my supervision."

"Put the fish in the refrigerator when you get the beer, it's cold enough now," said Gurdy as Johnny went through the cabin door. Then he added, "There's not enough fish to freeze, and we'll eat it tomorrow night when we have some more to go with it."

Neil always unplugged the refrigerators to save power in the cabins when they were not in use. Because of the camp's isolation, he had to use a diesel-powered generator to provide the camp with electricity.

6

The next morning, after a breakfast of pancakes and sausages, they packed a lunch, put some beer and ice into coolers, and headed down the French River. They also took two extra jerry cans of mixed gas with them, in case they ran into some difficulty that extended their trip.

Goolee told them they were going to a good spot for bass. He said he found it with his older brother a few years back. He thought it was about fifteen kilometres away from the camp, almost as far as the Dokis First Nations reserve.

The weather was still fine and warm. They all enjoyed the scenery. It had inspired pioneer Canadian painters like Paul Kane. The French River was about one hundred and ten kilometres long. It was broad and slow moving for the most part, and provided the drainage path from Lake Nipissing to Georgian Bay, which was part of Lake Huron, the third largest lake in the world. The river cut through the mostly pink and grey granitic, Precambrian-rock of the Canadian Shield. The route was used by the French explorers Brule, Champlain and Radisson; and the British explorers Fraser, Mackenzie and Thompson. It was also part of the Lake Superior to Montreal fur-trading, freight-canoe 'highway' until the 1820s.

The other men were impressed that Goolee quickly found the secluded, fully-enclosed little bay he was seeking. There were many little islands, and it was a place where one could get completely disoriented and hopelessly lost on a foggy day.

Goolee set Mac up with a hook and sinker for 'still fishing' with worms. He decided he would try some casting towards shore with a spinning reel. The others followed Goolee's lead, and rigged-up for either still fishing or casting.

Mac started to catch perch and sunfish, and also started to really enjoy himself. The perch were a good size. When Mac brought each one into the boat for Goolee to take off of the hook, they would all yell, "Atta boy, Mac, go get another one!" He also hooked a nice bass once, and it practically jumped into the boat. The fish came off when Mac got a massive backlash in the old bait-casting reel his father had given him.

When each boat had a nice stringer full of fish, they went ashore nearby for lunch. James McDuffie had told Goolee it was probably too early to give Mac a beer, but Goolee decided to give him half-a-cup full so he could be 'one of the boys'. Mac was in good spirits, and he didn't show any change in behaviour after drinking the beer.

When they finished their lunch, they decided to troll in a few places on the way back to the camp. They paced themselves to arrive back at the camp around three in the afternoon, so they could have a swim, and lie around on the beach for a while before dinner.

7

They slept in a bit the next day, which was Labour Day Monday in Canada. They had 'knocked-back' a few beers the night before, but had focused more on playing some 'serious' one dollar limit poker.

When they decided to go fishing, the sun was well up in the sky. Down at the dock, they met Steve and Philip about to depart in another of the camp's cedar-strip boats.

"How are you guys doing today?" asked Goolee cheerfully. Steve was trying to start the outboard motor, and Philip looked to be in a bad mood.

"I'll feel a lot better when I get this damn motor running," growled Steve who pulled the starter cord again without result. He was panting, and sweating heavily; his tee-shirt was completely soaked.

"It smells flooded," said Greg. Then he suggested, "Why don't you give it a rest for a couple of minutes, then maybe try pulling it over a few times without the choke. If it doesn't start, pull the choke out again, and have a few more pulls. It should go if it's not broken."

They loaded their own boats while Steve was trying what Greg had suggested. When Steve's motor suddenly sprang to life in a cloud of blue smoke, Steve gave a thumbs up sign to Greg and the others. "Okay, you better push the choke in now before it dies!" yelled Scotty. Steve did that, after fumbling to find the choke knob again. The motor started idling smoothly.

"How are you guys doing with the fishing?" asked Gurdy over the sound of the motor.

"Well, we've only been out once, and we didn't stay out very long," said Steve, looking sheepishly at Philip. "The wives aren't too keen on us going out."

"We're going to try Cross Point," said Scotty. "There's a deep hole out there that pickerel sometimes go down in on a bright day. I see you've got some worms. Why don't you join us? Then, if we have any problems, we can help each other out?"

Philip started nodding at Steve, and Steve said, "Yes, please!" with a big smile.

They all got underway, and Goolee took the lead with his boat. Everyone enjoyed the high-speed cruise in the warm mid-morning air. They could smell the spruce and pine trees nearby. Big flies or 'stouts' were racing along behind them, and Johnny had a lot of fun swatting them out of the air with a rolled-up tee-shirt.

Goolee slowed down about forty metres off the point, and stood up in his boat. He then went ninety degrees to shore, working his steering wheel and looking back at the shore the whole time. Mac was wearing a big, orange life preserver, and standing up in the bobbing little boat with his arms crossed. They could hear Goolee telling him to sit down, but Mac was refusing.

When Goolee was offshore a couple of hundred metres, he stopped his boat abruptly. He pointed down over the side, and yelled, "The hole's about here! With the north-east wind we have, it'll be best to drift fish over this spot, I think! You can use worm-harnesses, but a jig with a worm bouncing off bottom may be best! It might not be too bad either if we finish the drift well into the bay to the west!"

The fishing was slow, but every boat had at least one pickerel when the wind started *really* increasing in the afternoon, while veering to the east. Scotty had hooked a massive 'sheepshead', or freshwater drum fish, but he threw it back when Gurdy started laughing at him. They all considered a sheepshead a 'garbage fish', even though some people claimed they were okay to eat. The few people that ate them seemed to prefer calling them 'silver bass'.

The waves started building quickly after the wind came up. Mac had given up fishing, presumably in frustration. He was standing at the back of the boat with his arms crossed. Goolee's little boat rolled quite violently whenever they turned broadside to the waves.

Goolee yelled at Mac to sit down three or four times before Mac suddenly fell over the side into the water. His arms were still crossed when he hit the water.

Greg had been watching the ugly scene the whole time, and yelled to Dick and Johnny, "Pull in guys! We've got to help Goolee retrieve that moron!"

It was tricky business in the rough water. At one awkward point, Mac was bobbing between two heaving, rolling boats in a gap that was only a metre wide. But Dick and Goolee got a hold of Mac by his life preserver, and manoeuvred him over to the stern of Goolee's boat. Then Goolee hauled Mac over the stern, bringing in a gush of water at the same time. It was an amazing feat of strength as Mac made no effort to help him.

Mac was mumbling something the others could not hear. Goolee threw a towel at him and yelled, "Shut the hell up and use this, then put your jacket on!" Mac just sat there shivering in his wet tee-shirt with his arms crossed. His lips were starting to turn blue in the strong wind.

"I'll have to take the silly bugger to shore guys!" yelled Goolee while shaking his head with disgust. Then he added, "It's a shame! Because I think the fishing could *really* pick up with the weather change! *You* guys should stay a bit longer, though!"

Greg nodded, looked at Dick and Johnny for confirmation and then put his right thumb up in the air. Gurdy had also heard what Goolee said, and put his thumb up too.

Goolee stopped by Steve and Philip on his way back, and after a brief chat, they decided to follow him back to the camp. As Goolee's boat moved away from them, the others could see Mac at the back of the boat with his arms crossed again, sitting right in the wind stream.

Greg could hear Gurdy in the other boat cackling with his distinctive laugh. He knew they were joking about Mac. "Well, that was a close call, but at least Mac survived," said Greg, shaking his head.

"What could Goolee do?" replied Johnny angrily. Then he exploded with, "He must have told him *ten times* to hang on to something or to sit down! What a freaking idiot!"

"Unfortunately, that's what he is now for sure, an idiot," agreed Dick sadly.

Greg then showed Dick and Johnny a clear plastic box of cheap, small, silvery spoons that he had brought along on the trip. He took a yellow-striped spoon out of the box, and clipped it on his leader. Then he said, "Well, I'm going to try one of these now. We'll do a figure-eight over the hole, and see what happens."

"Can I try one of those too?" asked Johnny. "Maybe a green one, if you have that?"

"Sure thing, they were cheaper by the dozen," replied Greg with a laugh while handing Johnny the box of lures.

On the first turn, both Greg and Johnny hooked a fish. Dick netted them both. They were nice pickerel. Then Dick put one of the cheap spoons on his line too.

Greg yelled to Gurdy, "They're hitting those cheap spoons we bought on sale at 'crappy tire', whenever we make a turn!" They saw Gurdy put his thumb up in the air, then reach down for his tackle box.

The waves were *really* getting high now in the strong, east wind. The sun was still very bright in a wild-looking sky, with fast-moving, ragged little clouds.

On the next turn, all three young men hooked a fish. "Stay low, and in the centre of the boat, guys," cautioned Greg. Then he added, "We should stay at this as long as we can, I think. I've never seen anything like it!" His face was beaming with a big grin.

It was exhilarating to be pulling in fish after fish in the 'wicked' conditions. In less than half an hour, when Dick netted a fish for Johnny, Greg said, "That's it guys, we're maxed out, pull in!"

When they had their rods stowed away, Greg made his way carefully over to Gurdy's boat. The waves were splashing over the bow at times. "We've got eighteen!" he yelled to Gurdy.

Gurdy watched Scotty finish bringing in a nice walleye, and then he yelled back while reeling in, "So do we! Party time!"

They had great fun 'surfing' the waves on the way back to camp. As they eased their way around the rocky headland, the water became calmer due to the lee effect, and docking the boats was easy. It was actually warm again when they were out of the wind.

Later, Greg, Scotty and Gurdy started filleting the fish down at the distant point, showing Wally how they did it. When they were about halfway finished, Goolee arrived with a cooler of beer and a camera. He saw that Dick and Johnny were rinsing fillets in a large basin while the other guys were filleting and skinning the fish. "Geez, what a haul!" said Goolee with a laugh. "We better get some pictures."

When they had all taken turns posing behind the fillets and the many fish that still needed to be cleaned, Scotty asked, "So, where's Mac, Goolee?"

"Oh, he's still sitting in the sun on the beach," said Goolee. He was getting angry again, and he added loudly, "I tried *once* to get him to put on some sunscreen, but he knocked the bottle out of my hand! Then I said to myself, *what the hell*, I'm not his freaking mother, so *let him fry*! At least he's not hypothermic anymore."

They enjoyed their time together at the point. The wind was steadily dropping, and it promised to be a calm evening with a classic sunset. The gulls were swirling around, and the birds would fight with each other whenever the men flicked a fish carcass at them. When they were finally through, Goolee said, "We'll freeze most of these fillets. But let's have a proper fish fry tonight!" No one disagreed with Goolee's proposal.

Later in the evening, after taking their turn at doing the dishes, Greg and Johnny sat down with the others at the table in the cabin. Just then, Mac walked in the door with a bag of cookies. Mac's face looked a bit sunburned, but he looked okay otherwise.

Without saying a word, Mac laid a cookie down in front of everyone, except for Goolee. Then he smiled to himself, sat down on the couch nearby, and started eating cookies out of the bag.

Scotty stared hard at the cookie in front to him, then at Mac. Then he took a *big* sip of his rye and coke, raised his fist high in the air, then slammed it down hard, smashing the cookie to bits.

"That's what I think of your *freaking* cookie!" he yelled, while glaring intently at Mac. The others could not help laughing. Mac's smile turned into a pout. He stood up abruptly, and went flying out the door, slamming it hard behind him.

"Oh-oh, I think we pissed him off," said Wally with a laugh.

"I think it's going to be a whiskey night for me now too," said Goolee quietly, while shaking his head.

8

The next morning, they were just about to start eating their breakfast of bacon and eggs when Goolee came back in the door. He was frowning, and he growled, "He said he doesn't like me anymore, and won't go fishing again, with anybody." Mac had decided to sleep in the other cabin again by himself.

"Look, Goolee, Wally and I have been talking, and we'll take a day off and look after him," said Dick. Then he added, "You need a break. We'll *sit on him,* if we have to."

"Well, that would be great," replied Goolee with a smile of relief. Then he said, "But you *both* don't need to stay. I was thinking we should make a trip over to the Goose Islands in the middle of the lake. The cedar-strips are good on gas, so six guys can go in two boats, and I'll leave the 'Goolee Wog' here." Gurdy had just given Goolee a new name for his puny fibreglass boat.

"Then *I'll* stay with him," said Wally. He enjoyed fishing from time to time, but he was not 'right into it' like the others were.

"Okay, but don't try to hump any bears, Wally," said Gurdy.

"No, I'm *saving myself* for when I get back," laughed Wally.

"We know how that will go down," said Dick with a big grin. Then in a deep voice he said, "*Was that good for you too, dear?*" Then in a high falsetto voice, he added, "*What, is it in yet, Wally?*"

They all laughed at the crude joke, then started eating their breakfast. "We'll take a plate over to Mac before we head out," said Goolee with a mouth full of food.

Dick decided to go with Gurdy and Scotty this time 'to mix things up', so Goolee would go with Johnny and Greg. Goolee said Greg would be driving, as he, 'wanted to enjoy a real break, and finally do some serious fishing'.

They saw that the other paying guests were finally up and about when they pulled away from the dock in the two cedar-strip boats. The adults and their kids had just started carrying their stuff down the dock to the Lady Mic where Neil was waiting impatiently for them.

Jill was leaving that day too, with her big dog, 'to get things sorted-out', at their permanent home in Oshawa, Ontario. "Hope you all had a really good time!" yelled Goolee to the people on the dock. The short-stay guests and their kids all waved back with smiles. "See you next year, Jill!" added Goolee. She laughed and waved back, too.

They had an extra jerry can of mixed gas in each boat for the thirteen kilometre trip to the Goose Islands. They probably would not need the extra gas, but it provided some 'feel good' security.

It was really hot and muggy, and they felt better in the breeze made by their quick motion over the water. It was a bit breezier when they reached the islands, but it was still a hot, late summer day.

They trolled around a bit without success. Then Goolee saw a place where they could try still fishing and lure casting like they had done on Sunday with success on the French River.

Greg and Johnny rigged up for still fishing with worms, while Goolee started casting with a big, articulating minnow. They all took their shirts off. It was really hot in the sun and there was no wind at all now in the protected little bay they were in.

Greg was sipping his beer and feeling really drowsy when Goolee let out a yell. He was standing up and his rod had a severe bend in it. "That's a big fish, Goolee!" yelled Greg when he saw the rod twitch violently. "I thought you were just snagged for a minute!"

"He went to the bottom, and he's just staying there!" yelled Goolee while re-setting the tension on his spinning reel. Then he added with a grunt, "It's *got* to be a pike."

"Johnny, get your camera ready, and I'll do the netting if we get that far," said Greg calmly.

"He's going under the boat," said Goolee with another grunt from fighting the high strain on the fibreglass rod. "Coming through Johnny, sorry," he mumbled as he worked around Johnny at the front of the boat, and manoeuvred the line on to the other side of the boat. Thankfully, they were drifting and Goolee did not have to worry about an anchor line getting in the way.

"Here he comes!" yelled Goolee. The fish suddenly shot out of the water, rolled over on its side and came down with a big splash.

"It's a freaking monster!" cried Johnny. "I got that on film, I think!"

"He's sounding again, and running away from the boat!" yelled Goolee. The tension on the spinning rod was set correctly, and was resisting the pull of the big fish without straightening the hook or pulling it out of its mouth. The fish was actually pulling the boat a bit through the water.

Over the next twenty minutes, the fish worked in and out from the boat, sometimes running quickly away, and sometimes going back to the bottom and just slowly moving in circles around the boat.

Gurdy saw what was happening, and brought the other boat closer so they could watch too, and let Scotty take some photos.

"He's coming up now," said Goolee finally. "Get ready with the net, Professor!"

They could *see* the fish now, about a metre under the water. It was over a metre long. When the fish saw the men and the boat, it kicked its tail and made yet another run away from the boat.

After another five minutes the fish reappeared alongside the boat. Goolee said, "I think he might be finally tiring now. That couldn't happen soon enough for me, my arms are ready to fall off!" He was covered in sweat. Then he said, "Try to work the net over its head now, Greg."

Greg got himself in position, but every time he tried to slip the net over the fish from the head-side, the fish pulled away from the boat.

Then the fish actually surfaced at the side of the boat, and Greg saw his chance. He quickly slid the net over the fish from the tail-side, and hauled the fish up over the gunwale and into the boat.

Greg just barely had the fish over the gunwale when the net split apart. But thankfully the big, slimy northern pike fell into the boat. It was thrashing around like mad. The lure had come out of its mouth and was now hooked in the net.

"Hold him between your boots, Greg, and I'll smack him!" said Goolee. He grabbed a hammer he always brought with him, and when Greg nodded that he was ready, Goolee stunned the big fish by hitting it between the eyes three times.

Goolee then sat down with a grunt, and Greg offered him his hand. "Well done!" said Greg with a huge smile. Goolee gladly shook his hand, and then he reached around and shook Johnny's hand too.

"I've got about a dozen photos, Goolee," said Johnny with a laugh. "That was *great!*"

"That is a *big* bloody fish," said Goolee, looking down at it and shaking his head. "What do you think, Professor, sixteen pounds?"

"It's that anyway," agreed Greg. Johnny opened a beer bottle for Goolee, and handed it to him. Greg's boots were covered in slime from the fish, so he doused them with water using the bailing bucket in the boat to clean them a bit.

"That old cotton net must have been rotten," said Goolee, shaking his head. Then he added, "But it's never been used on a fish this big."

"It would have been a major *bummer* if we'd lost it at the end," said Greg still grinning. "But we didn't, and now we have something to talk about all winter."

"Stand up and show us the fish!" yelled Gurdy from the other boat. Goolee grabbed the fish firmly by the back of its head and held it up proudly so Scotty could take a picture.

"It's too small, you better throw it back!" yelled Gurdy with a laugh.

"No, this one's getting stuffed and mounted," said Goolee quietly with satisfaction.

It was starting to cloud over a bit, and they put their shirts back on. They stayed in the same spot for another hour or so with the boats closer together. They peed over the side when they had to. Johnny and Greg each caught a nice bass, and Gurdy and Dick in the other boat pulled in three bass as well.

Then the wind started really coming up. Greg stood up, looked west and said, "It's getting pretty dark over there, guys, I think we should start heading back."

Goolee stood up to look west too, and said, "Roger that." He motioned to Gurdy and yelled, "We're heading back, look at the freaking sky!" Gurdy held his thumb up in the air, and everyone reeled in.

The wind and waves were really starting to come up by the time they were halfway back to the camp. They could see flashes of lightning now in the west, and hear the odd roll of thunder. The wind was coming straight out of the north. Greg and Goolee knew it would be going directly into the bay.

"We might have to beach the boats, Greg!" yelled Goolee over the noise of the wind and the motor. Goolee was sitting on the middle seat facing Greg. Greg had a firm grip on the tiller of the motor. Greg just nodded grimly in response.

It started pouring rain in sheets, and the lake was suddenly full of white caps from breaking waves. The men pulled their baseball caps down more firmly on their heads. When they got into the bay, the waves were over two metres high with a very short period between them. "There's no way in hell we can turn safely to go into the docks!" yelled Greg. Then he added, "And he's tied up the Lady Mic to face into the waves! It's mostly blocking the way anyway!"

"Head for the beach then, Greg!" yelled Goolee. Then he turned around and yelled, "Come back on the middle seat with me, Johnny! Kill the motor and haul it up before we hit the sand, Greg!"

Gurdy could see what they were doing and brought his boat alongside. They found they were 'surfing' on the same wave. Gurdy and Greg killed their motors and brought the propellers up out of the water at the same time. Then they hit the beach like landing-craft on D-Day.

As soon as they were stopped, huge waves started breaking over the back of the boats. "We've got to get the engines off, and drag the boats further up the beach or they'll fill with sand!" yelled Goolee.

While they were struggling with the engines, they saw Neil running down the beach towards them. "What the *hell* are you idiots doing!" he yelled. "Get these boats over to the dock where they belong!"

When Neil reached them, Goolee grabbed him by the arm and yelled angrily, "Take a look at the *freaking water*, Neil! *No one* could turn one of these boats in those breakers without flipping over!"

Neil paused to look, and then he said, "Oh, okay, sorry, you're right." Then the look on his face changed from one of anger to one of worry. "Will you guys help me save the boats?"

"Of course we will, Neil!" said Goolee, letting go of his arm, and patting him on the back. Then he yelled, "Dick and Johnny, go get some branches or logs for rollers to put under the boats! Here comes Wally, ask him to help you!"

They got the motors off the two boats, and hauled them up under the trees. Then Goolee wrapped them in his boat tarp. Then they emptied the boats of their gear, the gas tanks and jerry cans and their fish. Then they bailed the water and sand out of the boats as best they could in the pounding surf.

They worked together to haul the boats over log rollers to get them higher up on to the beach, and further away from the pounding water. Then they flipped the boats over to keep them from filling with rainwater. The boats were water-logged, and it took all of their combined strength to flip them over.

When they were finally done, their clothes were completely soaked, and they were cold and exhausted. Neil patted them all on the back to say thanks and ran back to his house. The rain was coming down sideways when they got back to their 'deluxe cabin'.

Greg got the fire going in the wood stove before changing into dry clothes like the others were doing. Then Goolee came in the door dripping wet. He had laid his big fish out in the freezer in the shed near Neil's house.

"Where's Mac, Wally?" asked Goolee as he was taking off his shirt, and heading for his room to towel-off and change clothes.

"He's in the other cabin, moping," said Wally. Then he explained, "He wouldn't play cards with me, or go for a walk or a swim. I bought him an ice cream cone in Jill's little store before she left, and that seemed to cheer him up, but only for a minute. I showed him how to light the wood stove, and he's got that going over there still. I can see the smoke coming out of the chimney, going sideways." He was looking out the window in the door of the cabin. Then he said with a waver in his voice, "Geez, it's really howling out there now."

They could all hear the storm building in intensity. They had the hinged inner windows all down now inside their outer screens. The old windows were rattling in the wind gusts. The whole cabin was shaking at times. The lightning flashes were increasing, and the thunder was getting louder.

After about twenty minutes, when the storm seemed to be easing up a bit, they started to hear a strange howling noise. It increased in intensity and pitch like an approaching freight train. Then the wind *really* picked up.

They could see debris flying around outside. A large tree branch smacked into the side of the cabin, tore through a screen and knocked out a pane of glass. It seemed like the cabin was about to come off its pile foundation. Then the power went out, and Scotty lit a lantern.

And then the storm started easing again. It rained fairly heavily for another twenty minutes, then that eased off too. Then they could start seeing the sky again through the windows. It was dusk now.

9

When they emerged from the cabin, the devastation from the storm was obvious, even in the dim light. There were downed tree branches and wind-blown 'flotsam and jetsam' to be seen everywhere.

"Oh, my God, the house is knocked down!" yelled Goolee, as he started to run. The others started following closely behind him. "Check on Mac, Johnny!" Goolee yelled back over his shoulder.

"The boathouse has collapsed too!" yelled Gurdy between breaths. "It must have been a tornado!"

When they got to the wreckage of the house, they could see Neil trying to crawl on the wet sand just outside where the back entrance used to be.

When they reached Neil, Goolee knelt down to put an arm around his shoulders. Then he said calmly, "Easy buddy, you're all right, and you've got some help now."

Neil lay flat down on the ground, then he gasped, "It's my leg, I think it's broken."

Then Dick said, "I took some first-aid training, let me have a look at it." Neil was wearing shorts, and Dick felt very gently around a red, swollen area on his lower right leg. Neil grimaced in pain while Dick performed his mostly visual examination.

After a moment, Dick concluded, "It could be broken, but I don't think it's a compound fracture. It needs to be completely immobilised. We should put a splint on it."

Just then Johnny ran up to the others, looked down at Neil with concern, and then said while panting, "Mac's not... in his cabin... I don't know... where he is."

Goolee's jaw dropped open after hearing more bad news, and then he said loudly, "That's just freaking *great*! Greg, Johnny, Scotty, Gurdy, go check on the boats, and then start looking for Mac, while the rest of us take care of Neil. And don't get lost yourselves! Be back here in an hour. It'll be dark soon."

The four searchers had to walk around the wreckage of the boathouse. The usual route to the docks was right through the boathouse itself. When they could see the docks more clearly, it was obvious that three cedar-strip boats and the 'Goolee Wog' had been overturned and smashed. A fourth cedar-strip boat looked to be all right, but it had about a half-a-metre of water in it. The Lady Mic was on its side, and clearly resting on the bottom.

"When we came out of the cabin, I saw that the two boats we dragged up on the beach were okay," said Scotty. "The tarp was gone off the motors, but I bet they're okay too. So that gives us three cedar-strip boats left, hopefully."

When they went back along the trail, they saw Dick, Wally and Goolee inside the small vacant cabin nearest the wrecked house. They were tending to Neil in the pale, wavering light of a flashlight. Greg frowned, and gave a waggling, sideways thumb sign to Goolee. Goolee just shrugged and waved back from the shadows before returning his attention to Neil.

"There are only a few trails that go back into the woods," said Greg as he was walking towards the 'deluxe cabin' with the other members of the search party. Then he added, "Trails lead to an old dump, and a workshop, I think. So this shouldn't take us very long. There's no way Mac could travel along the shoreline or through the woods, it's all too thick with underbrush. Was Mac's stuff still in the other cabin, Johnny?"

"I forgot to look," said Johnny. "Let's check that out first. We're almost there anyway."

They quickly searched through the small cabin where Mac had been sleeping, and even in the weak light it was easy to confirm it was completely empty. Gurdy concluded, "Mac must have taken all of his stuff somewhere. Hey, do you smell smoke?"

When they went back out through the cabin door, Scotty yelled, "Hey, our cabin is on fire!" Greg ran back into the small cabin and came out with a dry chemical fire extinguisher. By the time he had rejoined his friends, they were all standing about twenty metres from the 'deluxe cabin', and backing away further because of the heat from a now raging fire.

The whole backside of the cabin was in flames. "You won't do any good with that puny fire extinguisher, Professor," said Gurdy sadly. Then he added, "It's already too late."

The cabin burned down very quickly. The wood timbers and siding were old and bone dry. Some of the surrounding trees started to smoke and flare up, but they were wet from the heavy rain, and didn't catch fire. Goolee and Wally ran up to join the group, and watched the end of the blaze with them.

It was dark now, and it was like watching a big bonfire.

After a few minutes of silently staring at the smouldering ruin, Greg asked, "You don't think Mac might have had something to do with this, do you?"

"That's exactly what I think," replied Goolee angrily. He was holding on to two small flashlights. "Let's split into two groups, and have a quick look for him. Here's a flashlight, Greg. You check things out from here to Neil's wrecked house, with Johnny and Gurdy. I'll check from there further on with Wally and Scotty. Dick is taking care of Neil. Don't go into the woods, you'll get lost now in the dark! Call out his name while you're looking. We'll meet back at the cabin where Dick and Neil are in half an hour."

Greg's group worked their way along the edge of the woods, calling out Mac's name the whole time. There was no sign of him. They decided to have a quick look around the back of Neil's ruined house, and they saw that the generator shed was still there. But the connecting wires had fallen down, and one wire had been pulled apart by a fallen tree. And they noted the master circuit-breaker had tripped.

Then they saw Goolee with a flashlight near the boathouse coming towards them. His search party was with him. They all met up at the door of the 'first-aid' cabin. Then Dick came out of the cabin, and Goolee asked, "So, how's Neil, Dick?"

"I think he'll be all right tonight," said Dick, looking a bit stressed. "But I'm no doctor or nurse, and we should get him to a hospital as soon as we can. Oh, and he says there's a forty ounce bottle of whiskey behind the freezer we can have, as long as we let him have a couple of shots. I think that might do him some good. It looks like he isn't a tee totalling 'Saint' after all!"

"And no sign of Mac, right?" asked Goolee. He looked around at everybody.

"Nope," replied Gurdy emphatically. "And he took all of his stuff with him, wherever he went."

"The radio-phone is trashed inside Neil's house, so we can't call for help," said Goolee. Then he added, "We'll just have to hope Mac comes back on his own accord, and look for him again when it's light in the morning."

"We probably can get three cedar-strippers to work," said Scotty. Then he shook his head, and added, "But your boat is 'toast', Goolee, sorry. On the plus side though, we can all get out of here in three boats, I think."

"Okay, let's get some heat and light on in this cabin, and the next one along the beach," said Goolee. Then he added, "Forget about the other two cabins, but check out the cupboards inside them. Neil and Jill provide matches and candles for when the generator is turned off, and the guests usually bring too much food with them, and just leave it.

"We should be able to scrape together a meal. We've got some fish in the freezer as you know, and I'll get the whiskey when I go get our fish. But it looks like we're *wearing* everything else we have.

"Oh, and let's tell Neil our cabin burned down, but we don't know how, maybe lightning hit it. And let's wait to tell him Mac is missing until the morning, okay?" Everyone agreed.

Then Goolee said, "We'll have to make sure someone is always outside looking out for Mac. He might not have *murder* on his mind, if he has a mind anymore, but I don't think we should take any chances either."

An hour later, they had a big pot of 'stew' warming on the wood stove. They had mixed together some canned tomatoes, brown beans, spaghetti sauce, corned beef and some actual beef stew. They democratically decided to leave out a can of sauerkraut; no one liked the stuff. They had canned corn heating in another pot. They found enough vegetable oil to fry their fish, and they mixed up some pancake mix to use as a wet batter. They had also found some saltine crackers, tinned sardines and mini-wieners for 'appetisers'. They even had some cola to mix with their rye whiskey.

But they had no ice to put in their drinks. No one seemed too upset about that, though.

They put pots of water on the wood stove in the other cabin. After they had eaten, they washed the dirty dishes in hot water. Then they got Neil settled in the bedroom of the 'first aid' cabin and mixed him one more drink as a night cap. Then Goolee motioned for them all to go outside with him.

"Look, I think Dick should stay in this cabin tonight to be close to Neil," said Goolee quietly when they were outside. Then he added, "It might be better if the rest of us all use the next cabin. We can keep a close watch on the two cabins at the same time."

Goolee stopped to listen to some wolves howling in the distance. Then he said, "It can get pretty scary outside on your own around here, at night anyway. So, we might want at least *two* guys on watch at the same time. We'll keep the wood stove and a candle lit the whole time inside both cabins. We should build a fire between the two cabins for a bit of light, and for something to warm the 'guards'. There are racoons, bears and skunks out at night. But we probably won't see any animals.

"And now of course we may have to fend off another 'Big Mac Attack', and I'm not talking about getting the munchies from smoking too much of Gurdy's dope!"

They all laughed quietly, and agreed with Goolee's plan.

10

As it turned out, no one managed to sleep much that night. They took turns lying down on the couch in Neil's cabin, and the bed in the other cabin. But their minds were racing, focused on their situation. They found even just resting was difficult.

It was cold outside, so they were constantly moving between the bonfire outside, and the cabins with their wood stoves. None of the men had a jacket, and most were just wearing tee-shirts. Neil was sleeping okay, so Dick didn't think he needed to be the only one that looked in on him occasionally.

It was a clear evening. With everything so dark around them, the show of stars and the Northern Lights were spectacular. They could see their breath outside towards morning.

Greg joined Scotty and Goolee at the bonfire just before sunrise. They were jumping around by the fire, trying to stay warm. "So, maybe The Prrrofessorrr can tell us," said Scotty in a phony Scottish accent while rubbing his bare arms. Then he added, "The Northerrrn Lights are just grrreat, but why do they glow like that, anyway?"

Greg was going to laugh, but instead he said in a monotone, robotic voice, "Plasma or the very hot charged atomic particles from solar flares travel along lines of geomagnetic flux heading for the North magnetic pole. And they ionise gas molecules in the upper atmosphere, causing them to glow in various spectral colours, depending upon the elements involved, as quanta of photons are released to restore their lower, more stable energy states."

Then Greg continued in his normal voice, "Or, the Viking god Odin is reforging his sword with the furnace he keeps in the heavens, and those are the sparks we're seeing from his mighty hammer blows."

Scotty and Goolee looked blankly at each other, and Goolee said, "I told you we should have asked Wally."

They all laughed together, and then Greg asked, "So, no sign of Mac yet?"

"No," replied Scotty. "Hey, here come Gurdy and Dick."

Then Goolee said to Scotty and Greg, "Come on then, you guys. They can stay here, while we have a look around. There's just enough light now."

They found the other cabins were still empty, and so was the generator shack.

But they found Mac in the shack with the freezer. He was on the wooden floor, shivering in the dark in a foetal position.

They looked at him for a few seconds, and their anger turned to pity.

"Mac, it's Goolee," said Goolee quietly, as he knelt down beside him. Then he added, "Come on Mac, it's time to go home now." He put his hand on Mac's shoulder, but Mac pulled away.

"No, I hate you athholes, go away!" said Mac angrily.

Goolee waited quietly another minute, looking at Scotty and Greg with concern. Then he said, "Come on, Mac, it's all right, we won't hurt you. But you can't stay here, you'll freeze to death. Come on, buddy, sit up."

Mac started whimpering, but he rolled over to sit upright. Goolee said, "That's great, Mac. Here, Scotty, give me a hand, and we'll get Mac up on his feet." Scotty and Goolee put their hands under Mac's armpits and hoisted him to his feet. Greg brushed the dirt and leaves off the back of Mac's tee-shirt.

"Where's your stuff, Mac?" asked Goolee.

"I don't know," replied Mac with a sniffle. "In the woods thumwhere, I guess."

"Okay, we won't worry about that right now," said Goolee. Then he said, "Come on, let's get those legs of yours working again, Mac, you're frozen stiff."

They walked Mac slowly back to the 'guard cabin'. The others saw them coming and gathered just outside the door of the cabin. Neil was still lying down inside the other cabin they were using.

When they reached the door, Goolee said, "Mac's chilled to the bone, guys, and he needs to sit by the fire for a while."

Gurdy said, "I'll get it stoked up good for him."

The others were instantly feeling nothing but pity as well. Mac looked at all of them, and gave them a bit of a smile. Gurdy and Dick both patted Mac on his back and went into the cabin to look after him.

11

They left Dick and Gurdy to look after Neil and Mac and went down to the dock to survey the storm damage in a better light.

"Five hundred bucks down the drain," said Goolee sadly when he saw his 'Goolee Wog' was upside down. The stern was submerged, and the old outboard engine was completely under water. There was also a prominent crack in the four metre long fibreglass hull.

They worked their way carefully out along the dock. It was missing a few planks, but it proved to be still sound enough to walk on. They made their way to the only camp cedar-strip boat that was still afloat. It was half-full of lake and rain water.

Goolee carefully stepped down into the boat, and started bailing out the water. Neil's practice was to tie a bailing bucket to each boat so guests would always have one available when needed. Scotty stepped down into the boat after about five minutes to force the stern further down. That way, Goolee could finish the bailing job.

When the open bilge in the boat was reasonably dry again, Goolee opened the vent on the fuel tank cap. Then he gave the gas line bulb a squeeze, checked that the engine was in neutral, pulled out the choke knob, pulled the starter cord and the engine started right up.

Everyone clapped, and Goolee stood up to take a bow with a big grin on his face. He pushed the choke knob back in, let the motor run for a minute then pushed the kill button to stop the engine. He looked at the gauge on the gas tank, and then he took off the fill cap to look inside the tank. "This tank is almost full, thankfully," he said. Then he added, "Let's get the two boats on the beach back in the water now. Then we'll use this boat to tow them over here. It will be easier to put the motors back on at the dock."

On their way to the beach, Goolee went to the busted-up door of the collapsed boathouse, and moved a few timbers aside. "Neil kept his boat-gas mix-oil just inside the door," he explained with a grunt. Then with a happier grunt he added, "Yep, here it is."

Goolee reached down and pulled four plastic bottles out from below some broken plywood. He threw the bottles on the ground at his feet and said, "After we get the two boats under tow, Greg, would you and Johnny drag the two boat fuel tanks over here, and fill them with our jerry cans of mixed gas? Then, cut up a bit of garden hose. I saw a hose behind Neil's old house. Then, use the hose to siphon some gas out of his tractor to re-fill the jerry cans, and then add the mix-oil. Make sure you follow the instructions on the mix-oil bottles. This way, we should have enough gas to get us all back to Parry's Landing."

"No sweat," said Greg. He didn't mention that he was a mechanical engineering student, and knew all about small boats too. Goolee was leading, and he was a very good leader.

When the boats were all ready to go, they put Neil on a wooden chair. Then Scotty, Goolee, Wally and Johnny carried him to one of the boats on the chair. Dick had put Neil's broken leg in a splint the night before using boards from the collapsed boathouse tied up with some old rags he found in a cabin.

Dick held Neil's leg while the others were carrying the chair. They took their time, especially when they were on the old dock. "Let's put the chair right in the middle of the boat," said Goolee, while puffing to catch his breath. Then he explained, "That way Neil can keep his leg up on the bench seat in front of him."

When they had Neil comfortably set up in the boat, they saw Neil had tears in his eyes. He was looking at the wreck of the Lady Mic on its side.

"Do you have storm insurance, Neil?" asked Goolee gently.

Neil paused for a few seconds, and then said, "Yes, thankfully. But it will still take a *lot* of hard work to recover from this disaster." Then he looked a little more cheerful, and he added forcefully, "But I'm going to do it, *damn it!*"

"What about your fish, Goolee?" asked Johnny.

"It was completely thawed out and starting to smell, so I threw it in the woods," said Goolee sadly, shaking his head.

"Well, at least we've got the photos," said Johnny. Then he smacked himself on the forehead with the palm of his right hand, and said, "No, I forgot, the camera got burned up in the fire."

They all looked at Mac. Mac did not seem to have heard what Johnny had said, or to be aware of any of the consequences of the fire. They had resolved not to say anything at all to Neil about what they thought probably had happened.

But to Mac's credit, he *had* let them all 'borrow' some of his clothing. They had found his big duffle bag in the woods not too far from the freezer shack. At least they would be *a bit* warmer travelling back than they would have otherwise been.

"Okay, let's get started," said Goolee. Then he said, "Everyone should get a drink of water, and have a pee. And then, Dick and Gurdy, why don't you get in this boat with Neil? I'll take Mac and Wally with me. Scotty and Johnny can go with The Professor. The weather is good, and the lake is calm again. We'll take it easy so Neil doesn't hurt his leg any further.

"But, hopefully, we'll be back in Parry's Landing in a couple of hours."

12

They had to go slower than Goolee was hoping for to keep Neil comfortable, but they all arrived safely at the landing just after noon.

There was no one else at the dock. They lifted Neil carefully out of the boat, leaving him on the chair the whole time.

Goolee was about to walk up the hill to his truck in the parking lot. But first, he had a hard look at Neil. He was sitting near the edge of the dock, and looking down at the three cedar-strip boats. Goolee could see Neil was worried about something, so he asked, "What's wrong, Neil?"

Neil seemed to appreciate the question, and he replied, "William, I don't want to leave these boats here like this. Someone will steal them, eventually," he said shaking his head. Then he asked, "Could we use your truck and trailer to haul the three boats up to where the cars are parked? Then, maybe you could take the motors off, and put them in my truck? I've got a canopy cover on the back of the truck, and I can lock the door."

"Sure thing, Neil, that shouldn't take very long with all of this help readily at hand," replied Goolee with a smile. Neil smiled back, said, "Thanks!", and handed Goolee his big key ring.

They hauled each boat out, then put the motors and everything stowed inside each boat, like paddles and life preservers, into the back of Neil's truck. Then they worked as a team to place the boats upside down on some concrete blocks to prevent them from rotting.

Then they all went back down to the dock, and carefully put Neil in the passenger side of Goolee's truck. Goolee gave Neil back his key ring, and drove the truck back up the hill to the parking area.

"Yes, that looks great," said Neil with a smile of approval when he saw how they had placed the boats for long-term storage.

"Look, Neil, let me give you my trailer," said Goolee. Then he added, "It's on its last legs anyway, and I'll get another one when I get a new boat. That way, you'll have a way to relaunch these boats when you want to."

"That's great, William, thanks very much," said Neil sincerely. They shook hands, and Goolee jumped out, then hooked the trailer up to the hitch of Neil's truck with the help of the other young men.

"Now, let's get you to a hospital," said Goolee after climbing back into the driver's seat of his truck. "North Bay, Neil?"

"Yes, I'll show you the way to the hospital when we get there," said Neil.

The other men had squeezed into the other two vehicles. "Wally and Scotty, follow me!" yelled Goolee out of his open truck window. Then he told them, "We're heading for North Bay!"

13

A male orderly pushed Neil in a wheelchair over to where all the young men were seated. They were in the waiting area near the emergency entrance of the hospital.

"Well, luckily it was a clean break," said Neil with a grim smile. Then he looked sad, and added, "They said three weeks with this heavy cast, then another x-ray, then another three weeks or so with a lighter cast."

"That doesn't sound too bad," said Goolee with a smile of support. Then he said, "Look, Neil, Wally just got us some rooms in a motel nearby. Why don't you check in there too, and we'll get some takeout food? And maybe you can call Jill from there?"

Neil looked relieved. "That's exactly what I was hoping for, thanks!"

"We're going to need our cash to pay for the motel, Neil," said Goolee. He wondered if this was going to be a problem. So, he asked Neil politely, "Can we *mail* you the money, Neil, for the rent of the cabin and the boats, and the gas we used?"

"Yes, that will be all right," replied Neil as if this sort of thing happened all of the time.

Goolee and the others were relieved. They were starting to think Neil wasn't such a bad guy after all.

Later in the evening, Goolee joined the other young men in the motel room that Wally and Dick were sharing.

"Well, I've got Mac settled in my room now with a fresh bag of cookies, and some pop," said Goolee. Then he added, "I called Jenny, and told her we're all right, but have to come home tomorrow 'because of the storm'. Jill is on her way right now from Oshawa with her son, so old Neil should be in good hands soon."

They handed Goolee a beer, and he sat down with a sigh. Then he said, "I'm not going to try to call James McDuffie. And I'm not sure what I'm going to tell him when I see him next."

"Look Goolee, we've been talking about that," said Greg for the group. Then he explained, "We don't think there's *anything* to be gained from linking Mac to the cause of the fire. And you know, ultimately, that is *still* just speculation on our part. We have no proof! And Mac has not owned up to it, although we haven't pressed him on the matter."

"Let's let it lie, then," said Goolee with a shrug. Then he said, "We'll head out first thing in the morning. Say, is there any pizza left? I'm still hungry."

14

The trip back was uneventful, and no one talked much. Scotty took Gurdy and Mac along with him in his small car. Greg rode with Goolee again, spelling him once at the wheel of the old pickup truck with the sloppy steering wheel. And Dick and Johnny went with Wally as they had before on the trip up.

Scotty followed Goolee back to Goolee's house, and parked behind Goolee's truck in the driveway. Then they all got out of the vehicles. Scotty opened the trunk of his car, and without saying anything, handed Mac his duffle bag, his sleeping bag and his fishing tackle. Mac was the only one with any baggage.

Goolee came over, took the duffle bag from Mac, and said, "Come on, Mac, I'll take you home."

James McDuffie answered the front door when Goolee knocked on it. He stood there for a few moments with a surprised look on his face. Mac walked past him into the house, and Goolee handed the duffle bag to James. "The fishing was really slow, so we came back a couple of days early," explained Goolee.

"Did you have any problem with Michael?" asked James.

"No, no problem at all," replied Goolee with no expression on his face. "I don't think he likes fishing much, though."

The Naive Neftyanik

1

Blake McTavish woke up with a snort. When he felt the tight seatbelt around his waist, he realised with a start that he had fallen asleep while sitting upright in a cushioned seat. Then he remembered he was on a Boeing 727 commercial airliner that he had boarded in Frankfurt, Germany.

It was July 3, 1992. This was his third trip to Russia, and the first time he would be travelling there alone. Blake was a petroleum engineer with Amoilco, an international, integrated oil and gas company with its headquarters in Atlanta, Georgia.

Blake was a thirty-six year old Canadian, currently working and living in Houston, Texas as an expatriate employee. He had just agreed to be a 'front man' for the company, setting up and running a small office out of a Soviet-era hotel in Neftezapadsibirsk, Western Siberia, Russia. He was working a twenty-eight-day-in, twenty-eight-day-out rotation.

It had taken him almost a week to recover from the eleven hour jet lag last time. And here he was, about to do it all to himself again.

The whole trip in would take seventeen hours of flying time, but with flight connections, it would actually require two days. The trip home would also take two days. So in reality, his time off would only amount to twenty-four days per rotation.

'Why am I doing this again?' he asked himself. Of course, he would receive his 'ex-pat salary uplift' of thirty percent, plus a bonus of one hundred and fifty US dollars per day after tax. But Blake was a realist, and he knew he had mostly agreed to do the job because he had perceived it as an adventure.

Another career consideration was that Amoilco was about to start another round of lay-offs. Times were tough in the oil and gas industry again. He was fortunate to have a three-year work contract.

He started to rehearse what he would say again at immigration in Sheremetyevo Airport in Moscow.

'*Zdrast-vuee-tye*,' he said to himself. 'Geez, what a tough word they use just for saying hello!'

'*Meenya zavut Blake McTavish*,' he continued, almost speaking out loud, and really struggling to remember what Lena the language instructor had just taught him in Houston. '*Ya Ingineer Neftyanik fe Amoilko, mezhdunarodnaya firma, eez Amerikii, buziness nefti ee gaza*'.

'*Neftyanik*' meant 'oil worker' or 'oilfield worker'.

Lena had told him, 'There's no way you'll pass for a Russian, but you don't have to. It usually goes a lot smoother, though, if you try to speak a few Russian words. Most people in any culture take that as a sign of respect, including customs and immigration officials.'

Lena had a doctorate in linguistics from Moscow University. It seemed like every Russian in the Houston office had an advanced degree and was glad to be no longer living in Russia, or the now ex-Soviet Union, with the demise of that 'superpower' in December 1991.

The middle-aged guy sitting beside Blake in business class had introduced himself as Colin Hawksley. He was a Brit, trying to get a, 'rope, soap and dope', contract set up for his oilfield service company based in Aberdeen, Scotland. Colin was now fast asleep and snoring loudly. Colin had knocked back three 'gin and tonics' in quick succession as soon as he had got on the plane.

Blake heard and felt the jet engines on the airplane throttle down. They were starting their descent into Moscow. Colin woke up beside him with a spasm of arm and leg twitches. He took a few moments to get reoriented, and then he said, "Oh, what joys are ahead of us now, the unique pleasures of entering the *worker's paradise* as a capitalist foreigner!"

Blake laughed nervously in agreement. He wasn't looking forward to this part either.

Blake had the window seat. He asked to get by Colin, and went to the washroom for a pee. He knew what the lines would be like in the airport.

The landing approach was normal, and the runway was rough. It seemed to Blake that *all* runways and roads in Russia were rough and uneven.

It was a grey, rainy day in Moscow. They had landed at about four p.m. local time. They waited for about an hour on the tarmac for their 'gate to clear'.

Most of the other people on the plane appeared to be European or American businessmen. There were a few older, wealthy-looking Russian men partnered with young, good-looking well-dressed women. Brad guessed every '*klassnaya baba*' on the plane was a mistress, not a wife.

Every one filed off the plane in an orderly fashion. They made two turns down dark hallways, and then bumped into the back of a stationary queue, ten-people wide.

It took one-and-a-half hours to get to the front of the immigration line. It was hot and stuffy in the cramped hallway, and there was a strong smell of body odour. Blake was glad he had not had drinks on the plane. He couldn't see Colin anywhere in the line. He hoped Colin was just 'lost in the shuffle'.

When it was finally his turn, Blake handed his passport and visa to the immigration agent. The agent immediately put the documents down in front of her under a purple-white, bright light. He could not see her desk surface. Blake guessed someone else actually was looking at the documents via a camera, and the agent's job was purely to turn pages, and follow instructions communicated by a simple on-off light system or a telephone.

"*Zdrastvueetye, Ya Ingineer Neftyanik fe Amoilko*," was all Blake could remember to say. He was a bit nervous.

The agent then looked up, and took a hard close look at his face. She smiled for one brief second before looking down again. This was all purely business.

The seven-minute wait at the immigration desk felt like half an hour to Blake. Finally, the agent started stamping his documents. That took another couple of minutes. Then she handed the visa and passport back to Blake. "*Dobra pazhalavat fe Moskvoo*," she said while motioning for the next person in line to come forward.

"*Spaseeba*," said Blake with a smile.

"*Pazhalusta*," said the agent without looking at him.

Blake then went down another darkened passageway to the baggage claim area. He was travelling with seven plastic containers that looked like big, camping coolers. They contained his clothes, token gifts for giving away to people, Western-style snacks and foodstuffs, a personal computer for sending emails over an Inmarsat telephone line, and some documents he was to deliver. He grabbed two rickety old push carts and waited with the other passengers for his baggage to appear. He also grabbed a blank declaration form and filled that out. The baggage finally appeared after a half hour wait. He looked around for Colin, but never saw him.

Blake then loaded up his two carts, and got himself in a 'nothing to declare' line. There were five other people ahead of him. Suddenly a guy with an overloaded cart came up from the side and started trying to push his way into the queue in front of Blake. He looked to be African, and was avoiding eye contact.

Blake asked angrily in English, "What's the problem, buddy?"

The man still avoided eye contact and said in reasonably good English, "I am in a hurry."

"And how do you know I'm not, asshole?" asked Blake loudly. His lack of sleep was catching up with him, and his patience had grown unusually thin.

A young man in a uniform then came over, and motioned with his baton to the African man to go over to the back of the 'something to declare' line. The African man hesitated for a second, and then he complied.

"*Spaseeba*," said Blake with a smile to the uniformed man.

The uniformed man just shrugged with a bit of a smile and said, "*Nye za shto*", which translated as 'not for that'.

Blake finally reached the front of the customs line after another half hour wait. The customs official took his declaration form, visa and passport, looked at the documents briefly and at his padlocked containers, gave him back his passport and visa and just waved him through. Blake suspected there were visas, and then there were visas. Some people were more equal than others here.

Blake smiled at the bored-looking customs official, and moved his seven containers down the short hallway towards the unsecured part of the airport. To make his way along, he had to push one wobbly cart forward a metre, and then the other wobbly cart forward a metre.

Things started to get *really* wild as soon as he got out of the customs section. Hordes of men claiming to be taxi drivers started trying to help him with his two carts. A gypsy boy was pulling at his leg. Finally, he recognized a man holding an 'Amoilco' sign in the crowd. It was his driver from the Moscow Amoilco office. "Sasha!" yelled Blake anxiously.

"Meester McTavish, *tavarich*!" yelled Sasha in return as he forced his way through the crowd. Sasha was grinning broadly and shook Blake's hand quickly. Then he started pushing the first cart and said, "Follow me, *moy droog*, stay close."

The crowd seemed to ease away a bit. Sasha and Blake made their way slowly to the main entrance, then out on to the sidewalk beside the passenger drop-off area. It was raining, and the traffic was in gridlock. The air stank heavily from car exhausts. Sasha led Blake about one hundred metres down the rough sidewalk to their right, then said, "Wait here, I get van."

After fifteen minutes, Blake could not hold it in any longer, and ducked behind a nearby sign for a piss. It smelled like many others had gone in the same place. Sasha arrived with the van after another fifteen minutes, and Blake helped Sasha load his baggage into the back of the van.

When they were seated beside each other in the front of the van, Sasha said, "*Paiyekali*? Go?"

"*Da, pazhalusta*!" replied Blake with relief.

Blake's hotel was in downtown Moscow. It was owned by a new European joint venture and was considered secure by Amoilco. It was a thirty-five kilometre drive away from Sheremetyevo Airport.

Blake perceived Moscow as a bleak, mostly concrete, dreary, dirty and air-polluted city full of ten million sad people. But it was all so foreign to him that all of the sights and sounds were fascinating. It really helped as well that Amoilco drivers like Sasha knew their way around the huge place so expertly. Blake could relax for the two hour drive to the hotel in heavy traffic, even though he could not yet manage a conversation with the mostly Russian-speaking Sasha.

Their drive eventually took them past the Russian Parliament Building, or 'White House', where Boris Yeltsin battled with the old system. Then they crossed the Moscow River. The top halves of the massive stone 'Stalin skyscrapers' were all in cloud. When they passed the Kievsky Railway Station, Blake knew they were finally getting close to his hotel.

When they got to the hotel, Sasha helped a porter load Blake's baggage on to a hotel cart, and then with a handshake and a wave, Sasha said, "*Da svidaniya*! Back five a.m." And then he drove away in the van.

The porter followed Blake into the hotel with his baggage. A young lady in a smart-looking hotel uniform at the hotel's front desk saw Blake coming towards her, put her hand out and said with no expression on her face, "Give passport, visa, credit carte." She would give him back his credit card, but the hotel security would keep his passport and visa until he left in the morning.

Blake looked at his watch. It was almost ten o'clock at night, six hours after he had landed.

2

Blake was back in the hotel lobby with his baggage at quarter to five the next morning. There were no other guests around, and he quickly checked out.

After putting his stuff in his room the night before, he had quaffed a pint of what proved to be very expensive Belgian beer in the hotel bar. He had thought the beer might help him sleep, but he was so jet lagged he had mostly just rolled around in the comfortable bed. He thought he might have been asleep for an hour once.

Sasha came in through the front door of the hotel at five minutes to five. "*Dobraye utra!*" he said to Blake with a big smile.

When Sasha opened the back doors to the company van, Blake saw the four cases of bottled water and two flats of canned Dutch beer that he had asked for. "Beer enough?" asked Sasha with a smile. "One week for Jeff." Blake assumed he was joking and just laughed. Jeff was his opposite number in the 28-28 day rotation. Jeff would be handing over to Blake later that day at the airport in Neftezapadsibirsk.

They quickly loaded Blake's stuff in the back of the van, and got started on the fifty-kilometre-long, two-hour-plus drive to Domodedovo, a domestic airport in Moscow. Sheremetyevo was mostly an international airport.

The rain had stopped. They passed two groups of police cars and ambulances on the Moscow ring road. Both times Sasha had made a walking motion with his fingers, and then swiped his right index finger across his throat as if he were slashing it.

The streets and ring roads of Moscow were as perilous for pedestrians seemingly as they were for drivers. Blake was seeing driving laws broken everywhere he looked, including people driving with their headlights off. He had heard one was supposed to drive with only parking lights on at night, but he could never confirm the rumour. It seemed insanely dangerous, if true.

This was to be Blake's second trip on the company charter aircraft. It was a Tu-134 that used to carry Russian 'communist-party big-wigs'. The Tu-134 looked like a DC-9, only it was a bit smaller with an 'anhedral' or downward swept wing. Like all Russian aircraft it also had very loud, low-bypass ratio turbojet engines.

Amoilco was also setting up a small presence in Baku, Azerbaijan, as well as in Nadym, a western Siberian town just south of the Yamal Peninsula in the Arctic. Amoilco had arranged the charter contract for the Tu-134 with Aeroflot to avoid the hassle and perceived safety risks of flying on regular, domestic flights.

During the long drive to Domodedovo, Blake remembered his first trip to Russia. It had two components.

He had travelled with a group of interpreters, reservoir engineers, production engineers and drilling specialists to visit a number of oilfield 'design institutes' in Moscow.

Then he had travelled to Neftezapadsibirsk with his boss, Roy Elliot, who was now the Moscow resident manager. Their guide had been a senior interpreter, Arman Assarian; he was Armenian and a very bright man, who knew 'all the ropes'. Blake, Roy and Arman had left Domodedovo on a regular Tu-154 Aeroflot flight. They went on to successfully persuade the Russian 'partner-to-be', KhantyRusNefteGaz, to support Amoilco's plan to set up a small office in Neftezapadsibirsk. They had also helped Blake hire a local interpreter, Elena Khalayeva, and a driver, Nikolai Kosygin.

The Tu-154 had resembled a Boeing 727 with three engines at the back, but it was a bit bigger. It also had an anhedral wing and very loud engines.

Roy had paid for the plane tickets in 'hard currency', or American dollars. The rouble was being devalued all of the time, and the country was experiencing hyperinflation. The Aeroflot people had taken them out to wait at the foot of a stairway positioned at the front door of the airplane. To their horror Roy and Blake had realised the aircraft had already been boarded.

Aeroflot officials went on the airplane and came back out with three very angry ex-passengers. Then, everyone on the plane had stared with anger as the three foreigners had taken seats together near the front of the plane.

Blake had tried to fasten his seat belt, but the strap had been double-sewn so that it would only work on a person with a *much* bigger belly. Roy had watched Blake struggling with his seat belt, and had said with a laugh, 'Well, they don't want people stealing their belt buckles, now do they. Welcome to Russia, Blake!'

Roy had then said, 'Let me tell you a true story that will give you a sense of this place. My last job was in Egypt, and while I was outside having a smoke waiting for a flight, I watched a group of airport workmen wheel a kind of forklift over to take off one of the rear engines of a Tu-154. As soon as they had the weight of the engine on the forklift, it toppled over, and the engine went careening across the tarmac, smashing itself to bits. About twenty minutes later I motioned one of the workmen over to the fence I was standing behind. He was crying. I asked him in Arabic what had happened, and he said they just found out the Russian engine was twice the weight of a Boeing 727 engine!' Roy had let that soak in a minute, and then he had added, 'This airplane is built like a Soviet World War Two tank, to work on *really* rough runways in all kinds of conditions. There are hardly any plastic or other lightweight materials in it. It is a 'gas hog'! It was built by a communist country with a false economy, where the price of fuel was set and kept artificially low. Hell, you'll soon see, they used to use *helicopters* here like *taxi cabs*. And all of that is coming to a screeching halt, as I speak.'

Blake left the recollection behind, and remembered where he was again. Sasha brought the van up to the main entrance of Domodedovo airport at seven thirty a.m. They pulled up to a secure gate at the side of the main terminal building. "Wait," said Sasha as he climbed out of the van. Sasha then went over to a guard shack by the gate, and handed some papers to the guard. Blake then saw the guard make a phone call. Sasha offered the guard an American cigarette, and the two had a smoke while they chatted to each other.

After half an hour, an Aeroflot official came over to the gate, looked at the papers Sasha had given the guard, then motioned for the gate to be partially opened. Sasha then walked over to the back of the van, and started unloading the baggage. Blake got out of the van and helped Sasha carry the stuff over to the gap in the gate. A tractor with a wagon in tow then pulled up on the inside of gate, and some airport workers loaded the baggage onto the wagon.

Sasha then offered Blake his hand. "Go now," he said pointing with his other hand at the Aeroflot official. "Follow."

Blake shook Sasha's hand, and said with a smile, "*Spaseeba, da svidaniya!*" Sasha waved at Blake and the guard with a smile, and went back to his van.

Blake followed the Aeroflot official through the gap in the gate and out onto the tarmac. The guard then closed the gate behind them. The Aeroflot official pointed at a spot on the tarmac, and walked away. Blake concluded he was to wait at that spot.

Twenty minutes later, a big tractor pulling a massive, empty, people-hauling trailer pulled up to Blake. Blake stepped inside the trailer, and grabbed on to a handrail. There was no place to sit down.

The tractor driver then drove through a maze of parked airplanes. The surrounding jet engine sounds were deafening. The driver finally pulled up and stopped next to a Tu-134 parked with its front door open. Blake stepped out of the people-hauling trailer and went up some rickety, trailer-mounted stairs to the open door of the airplane. He stuck his head through the door, and yelled, "Hello?" He yelled "Hello?" three more times until a pretty, blond Aeroflot stewardess appeared from the back of the plane.

"Goot morging," said the stewardess with a smile. "You Amoilko? *Gospadeen Mactavarich*?"

Blake smiled and said, "*Da. Dobraye utra.*"

"*Dobraye utra*," she said and made a formal hand gesture towards the cabin of the airplane. "*Pazhalusta.*"

The cabin of the aircraft was all fitted out with polished, varnished wood and grey fabric. It had a front section like a lounge area, with a bench cushion seat running down one side. Blake sat down on a big comfortable seat facing the 'conventional direction' towards the front of the plane. "*Kofye?*" asked the stewardess.

"*Da, pazhalusta*," replied Blake.

Blake was having a second cup of coffee when he heard, then saw through a small window, a tractor and wagon pull up to the plane, presumably with his baggage. The workers loaded the stuff in the tail baggage compartment. He remembered with an inward laugh that, had this been wintertime, the next step would be for a truck carrying a jet engine to violently blow the ice off the wings with heated exhaust. Presumably spraying ethylene glycol on wings was not something the Soviets had ever done, probably because of lack of supply.

Just before nine o'clock, two Aeroflot pilots boarded the aircraft and went straight into the cockpit, closing the door behind them. In Russia, pilots were the last to board, and the first to get off. Passenger movement efficiency and customer service was not part of the system.

When the pilots started the engines, the noise and vibration were incredible. Like the Douglas DC-9, however, the engine noise would be behind the aircraft in flight. The Tu-134, like the DC-9, was a development of the twin rear-engine Sud Aviation Caravelle. Unlike the DC-9, the Tu-134 had a longer take-off roll, probably because the wing was simpler and the airplane was heavier.

After traversing a long, convoluted taxi route, the Tu-134 finally pulled on to the active runway. Blake thought the ground speed was unbelievably high over the rough runway at rotation. He concluded the landing gear on the airplane must have been *way* over designed to put up with constant abuse.

The flight would be three hours in length and cover two time zones. Blake politely said '*nyet*' when the stewardess offered him some vodka. Before lunch, she brought him some deep-fried pieces of toast, orange caviar, and slices of cucumber. The toast was delicious, but very rich. Lunch was warmed chicken and potatoes, again very rich because the food had been cooked in what seemed to be animal fat.

Blake tried to doze for a few minutes, but the thought of soon 'hitting the ground' and literally going right to work had him stressed-out a bit.

It occurred to him suddenly that he was the only passenger on an airplane like a DC-9. The absurdity of that, and the waste of fuel, really bothered him. This was clearly an unsustainable practice. He could not *imagine* what the Russians would be thinking about it. Eventually, real-world economics would appear in this country, and Amoilco would have to rethink trying to impose 'Western' standards on everything.

But that was clearly the corporate strategy. Roy had told him, 'Just remember, the guys at the top literally believe, 'where there is crap, there is opportunity'. Amoilco's a bit desperate right now to return bigger profits in a low oil price environment. And you've already seen there's a *lot of crap* in Russia, and therefore *opportunity*. But just remember one thing, *no graft*. The big guys have to believe whatever deals we sign will be bulletproof under US Security and Exchange Commission scrutiny. A big part of your job will be to demonstrate that we can work profitably in Russia to American standards.'

As a Canadian, Blake perceived Amoilco was demonstrating from top to bottom an American form of arrogance; that American technology and methods were far superior; and that American-managed large-scale projects could be executed and operated more efficiently than Russians could ever do. Amoilco executives hoped the country would quickly move to an efficient, market-based economy, gladly accepting mentoring from their new American friends. But if that was delayed, Amoilco executives figured they could protect themselves with contractual language, with disputes ending up in American courts.

Blake was now deeply involved with a project to find out more about a massive oilfield called '*Podobskoye Mestorozhdeniye*'. The oil deposit was underneath a wide section of the Ob River floodplain, and about one hundred kilometres west of Neftezapadsibirsk. The Russian government was applying pressure on the regional 'Production Association' or 'PA', called '*KhantyRusNefteGaz*' or 'KhRNG', to find an American partner.

The Russian government wanted western technology and methodology, hoping to increase profitability and reduce environmental impacts. Amoilco thought they could get a deal with the Russians where, ultimately, they could 'share production'; Amoilco would take oil in kind out of the country and get world price, and KhRNG would keep selling their oil domestically.

Blake suspected the idea was hopeless, and he thought Roy Elliot did too. But his job as 'front man' was to assist the team with moving towards a deal, and behave at all times as a good ambassador according to 'western' standards. He was also expected to be a very good industrial spy, and never get caught doing that. That part of the 'mission' was never put in writing though, just implied.

But there were so many things to learn about Siberia; an ancient, mysterious, mostly Asian place that was once again in turmoil.

Blake then remembered with discomfort his *second* trip to Russia to open the office in Neftezapadsibirsk. He had boarded the charter airplane that first time with two American communications 'experts' from Amoilco's Denver office, Buzz Boyd and Henry Cody. Arman the interpreter had come along, too. The idea had been that after the Inmarsat telephone was up and running, Arman, Buzz and Henry would all return to Moscow together on the charter aircraft.

Buzz had looked like a cowboy, and had acted like one too. Henry had been a little more sedate, but had not been truthful with Blake about the official Russian approval to install the telephone in the Amoilco 'satellite' office. Blake had asked him twice, 'So everything is set up, right? We have formal written approval to use the telephone you're bringing in with you?' Henry and Buzz had both just blown him off with a laugh and a cavalier reply of, 'Of course, it's all in place.'

Buzz had pounded back vodka continuously on the charter flight, and had been drunk when they arrived. When they got to the hotel, and settled into the big, three-section room that was to be the Amoilco office, Blake had told Henry and Buzz to do *nothing* until he returned with Arman. 'We have to make our introductions to the Deputy General Director, and tell him about the phone,' he had said to Buzz and Henry.

Blake and Arman had come back to the hotel about two hours later. Their meeting with the PA had been a happy one. Blake had looked upwards in front of the hotel entrance, and he had seen a cable running up to the roof from a window on the third floor where the office was. 'Those stupid bastards have set up the phone!' Blake had yelled to Arman.

When they had rushed into the lobby, the new local Amoilco interpreter Elena had met them. She had looked really worried. She was a nice lady of forty or so, a former school teacher from Dagestan, with gold teeth. As they had made their way to the stairs, they saw maids standing around everywhere with their arms crossed. Some were crying, and some were just visibly angry.

'What are the maids crying for, Elena?' Blake had asked as they were climbing stairs two at a time.

'They say they're scared. They think they're being invaded by foreigners who are here to enslave them,' Elena had replied between breaths.

On the way to the Amoilco office, Blake had seen flower pots smashed on the floor under the hallway window where the cable had been run. Buzz and Henry had run the cable right down the hallway and into the Amoilco office! When they had got to the room, Blake had found the two men testing out the phone. They had both recoiled when they saw how angry Blake was.

Just then the red Russian telephone in the room had rung. Blake had motioned to Arman to answer it, and Arman had said, '*Allo*?' into the receiver. Over the duration of the three minute phone call, Arman had just said '*Da*' four times and '*Nyet*' twice. He had finished by saying '*Da, konechnya*', and then he had hung up the receiver. 'That was the KGB,' Arman had said calmly. 'They said not to turn the phone on until we show them our licence.'

'Okay,' Blake had replied calmly as well. 'Come on Henry, let's go with Arman and show them our licence.'

Henry had just looked sheepishly at Buzz and said, 'Well, we've actually only just *applied* for it.'

At the same time, Elena had been trying to introduce Blake to the very angry director of the hotel who had just stormed into the room. Blake had just about lost it completely then.

He had yelled at Henry and Buzz, 'You get your *lying asses* in gear and remove *everything* you've just done!' When they were running down the hallway, he had yelled after them, 'And don't break any more stuff, *you assholes*!'

The hotel director was smiling knowingly. She was a middle-aged, well-dressed woman with perfectly grey hair that almost looked purple. Blake suspected she had been the one that had called the KGB.

It had taken four days to get a faxed copy of the Inmarsat telephone licence from Moscow with the help of the Production Association, and the Amoilco Moscow office. Elena had gone to the post office every morning to pre-pay long-distance calls over the Russian system. Arman had requested each call from the operator on the red telephone in the Amoilco office. An hour after requesting a call, the phone would ring, and the operator would then place the connection manually. Then Arman would literally yell into the phone for three minutes during calls. Most of what he had yelled was, '*Shto*?' or 'What?' The connections had always been terrible, but at least they had *sort of* known what was happening in Neftezapadsibirsk back in the 'home' office.

It had all been very embarrassing for everyone, including the PA, who also owned the hotel. Buzz and Henry had cowered from Blake until the licence appeared. Then they had carefully run the cable from the small, self-standing antenna dish on the roof in through a window in the Amoilco office. Blake had made sure the hotel director approved of the installation.

Blake found out Buzz had later been fired, when he got drunk again and wandered off on his own during a trip to Baku.

3

For the second time during his long trip back to work in Siberia, Blake woke up to find he had slept upright in an airplane seat with his seat belt securely fastened. The Tu-134 charter had just started its decent into Neftezapadsibirsk.

He felt sweaty and a bit dizzy from jet lag and lack of sleep. His ears were hurting because of the rapid descent the pilots seemed to be making. He looked out of a window, and saw that it was a clear morning. They would be arriving at ten o'clock local time. The plane would take off at noon to return to Moscow with his counterpart, Jeff.

When they got closer to the ground, Blake could see tracks running everywhere over the barren areas of 'taiga', or sub-Arctic boreal forest and tundra. The tracks had been made, perhaps long ago, by wheeled and tracked vehicles that had damaged the active layer above the permafrost. The tracks would likely be there for centuries.

There were stunted, puny, hundred-year old trees in a few clumps here and there. Neftezapadsibirsk was at sixty-one degrees north latitude, on the south side of the mighty Ob River, right at the edge of the floodplain. It was minus forty degrees Celsius here for a week or so in the winter, and sometimes was over plus thirty degrees Celsius in the summer for a day or two. But it would typically get to a high temperature of about twenty Celsius at this time of year. Summer weather lasted only a couple of months.

The Soviet Union had started building the city of Neftezapadsibirsk in 1967 to house workers in a new oil development region within the Khanty-Mansiysk '*Okrug*', or

'Autonomous Region'. The city was designed for one hundred thousand people. It was built with standardised materials made elsewhere, including concrete slabs. The population was now about ninety-five thousand people. The Production Association's mission was to keep everyone gainfully employed and reasonably happy, and deliver the set production quotas, which were more than achievable as long as the supply chain associations did their bit and delivered *their* quotas.

Managers were rewarded if they met their quotas *exactly*. Overproduction created a myriad of problems within the planned economy. Therefore, there had actually been a disincentive to bring in new technology, or innovate to improve efficiency.

The PA followed a master plan to develop each oilfield that was prepared by a party-controlled 'institute'. Deviation was not allowed. The institutes sometimes revised their plans when 'reservoir surprises' were encountered. Successful PA managers were ones that could still meet their quotas when the supply chain failed them. The supply chain started *really* failing when the USSR started losing the Cold War. Then, worker safety and environmental protection had stopped being priorities, or even considerations.

The airport in Neftezapadsibirsk had one runway. It was made of standardised, pre-cast concrete blocks that had been laid on sand; then welded together where re-bar was exposed; and then paved over with asphalt. The concrete slabs had settled a bit unevenly. The runway was therefore really rough.

The Tu-134 pulled up to the small terminal building and the pilots shut down the engines. The silence was a welcome relief. There was no other activity at the small airport. There were about thirty helicopters parked near the terminal building on individual pre-cast concrete slabs. Blake saw they were mostly 'everyday workhorse' Mi-8 helicopters, but there were also a few massive Mi-6 helicopters and a few Ka-32A heavy-lift helicopters, with their twin, counter-rotating rotors, and no tail rotors, just steering fins. Only a few of the helicopters seemed to be serviceable, most had likely been scavenged for parts.

A small van with a stairway on its roof then pulled up to the front door of the plane. Blake could see Jeff Webb waiting just outside the airport gate next to the terminal building. Nikolai's car was behind Jeff. Elena would be in the car with Nikolai.

Blake waited about twenty minutes for the pilots to de-plane. Then he went down the stairs and waited for Jeff. Jeff walked over from the gate. A small truck with baggage arrived at the airplane at the same time Jeff did. Jeff looked really stressed, but he shook Blake's hand and said, "*Really* glad to see *you*, buddy! Let's do the baggage transfer thing first."

The 'ground crew' consisted of one bored-looking middle-aged man who drove the van with the stairs on top, and also the baggage truck. The airport worker opened the baggage compartment door at the back of the Tu-134, and just watched as Jeff and Blake first offloaded baggage, and then loaded baggage. Jeff was leaving with only a suitcase full of clothes.

When they were finished, the ground crew man closed the baggage compartment door, and drove the truck back to the gate. Nikolai would then supervise loading Blake's baggage on to a small hired truck that would follow them back to the hotel.

Blake and Jeff then went into the plane to do their 'handover'. Jeff handed Blake his handover notes; they were half a page of scribbled bullet points. Blake had given Jeff twelve pages of detailed, carefully typed text at their last handover.

Blake could see from the notes that Jeff had not done much on his twenty-eight day hitch. Jeff was a supply chain guy out of the Denver office who had experience with procurement. He was about forty-five, with a brush-cut and a big pot belly, and he smoked continuously. He had admitted to Blake when they first met that he was, 'just doing this gig for the money'. He said he had experienced some bad real estate deals that he was trying to recover from. Like Blake, he was single.

"So how did it go, Jeff?" Blake asked with a smile.

"Man, it sure dragged on at the end," said Jeff, shaking his head with disgust. Then he said loudly, "I almost went *nuts*. I don't know if I'll be back. The environmental guys just left, and they ran me ragged arranging cars and helicopters through the PA for their stupid field trips. And the geologists came in for a whole week. Same thing with them, a bunch of prima donnas! They wanted to go visit everyone and their dog, and look at hundreds of core samples. At least I had a way to bring in extra water and beer with the extra charter flights."

"Okay," said Blake. He was thinking what Jeff described was just the routine administrative part of the 'front man' job. Jeff was also supposed to be investigating how to procure office and oilfield supplies locally, and move things around through customs.

"I brought in two thousand American in cash so we can pay the staff, *et cetera*," added Blake. "How's the new office working out?"

"Well, we can change American dollars now to roubles in a local bank," said Jeff. Then he said proudly, "I set up a petty cash system. The key to the lock-box is on the key ring." Jeff paused to hand Blake a key ring. Then he added, "The Moscow office can now pay the hotel bill and the helicopter flights with wire transfers. The UPS is still alive, but it's been worked pretty hard with lots of brown-outs. The 220 volt power here is really dirty! We've got a printer now, sent in from Moscow. The Inmarsat phone and fax machine are working okay. Roy said we could call home as much as we wanted, but then he said to remember it costs eleven bucks a minute, so talk about a mixed message! Oh, and I didn't use your still. I figured Amoilco can afford to buy me as much bottled water as I want and have it sent it on the charter when I need it."

Blake waited a few moments for more from Jeff, and then he asked, "Anything else, Jeff?"

"Oh, Roy said it will cost over a hundred thousand dollars to bring a western-made vehicle in here, and he told me to look into buying one locally for now. So, Nikolai has a line on two new UAZ-469 jeeps for only four thousand bucks total! They came off the assembly line the same day, so we can use one for parts. They should be here next week, which means a month from now probably.

"But I'll never drive here. The cops can stick a needle into you for a blood sample if they think you've been drinking."

Blake then stood up, shook Jeff's hand, and said, "Well, enjoy your time off, Jeff."

"I'll enjoy it a *lot* more when I'm out of this *damn place* and drinking bourbon in business class," replied Jeff forcefully.

Blake chose not to say any more to Jeff. But he remembered what Roy Elliot had told him the first time they had met, 'Blake, I've been working my *whole career* for an opportunity like this one.'

Blake was of the same mindset as Roy. Most of the others on the team were as well. Jeff was the exception.

4

Nikolai and Elena were clearly pleased to see Blake again. While they were driving to the hotel in Nikolai's car, Elena chatted about what had been happening in town while Blake had been away.

It was only a short drive. Nikolai helped Blake unload the truck that had followed them back to the hotel, and then Nikolai released the truck and driver he had hired. Nikolai then helped carry all the stuff Blake had brought with him up the three flights of stairs to the Amoilco office. There was an elevator in the hotel, but it had never worked. Apparently missing parts just could not be found to fix it.

Then Blake released Nikolai for the rest of the day with a friendly handshake. Nikolai was working on a call-out basis with a daily retainer.

When they were alone in the office, Elena said angrily, "Jeff did *nothing* for a month. And every morning the garbage can was full of empty beer cans."

Blake put his hands up in the universal 'stop' sign, and said, "We're not going to talk about Jeff, Elena, especially when he's not here to defend himself. *I'm* here now, and I need your help. Now, are there any urgent matters for today?"

Elena then marched over to a stack of faxed documents in the left-hand section of the hotel room where Blake positioned his desk and the Inmarsat telephone. She picked up some documents, walked back to hand them to Blake, and said harshly, "Probably all of this stuff."

Blake flipped through the thick stack of printed A4 paper, and saw that some of the faxes were over a week old. Many required prior translation before delivery to people in the PA.

"Okay, can we see if we can catch up a bit today?" asked Blake. Then he added, "And then on Monday, maybe we can make some deliveries around town together?"

"All right, I *guess* I can work this afternoon," replied Elena abruptly. But she knew she would be getting overtime pay, so she added pleasantly, "Oh, and Brad White with Crackmeisters would like to meet with you in his office on Thursday. And you're invited to a party with his staff at his flat on Thursday night."

Crackmeisters was a Canadian-German oilfield hydraulic-fracturing joint venture.

Then Elena said, "And Roy Elliot and Penny Crawford are coming here a week from Monday, and would like you to set up some meetings for them." Penny was the team's community relations expert, and was a Canadian like Blake.

Blake's bedroom was at the other end of the three-section office. He could seal it off with a door. The middle section of the office was arranged like a living room, where they could sit with visitors comfortably. Elena also worked at a small desk in the middle section. She usually only worked during the week, Monday through Friday. The middle section also had a television that Blake had watched occasionally, to learn more about Russian culture. He stopped turning it on, however, when he heard the same model was blowing-up in other rooms in the hotel, and all over the country.

Blake usually ate in the hotel's restaurant. He could get soft cheese, chewy bread and black tea for breakfast, and weak soup and chewy bread for lunch. The restaurant made a nice borsht sometimes, and he always looked forward to that. For dinner, he could get a cutlet of some kind of meat that needed to be pounded by the cook to tenderise it. It always came with potatoes fried in fat, and greenhouse-grown cucumbers. Or sometimes they would serve him some kind of boiled wontons filled with pork. They called the dish '*pelmyeni*', and he enjoyed it with some Cajun spice he always brought into the restaurant with him.

On each trip to Neftezapadsibirsk, Blake also brought with him some canned and boxed food to occasionally make a 'western style' meal in his room. He had a 220 volt hot plate and a single pot. He also brought in *lots* of canned fruit, granola bars and multivitamins.

The water in the hotel was bright red with iron. The hot water was brighter red than the cold water. All water in the city moved through steel pipes. Copper and plastic pipe had never been available.

All hot water started out in the central heating plant in the city. Insulated, above-ground pipelines distributed the water around the city. The first pass of hot water through the hotel went through the radiators in the concrete walls. The second pass went to taps in the hotel rooms.

Blake had brought in a still to make distilled water that could be mixed with the bottled water. Amoilco sent bottled water to him from Moscow on the charter. He figured the still would reduce how much he had to lug up the stairs, and save the company a bit of money. He boiled the water he made with a 220 volt kettle for coffee and tea.

There was a small refrigerator in his office where he kept bottled water, and cans of beer, juice and pop. All of that stuff was sent in from Moscow on the charter.

The people in Neftezapadsibirsk had no choice but to drink the water that came out of the taps. Blake was *really* disturbed about that. Every week when he cleaned out the still it was filled with iron filings and bright red rust. Most of the people in the city, especially children, had kidney stones to some degree.

Blake woke up on his first Saturday night back on the job when the Inmarsat telephone started ringing. An angry accountant from the Atlanta corporate office complained loudly that Blake and Jeff were handling the petty cash 'all wrong'. He asked why Accounting had not been consulted. Blake replied politely, "Okay, sorry about that, sir. Please fax to us the spreadsheet we're supposed to use. Oh, and do you know what time it is here?" There was no reply, so Blake added, "Okay, well, it is three o'clock in the morning. Would you call back next time during our office hours, which are eight to five, *local time*? Thanks." And then Blake hung up without waiting for a reply.

He received at least one call a week like that. The extreme time zone difference was a new thing for most of corporate Amoilco.

The next morning, Blake's friend, Vadim Akhatov, dropped by for a visit. Blake was all alone; it was a quiet Sunday morning. "*Zdrastvueetye* Blake!" said Vadim with a big smile as he shook Blake's right hand with both of his hands. Then he added, "Welcome back, *moi droog*!"

Vadim had only been studying English for five months, but he was almost fluent now. He was a very bright, thirty year old engineer, married to a beautiful Russian lady named Natasha. They had a cute three-year-old daughter named Katya. Vadim was Tatarian, and looked like the American actor Charles Bronson, only skinnier. Vadim's uncle Ruslan had decided Blake needed a Russian mentor, and Vadim was given the job.

Ruslan Akhatov was the production chief of the small section of the Podobskoye Oilfield that was under development south of the flood plain. For environmental reasons, the PA had been forbidden from developing more of the field without a western partner. Blake was really glad Ruslan had given Vadim the assignment to basically look out for him.

Blake handed Vadim a compact disc. "A present for you, my friend," Blake said with a big grin. Then he explained, "It's the Pink Floyd album you liked." Vadim was clearly overjoyed to receive the gift. It was not something he could buy locally.

He had heard Pink Floyd for the first time during Blake's previous visit, and he thought it was 'fantastic music'.

Vadim and Blake then chatted for a while, and listened to the Pink Floyd album using Blake's 'boom box'. Then Blake arranged for Vadim to escort him around the Podobskoye Oilfield on Wednesday of that week, with Nikolai as their driver. No one from Amoilco, including Blake, had ever seen the small PA operation at Podobskoye.

Vadim also arranged to take Blake fishing the following Saturday, with Vadim's Tatarian best friend, Andrei Khuramovich.

5

Nikolai had borrowed an UAZ jeep from one of his friends for their day trip to Podobskoye. "Good machine, crap roads," said Nikolai after he and Blake picked up Vadim at the PA office. Vadim agreed with Nikolai about both of his observations.

Blake brought his international driver's licence with him. He would never 'drink and drive', but he also brought a syringe with him from his medical kit to offer to a policeman that might want to poke him for a blood sample for some reason. At least he would know the needle was clean that way. So, when they were outside of the city, Blake asked to take a turn at the wheel.

The UAZ or '*Oo-az*' drove like a tractor. None of its gears seemed to be synchromesh, so Blake had to double-clutch. It had thick rubber tyres, solid-axles, leaf-springs, crappy drum-brakes, and the door would open on the driver's side on hard turns to the right. Blake found it fun to drive in spite of all that, or maybe because of all that.

Blake asked Vadim why trees were dead or dying in a lot of places but only on one side of the road, not the other. Vadim replied, "We ran out of conduit pipes. The forest floods when it rains hard or a river rises, and the trees die." He said it in a cavalier manner, as if this was just a normal thing.

Vadim then explained how the PA built roads. The road to the oilfield, and ultimately to the regional capital of Khanty-Mansiysk, was under construction. So, Blake had the opportunity to observe for himself. Vadim explained, "Sand is available from the flood plain, but gravel and boulders are not. Trucks pour sand in strips about three metres high along the route where the road is to go. Then cranes place concrete slabs side-by-side on the sand. Then cars and trucks drive on the slabs for one year to compact the sand. Then cranes lift each slab up, and workers fill the holes in with sand to level them again. Then the slabs are laid again and welded together where the reinforcing bars are exposed. Then the road is opened for use. After another year some really important roads are paved with asphalt."

When they reached the part of the road where slabs had recently just been laid on sand, they let Vadim drive. After a few kilometres, they were on an oiled, sand road full of deep potholes. Blake could see the new road would be a major improvement over the alternative.

Vadim pointed out the sign marking where the oilfield began. He pulled on to a 'pad' where they were drilling, completing and producing wells. It was a large, flat area that had been cleared, then raised and levelled with sand. There were oil stains and even some puddles of crude oil in many places. They all got out of the UAZ for a look around.

The drilling rig was idle. It was on rails to allow it to drill a series of wells in a line. It was very old looking, but it was a rotary rig with a 'double drill pipe' derrick. Blake thought it could probably handle the twenty-five hundred metre wells he knew they were drilling, as long as the wells weren't too deviated, and they didn't get 'stuck in the hole'. But the wells would probably require a long time to drill, and side-track if the rig broke down a lot. And Blake had heard they got 'stuck in the hole' a lot because the drilling fluids they used were full of drilled solids. Blake could see some 'drilling mud' spilled on the pad in places, too. Drilled cuttings were directed to huge pits on the pad.

There was no 'service rig' currently on the pad for 'completing' or 'working-over' wells. There were about twenty small 'pump jacks' on the pad. About a third of the pump jacks were working. The pump jacks moved 'sucker rods' up and down. The rods were connected to double check-valves near the bottom of wells to 'lift' oil to surface.

So, Blake concluded the wells could not flow without help, or 'artificial lift', even if the field was under some kind of water-flood to maintain reservoir pressure.

The pump jacks were of at least three different types. Vadim explained to Blake, "We have to get them from wherever we can."

"So, is the field under water-flood?" asked Blake.

"No, not yet. We are still waiting for equipment," answered Vadim sadly. Blake knew they would recover only about a quarter of the 'oil in place' without water injection. They could recover up to half of the oil in place with a well-designed and operated 'water-flood'.

Blake could see a 'battery' facility nearby where the crude oil was de-pressurised, de-gassed and put into big 'atmospheric' tanks for storage. It would eventually be pumped down a pipeline to a refinery somewhere. There was a huge flare spurting intermittently at the battery, and Blake did not want to go near it.

As soon as they drove off the wellhead pad, they went down a hill. Vadim said, "We are now going down into the Ob River flood plain." The road ended at the edge of a river channel. They all got out of the UAZ again.

"This road continues on in the winter time," said Vadim. Then he explained, "There are many channels and islands in the summer, and one big river in the spring, during flood. The exploration wells were all drilled in winter time, in the 1960s."

"Amoilco thinks we should build 'artificial islands' or thick sand pads out in the floodplain, reinforced by concrete in places," said Blake. Then he added, "They want to bring in powerful western-made rigs and use clean drilling fluids. The plan is to drill highly-deviated wells to reduce the number of 'islands' required. And they want to put berms around the pads to contain spills, and plant bushes on the banks to stabilise the pads and prevent erosion during spring floods. Amoilco is doing some joint studies with a Russian institute right now to see what types of bushy plants might work best." Vadim seemed to be pleased to hear all of that, which Blake found reassuring.

6

It was Thursday morning, and Blake was acclimatised again after four full days in Neftezapadsibirsk.

Nikolai drove Blake to the Crackmeisters' office building for his nine o'clock meeting. Nikolai found a place nearby to park and wait. The office building looked to be a converted store of some kind. It was two-storeys tall, and made out of pre-cast concrete slabs. Blake was ushered right in to Brad White's office by a burly female security guard.

Blake had met Brad briefly once before. Brad was the director of the regional joint venture operation. He was from Edmonton, Alberta, and a graduate engineering-technologist. He was about forty years of age and slim, with premature grey hair that he kept fairly short.

Blake thought Brad looked older than the last time he had seen him, which had been only a few months before.

"Hi, Blake!" said Brad with a smile as they shook hands. Then he said casually, "Here, have a seat." Blake sat down on a chair in front of Brad's desk.

Brad studied Blake's face for a moment, then he said, "I figured I should follow up on my offer to explain more about what we're doing here."

"That would be great, Brad," said Blake. They waited while a pretty, petite, dark-haired woman placed a cup of coffee in front of each man.

"Thanks, Olga," said Brad with a smile. The woman smiled back as she left the room.

"Well, basically," Brad began, "We hydraulic fracture 'crap' wells, and split the incremental production with the

Russian side. The joint venture has gone through a number of evolutions, as the Russian rules are continually changed around us. And unfortunately, we may be about to go through yet another 'evolution' here that could end everything.

"The parent Canadian company hydraulic fractures wells as a service to oil companies, mostly in Alberta. Our German partner brought to our attention an opportunity here. The Russians use a 'dirty' drilling fluid and severely damage every sandstone reservoir they drill." Blake nodded as he was aware of that reality.

"Well, cutting to the chase," Brad continued. "We struck up a deal where we could read through the Russian well records, and select wells we thought had the best potential for 'stimulation'. We brought some 'frac' trucks and their crews in from Alberta. That took a bit of doing. We thought initially we would have to do moderately-sized 'fracs', you know, with thirty or forty tonnes of quartz sand 'proppant'. But we quickly found we only needed to do relatively small 'fracs' of ten tonnes or so, to just get past the near-wellbore damage.

"We quickly found we could turn wells making nothing, or a few barrels a day, into one thousand to three thousand barrel a day 'gushers'!" Blake reacted appropriately with a look of surprise on his face.

"Initially, the Russian side was really pleased, as they were getting half of the production increase," Brad continued. "The Russians sold all of the oil into their domestic market, and gave us half the proceeds.

"But here's what I really wanted you to know. The Russians *hate* the idea that foreigners can profit from doing business here. They inherently distrust us, and don't want us here. They want our technology and our money, and as soon as they have that, they use their system to *screw us*." Brad let that soak in a minute, and had a sip of his coffee.

"Now, here's what happened to us," Brad continued, while shaking his head. "Suddenly the Russian side announced *they* would select the wells we could consider for 'fracing'. When we *still* had great success, they suddenly announced the wells that were 'fraced' would have 'second priority' in their pipeline system. That started out meaning wells would be shut in for a few days a month.

"That has steadily increased to our wells being shut in *most of the time*! The Russians are now telling us they want a 'new deal' where we will have to take our oil 'in kind'. That means, we'll have to negotiate *our own* contracts with Russian pipeline companies to get our oil to a refinery where we can sell it."

Brad could see he had Blake's full attention. So he added, "I think you guys will have the same problem. The pipelines out of here are like a coral snake, sections are owned by different entities. You could cut fair deals with say, six of seven entities, or 'bands on the snake' if you will, and the seventh 'band' could demand *exorbitant* rates, believing they had you 'over a barrel'. If you were to agree to those terms to get them on-side, the other six 'bands' would suddenly want the same freaking deal."

"So, is there something else you are thinking of trying?" asked Blake.

"Yes, we've been working the last few months to see if we can hire ourselves out here as a conventional 'service' company," replied Brad. Then he explained, "You know, 'pay us a fee and we'll frac your well for you'. But we're encountering one bureaucratic obstacle after another, especially on the tax front. And we would insist on payment in 'hard' currency, which the Russians don't have.

"We'll keep trying for a while longer though. The crews really like it here. If you come to our party tonight, you can hear that from them yourself."

"Okay, Brad, that would be great," replied Blake with a smile. Then he asked, "What time?"

"Come around six," said Brad, standing up to shake Blake's hand. Then he added, "We'll have some food plates set out.

Elena knows where it is, she's been over a few times. She can tell your driver how to get there."

Blake stopped at the office door, and added, "You know Brad, I don't think we can blame the Russians too much for not trusting us. They've been attacked or invaded by Huns, Vikings, Swedes, Poles, Mongols, French, Japanese and Germans. They're scared *shitless* by the Chinese, and are always worried about the Koreans. They remember how American generals like Patton and Macarthur wanted to switch from fascists to communists to keep major wars going.

"Maybe they just see us as the latest bunch of exploiting invaders?"

Brad just nodded and picked up a document on his desk to go back to work.

7

Nikolai had no problem finding Crackmeisters' apartment building. It was the only one finished in a block of four concrete-slab buildings. When he dropped Blake off nearby, Nikolai said with a grin, "I wait here, Mister Blake, enjoy."

A young couple were at the door of the apartment building, laughing and smoking cigarettes. Blake walked up to them with a smile and said, "Hi, I'm Blake with Amoilco. I think Brad White is expecting me."

"Oh, yea," said the young man. He dropped his cigarette and stubbed it out with his shoe, shook Blake's hand, and said, "Hi, I'm Jack. And this is Tanya." The girl just smiled. She was really good-looking, and probably only eighteen years old. Then Jack said, "Come on, Blake, we'll take you up. Everyone's on the third floor." Blake followed behind as they climbed the stairs. He could see there was an elevator shaft, but no elevator. Non-working elevators seemed to be a very common local problem.

Brad greeted Blake at the top of the stairs, and led him into the first flat on the right. The door was wide open. The room was packed with muscular, young Canadian men, and local women. The women represented most of the ethnic groups in the former Soviet Union. Blake thought some were Uzbeks and Tatars, and obviously some were Russians, and maybe some were possibly Estonians. Some of the women were moderately good-looking, but most had clearly aged before their time.

Life was very hard here. Blake had come to the conclusion that women had made the USSR work. And things had not changed much. The average Russian man drank half a bottle of vodka a day. In the old system, you had to do something really bad to get fired and being hungover or even being a bit drunk was not considered all that bad for a man. Women usually worked as well and they had to keep the family running, stand in long queues to shop, and put up with a lot of 'crap' from their husbands or boyfriends. All of that took a huge mental and physical toll.

"Here's my number two," said Brad, stopping in front of a man standing alone with a mixed drink in his hand. Then he said, "I'll leave you two to get acquainted for a minute."

"Hi, I'm Blake, with Amoilco, from Calgary," said Blake offering his hand.

The man seemed to be reluctant at first to shake his hand. He was overweight and balding and he was perspiring heavily. "Wade, ah, Phillips, from Red Deer," he said finally, and then shook Blake's hand. Wade's grip was weak and his palm was wet.

"So, I heard you guys were trying to set up shop here, too?" Wade asked in a rather aloof manner. And then he added, "And you think you can do business here like you do in Texas or Alberta, eh? Well, *good luck* with that."

"Really?" asked Blake. And then he added, "What do you mean, Wade?"

"I mean, the only way you can get anything done around here is to 'grease palms'," said Wade. He paused to take a big sip of his drink. Then he explained, "If I want a helicopter, I just go to the airport and start flipping US dollars at people. Hell, I can go *anywhere* for a hundred, or two hundred bucks, tops. We pay a *lot* less than you guys will be paying."

Blake thought for a second, and then he said, "Well, Amoilco thinks once you start down that road, the money for bribes just keeps going up, and eventually you lose your licence to operate back in the States or Canada when regulators find out about it."

"Well, buddy, you're going to fail then," said Wade smugly. Then he said loudly, "Here, ask this guy. Hey, *Massimo*, come over here will you?"

A pleasant-looking man of average height then came over to join them. He was in his mid-forties, with curly-brown hair and olive-coloured skin. He was dressed in expensive-looking but casual Italian clothing, and he was wearing some gold jewellery.

"Massimo, this is another Canadian guy, Blake from Calgary, with Amoilco," said Wade. Then he snarled, "He thinks you don't have to pay bribes here. Well, see you. I'm going to get another drink."

As soon as Wade left, Blake offered his hand to the man and said with a smile, "Hi, I'm Blake McTavish. Pleased to meet you, Massimo."

The man smiled back warmly and said, "Massimo Bartolini, at your service, sir." Massimo sighed, and then he said, "I get tired of some of the crude things I hear at functions like this." Massimo's English was very good, with a slight Italian accent.

Blake nodded in agreement, and then he asked, "So, what are you doing here, Massimo?"

"Well, I run a construction company out of Naples, Italy," answered Massimo. Then he explained, "I have a staff of twenty artisans with me here now, and we renovate buildings to high standards using European methods and materials. The Production Association is letting us finish apartment buildings, and we've just started doing a hotel for them.

"You've probably noticed all of the unfinished buildings around the edge of town? The PA ran out of money, and they couldn't get Russian materials anymore, anyway, even if they had the money. We get paid back with part of the rent or revenue received when buildings are occupied."

Blake looked puzzled, and Massimo took a quick look around the crowded, noisy room. Then he said quietly, "There is a new class of rich people emerging here. They're calling them 'oligarchs' in Moscow. A lot of them are old communist party leaders. Some have connections to the Russian Mafia, but most are just opportunists with connections.

"We know all about these things in Italy. But if it costs us up-front money to get work, or to get things done, we know how to do it with *class*, so no one is offended. I'll give you one everyday example. I never use money. I carry bottles of nice Italian wine in my trunk. If a policeman stops me in my car, I casually open my trunk and pull out a couple of bottles of nice wine. Then I ask him about his family as we walk over to his guard house. Then I offer him a smoke and forget I put the packet of cigarettes with two more on his table. Then I put the wine discreetly somewhere, and forget I did that too. Then I shake his hand, we laugh, and I go on my way. No one is offended. A poor policeman and his wife are happier, and I get on with my business."

Brad then came over with an attractive, blonde-haired young woman, and said, "Oh, so I see you two have met, that's great! Blake, this is my girlfriend, Lyudmila. Lyudmila this is Blake McTavish, another 'Canuck'." Blake shook Lyudmila's hand, and she gave him a sly smile which could have meant anything. She was wearing a nice French perfume.

"Massimo fitted out this place for us, although he's still working on getting us an elevator," said Brad with a laugh. Then he added, "The concrete shell cost us next to nothing. Massimo brought everything in from Europe. Massimo's only competition around here is a Turkish company, but their work is not up to the same high standard as Massimo's."

"The Turks are *pigs*," said Lyudmila with disgust with a thick Russian accent. Then she spat out angrily, "They wash out their condoms to use them again."

Brad could see Blake was blushing, so he quickly said, "All of our crews have flats in this building. Most of the guys have girlfriends here now." Brad then kissed Lyudmila on the cheek, and she left them to talk to some other people.

"Most of these guys also have girlfriends or wives back in Canada too," Brad continued quietly. Then he confessed, "We've been kind of living a 'double life' here. It will be *really hard* to leave if we can't figure out how to stay in business."

Brad then looked sadly at Lyudmila at the other end of the room.

8

Blake was standing just outside the entrance to his hotel in Neftezapadsibirsk. He was wearing his tall rubber boots, a thick sweater under his insulated oilfield coveralls, and a stocking-cap or 'tuque'. The tuque had an Amoilco logo on it, only with the 'c' in Amoilco replaced by a 'k'. He was wearing leather gloves, and he was holding on to a disassembled spinning rod and a small tackle box.

It was a windy, cold, Saturday morning. He could see a few snow flurries, and realised it was only just above freezing temperature. 'I don't know about this,' he thought to himself, 'It's July 11, and there probably is better weather in Tuktoyaktuk.'

There were only a few people moving about. He could see the patriotic mural on the side of the PA building across the street. It was done in the 'heroic style' popular in the USSR in the mid-sixties. There was a metal statue of Lenin on a concrete block pedestal in front of the mural. Everything was still nicely maintained. Graffiti had not yet reached this part of Russia. Most people were still 'happy in their work', or were pretending to be so.

A small, two-door car pulled up in front of Blake, and Vadim got out of the car on the passenger side. "Good morning, Blake!" he cried loudly with a big grin. "Today we are '*reebokii*', fishermen, not oilmen."

Then a huge, dark-haired, Slavic-looking young man struggled out of the other side of the Russian-made car. He walked over to join them on the sidewalk, and Vadim said by way of introductions, "*Eta moi droog, Andrei. Andrei, eta Gospadeen McTavish.*"

"*Maya imya Blake, Andrei,*" said Blake with a smile as he shook hands with Andrei. Andrei's hands were also huge. He was almost two-and-a-half metres tall, and clearly all muscle like the smaller Vadim. Blake could tell instantly Andrei was a nice guy.

"Come, let's go," said Vadim, while taking the fishing gear out of Blake's hands. Andrei opened the trunk of the car, and Vadim somehow found a spot for Blake's stuff inside. Vadim then struggled into the back seat, and Blake took the front passenger seat.

As they were driving along, Vadim explained that Andrei also worked for the PA. Andrei did not speak English, but from Vadim's description of his work, Blake concluded he was either a reservoir engineer, or a technologist working for reservoir engineers. Not all Russian oilfield positions matched up with western ones.

They drove about twenty kilometres west of Neftezapadsibirsk on the main road, and then Andrei turned on to a rough sand road going north and down into the Ob River floodplain. The road soon became a narrow lane running through very tall, segmented grass that looked like a type of bamboo.

Andrei stopped the car in a small clearing at the side of a wide river channel. They all got out of the car, and Andrei started pulling everything out of the trunk. "Andrei found this place by accident last year," explained Vadim. Then he said, "No one else uses it. So, the fishing is good here."

Vadim and Andrei were both wearing a kind of green, military uniform obviously made for cold weather. Vadim saw Blake looking at what they were wearing, and said, "We were both in the militia together." Blake didn't know if the 'militia' in Russia was the same as the 'militia' in Canada, but decided it really didn't matter.

Blake then pulled down the zipper on the top of his coveralls, pulled out two tuques and handed one to Vadim and one to Andrei. "Amoilko," read Andrei out loud. "*Kharasho! Spaseeba balshoi!*"

"*Pazhalusta*," replied Blake with a smile. The 'I' and the 'L' used in the logo on the tuque were not Russian letters, but Blake was happy that Andrei had still figured it out. Penny would be pleased to hear about that.

Blake watched as his two Russian comrades pulled a small rubber raft out of the trunk of the puny little car, and then rolled it out on the ground. Vadim then started to inflate the raft with a foot-powered pump. At the same time, Andrei unravelled what looked like a cotton gill net, wrapped around two dozen or so one metre long sticks.

As Vadim was pumping with his foot he said, "We'll show you how we usually catch fish, and then you can show us your Canadian technology. Maybe we will see which way is better?" He laughed when he saw Blake suddenly looked a bit apprehensive.

When they had the raft in the water, Vadim pulled a wicker basket out of the trunk. He said, "We are now ready, but first we must toast to our success." He pulled three small glasses out of the basket, and a bottle of vodka. He handed Blake and Andrei each a glass, and then filled their glasses. Then he filled his own glass. "Blake, I said toast, but this is good vodka and I meant *sip it* and *enjoy it*." Vadim held his glass out and said solemnly, "*Na oozpekh*, to success!"

Andrei and Blake both said, "*Na oozpekh!*" in return, and took a sip of the vodka. Blake thought it actually did taste pretty good.

Blake then held his glass out and said, "*Za meer ee droozhba*, to peace and friendship!"

Vadim and Andrei looked at each other strangely. Then Vadim said, "Is good toast, Blake, but communists used it. But, *davaii*, let's sip anyway!"

When they finished their vodka, Andrei and Vadim somehow got into the small raft together. Vadim paddled them around while Andrei stuck the sticks in the muddy river bottom, then strung the net between the sticks under the water. It took them about half an hour to complete the job. Blake could not imagine how Andrei had tolerated the very cold water with his bare hands.

When they climbed out of the raft, Vadim said, "Okay, now show us the Canadian way!"

Blake had assembled his rod while Andrei and Vadim were in the raft. They watched as he clipped a red and white 'spoon' on to the leader. He made two casts, then hooked a small pike. "Is good!" cried Vadim. Then they all took turns using the rod. Blake showed them how to adjust the tension on the spinning-reel so they could play the fish without losing them.

Andrei and Vadim were keeping every fish. Blake realised this wasn't just for fun.

While Andrei was taking another turn with the fishing rod, Vadim looked through Blake's small tackle box, and pulled out a small hook. "Try next, Blake?" he asked.

"Okay, sure," replied Blake. Then he observed, "But we don't have any worms."

"We could dig for some, but Siberian worms are very small," said Vadim. Then he laughed, and said, "But I will show you a better thing. Put the hook on the line, then watch."

Blake then tied the hook on to the line, clipped a lead weight just above it, and then he watched as Vadim scooped a big green fly off his leg into his hand. Vadim stuck the small hook carefully through the abdomen of the fly without killing it. "Now watch," said Vadim, as he lowered the rod to place the fly on the water near the edge of the river bank. The buzzing fly was barely below the surface of the muddy water when he hooked a fish. After a pretty good fight, Vadim pulled a nice, two pound white fish of some kind up on to the bank.

Blake laughed and shook both Vadim's and Andrei's hands. "Now *that's* what I call 'fly-fishing'!" he yelled. Vadim translated, and Andrei laughed too.

Blake was feeling the cold, but he could tell Andrei and Vadim were not, so he pretended he didn't mind it either. These Siberian men were very tough 'hombres'. But they had also become fast friends.

They had a lunch of bread, cheese, cucumbers, caviar and cold smoked fish that Vadim pulled out of his basket. They had another glass of vodka with their lunch. Then Andrei and Vadim got back in their raft, and gathered in their net. When they got back to shore with it, they unravelled it again and plucked out about two dozen fish, mostly white fish and a species of small carp.

When they had everything back inside the car, Vadim said, "Blake, the Russian way was okay, the Canadian way was okay, but the *combined way* was best."

Blake laughed and said, "I think you're on to something, Vadim."

9

It was Monday morning, and Blake was now into the second week of his 'hitch'. Roy Elliot, Penny Crawford and Arman Assarian, the elite interpreter, arrived from Moscow on the charter. Roy and Arman immediately went over to the PA building for a private meeting with Sergei Artemiev, the 'number two man' with the PA. Nikolai drove Penny and Elena around to visit a number of local community organisations.

Blake manned the office by himself. He found he had time to examine some well test reports that Vadim had 'borrowed' for him to examine, with the stipulation that the reports must all be returned intact the next day.

Amoilco was paying a retainer fee for another room in the hotel. Blake and Jeff used the smaller room for storage when they did not have visitors. Roy had decided to stay in that room on this trip. Blake had arranged a third room for Penny to stay in during her visit.

The hotel rates had never changed since the hotel opened in the late 1960s. Amoilco paid the rouble equivalent of eight US dollars per day for the big three-section room they used for an office, and four US dollars per day for the other rooms they used.

Just after five o'clock in the afternoon, Penny and Roy came back into the office together. Roy looked tired, but Penny was bubbly and cheerful. Roy took off his tie, and asked, "What time is 'happy hour' around here, Blake?"

Blake said, "Right now, sir. They want us down in the restaurant at six thirty. I have cold water, cold pop, cold beer, twelve-year-old Canadian rye whiskey, but I have no ice. What will you have?"

Roy and Blake decided to have whiskey and cold bottled water. Penny selected cold cola and whiskey. They sat down together in the living area of the office with their drinks.

"How did it go today, Roy, or can you talk about that?" asked Blake.

"It went a lot better than it has up to now," said Roy, stretching his legs out. Then he explained, "It was a good idea to leave the lawyers behind for once. The PA 'big-wigs' now say they understand our concern about lack of tax and natural resource laws in the country. They promised to keep working with us on the basis that the Production Sharing Agreement or 'PSA' will be a 'stand-alone' document. They warned me, though, that the PSA will have to be approved by the Russian 'Duma', or parliament, to carry any weight, and override any other legislation that gets passed.

"We agreed on a timetable for completing the draft PSA. Tomorrow morning, we'll flesh that out to include who will meet with whom exactly, and when. The Russian side will write up a Memorandum of Understanding or 'MOU' this time to capture our interim agreement. They attach a lot more value to MOUs than we do. They call them 'Protokols'." Roy paused to take a big sip of his drink, then added, "They want to celebrate this 'Protokol' by treating us to a dinner with the general director tomorrow night. You're both invited."

"It sounds like real progress to me," offered Blake. "How about you, Penny, how did you do today?"

Penny had been lost in her own thoughts and had not really been listening to Roy. She looked at Roy and Blake, smiled awkwardly and said, "Sorry, I was 'wool-gathering' just now. But I heard your question at least! I think I did some good today. I finally got in to see my 'equivalent' at the PA. She likes my idea about jointly sponsoring the river cruise during the Finno-Yugric Reunion."

"What on earth is a 'Finno-Yugric Reunion'?" asked Roy with a confused look on his face.

Penny laughed, then explained, "Well, it seems that every ten years or so, ethnic groups that speak variations of Finnish, Hungarian and the local indigenous languages, Khanty and Mansi, have been getting together to 'bond and reconnect'. The communist government used to pay travel costs, and the propaganda press always made a big deal out of it. The Khanty and Mansi people used to be big reindeer herders, and some still do that. Their language has the same roots as Finnish and Hungarian."

"Really?" asked Roy. He seemed surprised, and sincerely interested.

"Yes, it's true," replied Penny, happy to see some interest. Then she added, "I have an anthropologist friend in Calgary that thinks our Inuit people may use some of the same words too and have some of the same religious beliefs. Something stemming from the land bridge that once connected Siberia to Alaska, I guess.

"So, my thought is we could offer to pay some of the reunion costs, and bring over an Inuit couple to attend. I know a 'bear dancer' from Copper Mine who would be just perfect. His wife plays a drum while he dances in his furry costume. She also keeps him away from the booze. We might get some free publicity, and make some cultural ties that we can build upon down the road. Everyone would get on a river cruise boat here in their native costumes, and then we would stop in a few places along the Ob River for scheduled celebrations on shore. We would sleep on the boat for security."

"I think that idea has *great* potential, Penny!" said Roy with a big smile. Then he added, "So, please keep working on it, and work up a cost estimate for me."

"Elena and I will help you every way we can, Penny," added Blake. Then he said, "That will be a lot of fun for us."

"Go ahead, make my day, guys!" said Penny with a laugh.

"We are advancing constantly," said Roy solemnly, holding his glass up for a toast. "We're going to grab the cynics by the nose, and we're going kick them in the butt! And we're going to kick the hell out of them, all of the time, and we're going to go through them like crap through a goose!"

"Amen, brother!" said Blake with a laugh, after sipping his drink.

"Halleluiah!" said Penny with passion. "Where did you get that, Roy?"

"Patton said something like that to inspire his troops," said Roy with a smile. Roy had been an artillery officer in the US Army. He went through university as an ROTC cadet.

After dinner, Roy was sitting with Blake in the Amoilco office having another drink. "Blake, at your age, if you're not feeling good, you're probably either not drinking enough or you're drinking too much," Roy said quite seriously. Then he added, "Finding the right balance is the key."

Blake smiled and said, "That's good advice, thanks."

Roy had an envelope in his shirt pocket, and handed it to Blake. Blake opened it, and saw it was a letter on Amoilco letterhead, signed by Roy. It thanked Blake for 'doing a great job' and opening the first office in Siberia. It was copied to his HR file.

When Blake had finished reading the letter, Roy said, "There's a brass clock coming as well, engraved with your name on it with the words, *First Amoilco Expat in Siberia.*"

Roy then shook Blake's hand and said, "I think you're doing a *great* job here, Blake, and I just want you to know that. You and Penny are our *secret weapons*. You are typical Canadians, which means you're polite, tolerant and respectful, and you make real friends."

Blake was a bit choked-up, but managed to say, "That means a *lot* to me Roy, coming from you. Thanks!"

Blake thought Roy was one of the best bosses he had ever worked for. He was a natural, sincere and inspirational leader.

Blake was making a lot of mental notes, so he could try to be the same one day if he was ever given the chance to be a manager.

After sipping their drinks for a while, Roy asked, "So, what did you get up to today, Blake?"

"Well, I looked carefully at some Russian exploration well 'drill stem test' data that Vadim lent me 'under the table' for a day," said Blake. Then he explained, "It looks like Institute drilling crews shot holes through casing set in an oil reservoir section picked from wireline logs. Then they used *air* to blow the fluid out of the well! It looks like they did that *twice*, once to remove the mud and bring in a volume of 'live oil', and then again while measuring how much oil they pulled out of the reservoir on the first 'blow'.

"Geez, they must have had the occasional blowout using that practice, and maybe some big explosions at times too! A fuel-air mixture makes a powerful bomb if there's a source of ignition. Sorry, you would know that better than me, being an artillery officer.

"Anyway, after the 'second blow', they had a way to monitor the rise of fluid in the cased well over time, maybe using a sonar device at the surface? I guess it was their way of estimating the productivity of wells using some approximating algorithms.

"We, of course, use downhole testing valves, sensitive downhole pressure gauges, and pressure-transient analysis. And for a land exploration well, we would try to do it 'open hole' without the expense of running casing. And we would use a downhole 'packer' to reduce the wellbore storage volume, and speed up the test.

"I converted their tabulated fluid levels to hydrostatic head using an assumed oil density. I then plotted the derived pressure build-up. I think there's a *lot* of 'near wellbore damage'. That's no surprise, considering the 'crap' drilling fluids they used.

"But I think I can show that the 'B-12' formation is really 'tight' in all of the wells. It probably has less than ten millidarcies of permeability. But the 'B-10' formation is much better, probably more than ten times better. I sent a spreadsheet with my work to Chuck, the reservoir engineer in Houston."

Roy sat thinking for a minute. Then he said, "Those numbers line up pretty well with what the geoscientists have guessed from looking at the Russian logs, and the bit of sandstone core they've been able to look at. Unfortunately, the Russians and our guys both think most of the oil is in the 'crappy B-12' formation.

"We may be able to eventually get comfortable about a commercial deal, but you can't do anything cheaply to overcome bad rock. And you have to be able to get the produced oil to market." Blake had told Roy over dinner about his meetings with Crackmeisters.

"I think the difference in well testing methods is just another example of the differences in our political systems," Roy continued. Then he explained, "The Russian explorers could get steel casing, cement, and air compressors, but not inflatable packers, sensitive downhole pressure gauges and reliable downhole tester-valves. They had to use drilling rig crews for their tests, not specialist technologists and service companies. Rig time meant mostly nothing to them because their economy was 'false'. And if you were hurting people anyway with other unsafe practices, why care if the odd well blew-out, or blew-up?"

Just then, the Inmarsat telephone started ringing. Blake got up to answer it. He came back in to the living area after a few minutes, and said, "Roy, it's a corporate lawyer from Atlanta. Something about our handout gifts."

"Okay, put him on the speaker-phone, and let's hear what he has to say," said Roy while standing up.

The Inmarsat phone was in a big aluminium suitcase. Blake had it opened up on top of a small table. Roy and Blake pulled some hard wooden chairs over to it, and Blake pushed the speaker-phone button on the control panel within the suitcase.

"Hello, this is Roy Elliot and Blake McTavish," said Roy in a loud voice. "Who are we talking to?"

"This is Phillip Sunderland, Corporate Law, in Atlanta," they heard in reply. Then there was a long pause, presumably for effect. Then they heard, "I know these calls are *expensive*, so I'll get *right to the point*. We understand someone on your staff, ah, a *Mrs. Penny Crawford*, has ordered, and is now *distributing*, corporate gifts with our logo, only with the 'c' replaced by a 'k'!"

Roy paused before answering, definitely for effect. "Yea, so?" he asked bluntly.

"So!" yelled Phillip. Then he yelled, "It's our *logo*, it's a registered trademark, and *no one* can change it!"

After a short pause, Roy said calmly, "Phillip, a 'c' in English is an 's' in Russian. Do you have *any idea* what 'amoilso' means in the local indigenous Khanty language?"

There was no reply after a long pause, so Roy added in a serious tone of voice, "Well, let's just say, Phillip, it's basically an unnatural act with a reindeer."

After another protracted pause, Phillip said in a very subdued voice, "Really? Well, hmmm. Then, could you folks just hand out gifts from now on *without* logos of any kind on them?"

"That we will do, Phillip, no problem," replied Roy cheerfully. Then he added, "Now, you have a nice day, Phillip. Goodbye."

"Yes, goodbye," said Phillip quietly.

Blake pushed a button on the Inmarsat phone panel to break the connection, and then he asked with a big grin, "How do you think that *fast*, Roy?"

"Practice," said Roy after a laugh. Then he confided, "Blake, you're going to find the higher you rise in any organisation, the more *bullshit* you have to contend with."

10

Nikolai arranged another car to help take Roy, Blake, Penny and Arman to the PA-hosted dinner.

KhantyRusNefteGaz had a traditional Russian wooden building at the edge of the city in a forest of tall evergreen trees. They used it for hosting 'distinguished visitors'.

They were met at the front entrance of the rustic PA facility by the deputy general director, Sergei Artemiev, and a tall, dark-haired, beautiful woman, that Arman introduced as Sergei's 'assistant', Tatyana. Artemiev by contrast was a large, rather ugly-looking older man, with a big reddish nose, and prominent purple veins on his face.

Arman translated as they took a quick tour together around the outside and inside of the building. It was basically a dining hall, with a couple of comfortable sitting areas that American executives probably would have called 'breakout rooms'. The wood outside was unpainted, but decorated with beautiful carvings and lathe-turned pieces of hardwood. The wood had all naturally aged to become a uniform shade of grey. The inside of the building was all panelled with knotty pine that had been varnished. There was a Scandinavian style sauna inside as well, with a shower and a change room.

There was also a traditional Siberian 'banya' outside, near the back of the building. It was made of sod and logs. Vadim had explained to Blake that the 'banya' was the only way original Siberians could get clean in the winter. They would stoke-up a fire inside, strip off their clothes, get really hot and work up a sweat and whip each other with birch branches to 'improve the circulation'. Then they would run out and roll in the snow, drink some cold vodka, then run inside to do it all again. When they eventually towelled off, they would be clean, both inside and out. Vadim had already invited Blake to try it in the approaching winter. Blake was not especially looking forward to that.

After their tour, they were ushered into the dining room. They were the first to arrive. Roy was seated in the middle of the long table, with Artemiev on the left side of him and Arman on the right. Blake and Penny were seated at the extreme left end of the table. Russian guests then started to arrive individually, and Artemiev introduced them all to Roy with Arman's help. They were all directors of some sort with the PA.

Blake and Penny were ignored completely through all of those formalities.

The very last to arrive was the general director, Vladimir Muratov. The Russians all leapt to their feet when he entered the room, and Roy, Arman, Blake and Penny followed their lead. Muratov was handsome, and looked a bit like Stalin, only taller with less of a moustache. His father was a very famous pioneer in the Russian oil industry; they had named a big nuclear-powered icebreaker after him.

Muratov looked quickly around the room with a pleasant smile, then he strolled over to the sole remaining vacant chair, directly opposite Roy. Then he very deliberately and slowly sat down, and everyone else in the room did the same.

Waiters and waitresses dressed in traditional Siberian costumes then appeared from a side door with platters full of appetisers. They used silver spoons to place the appetisers on everyone's plates. The appetisers were various types of raw, brined or cooked fish, black and red caviar, and pieces of deep-fried toast. Blake, Penny and Roy did not eat the raw fish. They had been warned about parasites by the Amoilco health department.

Then one very tall, handsome young man, or '*moladyets*' entered the room in a costume that might have come from a ballet. He went around with a vodka bottle, and poured a glass with great formality in front of each man. He offered the women some as well, but it seemed to be okay for them to refuse. Penny accepted half a glass.

Then Muratov slowly rose to his feet, and everyone followed his lead. He raised his glass of vodka, and delivered a formal toast. He stopped after each sentence to let Arman translate. He thanked Roy Elliot and his subordinates for joining the directors of *KhantyRusNefteGaz* at their favourite home in the Siberian forest, where they could celebrate together the execution of the first really significant '*Protokol*' with Amoilco. He said this was like the first step on the moon, only this time Americans and Russians were taking the first step together.

Roy had advised Blake and Penny to drink exactly what Muratov drank, and they would be all right. Muratov downed his glass of vodka in one gulp. Everyone else did the same. Blake and Penny almost gagged on the strong liquor, but successfully restrained the impulse. Then everyone sat down and sampled the appetisers while the vodka glasses were refilled. Penny only accepted a quarter of a glass this time.

Roy then stood up with his glass held forward, and everyone else remained seated because Muratov had remained seated. Then Roy delivered a toast with Arman's help. Roy thanked the general director for his encouraging and friendly words, and on behalf of Amoilco, he said everyone was greatly looking forward to working with all of the directors in the room. He said a 'lasting win-win agreement' could be achieved to develop the gigantic Podobskoye oilfield in a safe, environmentally-friendly and profitable manner. Roy then said, while looking all around the room, that Amoilco was not just an American company. In fact, he said, the local Amoilco representative, Blake McTavish, was a Canadian.

Roy stopped and motioned for Blake to stand up. Then Roy said his 'secret weapon', Penny Crawford, was also a Canadian. There was polite laughter in the room when he said that. He motioned for Penny to stand up as well. Then Muratov stood up and all the Russian side joined him. Then Roy said, "*Na Oozpekh*! To success!" and downed his glass of vodka with one gulp. Blake and Penny watched Muratov. He only downed half his glass, so that's what they did too.

When they sat down again the vodka glasses were refilled again. Penny refused any more. When the appetisers were gone, a hot meal was served. It was a kind of beef stroganoff over thick noodles. It was delicious.

After the meal, two directors gave short toasts towards a great future with new-found friends, and Blake and Penny each rose to do the same. Muratov just took a small sip at each toast, and Blake and Roy did the same. Most of the Russian men were still downing full glasses of vodka at each toast.

Muratov then stood up and everyone followed his lead. He apologised that he had to leave to attend another function, but he hoped everyone would linger a while longer for cake and coffee to become better acquainted. Then he left the room and all the Russians waited without talking until they saw him leave the building. Then they started talking with each other and moving around the room. They were eager to say things to Roy, and they took turns using Arman for interpreting. Blake and Penny shook hands with all of the directors, and just said 'hello' if Arman was not nearby and able to help them with more of a dialogue.

Many of the Russian men drank vodka with their cake and coffee. Only one man showed any ill effects from the strong drink, and he just looked sleepy. Blake's general sense was that the Russians were excited to be working with foreigners, and were optimistic about a better future.

After a while, many of the Russians were starting to look at their watches. It was a workday again tomorrow. Roy was starting to look a bit tired and anxious, so Blake went over when he was chatting one-on-one with Artemiev. With Arman's help, Blake explained that the drivers were probably ready to go now, and asked if that was all right. Roy looked relieved, expressed his apologies and thanks to Artemiev, and bid him farewell for now.

When they were in the car driving back to the hotel, Roy said, "Blake, you and Penny did great tonight, thanks. I think that went all right. Muratov is *impossible* to read. Artemiev has already got his hand out, but I'll let someone higher up slap it away through Muratov if it gets any worse."

11

The next Saturday morning, Blake and Nikolai drove over to Vadim's apartment building. They used one of Amoilco's new UAZ jeeps that had just arrived. They brought their bathing suits along with them. The plan was to drive around a bit and see what Vadim thought of the vehicle. Then they would take a tour of some sand quarries east of the city and do some swimming if the weather was okay.

It was really just an excuse for something to do. Nikolai waited by the UAZ while Blake went to fetch Vadim.

Vadim lived on the top floor of a ten-storey apartment building that was mostly unfinished. There was no elevator installed, naturally. Vadim said he and Natasha were the only people living on the tenth floor, and that one could easily tell because they had the only door.

Blake thought he was in pretty good shape, but he had to stop on the eighth floor landing to catch his breath. He waited until he was almost breathing normally again before knocking on Vadim's door.

Vadim opened the door, and asked him to come in. Natasha was cleaning up after their breakfast. Their little daughter was playing in the living room with a doll. Vadim said, "Please have some coffee with me and Natasha, then we will go, okay?"

"Okay, but I better go back and tell Nikolai that we'll be a few minutes," said Blake.

"No, I'll use the new, high-technology Russian intercom system," said Vadim. He opened a door to the balcony and yelled down to the street in Russian. Then he waved and yelled some more words in Russian. Then he came back in and said,

"That is a great system, but sometimes you have to hit the car with a stone to get a connection." Both he and Blake laughed.

Natasha was really shy, and a stunning beauty. Her white skin had no blemishes. She had high cheekbones and green eyes, and a slightly reddish tint in her long, brown hair. She sat down and Vadim translated for her as they drank coffee and talked.

Vadim explained that they were really fortunate to have a flat. They had applied five years ago for one. Most people had to crowd in with other people until they had somewhere to live. But they were both in really good shape now because of the stairs they had to climb, so that no longer concerned them. And their daughter had a proper place to live.

When they were back on the ground level, Vadim looked at the UAZ and said, "*Eta khoroshaya mashina*, good choice." Nikolai saw them coming, got out of the 'jeep' and opened the hood. They all looked inside at the engine.

Nikolai started talking in Russian and was getting steadily angrier. Vadim translated what he was saying as best he could. "He says this one is carburetted and the other one you bought is fuel injected. She was made the same damn day in the same damn plant as the other bitch. The wipers are different, the handles are different, and the tyres and the wheels and the shock absorbers are all different. Most things are different. What a screwed-up country Russia has become."

Blake put his hand on Nikolai's arm, and Vadim translated what he said. "That's okay, Nikolai, we did our best. The factory probably just had to meet their quota, and they had to use whatever parts they could scrape together. At least we still have two 'sets of wheels'. When one breaks down, we'll just drive the other one." Vadim and Nikolai both looked at Blake and nodded. Nikolai said some words in Russian, and Vadim said, "Nikolai thinks you are almost Russian now. You have an optimistic outlook, and it gives us hope."

It turned into a hot, sunny day. Blake thought it might be approaching thirty degrees Celsius. They took turns driving around town with the windows down. Both Nikolai and Vadim pointed things of interest out to Blake.

They made their way eventually out of the city to the east. "We are getting close to the quarries now, Blake," said Vadim. Then he explained, "This is where the construction sand comes from. The pits filled with water because they went into the water table below the river level. There is a good spot for swimming up ahead. I see there are people there. We should put on our bathing suits, I guess."

Blake was feeling sweaty. When he had changed into his bathing suit, he saw Vadim dive in from a spot on the bank, so he followed his lead and dove in head first. Nikolai was already in the water swimming around.

The water was cold but refreshing. When Blake came back to the surface, he started treading water beside Vadim. His eyes were blurry from the water, he thought. "What a great idea Vadim, thanks!" he yelled.

Vadim looked at him and said, "*Vashii otchki*! Your glasses!"

Blake put his hands to his face, and said, "Shit!" He had forgotten to take his prescription glasses off, and now they were gone.

Blake swam over to the step bank, and watched while both Vadim and Nikolai tried to swim down to the bottom to find his glasses. They tried about ten times each, but the water was five metres deep, and they had to feel around because it was dark and murky down there.

Blake knew it was a lost cause, and asked them to give it up and take him home. He had another pair with him in the hotel, but they were prescription sunglasses.

12

On the following Monday, Elena and Vadim escorted Blake to an optometrist in town. They found out from the attending nurse, with both Elena and Vadim translating, that the doctor was in Moscow for the summer on his ten week vacation. Then both Elena and Vadim told Blake that most non-PA professionals took the entire summer off.

Vadim asked if there was anything the nurse could do to help. She said there might be, and went into a back room for a minute. She came out with a cardboard box full of what she called, 'old glasses'. She said maybe Blake could try a few on to see if any helped.

Blake was going to laugh, but he was already fed up with trying to see with sunglasses indoors. And he was getting funny looks from people wherever he went. Besides, he really didn't want to offend Vadim, Elena and the nurse. This was just another everyday reality for them.

So, he tried on every pair of glasses in the box twice, and decided one pair actually seemed to work. With Elena's help he asked the nurse how much they cost. Elena translated what she replied as, "For a handsome guy like you, no charge!"

Blake tried to wear the 'new' glasses back in the office, but after a few hours he had a splitting headache. He realised he would be wearing his sunglasses until he could get a new pair of regular prescription glasses back in Houston. He was angry until he accepted the fact there was nothing he could do about it.

Blake and Elena got back into their regular administrative routine. Blake had set up an electronic 'mailbox' with an

American commercial service provider. He could dial up a number using the Inmarsat phone, then direct the call to the modem on his computer. He could then download and upload documents.

The geoscientists and engineers in Houston sent him requests for information from certain individuals in the PA. Then Blake and Elena would set up a meeting, make a visit, come back with the information, or a reason why it could not be provided, and then send a message back to the party in Houston that had made the request.

Blake also wrote a daily report to tell the whole team about what was happening, share the stuff he was learning about living and working in Neftezapadsibirsk, and share his thoughts about why certain people in the PA might be behaving the way they were. It was a 'Personal and Confidential' communication vehicle sent over a secure line. But he also tried to interject some humour where he thought he could do that without offending anybody. Some people on the team called him to say his reports were a 'real hit back home'.

Blake was also careful about what was said in the office, especially over the telephone. He was fairly certain the office was 'bugged' by the PA, or the KGB.

13

Towards the end of his third week in Neftezapadsibirsk, Blake received a fax then a phone call from the Amoilco aviation department in Atlanta. They wanted him to have a chat with the Aeroflot Commandant at the local airport. Amoilco had decided that they would let people fly only in the Mil Mi-8 MTV type of Russian helicopter.

Apparently the MTV was a variant of the more modern Mi-17 helicopter, which had a transmission that would automatically accelerate one of the two turbo-shaft engines if the other engine failed. That way, flight control and altitude could be maintained until the 'chopper pilot' could find somewhere safe to land.

If an engine failed on a regular Mi-8 helicopter, the rotor could stop turning entirely and cause an immediate crash. Also, the older Mi-8s liked to turn only in one direction, and had fuel tanks inside with the passengers to extend range. Some choppers were known to blow-up if someone was smoking nearby, and there was a leak in a tank. A man from Amoilco's logistics department had witnessed that happen on an early visit to Russia. The man smoking had been the pilot. Eight people had died in a flaming wreck.

The aviation department suspected that availability of an MTV helicopter, and spare parts for it, would be a problem. But they were willing to pay the international going-rate of about twelve hundred US dollars per hour for the use of a helicopter sized like the Mi-8. And they wanted the helicopter to be maintained to American FAA standards. The aviation department was pursuing a contract with Aeroflot through the

Moscow office, but they did not want to 'blind side' the local Aeroflot manager. Blake was impressed with their grasp of the 'bigger picture'.

Elena prepared a written translation of the fax from the aviation department. Then she set up a meeting with the commandant and went along with Blake to translate.

The commandant's office was on the second level of the small, concrete-slab terminal building at the airport. A uniformed guard at the door to the restricted part of the terminal led Blake and Elena upstairs to the door of the office. The commandant rose from his cluttered desk when he saw Elena and Blake at his door. He shook their hands over his desk as Elena made the introductions. Then he motioned for them to sit down on hard, wooden chairs facing his desk. Then he sat down himself.

Elena handed the translated fax to the commandant and he read it thoroughly without comment. Then he spoke in Russian and Elena translated what he said for Blake.

The commandant started by saying that as regional director he was actually Aeroflot, not people far away in Moscow. He said he could not see why Amoilco would want to pay ten times more for a helicopter that was hard to find parts for. He was keeping a number of standard Mi-8 helicopters flying by taking parts off other ones parked just outside the terminal building. Crashes were rare because his pilots were very competent. With a slowdown in activity, only the best pilots were flying.

Blake responded that the Mi-8 MTV had unique features of interest to his company, and the extra money was to help Aeroflot secure new parts when they were needed, and to pay for more frequent maintenance checks should the FAA methods require that. Blake said he was sure the Aeroflot methods were good, but this could be a chance for the commandant to try a different methodology, and have someone else pay for that experiment. If the FAA checks were more frequent, it was unlikely that the different approach might make things worse. At worst, the commandant would see no differences in reliability, and he would have more revenue.

The commandant nodded in agreement, and said for the extra money he would add a ground crew man to help Amoilco with their charter aircraft. Also, if they wanted to drive their own truck with their baggage right to the airplane, that would be okay from now on. He asked to be informed when the contract with Aeroflot Moscow was executed, and for a copy of the contract. He said he might never see the contract otherwise. Blake promised to do that for him, and they shook hands again. The meeting was over.

There really was no security at the airport. If the guard on duty recognised Elena and some people in an Amoilco group, he just waved them through the gate. None of the baggage was ever x-rayed or inspected. The security at other domestic airports in Russia was also lax by western standards. Part of the problem was that equipment like metal detectors always seemed to be broken.

When they got back to the office in the hotel, Blake saw that the door of the adjoining room was open a bit. As he put his key in the lock of the office door, he caught a glimpse of a man in a camouflage jacket sitting in the next room. He was wearing headphones, and there was a big tape recorder in front him. Blake and Elena both pretended not to notice.

They could hear the door next door close a few minutes later.

Blake knew for sure now that 'people of interest' were under surveillance in the hotel, presumably by the KGB. And he figured Amoilco people were high on the KGB's list, and the PA were getting reports from the KGB about what was being said inside the Amoilco office.

'Big Brother' was still alive and well and living next door. He felt a bit like Orwell's Winston Smith.

14

On Monday morning, at the start of Blake's fourth week in Neftezapadsibirsk, the hotel director walked through the open door of the Amoilco office, and started talking loudly with Elena. Blake liked to keep the office door open as a gesture of friendship to visitors, but he hoped visitors would knock before entering. The hotel director seemingly had no interest in such protocol. This was her empire to rule.

Blake came away from his desk and walked into the living area of the office, while taking off his sunglasses. The director was smiling smugly and was about to leave. Blake told Elena to ask her to stay for a minute. Then he told Elena to tell the director that he was the Amoilco representative in Neftezapadsibirsk, and she should address her concerns to him, not Elena.

Elena looked a bit sheepish, but she relayed the message. The director started to get angry, and Blake asked to know what was going on. Elena now functioned as a translator again.

The hotel director said the new rate for the 'big office room' was now two hundred US dollars per day, and the small rooms were one hundred US dollars per day. She said that was what foreigners were paying for hotel rooms in Moscow. Russians, of course, would keep paying the same rates as always. Also, Amoilco payments had to be in hard currency now, not roubles, and they had to be made a week in advance.

Blake asked what upgrades they could expect to receive in service, and in the quality of the furnishings, by paying twenty-five times more for rent.

The director then got very huffy, and said Amoilco already had the 'best room' in the hotel. Then she stomped out of the office. She was going to slam the door behind her, but Elena yelled something to her in a very commanding tone, and she left it open.

Blake then sat down at his desk, and drafted a letter to the hotel director's boss within the PA. It basically was just a comparison of what came with a two hundred dollar a night room in Moscow versus what they were getting in Neftezapadsibirsk. It also requested a face-to-face meeting.

When Elena read the letter, she said, "Her boss is Zakhar Snetskov. He is a very nasty man. He will not like this letter at all. He handles all of the payroll and 'special benefits' to workers for the PA, and people think he likes to be mean. He used to be very big in the Communist Party."

Blake thought for a minute, and then he said, "This is mostly about a fundamental principle, Elena. If the PA thinks they can unilaterally extort Amoilco out of more money without a challenge, we'll never be able to be their partner."

Elena smiled and said, "Then this is a very good letter."

Two days after delivering the letter, on Wednesday, Blake and Elena went over to the PA building for the meeting with Snetskov. His office was on the ground level, just behind where workers lined up to receive their pay in rouble notes, and the gifts of food or other perquisites that the PA occasionally gave out 'to improve morale'.

Snetskov was 'all smiles' when they entered his office. He motioned for them to sit down, but did not offer them his hand in greeting. His office was drab, and equipped with worn out, basic furniture. Blake guessed that was intentional so workers would believe Zakhar was just like them; another poor '*rabotnik*' or worker, just doing his job for the good of the cause. He was a sly-looking, skinny, bald-headed man who avoided eye contact. But he started talking immediately in a pleasant tone, and Elena translated what he said for Blake.

Snetskov thought Amoilco's letter made perfect sense. 'Of course' more should be provided with an increase in room rates. He had been in Moscow hotels himself, and everything on the list was reasonable. He had already given orders to put the changes in effect. And was there anything else today they wanted to talk about?

Blake said no, that's all Amoilco wanted to hear, and he thanked Snetskov for the meeting. Snetskov sat down at his desk with a smile. There were four telephones on his desk, all different colours. He picked up the handset on the yellow telephone and started dialling. Blake and Elena concluded the meeting was over, and left.

The next day, Blake started getting a fresh, thin, worn out hand towel every day. It was the only towel the hotel ever provided to him. There was also a spare roll of course, grey, toilet paper in the bathroom, so he would no longer have to ask a maid for a refill. They also took the broken, stand-up piano out of the living room, and replaced a broken table with an old one of the same type.

Nothing else changed. The maids still had no vacuum cleaners. They had to use coarse brooms to sweep the room floors and carpets. They had to use only rusty tap water, without detergents, for wiping and mopping. And they still only 'cleaned' the rooms every other day. So, the rooms were as filthy as always.

Blake figured the hotel director and her boss were now pocketing a nice kick-back in hard currency. All he felt he could do was relay another interesting anecdote in his daily report.

15

It was Friday night. Blake was scheduled to depart in the morning at the end of his twenty-eight day hitch. He was packing his suitcase in his bedroom when the Inmarsat telephone rang at the other end of the three-section hotel room.

He rushed into the office room without turning on the lights, picked up the handset and said, "Blake McTavish, Amoilco,"

"Blake, it's Roy, in Moscow," he heard in reply. Roy sounded anxious, and he added, "I read your report about the 'ears against your wall'. Maybe just listen and avoid saying much."

"Okay," was all Blake said in reply.

"Listen, we're in the emergency response mode here, and we just ramped it up to include the executive crisis management team in Atlanta," Roy said quickly. He paused a moment to let that sink in, then he added, "Brace yourself. Keith Samson has been shot, in the leg, and we're trying to arrange a 'medevac' with a corporate jet company out of London." Roy paused for a moment again, perhaps to take a drink of water this time.

Keith Samson was Blake's counterpart in Baku, Azerbaijan.

Then Roy said, "Someone got on board our charter with Keith, maybe by hiding in the baggage compartment in the rear. You know the compartment on the Tu-134 has a hatch into the passenger area.

"Anyway, it sounds like the guy was a Chechen rebel of some kind! He suddenly appeared in the passenger area with an automatic pistol, grabbed Keith as a hostage, and then barged into the cockpit. The pilots were about to start the engines for departure and return to Moscow with Keith.

"The guy was either a terrorist or an extortionist. He demanded a million US dollars in cash. He said he was supporting, 'the glorious cause of Chechen independence and the return of Sharia Law'.

"The pilots relayed what the terrorist had said to the control tower. They sat there for about half an hour on the tarmac.

"Then Russian assault troops stormed into the passenger area of the airplane! It sounds like they came in through the aft cargo compartment.

"You know the Russians don't negotiate with hijackers, right? There was a gun fight. Someone shot Keith in the leg, either the terrorist or an assault team member. The co-pilot and the terrorist were both killed. The fuselage of our charter airplane was shot-up and punctured in a few places.

"So, our charter is now out of commission."

Roy let Blake internalise all of the terrible news for a few moments, then added, "I just talked to some Aeroflot managers with our lawyer here. They started out by demanding *we* pay for the damage to *their* airplane, or replace the airplane in kind. They said the damage was clearly our fault!

"We quickly turned that nonsense around though, using the contract. Aeroflot provides a transportation service to us for a fee. It's not our airplane, they can use *any* of their airplanes that meet the contractually agreed specifications to fulfil the service. And obviously, security at airports is an Aeroflot and police matter, not ours.

"So, they're working cooperatively with us now to find another airplane to use as our charter."

Blake could hear Roy talking to someone in the background, Then Roy said, "Blake, our best guess here is they might have another aircraft ready for our use in about a week. So, we'd like you to stay put for now." Blake could tell that was an order, not a request.

Then Roy said, "We won't be sending *anyone* back to Baku until this 'emerging Chechen independence movement', or whatever, is resolved.

"There is some *more* bad news that directly affects our project, unfortunately. As soon as Jeff Webb heard about the attack in Baku, he called the receptionist in the office here, and told her to tell me he wasn't going to rotate to Russia anymore.

"I know they don't want Jeff back in the Denver office. I guess he 'burned bridges' there too. So, I'm going to release him with a package. That's probably better than he deserves."

Roy paused to talk again to someone beside him in Moscow, then he said. "Look, I've been talking with my wife, Sheila. If you can manage another week there, I'll fly in after next weekend, say on Monday, on the charter hopefully. I'll spell you for a few days, maybe until Friday of that week. Sheila's got a friend of hers coming in for a visit from the States. She thinks you'll really like her. My wife's a bit of a 'match maker', sorry.

"Anyway, you can have your own room in our dacha out in the countryside, and Sasha can drive you around. You know, maybe try to buy some new spectacles, and do some shopping. And Sheila has a list of restaurants she wants to take you and her friend to, and some tickets to the Bolshoi Ballet. Who knows, maybe you two will 'hit it off' well together? Now, how does all of that that sound?"

"That sounds great, Roy," said Blake, sincerely.

"That's really great, Blake!" Roy replied quickly. Then in a more relaxed manner, he said, "Now, let's get into the problem of replacing Jeff, and what we should do point forward.

"First, I think we've got to get you out of that 'crap' PA hotel you're in. We have to *know* we can talk openly without being spied upon, or blackmailed into lining somebody's pocket with our hard-earned cash. And if we're going to pay a lot more for rent, we should get some value for the money we spend.

"Second, we want to put more technical people on the ground there to extract information more quickly from the PA.

"So, we are now thinking we should build a 'proper' forty-person camp there, using a western contractor to build it. And we'll hire another western contractor to cater it, with good food and supplies sent in on the charter from Moscow. We'll need someone to oversee the construction of the camp when you're not there, and bring in some administration skills that you haven't quite learned yet. There's a guy in the Calgary office named Doug Koenig who says he might be interested in taking Jeff's place. Do you know him?"

"I know Doug very well, Roy, and he's a decent, competent guy," replied Blake with interest. Then he added, "He looked after the pipe-yard when we were working in the Beaufort Sea, and he used to build roads and leases for the land drillers in Alberta. He's perfect."

"Okay, that's all I needed to hear," said Roy with a little more cheer in his voice. Then he confessed, "Realistically, it will take at least a month to get him freed up for his first hitch with us though. Can you manage until then?"

Blake paused for a long moment, and then he said, "Sure Roy, I can handle that. Glad to help."

"That's really great, Blake, thanks!" said Roy happily. Then he said quickly, "Look, I've got to run now. We've got to get Keith out of Baku. You take care of yourself, Blake, and I'll call you again tomorrow."

"Okay, I will, Roy, don't you worry," replied Blake. Then he said quietly, "Bye for now."

Blake hung up the phone and sat there for a few minutes in the dark. The only illumination in the room came from a few glowing orange bulbs on the Inmarsat telephone panel.

'Well,' he thought to himself, 'It's a good thing they didn't offer me the Baku job.'

The Tesla Terrorist

1

Weldon Purdy was wiping his sweaty brow with an old rag. He had finally decided he better rest a minute on a flat rock near the top of the heavily wooded ridge. He looked down the slope, and yelled, "You're a good boy, Elroy, a very good boy!"

His son, Elroy, was continuing to struggle with a heavy length of braided insulated cable. He was using a hand-powered winch that was chained to a tree stump. He was trying to drag the cable a little further up towards their objective, a wooden tower as tall as the trees at the summit of the ridge above them.

The tower supported an intricate platform made of steel, copper, aluminium and glass. Above the platform was a metallic 'torus'. It was a ring, circular in cross-section, and it resembled a very large donut.

It was a fine, hot sunny day. The air was thick with black flies and mosquitoes, the nasty, biting, insect-demons of Labrador in the summer time.

Weldon had never paid any attention to bugs, even the biting variety. It helped that he had long greasy hair, a bushy beard, and dark clothing that stank horribly from never being washed.

Elroy was finally talking, even if just in monosyllables. Weldon's hillbilly wife had been especially worried about his stunted development. 'Tain't natural for a boy of three, Weldon, let alone one that's eight,' she had said to him a decade ago. That was just a few months before she had passed away of some kind of fever.

Weldon had never believed in doctors or hospitals, even if he could get to one in time. His obsessive mistrust of the 'system' no doubt led to his wife's premature death. But Weldon would always just blame it on fate.

Weldon didn't really care if Elroy talked at all, just as long as he listened carefully and did exactly what he was told. If he didn't, well, there would be another beating.

They were so close to being ready now, and there were far too many ways to screw things up with even a small mistake. And they *must* finish it all in the next few days.

The storm was coming, he was sure of it.

He hoped it would be the 'five hundred year' storm. *That* would really fire up the magnifying transmitter he had built.

They were about to do something beyond even the *wildest* dreams of the great Nikola Tesla.

Weldon hoped to 'crack the earth' at its natural frequency, after first shocking the *shit* out of some of those stupid bastards who had laughed at him.

Weldon had first heard about Tesla in basic training, from a smart but physically weak volunteer who had eventually 'washed-out' of the US Army. After completing his basic training, Weldon started reading all he could find about Tesla.

He had no moral problem with stealing books and documents he could not afford to buy, or could not find in libraries. While other young soldiers were busy getting drunk and finding whores on leave, Weldon was busy finding more Tesla documents to study.

Tesla was no doubt an electromechanical engineering genius, but he was always looking for practical uses for the things he devised. Weldon believed he had overlooked the fact that a 'magnifying transmitter' for sending electrical power without wires over long distances was *by itself* a very useful device.

Weldon thought Tesla had worried far too much about not having a practical device for *receiving* electrical energy sent through the air. Tesla's goals of course had been to make a lot of money, and win some accolades from his peers.

Weldon was only interested in destroying capitalists, and the things made by capitalists. He didn't know what a better world looked like exactly, but this one sure 'sucked'.

When his sergeant had overheard Weldon talking about Tesla, and how he could do things a lot better than Tesla had done, he had told him, 'Shut the hell up Weldon, and be a *soldier* if you want to stay in the army.'

So, Weldon shut up, and was a very good soldier. But he worked even harder, in private, on his self-study programme.

He looked at his son again. The boy had never been near a school, or a town for that matter. But he also had never been laughed at by a society of 'money-grubbing hedonists'. Elroy had never been anywhere but here. The only people he had ever known were his parents. And if things went to Weldon's plan, the only people Elroy ever would know would be his parents.

But Elroy was clearly an idiot. Weldon thought Tesla had been right about one thing in life. Selective breeding would make the world a *lot* better place. Well, maybe if Weldon helped reduce some excess population, he could do his bit for that cause. One could never underestimate the stupidity of the average person. And there were far too many stupid people in the world.

Weldon laughed to himself again at the name he had given his son. Elroy had been a television cartoon character when he was training in Appalachia for a covert operation in Central America.

Truly, Elroy was the son of a 'man of the future'. But his father was not a nice-guy 'boob' with a 'putt-putt space car'.

Weldon had met his woman in Tennessee, too. She had been watching from the trees as the CIA assassination experts put him through his paces. The instructors did not know she was there, but Weldon did. She had grown up in isolation like Weldon had, and knew how to survive in wilderness. A key survival skill they both had learned at a young age was how to move about without being seen or heard. And the one very brief moment when he managed to see her face was enough for him to see that she was beautiful.

Weldon had gone back into the woods by himself when he finally completed the CIA training. He waited for her to reappear in the spot where he had first seen her.

Her brothers had found him first, unfortunately. They were moonshiners, and they were about to kill him after giving him a severe beating. But wife-to-be had stopped them just in time. She had made them carry Weldon back to their shack deep in the woods so she could tend to his wounds.

No one had ever cared for Weldon like she had done. And when he found out she distrusted and hated the modern world as much as he did, he realised he was truly in love.

Weldon noted the trees in the hills of Tennessee were as tall as the trees around him now. The sight of the tower far above him brought him back to the task at hand.

"Another forty metres, Elroy, that's all!" he yelled. Then he yelled, "We'll terminate this end at the fourth Wardenclyffe tower to complete the telluric current oscillator loop!"

"Wha', Pa?"

"You're a good boy, Elroy. You're a very good boy."

2

The annual early summer trip to the Owl River in Labrador, Canada started as it usually did. Fred Antle sent a rather obnoxious email note to Curtis Furlong, copying the other 'regular' participants in the recurring adventure.

The note read, 'Looking forward to that first week on the river again, Curtis, when we can hook the big salmon ahead of the main run. And we know you're still freaking loaded, so no reason to charge your buddies for more than food and gas. Everyone expects another big run of grilse or first-run salmon this year, so you can rip-off the paying customers that come after us.'

Fred could be a pain, but every year no one else seemed to want to start the obvious necessary conversation.

The 'core group' had been going on the trip for years. Before they had purchased and renovated a small cabin together, Curtis Furlong and Jerome Efford had made the trip a few times with only a nylon tent, sleeping bags, cooking gear, their fly-fishing equipment and some really basic provisions. They took the ferry that used to run from Lewisporte, Newfoundland to Bowhead Arm, Labrador. At Bowhead Arm, Walter Cartwright, the local hotel owner and a good friend, made an open aluminium boat ready for them.

After putting on their foul-weather gear, the three men would depart in the deeply-laden boat for the thirty-five nautical mile trip across English Bay to the Owl River estuary.

Long and twisting English Bay opens to the North Atlantic Ocean. It is always frigid, and often rough, especially in the tidal-rips and during the frequent storms. It is also prone to grounded icebergs in the spring and summer.

A boat trip remained the only practical way to travel from Bowhead Arm to the Owl River, other than by expensive chartered helicopter or float plane. On some days, no trip of any kind could be made across the bay because of really bad weather, or fog. A snowmobile could theoretically make the trek in a few hours in the winter time. But only a few hardy, experienced fur trappers made such a trip, and well after the end of the salmon sport-fishing season.

It did not take long for Curtis and Jerome to start looking for a more comfortable way to enjoy 'The Owl', one of the finest Atlantic salmon fishing rivers in the world. Walter brought their attention to the last parcel of Crown Land that could be leased on the estuary of the river. After securing a long-term lease, Curtis and Jerome invited two other friends in St. John's, Brad Walsh and Fred Antle, to help refurbish the existing cabin on the leased land. The group also agreed to buy a couple of boats for the camp. Walter agreed to be a 'non-paying member', and to look in on the cabin a few times during the long offseason.

The group enjoyed the cabin together for almost a decade. It was agreed each man could bring a family member or a guest along, as the cabin had plenty of room. Still, it was hard work setting up their base camp every year. A generator, fuel, and a week's worth of food and drink had to be hauled in with their own baggage. In addition, a terrifying stretch of white water known as 'The Chute' had to be traversed every time they wanted to fish above the estuary. Some of the best pools on the river were above The Chute, next to the Owl River Salmon Club, the only commercial salmon fishing lodge on the river.

Unknown to the group, Curtis had had his eye on this lodge for years, and suddenly bought it.

Initially, the group had been a bit angry with Curtis, as his purchase threatened to end a fun and unique kind of partnership. But Curtis 'calmed the waters' by inviting them along on the first week of the salmon fishing season at a reduced rate. And the lodge was a luxurious step up from the 'self-catered' cabin. There was with a professional camp cook, and registered fishing guides. Furthermore, Curtis hired Walter's son, Dwayne, to run the lodge, which Walter really appreciated.

This year, Curtis came back immediately to Fred and the others with his own email message.

The message read, 'Yes, we can do it again this year. I'll be bringing my sons, Kelvin and Ryan, with us like last year. And this year I'm also bringing two business guests, Odvar Knudsen, a Norwegian, and Malcolm Smallbridge, a Brit, who lives in Houston. Odvar has done a lot of salmon fishing, but never on this side of the 'big pond'. It should be a good laugh having them both along. If you guys want to bring anyone but yourselves, it could be a bit cramped in the main lodge. If you don't bring anyone else, we can all go in a big company van I can borrow. We can now drive right from the Blanc Sablon ferry terminal in Quebec near the Labrador border to Bowhead Arm, thanks to a new high-grade road extension.'

They all quickly agreed that going together in the van was the best way to go. Everyone could catch up on personal news, and 'tell a few yarns'. And the guests could be briefed on what to expect on their upcoming adventure.

The rest of the arrangements were quickly made as well. Curtis owned a small brewery in St. John's that his oldest son, Kelvin, managed for him. So, Curtis would bring the beer. Fred and Jerome owned a wholesale food business, among other businesses, and would bring 'the specialty scoff', like crab legs and prime rib steaks. The food would be packed in coolers full of ice. Brad, who worked as an engineer in the offshore oil and gas industry, would pay for the boat gas, snacks and dry goods they would pick up in Bowhead Arm. They agreed to split the hotel and restaurant bills along the way.

Curtis called for everyone to meet at daybreak on the twenty-eighth of June at the hotel in St. John's that Jerome's family had owned for generations. With the early start, they would have enough time, with a few hours to spare, to drive across the entire island of Newfoundland. They had to arrive in time to catch the last ferry leaving the small port of St. Barbe, near the tip of the Northern Peninsula.

Malcolm and Odvar flew in to St. John's on the twenty-seventh of June. Curtis took them around the city to a number of stores to finish fitting them out for the trip. Then they went with Curtis and Brad to pick up the van at the offshore oil production platform construction site in Bull Arm. Brad drove the van back to St. John's by himself, while Curtis toured the construction site with his guests. They all met up again in the evening for drinks and a barbecue at Curtis' house. Curtis put them all up for the night so they could leave together first thing in the morning.

The next morning, Fred was the last to arrive at the parking lot of the hotel. The others had all stowed the coolers and their baggage in the back of the large, diesel-powered, twelve-seat van. Fred appeared to have a bit of a hangover, and was grumbling unhappily about the decision to leave 'so early'. When he realised no one was listening to him, he took a seat at the back of the van and closed his eyes.

Odvar and Malcolm were clearly looking forward to the road trip. They both worked in the oil industry and were well-travelled. But they were first time visitors to Canada, and thus had an endless string of questions. One answer seemed to lead to another question. The van was 'road quiet', so everyone could join the conversation.

Odvar had many fishing stories, which he always prefaced with, 'I have another interesting story to tell you… ' He owned a house on a prime salmon river in Norway, and had taken salmon fishing vacations in Iceland, and trout fishing vacations in New Zealand. He was also a very wealthy man, and talked about his custom collection of rods and reels crafted by artisans. There was nothing pretentious in his talk, he was clearly excited to be talking to people equally passionate about a sport that he loved.

Malcolm was an occasional trout fisherman, and enjoyed wilderness vacations, especially ones involving kayaking or whitewater rafting. As they drove across the city boundary of St. John's, Malcolm alerted Curtis to a large horse standing in the ditch along the Trans-Canada Highway.

"No, really?" asked Malcolm, when they told him his 'horse' was actually a bull moose.

"Look at the horns, b'y!" replied Jerome with a laugh.

They stopped the van and let Malcolm take a photograph of the moose with his cell phone. He then sent it off to his son in London, England.

Once they were back on the road, the moose encounter stories began, and there were many. Curtis interjected by asking everyone to help him keep a close eye out for the massive, wild creatures.

"A collision with a half-tonne moose will ruin anyone's day," said Jerome in support.

"Newfoundland is thick with moose, whereas we're more likely to see black bear and caribou in Labrador," said Curtis when the stories slowed down. That set off the many bear stories, which helped to pass some more time.

Just before Clarenville, Fred suddenly opened his eyes and blurted out, loudly, "Curtis, are we going to stop for breakfast, or what?"

"There's a gas station just ahead, Fred, with a restaurant!" yelled Curtis in return, looking in the rear-view mirror. "But thanks for the reminder, you glutton!" No one disagreed with Fred that it was time for a break, including Curtis.

After the men consumed some bacon, eggs and toast, the trip resumed with a much happier Fred now joining in the banter. The talk had turned to fishing on 'The Owl', and the additional equipment Curtis had helped Odvar and Malcolm purchase in St. John's.

"The risk with going so early to the river is the salmon run may not have started yet," said Curtis. Then he explained, "The run seems to start when the pack-ice leaves the coast, and warmer weather and heavier rain starts in the interior of Labrador. But no one seems to know why for sure. It might be the river 'smells' different to the fish?

"We *do* know the 'large' or 'return' salmon are the first to move, and usually on a really high tide. The regulations require us to release all salmon over sixty-one centimetres in length. Fish under that length are deemed 'small', while over-length fish are deemed 'large'. There's no such thing as 'medium' salmon around here! You're a lot less likely to hook a 'large' salmon when the grilse or first-run salmon are on the go, as the grilse are *so* aggressive. We'll be the first on the river by at least a week," he exclaimed, with satisfaction.

"Since we hope to play some big, heavy salmon, we use a leader of twenty-pound monofilament and twenty-pound nylon tippet material," Curtis continued. Then he added, "I like a long leader, say two-and-a-half metres of the monofilament and a metre of the tippet material. I use a 'rocket' or weight-forward, nine-weight floating line on a nine-weight graphite rod. And I like a 'large arbour' reel and *lots* of 'backing-material', a hundred metres worth anyway. The wind usually comes up in the afternoons on The Owl, so I also have a twelve-weight rod with me."

Odvar was intrigued by all of this technical talk, and talked about his own theories of how best to fish a salmon river. Odvar explained how using a Scottish two-handed Spey rod differed from the now common one-handed variety.

Most of this talk went over Malcolm's head, but he didn't seem to mind. As for the others, they had always just accepted Curtis as their technical expert. Over the years they had bought what he suggested, usually with fantastic results, and they used the same fly patterns that he did.

Curtis tied his own flies, and always hooked the most fish, although his younger son, Ryan, was now coming close in the overall count. Curtis had also landed the largest salmon of the group, a twenty-three pounder. The 'normal' return salmon on The Owl were consistently around fifteen pounds. The grilse ran about four to six pounds. But even the smaller grilse were powerful, wild fish. They were strengthened by their short but perilous life in the ocean, a place richer in food than a northern river.

When they reached the Deer Lake turnoff to start travelling north, they stopped to eat some lunch in a diner and stretch their legs. After lunch, Curtis asked Brad if he felt up to driving for a while, and Brad said he would enjoy that. Brad got behind the wheel and Malcolm moved into the front seat that Brad had just occupied. Curtis took a seat in the back and closed his eyes. Everyone then spoke quietly so Curtis could get some sleep.

Brad turned the radio on to low volume so he and Malcolm could catch the news before they moved out of range of a station.

Towards the end of the news segment, the announcer replayed a recent interview with the science reporter for the network. The topic was the magnetic field surrounding the earth, which was said to be weakening, perhaps at an accelerating rate. Brad and Malcolm looked at each other with concern, as they had talked about this emerging story at Curtis' barbecue dinner party. Susan, Curtis' wife, had also seemed interested at the time. She had been angry with Curtis when he had blown the theories off with a laugh.

The reporter ran through various opinions from the scientific community about what the change might mean in practical terms. The growing fear was that a pole reversal could be imminent. The reporter said such an event has likely happened a number of times in the earth's history, judging by 'magnetic signatures' left in newly-formed rock on both sides of the mid-Atlantic trench.

It sounded like most experts were agreeing that a relatively quick pole reversal might not be all that serious, but it would certainly force a significant correction in compass readings to find True North. Some of the experts also seemed to be agreeing that a prolonged period of weak or non-existent geomagnetic flux could be *very* serious for life on Earth. They said the field provides the first 'line of defence' against solar radiation. They added that layers in the earth's upper atmosphere provide another 'line of defence'.

"I'll find the right time to talk again to Curtis about this," said Brad as they drove along. Then he added, "I don't want to be alarmist, but he at least needs to know that compass headings might 'go walkabout' for a while. I don't think GPS readings would be affected. And those are all in relation to True North, not Magnetic North, I think."

"There actually might be more to be alarmed about than we just heard, Brad," said Malcolm with a waver in his voice. Then he explained, "This is a maximum sun spot year, you know, in the eleven year cycle. And solar flares are *fifty times* more likely during a maximum."

"I think maybe we should listen to some music now, and try to remember *somehow* that this is a vacation," suggested Brad, as he reached for the volume knob on the vehicle sound system. Then he smiled and asked, "Okay, Malcolm? I'm sure you *must* be familiar in England with '*Buddy, Wasisname*'?"

Malcolm laughed, and after a while, he seemed to relax again. He said he liked the Newfoundland music that Brad played. Their talk turned again to the obviously healthy moose population as they crossed the Long Range Mountains of the Northern Peninsula into Gros Morne National Park.

"Moose are not a native species to the island of Newfoundland," said Brad. Then he explained, "Humans are their only predators here. A lot of moose culling occurs by accident through vehicle collisions, unfortunately, for both humans and moose. And of course there is no hunting allowed in parks like this one."

"I thought the wolf hunted deer and moose," said Malcolm. Then he asked, "Is that not true?"

"They do," said Brad. Then he added, "But you will not find the wolf here, or deer for that matter. Also, there are no porcupines, racoons, snakes, or skunks. Newfoundland is truly an island, and it's been that way for a very long time."

"If I did not know better, I would say this island is in Norway by all the fiords we are seeing!" Odvar said with excitement. He was been sitting right behind Brad and Malcolm, and had been listening to their conversation while watching the scenery.

"Actually, this could have been Norway, I suppose, Odvar, if things had worked out differently," said Brad thoughtfully. Then he explained, "If we went about one hundred and forty kilometres further up this road than we'll be going, we would come to a place now called L'Anse aux Meadows. There's strong evidence some Norse or Viking people tried to live there around 1,000 AD."

As they drove further north and out of the park, the mountains retreated from the coastline where the highway ran, and the trees became stunted and 'flagged' by the very strong prevailing wind. Stacks of lobster pots were seen near weather-beaten fishing shacks on stony beaches.

"All of these little rivers we are crossing are famous salmon rivers!" said Curtis loudly from his back seat after suddenly waking up. Then he yelled, "The runs usually start later, but as you can see there are a few folks fishing! The water seems unusually low for this time of year! I don't think they've been getting the rain here that Walter says they've been getting up in Labrador!"

Finally, the group arrived at their destination, the ferry terminal in St. Barbe. It was slightly before five o'clock in the afternoon, and the ferry was just pulling up to the dock.

3

It was five o'clock in the morning and the river was steaming in the first light of what probably would become a cloudy, drizzly day.

Brad had just waded out up river from a spot where young Ryan said fish might 'hang up'. Ryan had already started casting into the next 'pool' down from him.

Brad stopped fiddling with the lid of his fly-box and watched Ryan for a few minutes.

Ryan was a natural at most sports. A strong young man of almost twenty now, he had been 'throwing a fly' and 'hooking salmon' since he was six years old. He could throw the whole fly-line, 'right to the backing' whenever he wanted to. And he could place a fly anywhere he wanted to in any wind. Brad was a jealous 'comes from afar mainlander', and he knew it. But he really loved this sport too, even if he could not make it look as easy as Ryan and his father could.

Curtis was across the broad, fast-moving, boulder-strewn river, standing on a big flat rock with his European guests. He was using his long fly-rod like a teacher would use a pointer in school to point out aspects of interest to his 'pupils'. Brad could not hear what was being said, but he could guess. Curtis had given him that kind of coaching many times.

Brad figured Curtis must have used one of the camp boats to get over there. Then Brad could see a boat pulled up on the river bank down river from where Curtis and his guests were positioning themselves. Brad waved, and through the mist he saw one of the guests, probably Odvar, wave back. The man was decked-out as a Scottish fisherman, with woollen knickers, knee socks, and a woollen, broad-brimmed cap like the fictional Sherlock Holmes was said to have worn.

Brad decided to try his favourite fly first, a 'green bug fished wet'. It was a Curtis Furlong variation of what some people called a 'Green Machine'. Brad saw there a nice 'vee' in front of him at the base of the 'pool', or section of smooth water on the river surface. 'Vees' were caused by submerged rocks, and this one was almost twenty metres away from him. A fish might be lying beside and behind the submerged rock, resting there in the backwash before advancing further upstream.

It would be a stretch for his clumsy skills, but Brad thought he might *just* be able to drift the fly down to the 'vee' with the wind coming from the upstream direction. But he would not try right away. Brad had enough experience to know you have to 'fish down' to a salmon, not *over* a salmon. Patience and a series of progressively longer casts were required.

Brad stripped out line while waving the rod tip back and forth above him. 'Cast out about eighty degrees to the downstream bank,' he remembered. 'At the end of the cast, point the rod tip at where the fly is at the end of the 'invisible' three-metre-long leader. Strip the line in to keep the line straight on the water, and the fly properly 'presented' to the fish. Let the cast complete itself, moving the rod tip and stripping in by hand pulls to adjust the drift of the fly. Lower the rod tip to the water. Then strip *really hard* while pulling the rod tip up hard to free the line from the suction of the water. Pull the rod tip up past twelve o'clock while pulling the line down to your side with your other hand. Wait! Wait for the weight of the line shooting out behind to start bending the rod tip back. Then move the rod quickly ahead at your new target. Wait! Wait to let go of the line so the strain energy in the rod can shoot the line forward.'

Every time Brad cast, he stripped out about thirty centimetres more of the line. A salmon jumped up river with a big splash. 'That's a good sign, but that fish has gone past me now,' thought Brad to himself. 'Now, was that a swirl near my fly, just ahead of the 'vee'?' 'Yes! A salmon has come for a close look. Did it strike the fly? No! Then this one might come back again.'

There was a 'hoot' like an owl from down river. Young Ryan had one on, and he somehow managed to wave at Brad while fighting the fish.

"I raised him *four times* before he took it!" yelled Ryan as the fish jumped right in front of him.

"That's great, Ryan!" yelled back Brad. Then he mumbled to himself, "You bugger."

'What to do next?' Brad asked himself. 'Keep fishing the same fly? No, let's slow this down. The fish are 'flying', which means they're moving, probably on a tidal pulse. But this fish probably likes that 'vee' and might stay right there a bit longer. Try a 'brown bomber', tease him with that, then go back to a wet fly.'

Brad didn't like using a dry fly. There is a definite art to hooking a salmon with one. Brad could watch Jerome for hours playing with one, as he was a true master. The cast is different, actually made up river, and the fly floats by with a bit of slack line. But you cannot use *too much* slack line, as you must strip in quickly to try to set the hook when you see a fish is coming for it. And, to make it worse, the water in the mouth of the moving fish tends to plough the fly out of the way.

But Brad knew you could really 'stir up a fish' with a 'bomber', and keep it interested.

He smeared a bit of specialty 'gunk' on a furry brown 'bomber' and its front and back, polar bear fur 'tails'. The gooey substance would change the 'wettability' of the fly and make it sit high out of the water. Then he made a few awkward casts. Then he saw a *definite* swirl and a dorsal fin right in the same spot as before!

'Okay, take it easy,' Brad said to himself. 'Back to a wet fly now, but which one? It's kind of a grey day today. Number six hook, an 'Undertaker', that's the ticket.'

He worked eight casts to get down to the spot again. Then there was a *big* pull, and not even a swirl. 'Fish on?' he asked himself. 'Yes! It took the fly under the water, and then went deep!'

Brad looked up when he heard another 'hoot' from Ryan. Ryan had just released a large grilse. Then Brad's fish jumped. It was a large or 'return' salmon. There was a yell from Ryan, "Right freaking on, Brad!"

Brad's heart was pounding now. When the fish jumped again, the line went slack. Brad madly stripped in line to try to catch up to the fish. But he did catch up. It was still on, and pulling like hell.

Brad cupped the reel in his palm to control line tension by feel. He remembered to keep the rod tip up. The fish suddenly decided to run downstream out of the pool! Brad knew he was just along for the ride now. This fish was fresh from the ocean, far from being played out, and it was really pissed off.

Brad started wading back to the river bank. He slipped and fell in up to the very top of his chest waders. Thankfully, the belt that kept water from turning his waders into an instant sea anchor worked, and he staggered to his feet. 'Move!' Brad told himself. 'And don't let the line wrap around a rock!' The fish had pulled line out well into the 'backing' now, and it was stripping more line out all of the time.

Brad half staggered, half floated past Ryan in a fast-moving blur, while avoiding and not avoiding boulders in the cold water of a river that had become a series of rapids.

"There's a steady just ahead, Brad!" yelled Ryan, who was following along behind him like Kipling's jungle boy, Mowgli. Only this Mowgli was carrying a dip net! Then Ryan yelled, "We might be able to play him out in the quiet water!"

And then somehow they were there, at the base of the rapids in quiet water. Over the next twenty minutes, the fish jumped and ran in and out three more times.

The regulations no longer allowed retention of a 'large' salmon, so Brad did not want to tire this fish out completely, or use a dip net that could hurt it. As he was putting on a cotton glove, Ryan yelled, "When he floats on his side with his head up, I'll tail him for you, Brad!"

It was really hard with the long leader to manoeuvre the fish with short line. The knot of the leader was working inside the last 'eyelet' on the rod. But eventually, Ryan was able to make an accurate stab with his wet, gloved hand, and had the fish firmly by the tail. Brad waded out to him, and easily pulled the barbless hook out of the lower jaw of the fish.

"Fifteen pounds for sure, Brad! I'll get a picture!" said a grinning Ryan as they shook hands.

Brad's hands were shaking, but he somehow managed to pull on his own cotton gloves for the photo. He remembered to wet his gloves before handling the fish to avoid damaging its scales. Then he and Ryan cradled the fish over to the base of the fast water, and held the fish there until it revived. When the gills were working fully, the fish gave a huge kick. They gladly let go, and it turned and went deep into the pool.

Hopefully, after just a short rest, it would resume its primal mission to spawn.

4

"There's no such thing as a bad day on The Owl," said Jerome with a big smile as he sipped his rum and coke.

Everyone had gathered on the large wooden deck in front of the main lodge. They were leaning on the perimeter railing, and taking in the spectacular, panoramic view of the pools below them. The sun had come out in the late afternoon, and there was great promise for a classic Labrador sunset.

After their first full day of fishing on the river, it was starting to feel like a vacation. The men could hear the roar of the whitewater in The Chute downstream from where they were standing, but they could not quite see it.

The trip in had gone smoothly, and Curtis was especially thankful about that. The Strait of Belle Isle ferry had left on time. The short drive from Blanc Sablon, Quebec to the hotel and restaurant in L'Anse au Clair, Labrador had been easy on fairly good paved road. They had set out early the next day in bright sunshine, and the guests were able to see the many sights, including the spectacular Pinware River gorge that the road had to cross. Further along, the group had done their best to answer questions from Odvar and Malcolm.

They had told them about the history of Red Bay. Basque whalers had once lived at the desolate place in the 1500s and had also wiped out the Bowhead whale population in the Strait. The Bowhead had somehow survived the whaling era, but only as an Arctic species. Basques had used fired, red clay roofing tiles for ship ballast on their dangerous journey over from Europe. The bay got its name because Basques had offloaded their ballast to free up space in ships' holds for their perilous journey back to Europe with whale oil.

The paved road had ended north of the Red Bay National Historic and World Heritage Site, although more asphalt had clearly been added recently. On the long, dusty, gravel road to Bowhead Arm, they had seen a black bear. Everyone had been content to watch it in safety from within the van.

They had only passed eight vehicles during their five hour drive, and one of those was a road grader. The group had pointed out to Malcolm and Odvar where forest fires had occurred. And at one of the few gas stations they passed, they had stopped for ice cream cones, and a 'pee break'.

When they had finally reached Bowhead Arm, the men were pleasantly surprised to find that Walter and Dwayne had everything ready to go for them. They had met first at Walter's hotel. Then they all had driven down to the crab plant wharf where the boats were all tied up.

English Bay had been relatively calm for the crossing. They had even been able to stop for an hour on the bay to cast treble-hooked 'spoons' with spinning-reels towards a rocky beach. They had managed to catch about a dozen sea-run Brook trout.

They had arrived at the lodge before dusk, in time for 'a few flicks' or casts for salmon on the river.

The water in the river was very high from recent rain storms, and there were huge standing waves and deep 'holes' in The Chute.

Curtis and Walter had driven two camp boats with their forty horsepower outboard motors from Bowhead Arm.

Dwayne had gone ahead of Curtis and Walter, with Brad and the European guests, in his larger, faster, shallow-draft, stainless-steel boat. Dwayne's boat was powered by a hundred and fifty horsepower 'jet' outboard motor, and he had taken an almost direct route through the rapids. The new guests had been thrilled by their adventure.

Curtis had made sure he followed Walter's route exactly through the more violent rapids in The Chute. The character of the rapids changed dramatically with changes in water level, and a lot of experience was required to choose the safest path to take. The camp boats had *just* enough power to get over the steep lip of smooth, rushing water at the top of The Chute.

Rob and Diane Dixon had the lodge in full working order a day or so ahead of the group's arrival. Diane was the chef, and Rob, a retired Ontario high school teacher, helped with the catering.

The only other staff member so far was Bobby Clarke, the head guide. Bobby was married, and did 'handyman work' when he could get it in Goose Bay, Labrador. So, he was really dependent upon the extra bit of money he made by guiding every year.

Rob and Diane mostly just loved the job of running the lodge with Dwayne, and the chance to meet some interesting people in a wilderness setting.

"Who wants some fresh sea trout?" cried Diane to the men on the deck as Rob carried out a large, steaming platter through the door of the lodge.

"Stupid question I think, Diane!" replied Fred, grabbing a fork.

"You can only beat fresh wild salmon with fresh sea trout," said Jerome, as he elbowed Fred aside in the race to the table on the deck. Then he yelled, "Excellent! They're pan fried with the skins left on! This is Labrador candy, b'ys!"

The fish had been cleaned, but not filleted, then lightly battered and fried with their heads left on. Curtis showed Malcolm how to pull the flesh off on one side of the fish with a fork, leaving the bones behind; and then how to hold the tail and peel the spine back to remove the bones completely from the other side of the fish as well.

The perfectly cooked flesh was salted and peppered, deep-orange in colour, and naturally rich with oil. Diane clearly knew what she was doing in a kitchen. "The skin is crunchy and delicious, don't throw it away!" Curtis told his guests.

As she re-entered the lodge, Diane shouted back over her shoulder, "Jerome and Ryan have each donated a grilse for our dinner! I think some thanks to them are in order."

The thanks were said over another round of drinks.

It seemed that everyone had enjoyed the day. Even the novice Malcolm had hooked a salmon.

"How big was it?" asked Fred.

"Never saw it actually, it was only on for a second," said Malcolm.

"No, Malcolm, for situations like this, you're supposed to say, 'Large one for sure, b'y!'" advised Fred.

"I say, thank you very much *indeed* for that, old boy," replied Malcolm, with an exaggerated, old-English accent, and a friendly wink.

"I am pleased to say I have a few more interesting stories now, Curtis," said Odvar, sensing his moment.

"We'll want to hear those, Odvar, for sure, but what's that sound?" said Curtis, looking towards the river.

"There's something coming up The Chute," said Jerome. "And it doesn't sound like a boat."

"It's a small hovercraft!" yelled Kelvin, while leaning far out over the railing to look down river. "But something's really wrong with this picture. It's got wings! And it's flying!"

Everyone could see the strange craft now. It was just large enough for two seats in tandem that were open to the air behind a windscreen. It had a single wing that looked to be covered with rubber. It also had the 'skirt' of a hovercraft; and a pusher-propeller in a protective cage at the back, with controllable vertical and horizontal fins. And it was about three metres off the water, making about seventy kilometres per hour.

"I saw something like that on the internet once. It was about to go commercial," said Malcolm. Then he added, "But that thing looks like a prototype; a bit crude around the edges, if you know what I mean."

"That's Weldon Purdy!" yelled Curtis and Jerome, almost at the same time.

Curtis shook his head, and said, "No doubt he made that himself, from scratch. The guides say he's a genius. And a complete 'nut case'."

"You'd be *nuts*, too, Curtis, if you lived most of your life up here alone, year round, like he has," said Fred.

"Not always alone," said Walter, who was also shaking his head as the strange craft 'flew' out of sight up the river. Then he explained, "He had a wife of sorts for a while, they say. And they had a boy too, maybe. He has a cabin below The Chute, up on a ridge. And they say he has another one up the river about sixteen kilometres from here, at the end of a long 'steady'. That's probably where he's headed now, for some reason."

"Bobby the guide talked about him a *lot* today," said Malcolm. Then he added, "He said he is a, 'thieving, poaching, fur trapping Métis', whatever that means."

Everyone then got really quiet, and looked sheepishly at Walter and Dwayne.

Walter took a long sip of his drink, and said, "It's okay, guys. Malcolm is a bit out of his element here. He had no way to know."

Walter then explained to Malcolm and Odvar that he was Inuit Métis, in his case a cross between English settlers and aboriginal people, like many people living in coastal Labrador.

"Bobby was born in Wabash in western Labrador," Walter explained. Then he said, "There's a good chance he's Innu Métis, and just doesn't know it. The Innu are what white people used to call Indians, while the Inuit were called Eskimos. Now they're all called First Nations people, while the Métis continue the struggle for the same rights to the land and their heritage.

"Native people had to go through the *hell* of 'residential schools' in the sixties. And they have been *crapped on* for years by prejudiced white people." He knew he was venting, so he paused to cool down a bit and take a sip of his drink.

"Look, Labrador is the same size as Arizona," Walter continued, as Odvar and Malcolm looked sincerely interested in what he had been saying. He had had this conversation before with tourists. Then he explained, "Even with all of the desert space, there are six million people living in Arizona. That's two hundred people for every ten square kilometres. There are not even thirty thousand people in all of Labrador, and half of those folks live around Happy Valley-Goose Bay. That's one person for every ten square kilometres."

Walter paused for a minute to let that 'sink in'. Then he said, "Guys like Bobby baffle me. I mean, if you're not Métis now in Labrador, your kids and their kids are going to be. And what the hell's wrong with that?"

Everyone agreed when Curtis said, "There's nothing the hell wrong with that, Walter."

After another sip of his drink, Walter said, "As for Weldon Purdy, I'm probably related to the *crazy bugger*. And I hope I don't have any of those genes! But maybe I do, and that explains what's wrong with you, Dwayne?"

Dwayne laughed, and then he said, "You know, Dad, there's always been a lot of theft up here. We found a lot of *strange shit* missing again this year when we first opened up. Like, all the wire and copper pipe carefully stripped-out of four of the cabins.

"But not *all* of the cabins were touched, or the main lodge. An outboard motor was missing. A starter motor and a wheel were missing from an ATV. All the nails, screws, glue, tape, grease and a few wrenches were gone. And the diesel tank was *bone dry* again after topping it up as always for winter. We do that to keep the diesel from adsorbing water that condenses on the inside walls of the tank.

"Nothing was damaged and there was no vandalism. It's like someone can't resist thinking this is a handy store. We report it every year to the Mounties in Goose Bay. They keep telling me Weldon is a suspect and under watch, but I think he scares the crap out of them, or something."

"He *is* a scary person," said Curtis quietly as Rob called them to dinner. "He came up behind me last year when I was fishing the lower river. I offered him a beer from my pack, and when he took it he said, 'You know, I have no respect for a human life, but I will take a beer from *some* humans when offered one.' And then he went off in the woods, I guess to drink it somewhere else. I got the hell out of there fast. My hands are starting to shake again just thinking about it."

5

Young Elroy was nowhere in sight when Weldon Purdy drove his 'hover plane' up on to the sandy beach, and into a purposely cleared space within some alder bushes. When he shut down the three 'converted' snowmobile engines, Weldon called out to the nearby trees, "Elroy boy, it's Pa!"

Elroy then appeared from the trees, exactly as he had been told to do. He was holding a cocked, single-barrelled shot gun in his hands.

"Did you see anyone, Elroy?" Weldon asked forcefully.

"No, Pa." Elroy replied meekly.

"You're a good boy, Elroy," Weldon said quietly. Then he growled, "Now uncock and break open that shotgun before you hurt one of us. Then help me with this circuit-breaker. It's the last thing we need."

Weldon and Elroy then lifted the stolen fifty kilogram electrical device out of the baggage compartment at the rear of the hover plane. Then they somehow managed to carry it over the wet, uneven sand beach without stumbling, and placed it carefully in a wagon attached to a 'quad' all-terrain vehicle.

Then Weldon followed behind with the shotgun as Elroy drove the 'quad' up the long, well-travelled path through the trees to the 'control cabin'.

The circuit-breaker had come from a bussing station many kilometres away. It was taken on a dark night one winter ago.

Weldon did his best work at night. And winters made it easy to get around. He knew all the snowmobile trails in Labrador, so very well.

During the long walk up the hill, Weldon remembered how his grandfather and father, as fur trappers, had also done their best work during the long Labrador winters. But fur trapping was simple, tough, mind-numbing work.

To Weldon, fur trapping was just a means to buy stuff a smart person like himself could not acquire otherwise through cunning and stealth. And it was a way to look legitimate to anyone stupid enough to sniff around.

His grandfather had been a trapper before snowmobiles were common or affordable. He was the toughest man Weldon had ever known. And he had talked to himself a lot as a result of his many years living in isolation.

Every autumn, his grandfather would load his wolf-like dog, his rifle and his shotgun, some flour and cooking oil, some kerosene, and not much else, into a wooden row boat. Then he would kiss his wife goodbye and head across English Bay and then up the Owl River until the boat would go no further. Then he would find his wooden sled, and with the help of the dog, haul everything up to his cabin.

No one ever messed with his grandfather's cabin. Everyone knew how much he depended upon it. He had all the other stuff there that he would need for the long winter.

The first thing he had to do was get a moose. That was not an easy task in the heavy timber, and the massive beasts have never been as common in Labrador as they are in Newfoundland. He would cut the moose he shot into pieces, and haul those pieces up on ropes to hang from tree branches, away from the reach of hungry animals. Then he would get his traps ready.

The winters were always long and dark and cold. After skinning the pine martens, and everything else he managed to trap, he would eat their flesh. Everything trapped in the forest was instantly frozen, and therefore safe to eat. Except, that is, for any porcupine that had managed to find some plywood to eat. The glue in the plywood ruined that meat. Some meat tasted stranger than others, but meat was meat. He thought the Great Horned Owl was the best, but he had to use a shotgun shell to get one of those, and those shells were dear.

He would walk his trap lines in the mornings in snowshoes, and scrape, stretch and cure the furs on wooden racks in the afternoons before it got too dark. Then he would talk to the dog in the cabin by a wood stove until they both fell asleep.

Getting everything out in the spring was the worst part. The fur pelts were heavy and awkward, and pulling the sled down the river back to the boat during 'break-up' was dangerous, heavy going.

But it all paid the bills, and his wife was usually glad to see him; at least after the first week or so, when he finally started talking more to her than the dog, or himself.

Weldon's father had it a bit easier than his grandfather. He had a powerboat, a 'Ski doo' snowmobile, a metal tow-sled and a gasoline-powered generator. When Weldon turned thirteen years of age, and his mother died, his father had told him, 'School and the easy life are over, Weldon'. Then he started taking Weldon with him into the forest each winter. His father had told him having him along would be a bit better for him than talking to his dog all winter; but not much better.

Weldon was a tough strong kid, far smarter than he looked. And like any child or teenager, he had craved the love of his parents. When anything broke, he would fix it. It seemed he could fix anything. He always made things work better than they had before they broke. His father just seemed to expect it, as if *anyone* could do things like that. He never thanked Weldon, ever. Instead, he kicked Weldon around as much as he kicked his useless dog around. And Weldon's father was a mean drunk.

Weldon ran away at eighteen. Being, in fact, very smart, he guessed there might be more to life than fur trapping and putting up with continuous abuse from a drunken father.

He made it all the way to New Orleans somehow, mostly by hitch-hiking. He was in a very bad way when he met the kind, old army recruiter. After a good meal, he found himself signed, sealed and delivered to the US Army.

After four years, he decided the army was not for him either. But he was a crack shot and a natural soldier who could take any deprivation, and live anywhere on anything. And he could kill efficiently without remorse. All of that got noticed, which led to a second career as an 'assassin'. He could never talk about that part of his life, not even to the 'wife' he ultimately brought back to Labrador with him, with all of his books.

The books were all up in the control cabin now, waiting for him. People had laughed at his books, and his ideas, just like they had laughed at Tesla.

But Weldon was a self-made man. He could still build anything, from just about anything; even stuff others had only dreamed of, like Tesla.

6

Diane had cut the two grilse salmon into chunks, then poached the chunks in white wine, with a selection of herbs, sliced ginger and green onions. The result was exotic and delicious, and not something a group of vacationing fisherman on their own would have made an effort to try. For dessert she served strawberries and ice cream

After dinner, Curtis, Jerome and Fred all talked to their wives on the satellite phone. In addition to the satellite phone, this year Dwayne had managed to install an internet connection in the lodge. Right after dessert, Kelvin had 'gone on the web', and read about the solar flare.

"Susan is freaking out a bit about this solar flare," Curtis said to Jerome, after taking his first sip of neat, single-malt, Scotch whisky. Then he added, "So, I told her she should pull out all the plugs around the house, like the news stations are advising. And I said she should stay inside until we find out this is just another 'Y2K' or 'Mayan calendar doomsday' bunch of crap."

Malcolm and Brad were struggling to look over Kelvin's shoulders as he was continuing to monitor updates with his laptop computer.

"There's been another major CME," Brad announced loudly. Then he said, "That means bad things could start happening here in only a few hours, just like they did back in 1859. They think the first CME paved the way, so to speak, for a second and more serious one."

"What the *hell* is a 'CME', Brad, and what do you mean by *bad things*?" asked Fred, angrily. Then he fumed, "Not all of us read the same books you know, or went to the same schools!"

"CME stands for 'Coronal Mass Ejection', Fred, sorry," said Brad sheepishly. Then he explained, "A huge mass of plasma, or electrically-charged super-heated gas, has burst out of the sun, and is coming right at the earth! And a whole bunch of radiation is coming, too!"

"Expect a very bright Northern Lights show at the very least, Fred," continued Malcolm in support of Brad. Both he and Brad were looking and sounding very worried. Then he added, "But the last time one of these big solar events happened was in 1989. That one knocked out the *entire* Hydro Quebec power system of twenty thousand megawatts for over nine hours. But they're saying this one will be a *lot* worse, especially with the weaker magnetic field around the earth."

"The world was not very electrified in 1859, Fred," added Brad. Then he explained, "That CME was a lot larger than the one in 1989. It was called the 'Carrington Event' after the British astronomer who first observed the massive solar flare. They saw Northern Lights in the Caribbean! Supposedly you could read a newspaper at midnight by the light of the 'aurora borealis' in Boston! Telegraph systems failed all over Europe and North America. Telegraph clickers continued to send and receive even after they were disconnected, literally and figuratively shocking their operators!"

"Electromagnetic induction from the electrically-charged stuff in the solar storm drove huge current surges down wires," said Malcolm, now with real stress in his voice. Then in a louder voice he said, "There are a *hell* of a lot more wires in the world now than in 1859, folks! We are now almost *totally* dependent on electricity and all things electrical!" He was shouting now, almost hysterically. "And, *oh yes*, all the satellites up there, for communication and our global positioning system, they are *completely unprotected*, just like the space station is with the three astronauts on board!"

Curtis put his drink down, walked over, put his hand on Malcolm's shoulder. Then he looked him in the eyes and said, "I haven't been listening to you and Brad properly, and I'm sorry. Now, what should we do?"

"We just lost the internet connection", interjected Kelvin.

"And the phone has just gone dead," added Dwayne.

"Pull out all of the plugs everyone, and kill the generator, Dwayne," said Walter calmly.

"I'm on it!" Dwayne yelled back, while running out the door in the back of the lodge.

After a minute, Fred said, "It didn't get dark in here, guys, when the generator stopped." He was standing at the door to the front deck, looking out towards the river. Then he said nervously, "That's because it's getting like noon outside. Only, the sky is all pulsing in purple and green and yellow streaks."

7

Weldon and Elroy Purdy were standing together inside the biggest shack on the ridge. It was evening now, but there was no need for interior lighting. Bright pulses of green, red and purple light were entering the cabin through a few greasy windows. If it had been a happier place, one could have imagined the colourful light was coming from a big Christmas tree outside.

"I'm going into this 'Faraday Cage' now, Elroy," said Weldon happily. It was great to finally be putting his plan into action. Then he ordered, "You go get in the other one down by the river. You won't need a flash light now, the sky is all lit up. Put on the wooden shoes and the leather gloves like I showed you how to do. Put the wooden chair right in the middle on the plywood. *Don't move* from that chair until I come and get you! *Don't touch the cage, ever*!

"If any one comes before I do, shoot them through a hole in the cage. Don't touch the cage with the barrel! Put another shell in the gun every time you shoot someone. Shoot anybody that tries to come up here. You got all of that, boy?"

"Yes, Pa," Elroy said calmly. His low intelligence and profound ignorance were blessings at times like this. He was not remotely aware enough of the immense risks to be afraid.

"You're a good boy, Elroy," Weldon said without feeling. Then he growled, "Now git!"

After Elroy left him to walk down to the river, Weldon pulled on some leather motorcycle pants. Then he buttoned a leather jacket with 'Harley Davidson Acapulco' on the back. He had sewn on the buttons of the coat himself after he had ripped out the metal zipper. He had also removed all of the fancy metal studs. The original owner was no longer around to complain how his clothes had been made more 'functional'. He stepped into the wooden clogs he had carved, put in some earplugs, pulled on some old ice hockey gloves, and put a welder's mask on his head.

He didn't know *exactly* what was about to happen, but he had a fair idea. And it was going to be a *really* good show.

Weldon went into the cage and closed its metal door. There was a plywood floor in the cage. He sat on a wooden chair, and positioned it so he could poke buttons on the nearby control panel using the shaft of a wooden hockey stick. He made sure the openings in the cage lined up with where he had to poke the stick.

There were not many controls, really. He only wanted to do two things, in sequence. And all he had to do was start one process, and then initiate the other process in parallel, when he thought the time was right.

The 'intensifier' gauges were showing that his charge-collecting and accumulating arrays were beginning to work. The front edge of the solar storm had *definitely* arrived. An *unimaginable* energy source would soon be available to exploit and re-direct, if someone bright enough and brave enough was willing to try.

The 'collecting array' was his idea. He had borrowed the rest from Tesla, and a few others. The charge was now quickly accumulating in banks of high-frequency, high-voltage Tesla coils, and capacitors and helical-resonators. A few of these complicated devices were around the Faraday Cage he was sitting in. The steel cage was stoutly grounded, and would protect him from errant electrical discharges. He mostly believed that.

Sparks, flashes and loud crackling sounds were suddenly starting up all around him. He poked the first button with his hockey stick. He had trimmed it to remove the blade, and shaped the end to conform to the rounded-shape of the control knobs. Then he pulled down the welding mask.

He could smell ozone, burnt dust and smoke accumulating in the normally just stuffy interior of the control cabin. It was starting to get *really* hot, and he was 'sweating buckets'.

He checked that the aim of the 'spark-emitting array' was still pointed at 'Churchill Falls'. When enough charge had accumulated to leap the *gigantic* potential difference, the longest bolt of electricity in history would shoot out from his modified Wardenclyffe towers. And the unprecedented 'spark-emitting' process would repeat itself until the energy source, the solar storm, finally abated.

And then it happened. The sonic shockwave from the massive electrical discharge above him smashed all of the windows and shook the walls of the control cabin almost to pieces.

Weldon was stunned, and his ears were ringing, even though he was wearing ear plugs. He had fallen off the chair onto the plywood floor of the cage. And he saw through the little viewing port on his welder's mask that the cage was all brilliant white now, with *spectacular* sparks and flashes.

He looked for his hockey stick, and he held it tighter when he finally found it. One bolt was *just not good enough*. He must take as many of these punishing blows as he could stand, then push the other button. He just *had* to give 'Muskrat Falls' some of the lightning bolt business, too, before he pushed the last button.

8

It was late in the evening, but no one was even thinking about going to bed yet. Ryan came into the large, communal section of the lodge from the back hallway that led to the kitchen. He said loudly, "Uh, Dad, Diane says there's 'purple lightning' coming out of the tap in the kitchen! And, hey, the lights are coming back on with the generator off!"

"Just like in Colorado Springs when Tesla was doing his high-frequency, high-voltage experiments," gasped Malcolm. Only Brad seemed to have heard him.

"Jerome, what are you at, b'y?" said Fred nervously as Jerome came in from the front deck. Then he said, "Hey, lift your foot again. I don't want to scare you, buddy, but, uh, you've got a *big spark* under your shoe."

"I can *feel* it, and my hair's standing on end!" yelled Jerome.

"Grab a dining room chair, and head for the deck everyone!" yelled Brad. After the mad rush to get through the front door in single file, he added, "Now, put your chair down on the deck where it's dry, and stand up on it!"

"This would make a great picture," gasped Walter. He was trying to catch his breath, and correct his balance on a wobbly chair, at the same time. Then he yelled, "And what's up with the flag pole? It's *glowing*!"

"That's 'St Elmo's Fire'," said Curtis with wonder. Then he added, "I saw it once before, on a mast, when I was sailing during a thunderstorm."

It was midnight, but it was alarmingly bright outside.

Suddenly, there was a blinding flash in the sky. Less than a minute later there was a deafening, concussive crash of sound, and a rush of air.

They were all knocked off their chairs.

"*Lord thundering, Jesus*, what the hell was that?" cried Jerome. Then he croaked, "Thunder and lightning, in *clear air*?"

"I don't know," said Brad while trying to clear his throat and his head. Then he yelled, "Get back on your chairs everyone! I don't think we have to actually *stand up* on them, just try to keep our feet off the deck. The ground is *electrically-charged* now, somehow! Here Fred, let me help you up. Are you all right?"

Fred sat down hard with a grunt. Then he said sarcastically, "Other than ringing ears and retina burns, sure thing, Brad, I feel just great! Now, my *expert* advice, for what it's worth, is for everyone to start *drinking heavily*!"

"You go back in and get a bottle, Fred, of anything, and I'll drink it with you," said Jerome.

9

'Was that ten'? Yes, Weldon thought, that was 'Number Ten'.

Through the pain and the daze, Weldon remembered the other button. And he now wanted to push that button *very badly*.

He thought, 'Where is the damn stick?' 'Oh', he realised; it was in his hand.

He stabbed with the stick. He thought with frustration, 'Why is this so *freaking* hard'?

On the eighth try, he was sure he got it.

And then the 'mechanical-oscillator' kicked in. He could *feel* it! It was working as it should, in tandem with the 'electrical-oscillator'.

Tesla had discovered that the resonant frequency of the earth was about eight Hertz. He thought, 'How had that smart son-of-a-bitch done that?'

And Weldon's oscillators were tuned *precisely* to excite vibration at that very same frequency. They were all really thumping like crazy now.

The ground was shaking wildly. The roof of the control cabin was falling in. Inexorably, Weldon was bounced and rolled towards the side of the cage that was white-hot with sparks.

Before he could raise his hands to protect himself or readjust his welder's mask, Weldon Purdy died with his face baked to carbon on the wire of the cage he thought would protect him.

10

They were hanging on to each other in a tight circle of chairs on the front deck of the lodge.

"I make that number *ten* of those sons-of-bitches!" yelled Rob.

"Ya, that is so," said Odvar, with a remarkably calm tone of voice.

"Canada Day", said Fred bluntly. Then he explained, "It's after midnight now, so it's now Canada Day, the first of July. This must be the local idea of a fireworks display, right Walter?"

"Shut the hell up, Fred," said Jerome.

"Everyone still okay?" asked Diane.

There were nods all around.

"I think the ground is starting to shake," observed Odvar calmly.

"It's *definitely* starting to shake!" yelled Curtis. Then he yelled, "Hold on *tighter* everybody! Now what?"

There was a deep rumble all around them, growing steadily in intensity. They were suddenly all thrown off their chairs, but everyone held tightly to each other.

Then the deck started falling down at one end. Then the rock wall beside the lodge broke away, and slid down the bank into the river with a thunderous crash.

And then, all of sudden, the shaking stopped.

The pulsing, bright sky was full of crying birds, mostly gulls, whirling around in the eerie light.

They all staggered to their feet on the now sloping deck.

"I think we better get to solid flat ground now," Dwayne somehow managed to say.

"Hey, look at the banks of the river!" cried Ryan. Then he yelled, "There's salmon *everywhere*!"

"Jumped right out in fright, I'd say," said Jerome with wonder. Then he predicted, "The surviving bears won't go hungry for a while, that's for sure. And, we might want to grab a few of those salmon ourselves."

"There are lots of things to do like that, if there isn't another freaking Armageddon lightning bolt," said Curtis.

Thankfully, there was no 'Number Eleven lightning bolt'.

11

Curtis was sitting at the end of the long dining room table in the main section of the lodge. He quickly scanned around the table, and then he said, "Okay, I know we're all really tired, especially just after eating a big meal, and with no sleep last night. But I think before we break up for the evening, we should go around the table to see where we're at.

"Diane and Rob, why don't you sit down and join us? Thanks. And you stay too, Bobby. Thanks. I think that's the *first thing* that needs to be said. We're in 'survival mode' now. There are no bosses or staff people around here anymore. We're all in this together! Everyone okay with that?"

Everybody was nodding, so Curtis said, "Okay then, Dwayne, why don't you start us off?"

"Well, first off, none of us are seriously hurt, although some folks still have some ringing in their ears, and some have a few bruises from falling down," said Dwayne. Then he added, "And we still have an intact roof over our heads, somehow. We've got the fireplace for heat at night in the main lodge, and lots of stacked, dry wood.

"We should talk about the power next, I guess. The main camp generator is completely burned out. It's clearly been on fire, insulation and other stuff has melted inside of it. I disconnected it from the drive shaft, and I can start the diesel engine from the battery, so somehow the starter motor and, I think, the glow plugs survived. When I turned the generator off last night, I disconnected the battery leads to the diesel engine, too. I'm really glad I did that. But right now, that engine is no good to us.

"We had a spare generator for it once, but that 'disappeared' two winters ago. It was stolen, no doubt. We're running a deep freeze, a refrigerator and a few lights using a four thousand watt backup gasoline generator. But we shouldn't put any more load on it, and we should watch our gasoline consumption closely. We've got one drum of gasoline, and you guys and Bobby brought in twenty jerry cans of gas, so…"

"Sorry to interrupt, Dwayne," interjected Bobby. Then he said, "I mixed five of those jerry cans up for the outboard motors. And I just checked all of the camp outboards. Only one would start, but it didn't sound right. We've got ten outboards in total here, and some spare parts. I swapped out some parts and finally got *two* to work, *that's it*! And I also got *mine* to work. Then I helped to get Dwayne's to work. It runs on unmixed gas."

"Thanks, Bobby, it's good to know we can get out of here, at least as far as Bowhead Arm," said Dwayne. "We've got *lots* of diesel for what that's worth, and propane so we can cook in the kitchen and with the barbecue. The barbecue fell to the ground when the deck collapsed, but Rob put it back together again, just like 'Humpty Dumpty'. The ATV won't start, but we won't need it, with all you strong folks around to carry stuff. Yes, you too, Fred!" he laughed when he heard Fred groan.

Then Dwayne said, "The gravity-feed fish-box water tank up behind the lodge is full, but the electric pump for filling it is 'fried'. So, we should go easy with the water, unless we want to haul more up from the river by hand.

"The phone and internet don't work, but you all knew that. The Citizen Band radio in my boat just gives static, as does Diane's AM/FM radio in the kitchen. My handheld GPS turns on, but it's not seeing any satellites.

"The compass in my boat is just swinging around in circles on its own! Oh, and we've got *lots* of canned food, and other food that we will lose if we have to turn off the freezer and the refrigerator. We've been stocking up for the season that was supposed to start in three days.

"God only knows where the first real guests are!

"We will have to keep putting our garbage in the big bin out back with the heavy lid. The bears are probably busy with all the dead salmon on the bank, but you never know. I've never actually had to shoot a bear up here, and I really don't want to. I've got a double-barrelled, twelve-gauge shotgun, and a box of buckshot shells by my bed."

"So, all in all, we're in pretty fair shape around here, considering," said Curtis, looking at the faces around the table. Everyone was looking stressed. Then he asked, "But what about the *rest of the world*, how is it doing?" He was thinking of his wife, and the rest of his family. He wasn't alone with his thoughts.

No one said anything, so Curtis asked, "Brad and Malcolm? What do you guys think happened, and what could be next for us?"

"Okay, first off, Malcolm and I are mechanical engineers," said Brad. Then he explained, "I have a Bachelor's degree, and Malcolm has a Master's. So we're not astrophysicists, or electrical 'gurus'. But we *do* apply science for a living, and are 'observant nerds', I guess.

"And we *have* been 'putting our heads together'. Did you notice the how long it took between each of the ten 'lightning bolts'? Well, I did, and it ranged from forty to fifty-five minutes. And did you notice the time between the flash of the 'bolt' and the thunder noise was always exactly the same, fifty seconds?

"That means if it was lightning, it was *always* about sixteen kilometres away, you know, using the three-second-per kilometre rule for the speed of sound in air. Thunderstorms *move*, meaning the time between 'flash and boom', or lightning and thunder, is supposed to *change*. So, we'll be *damned* if we know what was happening around here."

"And, the light and the noise was coming from upstream, or the west," said Walter. Then he added, "That's where Purdy has his other place." Everyone mulled that over a moment.

"He's *definitely* got a place up there!" said Bobby suddenly and loudly. Then he added, "He parks his stolen boat on the bank, and goes up the hill. He always seems to have a *different* boat, and now that flying thing he built. But *none* of us have ever gone very close. And you have to drag a boat around two sets of rapids to get up there. He shot at old Sid a few years ago, or at least that's what Sid said right before he quit."

"Okay, we'll get back to that, thanks, Bobby," said Curtis. Then he asked, "Brad and Malcolm, anything else?"

"It's getting dark outside now, and there still are Northern Lights in the sky, but nothing like last night," said Malcolm. Then he added, "The static on the radio might mean the solar storm is still happening, and messing with the ionosphere. Or the radio stations were 'fried', as you say, and are now under repair, or waiting for power to be restored. Or all of those things combined!

"I checked before dinner, and Dwayne's compass is still spinning around. That means we may also be experiencing a 'magnetic pole reversal'. There may even be multiple poles right now. A 'magnetic pole' is where the geomagnetic flux enters or leaves the earth. The bottom line is, we should *not* use a compass for navigation, maybe for a long while."

"We probably shouldn't count on having GPS, or a satellite phone, for a long while either," said Brad sadly. Then he added, "At least until replacement satellites are built and launched, and we're talking about needing to replace hundreds of those, I imagine."

There was a long pause while people tried to rationalise these terrible developments in their own minds. Then Malcolm said, "The electrification of the ground is really puzzling. Do you remember that it stopped when the ground stopped shaking?"

"And do you remember in the 'heat of the moment' when I talked about Tesla and Colorado Springs? No? Well, he caused something like what we experienced when he was experimenting with high-frequency, high-voltage gizmos in his lab.

"What happened here may have been linked to the solar storm I suppose, but I'm not smart enough to tell you that for sure. The water in the river must have been electrified for a while too, to drive salmon up on the banks."

When he saw the blank faces, Brad explained. "Nikola Tesla was a Serbian-American, electro-mechanical engineer, and a true genius. He studied in universities, but I don't think he ever received a degree. He had *hundreds* of patents. He invented practical stuff that we have long taken for granted, like efficient, reliable and relatively inexpensive alternating current induction motors. George Westinghouse worked with his ideas to beat out Thomas Edison, who was pushing direct current for public power distribution and use.

"Tesla was also a bit of a 'mad scientist' type of guy, and a contrarian in the science world. For instance, he didn't believe in the electron, rather in the nineteenth century concept of something called the 'ether' that transmitted electrical energy. He said machinery in the future would all run by a power obtainable at any point in the universe."

"Brad, think about that for a second," said Malcolm. Then he said with excitement, "Maybe Tesla was talking about the mysterious 'dark mass' and 'dark energy', you know, what cosmologists say they can't detect, but they need in their equations for explaining why the expansion of the universe is accelerating?"

"It seems to be back to normal now," said Ryan while looking out of the front window of the lodge. Then he added, "The river, I mean. I saw fish jumping as always this afternoon. At least there are still salmon on the go." There was a moment of confused silence, and then laughter all around.

"Time to return to Earth, thanks, Ryan!" yelled Brad with a laugh. Then he became serious again, and said, "But remember, our earth was shaking not so long ago. Did you feel it build steadily in intensity? And did you feel the regular pulse of the vibration?

"I'm not a seismologist, but I don't think that's how natural earthquakes behave. Another thing 'old Tesla' played around with was setting up resonant vibrations in the earth. He was busting up something with a sledge hammer when the cops arrived one day to find out why all buildings around his lab where shaking like crazy."

"This Tesla stuff is all really interesting I guess, and a disturbing recurring theme," said Rob, while looking at Diane. Then he asked, "But can we get right down to earth now, pun intended? What do you think has happened around us, in *practical* terms?"

"And that's more guess work, unfortunately," said Brad. Then he added, "I think we should assume there's been a widespread power outage from a solar storm, like what happened in Quebec in 1989. Only, if this solar storm was worse, like we think it was, a lot of the electrical distribution system may have been *really* damaged, meaning no power in some places, or maybe most places. Big, high-voltage, high-current transformers, switches, circuit-breakers, *et cetera*, are not 'off the shelf' items. It might take *months* to get things working again everywhere."

"There also might be ships that have lost power and control, and are just drifting at sea," added Malcolm sadly. Then he added, "Let's hope governments grounded all airplanes at the start of the storm. It might take a long time for airports and air traffic control to be functional again. And think about all the refineries, chemical plants and nuclear reactors! Hopefully they were all shut down and de-pressurised safely.

"And we all probably received, and still may be receiving, large doses of radiation; gamma, cosmic, and the rest."

"Just think about all the things electrical in our lives," said Brad quietly. He could sense the high level of confusion and stress around the table. After a moment, he added, "People now might not have some or most of the things they have become used to. Maybe that will go on for a long time. We just don't know right now. And we also don't know if our 'shaking ground' was a local thing, or something wider-spread. Or, if it was a natural phenomenon."

Curtis looked up and down the table, and saw the anguish on people's faces. So he said, "Okay, that's probably enough for tonight folks, unless someone wants to join me for a nightcap?" Most people seemed to be nodding at his suggestion. So he added, "Yes, all of you? Well, okay then!

"And I think tomorrow we should start planning our trip back to Bowhead Arm. Unfortunately, that's really the only way to get a better idea of what happened outside of this area."

"Ah, there's one other thing to consider, Curtis," said Walter quietly. Then he said, "We know there is one other person up here for sure, Weldon Purdy. And maybe he's got a son too, like some of the guides think he does. They could be hurt, and I don't think we should just leave without checking on them. He might not be a 'civil' or 'social' man, but I am.

"I'll go look for him, even if I have to go by myself."

"I'll go with you too, Walter," said Brad quickly. Then he said, "I'm curious as *hell*, and I've never been up the river from here."

"We'll need some more help with the boat," said Walter. Then he explained, "We'll have to haul it up or around those two sets of rapids."

"Then we'll come along too, right, Ryan?" said Kelvin with a grin. Ryan grinned back.

"Will that be okay with you, Curtis?" asked Walter.

"They're both grown men now," said Curtis bluntly. Then he said, "They can make up their own minds. And now, can I talk with you for a minute, Walter, in private?"

Walter looked puzzled by the request, but nodded his head.

Curtis and Walter then stood up, and Walter followed Curtis and his flashlight beam back to Curtis' room in the main lodge. Curtis closed the door, and pulled a zipped-up leather pouch out of a drawer. Then he said, "I want you to take this with you, Walter."

"What is it, Curtis?"

"It's a forty-four Magnum revolver and twenty rounds."

"Are you *nuts,* Curtis? You can't carry that around, or give it to me! This is Canada, remember? The land of the 'restricted weapon'!"

"It's registered to me, and I think we can explain it to a cop if we have to, all things considered. I started bringing it up here after young Ryan and I had a bear tear up our coolers outside the cabin one night, then try to come through our front door! All we could do was bang pots and pans together, and throw things at the door. For some reason, that was enough for that particular bear. But I figured an 'equaliser' might let us sleep easier on future trips. Another bear might be sicker, or hungrier."

"All right, Curtis, I'll be glad to have it along. Dwayne will still have his shotgun handy here if it's needed."

"Oh, and Walter, there is one more thing. If that *crazed son-of-a-bitch* tries to hurt my boys, you'll plug him like 'Dirty Harry', won't you?"

"Count on that, Curtis, in a heartbeat."

12

They were finally in the long, steady section of the river above the second set of rapids. Brad was sitting in the bow of the boat, looking ahead for hazards below the surface of the water. Rocks, and partially-sunken logs, or 'deadheads', were sometimes hidden under smooth, innocuous-looking water.

Kelvin and Ryan were sitting side-by-side in the middle of the five metre long, aluminium boat. Walter was at the stern, operating the outboard motor, and thoroughly enjoying the sunshine. The speed of the boat was creating a refreshing breeze.

Walter and Brad were really glad to have Kelvin and Ryan along. They had helped make the two portages relatively easy. The two young men were strong and wiry, and fit as hell. Ryan played rugby and had just started framing houses, and Kelvin ran every day, and got his 'hands dirty' as much as he could in his father's brewery.

"My wife's father used to have a cabin right there!" yelled Walter over the engine noise. He pointed at a spot above the right bank that appeared to have younger trees than the surrounding heavy timber.

"He was a fur trapper, and that's where he stayed in the winters!" continued Walter. He slowed down a bit so he could tell his story in a more normal tone of voice. Then he said, "He was also a commercial salmon fisherman, when the government used to allow that business. He's dead now, unfortunately.

"But he came along with me, Curtis and Jerome once, to see what 'sport' salmon fishing was all about. All he had with him were some tobacco, and some papers for rolling cigarettes. They used to do that in those days. And he was only wearing a pair of dirty, old coveralls over his tee-shirt and jeans, and he wore his rubber fishing boots. You know how cold it gets up here, but that never bothered him. His skin was like dark-leather from being outside all of the time.

"Anyway, he spent hours watching Curtis with his fly-fishing. Curtis, of course, was all rigged-out in his 'high-tech' chest waders, collapsible wading stick, felt-bottomed boots, flashy vest with a hundred pockets, *et cetera*. Then I guess he got up enough nerve to beg a bit of monofilament line off Curtis. Curtis, of course, had no problem with that. Then he asked Curtis if he could spare a fly, too. Curtis was wondering what he was up to, but he let him pick one out of his box. Curtis offered him a few more, but he said, 'No, one is enough'.

"Then he went off into the woods and came back with a long, skinny, dead tree. He cut the limbs off the 'big stick' with a knife, and stripped off all the bark until he had a smooth, four metre long pole. Then he tied the monofilament line to the skinnier end of the pole, and then he tied the fly on to the end of the line.

"Then he went upstream a bit to a 'dabbling pool' where he had seen some fish hanging up. He put a large boulder between himself and the pool, and stuck the pole over the boulder so the fly could dangle in the water without a fish ever seeing him. It took less than a minute for a salmon to take the fly! When that happened, he hauled up, and hurled everything, the pole, the line and the wild surprised fish, everything, up into the alder bushes above the bank. Then he ran into the bushes and beat the fish senseless with a rock.

"When he had gutted and cleaned the fish, he came back to Curtis with it and said, 'You know, you don't need all of that fancy gear you've got.' Curtis smiled at him and handed him a tag. Then he said, 'You better put this tag in the mouth of that fish, or else a warden will take it away. You don't have a licence, so they might take all of my fancy gear away, too.'"

Everyone enjoyed the story. They liked being with Walter. Walter knew this country so well and clearly liked having people along with him who saw it all with fresh eyes and wonder. Walter didn't go much for what he called 'fancy gear' either. He really appreciated the engraved fly-box, graphite rod and English-made large arbour reel that Curtis, Jerome, Brad and Fred had given him. But when he was fishing, he usually only wore a tee-shirt and a nylon pull-over jacket, with sweat pants and rubber boots. He didn't care if he got wet, and would actually swim out with his rod between his teeth to places the others could not safely reach with their chest waders.

And Walter could catch salmon.

"Let me know when you think you can see the next set of rapids, Brad," said Walter. He kept his speed low, so they could hear each other clearly. Then he added, "They may be around the next bend in the river."

The boat moved smoothly, with a fine 'rooster-tail' trailing behind, as it followed the bend in the river. "Some falls are ahead, Walter!" yelled Brad suddenly, while looking forward. Then he guessed, "Maybe three hundred metres away!"

Walter slowed the boat gradually to a stop and put the motor in neutral and a slow idle. The others turned to look at him.

Walter's tone was serious and calm. He said, "Look, guys. None of us know what's up ahead. All we *really* want to do is see if Weldon's all right. But I don't know how this will 'go down', at all. We've all heard the stories about him. Some of them may be true."

Walter reached into a bag at his feet. Then he said, "Kelvin and Ryan, your dad gave me this to bring along. I'm going to load it now." Walter took the revolver out of its pouch, opened it to expose the breech and put six bullets in place in the cylinder. He flipped the cylinder closed, and added, "Let's hope we won't need to use it." He looked up to see three wide-eyed, silent, nodding heads. Brad may have been the most surprised.

"Let's treat this guy like a bad bear," said Walter quietly. Then he said, "So, we won't surprise him. As soon as we start moving again, everyone start yelling his name. Keep your 'eyes peeled', and holler if you see something."

Walter then put the boat in forward gear, and turned the throttle handle *just* a touch to move the boat along at a walking pace.

Then the 'Weldon!' yells began.

Their voices were hoarse when they finally approached the base of the falls. A fog bank had rolled in, and a drizzle of rain had started.

"'Arn'?" asked Walter, over the low burble of the motor. "I mean, do you see anything?"

"'Narn'!" answered Brad with a nervous laugh. "I mean, no, nothing! No, wait, there's a boat on the right beach."

"And there's his hover plane in the alders up a bit further," said Kelvin.

Ryan, whose eyes were the best said, "There's something 'weird looking' past the hover plane. It looks like black and mangled metal, or something."

"Okay, I'm going to beach us here," said Walter. Then he said, "Keep yelling his name, you guys!"

They dragged the boat out of the water as far as they could with the propeller out of the water. Walter threw a grapple tied to a rope into some alder bushes, and tied the other end of the rope to the bow-cleat.

"I'll go on ahead with Brad," said Walter. Then he said, "Kelvin and Ryan, you follow us about thirty metres back. Keep yelling his name and looking for him."

When Walter and Brad reached the hover plane, Brad yelled back to Kelvin and Ryan, "Better stay right where you are for a bit, guys!"

At the base of a wide path that went up a steep slope through the trees, there was a blackened, bullet-shaped 'cage' made of welded 're-bars', or the steel reinforcing rods used in concrete. The cage was wrapped in chicken wire. It was laying on its side, and lying on what looked like a door to the 'cage', was the blackened, burned and partially-molten corpse of a teenage boy, or very young man.

The corpse was looking up to the sky with eyes open. Ravens had picked at the eyes and the flesh; some of the big black carrion-eating birds were nearby, looking down from trees and boulders. A blackened, skeleton hand was holding on to the door. A shotgun was lying in the cage beside a singed, wooden chair and a charred piece of plywood. It all smelled of burned wood and rotting flesh.

They stood there in shock for a minute, taking it all in. Then Walter took off his nylon, softball team coat, and laid it over the top half of the corpse. "You better go back and get those two, Brad," he said quictly. Then he added, "And maybe take a moment to prepare them for this, as best you can."

Walter went a few paces further ahead, and looked up the foggy path. There were fresh rock slides in places, and he could see a lot of big boulders and thinly rooted black spruce trees had recently been toppled over.

Walter and Brad let Ryan and Kelvin have a few minutes over the corpse. "Oh man, what a way to go," said Ryan finally, while staring and shaking his head. Kelvin said nothing, but he was clearly shaken.

"Look, it might be worse up ahead, guys, I don't know," said Walter. Then he said, "I'm the one who felt there was a reason to come here. If you guys want to stay here, or go back to the boat, that's all right. I've *got* to take a look up the hill though. That's not Weldon laying there."

"No, we'll come with you, Walter." It was Kelvin who said it.

Walter grabbed his shoulder, and said, "Thanks, man. I could still use some support."

Ryan was the first to start yelling 'Weldon!' again, this time without any prompting.

A few paces up the trail, they saw a metal plate lying on the ground. Someone had scrawled on it in black paint, 'KEEP OUT OR BE SHOT'.

The trail was hard going, with loose rock and freshly fallen trees and branches. It looked to have been well used. There were wheel tracks and ruts in it.

As they climbed further along, they started seeing metal rubbish and rotting wooden planks by the side of the trail. Then they started seeing old snowmobiles, parts of outboard motors, car and truck engines, electrical motors, rusty old winches, and pieces of machinery, including what looked like a homemade welding machine. There was a bent antenna tower, and in a bit of a clearing, what looked like a partially completed ultralight airplane on floats.

"This is a freaking junkyard!" said Ryan loudly. Then he yelled, "Weldon!"

They could see the trail was going to end at a clearing at the top of a ridge. "Be ready for anything now, guys," said Walter quietly. Then he added, "Take it slower, and follow me." He had the revolver in his hand, cocked and ready to fire.

When they reached the top of the ridge, what they saw poking through the fog in places made no sense.

There were a number of shacks in a series of connected clearings. The shacks had all collapsed. There were columns of tubular metal, tightly wrapped with bare copper wires poking out of metal and wooden wreckage. There were intact and broken electrical-insulators made of glass lying everywhere. There were shiny aluminium globes on metal sticks. There were transformers of all sizes, and cylindrical cans of all sizes that were labelled 'capacitors'. There were oily and smelly chemical puddles everywhere. There was evidence of recent, intense fires in many places, and the smell of chemical and wood smoke was everywhere.

As they moved further along, they saw huge busted-up 'cribs' made of telephone poles. They had been filled with boulders. There were metallic things that looked like coil-springs, leaf-springs and connecting-rods poking through the boulders in places.

"For fun once," croaked Brad. He cleared his throat, pointed to his right, and said, "My friend made a much smaller version of a thing that looked like that. He called it a 'Tesla Coil'. It generated high-voltage, high-frequency sparks. My friend was a bit odd, and thought it was great fun at a party. Tesla Coil discharges are not completely understood."

"This looks like the set from an old Frankenstein movie," said Kelvin. Then he added, "After a Hollywood earthquake."

"I'd say old Frankenstein Weldon has been a pretty busy boy around here," said Walter. Then he concluded, "And I think there's been much more than an earthquake around here."

Ryan had gone off to the side a bit. "Hey, there's a bigger shack over here!" he yelled. Then he said, "And it looks like a lot of cables went into it. And there's a fallen down tower or something beyond it."

"This is probably a crime scene," said Brad slowly. Then he added, "We should avoid disturbing or touching anything. But I'd like to work my way into the one Ryan just found for a peek inside."

"Too bad we didn't bring a camera," said Walter.

"I did," said Kelvin. Then he said, "It's a small digital one. I took the battery out when we were pulling the plugs in the lodge. It seems to work okay."

Brad looked at Walter and said quietly, "I think Kelvin should come with me, Walter. We'll be careful, I promise."

"Okay," said Walter. "But it looks really unstable. Don't push it too far."

After about ten minutes, Brad and Kelvin re-emerged through a broken window in a partially collapsed wall of the largest shack. They were both completely covered in black grime, and they smelled heavily of wood smoke. "There's another one of those strange 'cages' in there," said Brad, while panting.

Brad and Kelvin looked pretty shaken up by what they had seen. Brad took a deep breath and added, "And there's another corpse in there too. It was a man, we think, charred up the same way as the one we found down by the river, or worse.

"We also saw what looked like some kind of a control panel, and busted up electrical contraptions we could not recognise. And a *lot* of books, and drawings like old blueprints. Kelvin took some pictures."

"Okay," said Walter. "Fair conclusion, I think, that we just found our 'buddy', Weldon. Kelvin, you better use up the rest of the data storage in that camera. No, on second thought, maybe you better save a couple of shots for the other mess down by the water."

Ryan then walked around with Kelvin, and helped him decide what to photograph. When the two young men were out of earshot, Brad said quietly "Walter, there was a big, handmade 'gauge' of sorts in there that looked like a clock face, but with only one hand. It was pointing to a mark made with a wide felt pen. Above the mark was written 'Churchill Falls'. And there was a second mark on the 'gauge' labelled 'Muskrat Falls'." After a minute he added, "There may have been more than *one* crime committed here, Walter."

Walter took a couple of slow, deep breaths. Then he said, "Let's get the hell out of here now, Brad. We can *just* get back to the lodge before dark, I think."

When they reached the base of the trail again, Brad said, "Walter and I will do this, Kelvin. You go ahead with Ryan. It will only be a minute."

Walter lifted his coat away, and Brad used up the last two photos in Kelvin's camera. Then Walter put the coat back over the corpse of the teenage boy. Then he said quietly, "We'll leave the coat like that. I could never wear it again without thinking of this nightmare."

"I think it will be right not to bury the two corpses," said Brad. Then he explained, "There might be forensic evidence of use in an investigation, even if the animals get at them some more."

"That definitely works for me," said Walter with relief.

As they passed by Weldon's boat, Walter reached into it and pulled out an old, plaid, woollen coat. "There's nothing in the pockets," he said after checking them all. Then he added, "It's a bit damp, but if I wear it, I'll find it a bit warmer going home. I think a forensic investigator will understand."

After the others had climbed into the boat, Ryan pushed it away from the beach with a dangling foot, and climbed in over the bow. Walter started the motor, but left it in idle and let the boat just drift along in the slow moving current. He put the gun back in his bag, then pulled out a plastic 'Mickey bottle' of dark, Demerara rum. Then he said, "I know it's getting late, but let's pass this around, and 'kill it' before we leave. I bet that will take us less than five minutes."

The bottle was soon making its last round. Brad took a swig, wiped his mouth, passed the bottle to Kelvin, and said with a gasp, "Old Weldon was sure 'well done', wasn't he?"

Kelvin giggled during his swig, passed the bottle to Ryan, and choked-out, "Yes, and he was pretty, 'well welded on', too."

Ryan took his swig with a straight face, passed the bottle to Walter, and said, "I just hope we're not having *char* for dinner."

Walter finished off the bottle, put it back in his bag, and said, "You guys are a bunch of *sick puppies*." But he was laughing now, too.

13

Curtis was huddled closely together with Kelvin and Ryan. They were sitting on the old leather couch in the cabin Kelvin and Ryan were using. Kelvin was sitting in the middle of the couch, operating his digital camera. A candle was lit in the room, but it was dark enough to clearly see the images on the small viewing screen of the camera.

"So, what the *hell* is that?" asked Curtis loudly. They were about a third of the way through the pictures that Kelvin had taken.

"You tell me," mumbled Kelvin. He took a sip from his beer bottle, put it back between his knees, and then flipped to the next photo.

"You say there were a bunch of clearings up there, with 'structures' or whatever in each one?" asked Curtis.

"Yes, Dad," Kelvin confirmed. Then he added, "Walter thought Weldon must have cleared at least four or five acres all together. Just doing the clearing work up there would have been 'brutal'. There were wires and cables running everywhere, some obviously connecting structures or devices, and some just carefully wound round and round many times on other structures, for some reason."

"*That* looks like a collapsed wooden tower of some kind," said Curtis pointing to the screen with a sharp pencil. Then he said, "And *that* looks like some kind of weird antenna, shaped like a doughnut! It must have been at, or near, the top of the tower."

Kelvin kept moving through the pictures, and Ryan was looking over his shoulder.

"You haven't seen the next ones, Ryan," said Kelvin. "They're pretty gross."

"Holy shit," said Curtis when Kelvin opened the digital photographs he had taken with Brad inside the biggest building. Then Curtis said quietly, "It looks like he put himself in some kind of a *cage*, but why?"

"Every building was knocked to pieces up there," said Ryan. Then he speculated, "Maybe he was looking for protection from an earthquake, or maybe one he was going to cause?"

"Brad thinks the cage was mostly an electrical shield of some kind," said Kelvin. He added, "He called it a 'Faraday Cage'. He said it works like the steel body of a car in a thunderstorm. If lightning hits the car, it just electrifies the metal around you on the way to the ground."

"Well, Weldon might have believed that too," said Curtis. Then he said, "It looks like there were *lots* of books and drawings in there, too. It must have been a 'home away from home', or something like that. Hey, I read 'Churchill Falls' and 'Muskrat Falls' on that thing. Holy shit!"

"Yes," said Kelvin with a wry smile. Then he added, "That's what Brad said too, at the time. He thinks it may be the 'smoking gun' in the case, perhaps."

"And that's the other body, in another cage," said Curtis quietly. He looked at Ryan with concern, and asked, "This is not easy, is it, son?"

"No, he looked about the same age as me," said Ryan. Then he took a long sip of his beer.

"So, everything wrecked, and fires in many places," Curtis said in summary. Then he added, "And maybe a 'smoking gun' was found. Two dead human bodies were definitely found. And the two humans may have died the same way, probably by accident.

"I'd say if Weldon had a plan, dying was not in the script."

"That's what Walter and Brad think, too," said Kelvin.

"Well, let's get back to the lodge now, and join up with the others again," said Curtis. Then he said to Kelvin, "You better ask Dwayne to let you plug in the charger for that camera. I know they're not *supposed* to lose pictures with a dead battery, but, 'better safe than sorry'."

"What are we having for dinner?" asked Ryan.

"I think Diane said spaghetti, with salmon chunks in the sauce," said Curtis.

"That's salmon, not *char*," said Kelvin, while looking at his brother.

14

Dwayne and Walter were having a private conversation in the early morning. They were standing at the top of the wooden stairs that led down to the beach where the camp boats were all gathered. It was cool and misty, and the wooden planking was wet and slippery with heavy dew.

"I know Curtis wants to ask me to 'mind his investments' here, and I know what's holding him back," confided Dwayne to his father. Then he asked, "Could you check in on Rachelle, and the new baby? Then find a way to let me know how they're doing? If I know they're all right, I'll stay here for a while longer."

"No sweat, Dwayne," replied Walter, "Consider it done."

Then Dwayne said, "Rob and Diane have a married daughter in Ottawa, and they said they will stay too, if they can also confirm somehow that she's all right."

"I don't know how long I'll be in Bowhead Arm, but I should be able to send somebody back with word right away, if I can't make it back here myself," said Walter. Then he added, "I need to check on your mother of course, and the hotel. I bet she's got everything organised though and has Rachelle and the baby really close by her. So I don't think you have to worry much about that. 'Easier said than done', I know.

"And I really want to help Curtis and everybody else figure out a way to get back to St. John's." He paused for a second, then asked, "So, what about Bobby?"

"He basically just quit," said Dwayne while shaking his head. Then he added, "I said he could have some more gas for his boat, but we'll need the bulk of it for ourselves. What he's got for gas won't get him anywhere *close* to Goose Bay, and he's really 'pissed' about it."

"Curtis and the others brought more booze up here than you could find in a George Street bar," said Walter with a smile. Then he said, "If they 'coughed-up' some of their 'swill', Bobby could probably barter for more gas on his way home. I don't think it will take much 'arm twisting' to get Curtis and his crew to contribute to a good cause."

"I think Bobby will go quietly if they do that," said Dwayne. Then he said, "Thanks for the idea, Dad, and for your help 'in advance' for getting the booze."

"As for Rob and Diane, the most I may be able to find out is if anyone can actually phone Ottawa right now, let alone get in or out of the place," said Walter. Then he said, "This could be a hard reality to accept. There could be a *lot* of people in similar straits if Brad and Malcolm are even *close* to being right about what happened."

"There's a high tide tomorrow morning at seven thirty," said Dwayne. Then he added, "Well, not a *really* high tide, according to the tables. But you should *just* be able to weave your way through the shoals in the estuary in 'shallow water drive'. But you know the way better than anybody! That is, as long as your landmarks are still there, and line up the same way."

"I'm sure we can figure it out, son," said Walter with a handshake, and then a hug.

15

The ride through The Chute was thrilling. The three boats got through intact and had stayed reasonably dry.

"It was a lot faster going down than up!" yelled Odvar back over his shoulder to Curtis, who was steering their boat. Odvar was clearly exhilarated from the wild ride. He was sitting on the middle seat with Malcolm, right in front of Curtis. Odvar then looked more closely at Curtis, and he noted his eyes were fully dilated.

His closer friends knew that was the only way to tell when Curtis had been a bit scared.

Curtis sat down again after standing up to take a quick look ahead. Then he let go of the short length of rope he always tied to a gunwale to use as a brace. Then he said, "The water is down a bit from when we went up. You have to cross over the standing waves in *just* the right spot to avoid wrecking the 'prop' on some boulders, where the river bends a bit."

Walter was leading the 'convoy' with Dwayne's jet boat. He had Fred, Jerome and Brad with him, and most of their gear. Ryan was piloting the next boat, and he had his brother, Kelvin, with him. Ryan had started 'running The Chute' himself two years before when he had spent a full summer as a guide at the lodge. He was a very proficient boat handler. Curtis was 'tail end Charlie', as he called it, with Odvar and Malcolm.

Everyone was wearing foul-weather suits and life preservers. It was raining a bit, and windy. "The bay will be rough," said Curtis to Odvar and Malcolm. Then he said, "But Walter will keep us in the lee of islands wherever he can. First things first, though! We've got to get through some shallow spots in the river, and the estuary."

They weaved their way down through the bends in the river. There was fast water in a few places where power was really needed for control with the propeller fully down in the water. The propeller skid-plates touched with a lurch in a few places 'on things unseen' beneath the water. They had to use shallow water drive in other places, and actually had to get out and walk the boats along in one place.

"That white blob is a Federal Fisheries sign tacked on to a tree," said Curtis to Odvar and Malcolm, pointing to a spot on the closer left bank. Then he added, "There's another one far away on the right bank, directly opposite this one. Together they mark the end of the river, and the start of the estuary and the brackish water. You can only fish for salmon legally above that sign. That is, during the season of course."

"And what will I do with my legally caught fish, I wonder?" asked Odvar. Rob and Diane had made a bit of a scene on the beach. As they always liked to do with foreign guests, they presented Odvar with the grilse he had caught and tagged, packed in a long styrofoam box full of ice, and all taped up for travel. They had neatly written on it, 'Dear customs official, *kan du snakkes Norske*? This man now speaks some 'Newfoundlander', but talk slowly please.'

'We hope you come back again next year for another one!' they had said. Handshakes had not been enough; there had been hugs all around.

"I'm only worried about how we're going to get you and Malcolm home, not your fish," said Curtis. Then he quickly added, "Now, I'll need you to sit in the bow, Malcolm, just for a bit, to see if we can get the boat up on a plane. I'll ask you to come back to the middle seat with Odvar again when I need that."

Walter slowed at one point in the estuary, and the boats all bunched together more closely. With full right-arm swings over his head, he pointed three times at the right bank while keeping his eyes on the river ahead, and his left hand firmly on his motor steering wheel. Then Walter increased speed again.

The only things the other men could see where Walter had pointed was an overturned, engineless, aluminium boat on the bank, and a well-travelled, fairly wide path running up into the trees. The trail was marked by a sign. They were moving a bit too fast to read the sign.

"That would be Weldon's other place," said Curtis. They had previously agreed they would not stop there for a look. Rather, that would be something for the police to check out.

"I bet that sign doesn't say, 'Welcome Norwegian Trespassers!'" said Malcolm to Odvar, with an attempt at a laugh.

It was a cold, rough day on the bay. They had all prepared themselves properly. They had put on their rubber boots, with waterproof pants pulled down over their boots so water would stay out of them. And they wore extra layers of clothing under their foul-weather coats.

All the boats took on some water. The motor operators had to pull a drain plug at the stern to self-bail the open bilge. The men could taste the salt from the ocean spray, and that caused some retching at times. They pulled the drawstrings on their rubberised hoods tight around their faces and tried to time looking away at the right moment to avoid the worst from a breaking wave. The route they took was crooked, so they could meet the biggest 'rollers' head-on.

They saw no other boats during their five hours of misery.

"That is the buoy at the entrance to the harbour," said Curtis to Odvar and Malcom finally. There was only one buoy in sight, so he didn't bother pointing it out. Also, he was stiff with cold and he knew the extra effort of pointing would hurt. Then he added, "Walter is heading towards the crab plant dock, where we parked the van."

The water became progressively calmer as they moved up into the harbour, and the air got noticeably warmer. They could see a few people near the shoreline on both sides of the harbour, but no lights anywhere. A few homes looked damaged. There were a few boats tied up to the wharf. Everything was very quiet.

Walter slowed down his boat until it was right beside Curtis' boat. Ryan slowed down as well to position his boat on the other side of Curtis' boat.

"That's not the whole snow-crab fishing fleet tied up there!" Walter said loudly. Then he added, "I hope the missing guys are all right. The plant is not operational like it should be this time of year. It looks like the power is off *everywhere*. Let's tie up at the start of the wharf where it gets shallower. It will be easier to get our gear ashore from there.

"We'll have to pole ourselves in there, to get by the rocks. When we do get in, I better walk up to the 'cop shop', like we talked about, with Brad, Kelvin and Ryan. If the water tap works on this side of the crab plant, you should be able to wash the salt off everything. Then load all the baggage into the van, I guess, and wait until we get back."

Everyone's muscles were stiff from the cold. They had protected everything they could using taped-up green garbage bags as crude tarpaulins. Their clothes were soaked from sweat. Their waterproof suits were not ventilated.

When they had all of their stuff out of the boats, the men dove into their duffle bags for fresh clothes.

Walter found it especially hard to get his legs working again on the two kilometre long walk to the local RCMP office. "I always get cramped, but that was a bad one today," he said, while stopping to rub a thigh.

They followed an oiled, gravel road through the village. They saw a few kids playing, but they were clearly shy of strangers, and did not come close to them. Some mothers called their children back into their homes when they saw the four men approaching.

A group of pre-teen girls were standing in front of the single general store in the village. They giggled and whispered to themselves when they saw Ryan and Kelvin, but the young men acted like they did not see or hear them.

There were no cars driving around, which was unusual, even in such a small village. They noted smoke was coming out of most of the house chimneys. "There won't be a shortage of wood or fuel oil for a long while, and that's a good thing," said Walter.

The RCMP office was a converted trailer-home. It was marked by an impressive official sign, with a cruiser parked on the wide, gravel driveway. The men could hear the drone of a portable gasoline generator outside the back of the building.

A few sad-looking people were standing by the porch steps at the main door. When Walter asked politely to go by them, they quickly stepped aside.

The constable behind the desk was talking quietly with a crying young woman who had a baby in her arms. The police officer was writing on an official looking form, with a look of concern and sympathy on his face. There were six other people seated in the little waiting area inside the door. The constable looked up towards Walter, and said quietly, "Excuse me for one second, Sally, sorry. Walter, I'm glad to see you're back. Get any fish?"

"Officer Dan, I can see you're really busy, and I can only guess what with," said Walter quietly as well. Then he explained, "But we need to tell you about something really serious, when you get a minute." Quiet seemed to be the established protocol in the office. It seemed like a sensible 'norm' to Walter and the others.

"Okay," said Constable Daniel Lukianow. "As you can see, we've run out of seats, but 'hang tight'."

The constable started quietly talking again to the clearly distressed woman sitting by his desk. After five minutes, he stood up, put his hand on the baby's head, and came over to Walter and the others. He motioned for them to follow him out of the door. He was a tall, burly, Russian-looking, dark-haired man in his early thirties. He was from Saskatchewan, and his ancestors were from the Ukraine. He was wearing his working uniform, and looked very 'spit and polished', in spite of also looking a bit tired.

Once outside the office and well away from the people standing by the porch, Constable Dan turned around and said, "What is it, Walter?"

"Well, either a double murder or a double suicide or something else, and maybe something extra-terrestrial on top of that, we just don't know," said Walter very quietly.

"No shit, Walter?" asked Constable Dan. He sighed when Walter nodded his head slowly. Then he said, "Sorry about the language, folks. It's already been a very long day after a very long night. I'm the only 'sheriff' in town you know, and this place has become the 'Wild Northeast'. Why don't you come back in, and I'll set you up in my back office? Write it all down for me, carefully. Then you can read it to me when you're done. I've got to talk to a few people while you're doing that, as you can see.

"Oh, and Walter, it's like an *oath*. Tell it like it was, *exactly*. Leave nothing out. And sign it. And if these guys were involved, get them to sign it too. And *neatly* write out your names in block letters too, at the bottom, with addresses and phone numbers. Okay?"

"Okay, Officer Dan," said Walter. "Lead on, sir."

Constable Dan then led them to an interior office, and went back to his front desk. The men sat down around the tidy desk and closed the door. It was quickly established that Kelvin was a very neat writer, and he wrote down what they all agreed should be said. By the time it was all 'said and done', the men were surprised that it had taken them about an hour and a half of steady work.

Brad went out to tell Constable Dan they were ready for him. After a few more minutes, the big police officer squeezed by them to take his seat behind the desk. The others moved around to stand in front of his desk in the small office.

"Okay, close the door, son," said Constable Dan. "What's your name?"

"Ryan Furlong, sir."

"And yours?"

"I'm his brother, Kelvin Furlong, sir."

"And yours, sir?"

"I'm Brad Walsh, Constable, from St. John's."

"Not originally. You sound like me. Where did you grow up?"

"London, Ontario," said Brad with a smile. Then he added, "Sir."

"And you're Walter Cartwright. Okay, now who's going to read it?"

"We thought Kelvin should read it, as he did the writing," said Walter.

Kelvin carefully started to read the document out loud. The constable picked up a pen and made some notes from time to time on a scratch-pad. But most of the time, he just scanned the faces of the four men standing in front of him. His eye scan was really moving fast by the time Kelvin had finished.

"Phew", said Constable Dan. "Wow. Where's the camera?"

"I've got it in my pocket," said Kelvin.

"Do you think you could figure out how to download the pictures to my computer here?" asked Constable Dan. Then he said, "It's on an uninterruptable power supply with a surge protector, so it still works okay, same as the printer beside it. We have no internet or email yet, though."

"I think I can do that," said Kelvin. "It came with a connecting cord."

Constable Dan typed in a password to bring up the computer. Then he asked, "Would you give it a try then, son? Here, come around behind me."

"Where's the hand gun now?" asked Constable Dan while watching Kelvin look for a plug-in port on the computer.

"Curtis has got it with him," said Walter. "The others are all down on the wharf with the van."

They watched while Kelvin worked proficiently with the camera, the mouse and the keyboard of the desktop computer. "There," said Kelvin after only a few minutes. "Click on this icon and you can pull up the file."

The Constable took the mouse, opened the file and flipped through some of the photographs, shaking his head in a few places. Then he took out a 'memory stick' from a desk drawer, plugged it into a 'USB port', and copied the file over to it.

"We sure don't want to lose these photos," he said. Then he added, "The camera is evidence, so I'll have to take that." He put the small camera and its cord in a big brown envelope, then licked the flap of the envelope and sealed it. Then he wrote something on the outside of the envelope, and locked it in a cabinet behind the desk.

"Okay, I'll look at the photos more closely later when I read your statement again," said Constable Dan. He then put their written statement in another brown envelope, left it open and locked it as well in the cabinet. Then he said, "I think you guys did *really* well with the statement, not an easy thing to do after seeing what you saw.

"Now, after we get a drink of water from the cooler outside this office, we're all going down to the wharf in my car while there's a 'bit of a lull' here."

As the police car approached the wharf, the men could see everyone else in their group was standing at the back of the van. The van's two backdoors were open. Their bags and Odvar's styrofoam fish box were open on the ground. There was a man they didn't know with their group. The man was wearing a green uniform and a winter-style baseball cap that had an impressive looking emblem sewn on to it.

"That will be Federal Fisheries Officer Percy Snodgrass," Constable Dan said to them, or to himself, before he got out of the car. "Now, what's all this all about?"

"Very good, Constable," said Officer Snodgrass as they all approached as a group. "You're just in time to witness an arrest."

"An arrest for what, Percy?" asked Constable Dan.

Fisheries Officer Snodgrass ignored what he took as a mild slight, and replied, "This Norwegian man has a tagged salmon that is a centimetre over the limit."

"It's a centimetre under the limit," said Curtis. "I measured it myself, *three times* on the river and again just now."

"And I say, by my measurement, it's *over* the limit," said Officer Snodgrass. Then he looked at his notes, and added, "Mister, ah, Curtis Furlong."

"You're Curtis?" asked Constable Dan. Curtis nodded in response. Then Constable Dan demanded firmly, "I want the restricted weapon. Right now."

"Yes, Officer." Curtis reached into his duffle bag, pulled out the gun, still zipped into its leather pouch, and handed it to the RCMP officer.

Constable Dan took a quick look inside the pouch, and then he weighed the pouch in his hand for a few seconds. Then he walked over, looked down at the fish, and said, "You'll find it hard to keep that on ice around here. Do you really want it?" He was now looking hard at Odvar.

"I knew we would have a problem like this with ice," said Odvar. "I never really wanted it at all."

"Then please give it to me," said Constable Dan. "I know a single mother who could really use it."

"You are interfering with a federal fisheries officer in the performance of his duties, Constable," said Officer Percy with a red face.

"It's time you got your *head out of your arse*, Percy, and realised with the rest of us how *bad* the situation is around here!" said Constable Dan angrily.

"I have jurisdiction," Officer Percy started to say.

"No, *I* have jurisdiction, over everything, and *full authority* here now, Snodgrass," said Constable Dan. Then he added, "Before the power went off and the communications went down, I got a fax from Ottawa. Since there is no military here, by the 'Emergency Planning Order', I'm the federal authority until further notice. You are actually working for me now."

"I received no fax from my office," said Officer Percy. "So, I do not recognise your authority."

"Guys, you want to just back away for a minute?" asked Constable Dan sternly. The men quickly obliged and moved further away. "Thanks," said the Constable calmly.

Constable Dan then walked over and handed the pouch with the gun in it to Kelvin, and asked him, "Would you and your brother put that on the front seat of my car for me? Thanks."

Kelvin and Ryan walked over to the police car. Kelvin reached through the open window of the car and laid the gun on the driver's seat. Then he and Ryan stayed beside the car. They both figured that's what Constable Dan had really wanted them to do.

Constable Dan then walked back to within a metre of Officer Percy, and put his hand on the flap of his holster. "Now give me your service pistol, Percy." Percy hesitated. "Don't push me *one more second*," Constable Dan warned.

Officer Percy unfastened a waist belt with a holster attached, and handed it to Constable Dan. "Okay, I'm going to lock this up with the other gun in my office," said Constable Dan. Then he said, "Now, I also want the keys to your government truck and your government patrol boat, Percy." Officer Percy grudgingly handed a bulky key ring over to him.

Then Constable Dan said, "Okay, thanks. Now, you're going to walk home, Percy. Maybe talk to the wife about finally joining this community. And until things are sorted out, we're going to let people take a salmon, a cod fish, a moose or a *freaking sculpin* for that matter, so everybody has something to eat. You can have everything back if you decide to help me, because I could *really* use your help, Percy."

"Screw you," said Officer Percy angrily. "You'll be in my report, Constable."

"You'll be in *mine* too," said Constable Dan. When Officer Percy had stomped out of hearing range, Constable Dan added, "*Dickhead.*"

Constable Dan then walked over to the other men, and said, "Sorry you had to see, and probably hear that, guys. Like I really needed that right now."

"I'd say his head is pretty tightly wedged up in there," said Walter. "Glad to help you get it out any time, Officer, with a *crow bar*." The men all laughed at Walter's quip.

"I might need that help, Walter, thanks!" said Constable Dan with a laugh as well. Then turning serious again, he said, "Mr. Furlong, you don't have an 'ATT', an 'Authorisation to Transport', do you?"

"No, Officer," Curtis replied. "It's correctly registered to me, though."

"Come back to my office with me, then," said Constable Dan. "I'll look at all of your documents, and if they're okay, I will cite you for a violation, but I'll write it up as a warning. It might end up going further than that, but that's up to higher authorities. And Curtis, I may need to use the weapon myself if things get *really* bad around here. Consider it confiscated, for the good of the country."

"I fully understand, Officer," said Curtis. "And I hope it never comes to your needing to use it."

"So, what are the rest of you guys going to do now?" asked Constable Dan after taking a slow breath.

"The van won't start," said Jerome. "It might make a good locker though."

"I saw your wife, Phyllis, driving your hotel truck around today, Walter," said Constable Dan. Then he added, "Someone got it running for her, I guess. I'd 'deputise' her if she wasn't needed elsewhere, or everywhere. She's really helping out around here!

"Why don't you come with us, Walter, and I'll drop you and Mr. Furlong off at the hotel when we're done in my office? Then you could drive the hotel truck down here to pick up these guys with what they will need for tonight?"

"That would be *great*, Dan, thanks," said Walter. "I mean, *Constable Dan*," he added with a grin. "I think we can squeeze these guys into a few rooms tonight. But it will be cosy! And some of them snore like '*banshees*'."

"Okay, I'll come by in the morning," said Constable Dan with a laugh. Then with a serious tone, he added, "I'll want to talk to everyone again. I'll have thought some more about what you wrote up by then, hopefully with a clearer head."

"The coffee will be on us," said Walter.

16

The next morning, after a reasonably comfortable night in Walter's hotel, the men were all sitting near each other in the hotel dining room, enjoying a second cup of coffee.

"That was really great, Phyllis, thanks," said Curtis, pushing his empty plate away. Phyllis had just come into the dining room, and was wiping her hands on her apron.

"I think I'll let Jan carry on in the kitchen for a bit, and sit down with you guys for a coffee, if that's all right?" asked Phyllis. "Walter said he'll be back soon."

"That's *more* than all right," said Jerome with a smile, and pulled a chair out for her. "Yes, take a 'load off your feet', Phyllis. And here, let me pour you a cup of coffee." Jerome poured the remainder of the coffee in an insulated jug into a cup, and gave it to Phyllis. Rachelle was sitting next to Jerome with a sleeping baby in her arms. She was smiling shyly at everyone.

"Walter went to find some of Dwayne's friends," said Phyllis, after she took a sip of coffee. Then she said, "He's going to ask them if they could manage a round trip in a boat to tell Dwayne that we're all okay here. But there are *still* no phones working. Poor Rob and Diane!"

Everyone was having similar thoughts, and the room became very quiet.

"Here's Walter now, with Constable Dan," said Phyllis. They could see through the 'picture window' in the restaurant that a police cruiser had just pulled into the gravel parking lot.

"I found this *vagrant* walking on the road," said Constable Dan sternly as he came into the dining room. "Anybody know him?" Then he started laughing. It looked like he had finally managed to get some sleep.

Phyllis leaped up to get the RCMP officer a cup of fresh coffee from the kitchen.

"You folks look a little better than the last time I saw you, no offence, but maybe I do too?" asked Constable Dan with a smile. He took a seat at an empty table and took off his cap.

There were ten, four-place tables in the dining room. There was a local young couple at the far end of the dining room who were suddenly packing up to leave. "Good morning!" said Constable Dan to them. "Are you folks okay, too?" They just smiled and nodded as they walked past him.

"Phyllis, I got it all set up," said Walter as he was sitting down next to Constable Dan. Then he explained, "Chris and Mike are on their way in to see Dwayne. They said if there's any beer left, they'll stay the night. I think they'll stay the night, anyway." Phyllis and Rachelle both looked visibly relieved.

"I can't stay very long, folks," interjected Constable Dan. Then he said, "But I thought I should share a few things with you, then check in with you later when I have some more time."

They all turned their chairs to face him, and gathered round.

"There are a few things that completely line up with your statement, some scary things actually," said Constable Dan as an opener. Then he elaborated by saying, "Three days ago, Phyllis 'flagged me down' to tell me a German tourist had checked into the hotel the night before, and that he was about to check out. When I got to the hotel with Phyllis, we could see the guy had a big German motorcycle that looked like an off-road model, only it had a sort of sidecar with a rack of jerry cans.

"He was standing by his bike when we pulled up. He was wearing a dusty, full-leather suit, and a 'high-tech' exotic helmet with a built-in dust mask. When he took the helmet off, I could see he was a blond guy in his early thirties. Anyway, his English was really bad, and he seemed to be in a *heck* of a hurry to get going. He said he wanted to get to the Blanc Sablon ferry terminal right away. But he did make time to answer my questions.

"He said he had been on the Trans-Labrador Highway, and had come up from the junction south of here, hoping he could get some gas, some food and drink, and a night's rest in a proper bed.

"He said he had seen and heard the 'mother of all thunder storms' as he was coming up on Churchill Falls. When he got there, he said the *whole town* was on fire, and so were a lot of surrounding trees. I asked him about the underground power station there, but he said all he saw was a huge electrical yard 'all ablaze'. He said he got through all of that mess somehow.

"He looked a bit 'sheepish' about that, but I guess a lot of tourist folks might have done the same thing in his place, and just kept motoring along."

He paused for a sip of coffee. The group that had gathered around him were nodding to encourage him to say more.

So, Constable Dan added, "Further on, he met a pickup truck coming the other way from Happy Valley-Goose Bay, driven by a 'scared looking young guy' who said he was going to try to get to his family in Labrador City. They quickly exchanged stories.

"The young guy told the German guy, 'don't even try to get into Goose Bay', it was on fire too. And the young guy said the new Muskrat Falls power plant was 'gone'. I asked the German guy three times, and he said the right word was definitely 'gone', as he had seen that for himself later. The German guy went on to say he got around all of that mess somehow too, but really wanted to get going, did I mind?

"I told him the only other vehicle that has come up from the south, or from the west for that matter, was a pickup truck driven by an older couple that live here. They had been down south to Mary's Harbour to visit relatives. The gas station in Port Hope-Simpson was under lock and key. They had to ask the Mountie there for enough gas to make it back to here, and they had to get some help with a hand pump to put some gas into their truck.

"We have the same 'deal' going on here now with your pumps, Walter. Phyllis lets me have as much as I need, and I'm being frugal. And she decides who else gets any, and they have to have an 'emergency need', and she gets to ask a lot of verification questions.

"Anyway, the German guy said he had enough gas to get to Blanc Sablon and a bit beyond, and took off down the road after paying Phyllis in cash. I hope that fancy bike of his also *floats* too, because I very much doubt there's a working ferry in Blanc Sablon."

Constable Dan stopped, looked hard at Brad and said, "I looked on a map, and it's at least four hundred kilometres, as the crow flies, from Churchill Falls to where you said you found Weldon Purdy and the other body. And it's about two hundred kilometres from that spot to Muskrat Falls, and nearby Goose Bay. All of those places line up pretty close to a straight line on a map."

Then Brad said slowly, "There was a scientist guy named Nikola Tesla that I mentioned in the statement. Over a hundred years ago, he said he knew how to send electrical power over distances like that without using a wire. No one believed him."

Constable Dan stared intently at Brad and said, "Wow. And you think old Weldon Purdy thought he'd 'carry on the dream' or something?"

"Malcolm and I think it could have been something like that, yes," said Brad.

Everyone was quiet for a few moments. Then Constable Dan said, "There is another thing that may be relevant. You probably all remember seeing in the press how the pilfering at Muskrat Falls during construction was really bad? The RCMP still have a lot of files open. The main suspects so far have been contractors. But the evidence against them is weak or non-existent. I'll be recommending that a new file should be opened now, with Weldon Purdy's name on it. Getting that underway, and checking out what I guess we'll keep calling the 'alleged crime scene', and Weldon's home, will have to wait until more help arrives. This is my post, you see, and I can't leave it."

Constable Dan finished his coffee with a gulp, stood up and put his cap back on his head. Then he said, "Look, folks, I need to get going now. I know you'll be thinking today about how to get out of here. The road south is no good at all I think, even if you get your van working. The ferry cannot be working. And nothing is flying, in or out of here. And there haven't been any contrails high in the sky either, since the power went out and we had the earthquake, or whatever it was."

"We've been thinking the same thing, Dan", said Walter. "But there *may* be a way by boat, and that's an idea we'll pursue a bit today."

"It's a long way to St. John's, especially without a means to navigate," added Curtis. "But that could be our best option."

"Well, I really do hope that 'shakes out' for you," said Constable Dan as he started to leave. "Good luck everyone, and I'll see you later."

"You too, Dan," said Phyllis for everybody.

Constable Dan stopped suddenly in the doorway, and said in a professional tone, "Oh, and I don't want you all to leave without a final okay from me. And when you do go, I might ask you to take some mail along for me, and maybe another person or two."

As they watched through the window as Constable Dan drove away in his cruiser, Walter said sadly, "Bobby Clarke might be having a *bad day* right now if he got to Goose Bay. Poor bastard!"

17

The next morning, Malcolm, Kelvin and Ryan decided to take a walk, and explore the village of Bowhead Arm together. Jerome and Curtis left with Walter in his truck to talk to a friend of Walter's. The young man was a crab fisherman with his own boat.

Brad, Odvar and Fred found themselves sitting together in the bar of Walter's hotel. The bar had not actually opened for the day yet, and they were alone.

"I have not mentioned it yet, but I do not know why 'Churchill Falls' and 'Muskrat Falls' are especially troubling to everyone," said Odvar to Brad and Fred.

"There are, or possibly were, major hydroelectric generating stations at each place, Odvar," explained Brad. Then he added, "And some people have been living and working in those places to operate the facilities. Both projects as well have a bit of a history that gets some, or most, Newfoundlanders and Labradoreans 'worked-up' a bit."

"Premier Joey Smallwood *completely screwed* us, that is *all* you need to know, Odvar!" yelled Fred angrily. Then he yelled, "*Free* power for Quebec until the contract runs out in *2041!*"

"I *may* be a little more objective, being a transplanted Newfoundlander," continued Brad calmly. Fred glared at Brad for a moment, then he just shrugged his shoulders as a sign that he didn't really care if Brad continued with the story. So Brad said, "Churchill Falls was the bigger project, and it cost almost a billion dollars to build it in the 1970s. Power was on full-time in 1974. The plant has eleven turbines, and an underground power house of over five thousand megawatts. It is a joint venture. About two-thirds is owned by Quebec, and one-third is owned by Newfoundland and Labrador, through a 'Crown' or provincially-owned corporation.

"Fred and many other people get angry because most of the power, by long-term contract, gets sold to Quebec at a fixed, low price. Right now, Quebec makes about two billion 'bucks' a year in profit, and Newfoundland and Labrador only gets about seventy *million*.

"The contract has been challenged a few times in court by Newfoundland and Labrador, and Quebec always wins." Brad paused and shrugged his shoulders. Then he said, "'A deal is a deal' is the tested judicial viewpoint, I guess."

"The Quebec side changed the terms at the *last minute*, and Premier Joey Smallwood *caved in*!" said Fred angrily.

"You hear all kinds of reasons for it, Odvar," continued Brad calmly. Then he explained, "There may have been some bad legal or business advice. There *was* a sincere desire to put people back to work during a period of high unemployment.

"The 'other' side had a *lot* of stroke in the negotiation, too. Hydro Quebec is the biggest hydroelectric power producer in the world. They're up to about thirty-seven thousand megawatts now!

"Anyway, with the help of the Churchill Falls Project, Quebec can meet its own needs *and* sell power under contract to New England states, and to the province of Ontario, for profit.

"So, if the Churchill Falls power facility is now damaged or 'gone', there will be a *lot* of 'unhappy' electricity customers, and an immediate blow to the Quebec economy. And, there will be a future blow to the Newfoundland and Labrador economy."

Brad paused to think for a moment. Then he looked worried, and said, "But there is another twist, possibly. Churchill Falls is connected by the electric-power transmission-grid into Ontario, Newfoundland and Labrador, and the United States. Power could have *surged* down all the power lines from the solar storm, and from whatever this 'Weldon guy' may have done. The damage may be severe, requiring a very long time to fix. And we're talking about *millions of people* without power for *many months,* maybe."

"Muskrat Falls is smaller but a better deal for us," said Fred a bit more calmly. Then he explained, "It's a Newfoundland and Labrador joint venture with a Nova Scotia private utility. We had to borrow the money to build it, with the Federal government as co-signer. We've barely started paying off the *thirteen billion dollar* debt to build it though. If it's damaged or gone… " He trailed off with his own look of worry.

"Just as many bad possibilities with this one," agreed Brad. Then he explained, "Muskrat Falls came on *way over* budget and a couple years late in 2019, with over eight hundred megawatts of power generation. A seven hundred mile power link had to be built to get the power to the island of Newfoundland. It probably would not have been built today due to poor economics. Natural gas prices have been depressed for years, killing coal-fired thermal generating plants on the mainland, especially in the US. And solar cells and wind farms are getting cheaper all of the time.

"Anyway, they had to lay a submarine cable across the Strait of Belle Isle, and another one across Cabot Strait to Cape Breton Island, which is part of Nova Scotia. Newfoundland and Labrador started decommissioning the oil-burning, five hundred megawatt Holyrood thermal-electric generating station after the power started flowing from Muskrat Falls. That work may be just about done by now.

"One of the controversies was that the Holyrood plant could have been upgraded or expanded for a lot less money. The plant could have been converted to use a cleaner fuel, such as liquefied natural gas. There is a lot of offshore gas waiting for discovery or development in the province.

"Or, Newfoundland and Labrador could have 'swallowed some pride' and contracted to buy Churchill Falls power from Hydro Quebec until a new deal is triggered in 2041.

"There's about thirteen hundred megawatts of hydroelectric power generated on the island, not always enough to match demand. So, with Muskrat Falls and Holyrood gone, power rationing of some kind must be going on now, at least where the transmission infrastructure was not damaged by power surges from the solar storm, and by our 'buddy' Weldon. Power customers in Nova Scotia must also be struggling.

"People have probably been killed and hurt, and livelihoods have been ruined, with more hardship to come possibly. This might be one of the biggest acts of terrorism, ever."

"Why would someone do it?" asked Odvar.

"There's no sense to terrorism," said Fred. "It's insane, and perverted."

"I think that's well said, Fred," said Brad.

18

That evening, most of the men were having some dinner in Walter's hotel restaurant, and some were also sampling the last of Curtis' specialty beer. Malcolm, Fred and Odvar were sitting at a table together.

Jerome sat down across the table from Malcolm with a tall glass of rum and coke in his hand. He had just mixed the drink in his hotel room. No one working for the hotel seemed to have a problem with that. Then Jerome asked with a smile, "So, how was your first caribou cheeseburger, Malcolm?"

"Really great, thanks Jerome, like good lean beef, actually," replied Malcolm. Then he added, "And it was *nice* to be offered vinegar with the chips. You get interesting looks when you ask for vinegar in Houston."

Fred was sitting next to Malcolm. He said, "Caribou tastes a bit wild on the island. Walter says their diet is different here." He looked at Odvar on the other side of the table, and asked, "How was the Arctic char, Odvar?"

"A very nice fish," replied Odvar. Then he added, "It was pale orange, and nicely cooked. No Norwegian would complain. And we *know* our fish. And we don't put either vinegar or ketchup on them. Of course, most foreigners won't try our many kinds of pickled herring. Every culture has its own concept of good food, I guess."

"Where's Curtis, Jerome?" asked Brad. He was sitting at the next table with Kelvin and Ryan.

"He and Walter are in the hotel office talking to Officer Dan," said Jerome. "They have the door shut."

"How did you guys get on today?" asked Brad.

"Well, that's a bit of a story," said Jerome. He paused to swirl the ice in his drink, then said, "Walter and Curtis seem pretty happy now. There's a crab fisherman who is keen to get to St. John's. His mother is in the Health Sciences Centre there. He's got his boat working okay, and the electronic stuff working too, you know, the radar, the depth-sounder and the fish-finder. He said we could possibly work out a deal to go along with him.

"There's still only static on the radio. And definitely no working GPS or satellite phones, or compasses that can be believed. All the fishermen we talked to confirmed that sad reality.

"Anyway, Walter and Curtis eventually agreed with the crab fisherman that we will buy all of the food and the diesel for the trip. The fisherman will loan us what we can't pay for right now, and we will pay him the balance in cash when we get to St. John's.

"The ATM machines and credit cards don't work, and the bank in the village will only give you a hundred dollars every other day in cash, if you write out a cheque.

"Oh, and we will have to leave the keys to the van with the fisherman's girlfriend here, for 'collateral'."

"What about the navigation, how will that work?" asked Malcolm with interest.

"Well, the fisherman figures it might just add a few days to the trip," said Jerome. He paused to take a sip of his drink. Then he explained, "Fog will be our worst enemy. Groundings and collisions are the major risks. And, there are a *lot* of icebergs this season. That may be good for brewers like Curtis, who make expensive nightclub beer out of the 'mined' and barged iceberg melt-water, but that's about it.

"The plan is to hug the coast, and drop an anchor, or 'duck into' a port, when we lose sight of the shoreline, or the charted shoal markers and buoys. The radar will only help us so much. The fisherman has up-to-date charts. Curtis offered to help him stay located on the charts at all times. Curtis has sailed a lot. The fisherman said he was okay with that, 'as long as everyone remembers who the skipper is'."

Jerome then looked in turn at Malcolm and Odvar, and said in a serious tone, "We don't know what we might be able to do for you guys. That is, other than put you up as long as it takes in our homes in St. John's."

"We know everyone is doing their best, and we appreciate it, very much indeed," replied Malcolm with a smile, then a frown. Then he said, "We just wish we had called our wives more than once since being away. Now, I don't think anyone saw this 'rather awkward scene' coming, but that doesn't make it any easier."

19

Walter, Curtis and Constable Dan were huddled together in Walter's small office in the hotel. The door was shut, and it was getting uncomfortably warm inside the room even with the window open. A deer fly was buzzing incessantly while trying futilely to get through the screen in the window.

"I just got back from the radar site Walter, and Mr. Furlong," said Constable Dan. Then he said, "You know, the radar installation operated by NORAD, about thirty kilometres away from here. There are two technicians there now, one American and one Canadian. They said if the weather is good or 'VFR', a Twin Otter is going to land here for a few minutes tomorrow morning around nine o'clock. It is bringing in some spare parts for them, and some 'expanded orders' and a radio-telephone for me.

"Apparently the United States and Canada want to set up some kind of radio-telephone network to move messages around cooperatively until the power is back up in most places, or in all places, and when the wireline telephones and cell phones work again."

"How did the technicians find all that out?" asked Walter.

"They said that was a 'secret'," said Constable Dan.

"Some smart people in high places probably thought something like this could happen someday, and prepared for it," offered Curtis.

"Did they share any news, I mean, from outside of this place?" asked Walter.

"They said the 'full picture' is unclear, but pretty bad," said Constable Dan. Then he said, "There are massive power outages worldwide. The centre of North America might have got it the worst. Canada is basically in a state-of-war alert. The US is not quite there yet, but they are really watching a few 'rogue states' that might try to exploit our crippled situation.

"Government seismographs show massive earthquakes began at about the same time in unlikely places, like Baffin Bay, New Brunswick, southern Quebec, south of Newfoundland in the ocean, and even Missouri! The earthquakes all happened, or mostly happened, around the time the ground shook here. The technicians suspected a possible connection, but I didn't tell them anything about Weldon."

Constable Dan then glanced around the office, and said, "Please don't talk about what I just said *to anyone,* until an investigation is complete, and something is released to the public, all right? And please tell the others to 'button it up', too."

"Will do of course, Constable," said Curtis. He stopped to think for a minute. Then he said, "I believe an earthquake occurred in the 1920s south of Newfoundland, and it caused a tsunami that wiped out parts of the Burin Peninsula. Also, I think there were some strong, deep-down earthquakes within the modern-day boundaries of Missouri in the early 1800s, at least 'Magnitude Seven' I think. The tremors were felt as far away as Montreal and Boston! The widespread damage was blamed on the efficient transmission of seismic energy through mechanically-strong igneous rock. The Canadian Shield is Precambrian, or igneous rock. Labrador and maybe half of Canada are within the Canadian Shield area. And that's just where the igneous rock is exposed on the surface. It's *bedrock* below most of the US and Canada."

"That *is* interesting", said Constable Dan sincerely. Then he said, "Anyway, I'll get a copy of your statement somehow on the plane that comes here, with a 'memory stick' of the photos you took. It will all be stamped, 'URGENT, TOP PRIORITY'.

"I'm going to ask you guys to take another envelope with the same things in it to St. John's to give to the RCMP office there. You see, I want to 'cover all angles'.

"Also, I'll probably need some help getting a taller antenna set up somewhere, Walter. It will be a line-of-sight radio hook-up, so the higher, the better."

"You'll have lots of willing hands for that," said Walter. Then he said, "No doubt I could find you some keen volunteers to be radio-telephone operators too, if you want that?"

"That sounds great, Walter, thanks," said Constable Dan with a smile. Then he said, "Until then, there's a lady in town, Alice Ferguson, who is a 'Ham' radio operator. Her late husband was 'right into it', and he thought she should learn Morse code, and how to work the shortwave radio, too. She told me this morning that the static has cleared up a bit now, and she can hear some code messages now and then. She just managed to have a partial exchange with somebody in Florida this morning. Things don't sound so good there either."

Constable Dan paused for a second to gather his thoughts. Then he said, "Alice told me Ham operators bounce radio waves off the ionosphere, and it is bit of hit and miss even in normal times. She also said the Ham people have their own established network to help society in emergencies like this. It's a bit of a 'club for purists', she admitted, who wish they had more bandwidth to work with. And they don't trust cell phones or even wireline telephones. They may have just been proved right to some extent.

"Anyway, she said you guys could give her some short messages if you wanted to, in 'old-style telegram format', and she'll try to get them through for you. Apparently, the Ham operators bounce messages around between themselves until they get it through to someone close to the target recipient. Then I guess the last person in the 'Ham chain' will send it over somehow, or even hand-deliver it. I told her she can have enough gasoline to run her generator for two hours a day."

Constable Dan paused and smiled. Then he added, "I think she's going to be *really* busy helping *other* people out too. But she's clearly getting a 'kick' out of it all."

"So, Constable Dan, are you okay for Curtis and the others to head out in the morning with Will White Bear, the crab fisherman?" asked Walter.

"I think so," replied Constable Dan slowly. Then he said, "Our only medical provider here is a nurse. She's really overloaded right now, as you can probably well imagine, mostly with people that seem to have been 'closet' drug addicts, and can no longer get a 'fix'. The alcoholics will be next, I guess, when the 'booze' supply gets short.

"She says there's a sick little girl in the village who should get to a hospital right away. But I'm going to try to get her and her mother on the plane that comes here tomorrow." Constable Dan paused for a second in thought, then added, "That is, of course, if it's going to go back to a major centre within a day or so, and it's not a 'state secret' to tell me about that. Now, when are you planning to leave?"

"Will White Bear said we'll leave at daybreak," said Curtis.

"Could you make that ten o'clock?" asked Constable Dan. "I'd like to see you off."

They knew it was an order, not a request. Walter and Curtis could tell Constable Dan was truly 'covering all angles'.

"Yes, I think we can talk Skipper Will into that," said Curtis after only a short pause to consider the ramifications. Then he added, "After all, we 'paying customers' must have *some* rights! We'll 'name drop' though, and mention who will be in the 'send-off committee'."

20

URGENT MESSAGE FOR SUSAN FURLONG 12
BARRINGTON PLACE ST JOHNS NL CANADA FROM
CURTIS STOP ALL OK STOP ON CRAB BOAT
MARTHAS NIECES STOP JEROME FRED BRAD KELVIN
RYAN TOO STOP ETA 11 JULY DEPENDING ON FOG
STOP ODVAR AND MALCOLM WILL NEED BEDS STOP
WE LOVES U STOP IF YOU LOVES US DONT STOP
DONT STOP

21

Just before ten o'clock the next morning, Constable Dan arrived at the crab plant wharf in a police cruiser. He parked the vehicle where the fishing boat 'Martha's Nieces' was tied up. Everyone on the boat then climbed back up a ladder to join the RCMP officer, and Walter and Phyllis, on the dock.

Constable Dan stepped out of the car, then reached into the back seat through an open rear window for a package.

"Any luck, Constable?" called Walter and Phyllis almost together.

Constable Dan put his hat on as he walked up to them. He was smiling. He said cheerfully, "Yep, that went well. The Twin Otter pilot was a bit worried about the weather. So, they're going to start working their way back down the coast towards Newfoundland. But they've got a little girl and her mother with them now."

"Is that for us?" asked Curtis, pointing at the package.

"Yes, as we talked about," said Constable Dan. He handed the bulky package to Curtis, and said, "The photos are in the envelope on a 'memory stick', and there are some other documents in there besides your statement. It's officially sealed, so don't open it."

"We're glad to help," said Curtis. Then he promised, "As soon as we get to St. John's, we'll hike it over to your colleagues."

Constable Dan nodded with a smile, then walked over and looked down into the boat. Then he said, "It looks like it's going to be cosy. Good thing you're all friends!"

"I gave them some plastic lawn chairs from my backyard, and some blankets," said Walter. Then he added, "Also, the coolers they brought are going back with them, packed with food and ice."

"We've got some rum too, but Fred drank most of the beer," said Jerome. Fred slapped him on the shoulder in mock anger.

"There are no weather forecasts available right now, of course, but does it look okay to go, Will?" asked Constable Dan.

"We'll get on all right," said Will White Bear. He was a man of few words and was clearly eager to cast off.

"Okay, I won't keep you then," said Constable Dan. He took his hat off, and shook everyone's hand. Then he said, "I really hope to see you all up here again next year!"

"We feel the same way, Constable Dan," said Curtis for the group. "Best of luck to you!"

"Oh, we'll 'get on all right', too," said Constable Dan with a smile. Then he said, "Most people here have been through worse than this at one time or another. And Walter and Phyllis here are great 'deputies', even if I can't give them official badges in this country."

It was finally time to say goodbye to Walter and Phyllis. Phyllis was crying and laughing at the same time. She hugged everybody, including Constable Dan, who was not leaving on the boat. She even hugged Will White Bear, who she hardly knew.

"Keep a strain on her, b'y!" Jerome called up to Walter from the back of the boat.

Curtis was standing beside Jerome, and yelled, "As soon as we can, we'll be calling you! You folks take good care of yourselves!"

Walter yelled from the dock, "I'll get the lines, Will! Don't stop for any hitch-hiking seals!"

The two groups waved to each other as the boat pulled away from the dock. They waved again when the view was about to be obscured by a big rock standing proud of the water in the harbour.

22

It was just after dawn on the fourth day of their ocean journey to St. John's. Curtis had just come up from below. The others were making some breakfast or were still lying in their bunks.

"Man, the fog is *still* as thick as pea soup," said Curtis, while squinting through a forward-looking glass window in the small wheelhouse. Then he sighed, and said, "Day Two of this 'crap', Skipper, and it doesn't look like it will be lifting any time soon."

Then Malcolm came up the stairs from below, and said, "Here's something to cheer you up, Mister White Bear." Then he carefully handed 'the Skipper' an obviously hot, steaming cup of coffee.

Will was sitting behind the wheel on the only chair in the wheelhouse. It was a cushioned, swivel-chair; and it was high enough up so he could see most things on the water surrounding the boat.

Malcolm and Curtis pulled some plastic chairs over a bit closer to Will, and sat down with their own cups of coffee.

"It's Ikkusek," said Will suddenly.

"What is?" asked Malcolm, looking puzzled. He was thinking he was having yet another problem with a local dialect.

"My last name is actually 'Ikkusek'," said Will. He smiled for the first time on the trip. Then he explained, "My friends started calling me 'White Bear' after I killed a polar bear that came into town. It tried to come into the back of our house when just my little sister and I were at home. I shot him *right between the eyes* with my father's rifle. I was thirteen years old."

"Really!" said Malcolm with sincere astonishment. Then he exclaimed, "You have black bears *and* polar bears around Bowhead Arm?"

Malcolm had seen a baited bear-trap set up right beside Walter's hotel. The bear-trap was a big piece of metal culvert with steel mesh at both ends, mounted on a trailer, with a ramp and trap door on one end, and a plucked chicken carcass hanging inside at the other end.

"Black bears are local," Will explained. Then he added, "A polar bear will sometimes come off grounded ice, and hunt people when it can't get a seal."

"Polar bears have no natural predators," said Curtis. Then he said, "They will stalk a human being, and they are fearless. We're just another source of food to them."

"And they ride icebergs here?" asked Malcolm, with continued astonishment.

"I'm sure not intentionally," said Curtis. Then he explained, "One of their natural food sources is seal meat. They hunt seal on pack ice in the Arctic. You see, the seals are air-breathing mammals. They have to come up through holes in the ice, and the polar bears wait by the holes to 'nail them' there.

"The pack ice grows on the Labrador coast every winter. It also 'flows' with the Labrador Current. It can extend down over the Grand Banks some years, interfering with offshore oilfield operations. Embedded within the pack ice are icebergs and even remnants of huge, tabular 'ice islands'. They come from glaciers that break off up in Greenland or Baffin Island, where the polar bears are.

"As the pack ice melts back in the spring, the icebergs are freed up and become menaces to shipping until they eventually break apart and melt."

Curtis paused, and took a sip of his coffee. Then he said, "The Titanic hit an iceberg a long way south of the Grand

Banks. The US and Canada monitor the track of icebergs with long-range patrol aircraft. They do it as a service to commercial shipping, and for their own navies. The oil industry has a shorter-range patrol service, and the information is shared. With 'global warming', there are a lot more big icebergs now from broken apart ice islands. Unfortunately, the glaciers are melting fast in Greenland."

"There's a big grounded ice island nearby," said Will. Then he added, "That's why it's so cold here. And it's probably helping to make the fog."

They were anchored off Cape St. John on the north coast of Newfoundland. Will had dropped the anchor at dusk when the fog had set in. At the time he had said, 'I really don't want to go too far into Notre Dame Bay unless we have to. There are many islands and shoals there, and a jagged coastline. I'm hoping we can cut straight across. The compass is steady again. We can set an easterly course using the sun, when we see it again, and hold whatever the compass says the course is when we lose sight of land.'

The trip had been fairly easy to this point, and Will was a lot more relaxed now because everyone was pitching in to help him.

Before he set the anchor last night in about forty metres of water, Will had told Ryan he could see some fish *just* off bottom on the 'fish-finder' sonar unit. Ryan had then put a treble-hooked jig on a hand-line. The jig Will liked to use was made of silvery-metal. It was about twenty centimetres long with a triangular body. There was no need to bait a jig, and Ryan had quickly run it to bottom. It took no more than four upward pulls for Ryan to hook the first fish. Will had let him keep four, six-pound cod fish, declaring that was enough. Their food supply was in pretty good shape.

Curtis and Will had shown Jerome how to use the radar. Jerome took an immediate interest in the device, and was now the 'official radar watchman'.

Jerome came up the short ladder from the cabin below. He stood on the top rung, and yelled, "Morning, gents! Say, Skipper, there's a boat, I guess, moving left to right about twelve kilometres out from shore. It looks pretty big on the screen."

Will went over to the radio, adjusted a knob and said into the handheld microphone, "Vessel travelling east twelve kilometres off Cape St. John, do you copy, over?" They all listened very intently for a reply. They could only hear the normal hissing sound of background static. Will repeated the message two more times. There were no replies.

This had been the routine three times before when they had seen a distant boat either visually, or on radar. There was very little activity on the ocean, and nobody was answering to hails.

Will then said into the radio microphone, "All vessels near Cape St. John, fishing vessel Martha's Nieces is anchored in fog in Manful Bight." Then he hung the microphone back up, and took his seat again.

Malcolm stood up to stretch his back, and to look at a small, faded chart he had noticed on the wall in the wheelhouse. It was a photocopy, and it was protected by clear plastic. "Newfoundland," he read out loud.

"That was on the boat when I bought it," said Will. "The charts below are better."

"But not much better," said Curtis. "Take a look at who made that chart, Malcolm."

Malcolm read out loud, "James Cook and Michael Lane, Surveyors, on orders of the British Admiralty, published by Act of Parliament, 1775." After a pause, Malcolm asked, "Is that our famous Captain Cook?"

"Yep, and he did such a good job of it, no one could better it for over a century," said Curtis. Then he added, "He made a similar one of Hawaii and another one of New Zealand. He was a *hell* of a navigator, and a great seaman too. He found Australia, and in the Seven Years War, he found a way to get the British fleet through the uncharted shoals of the Saint Lawrence River. That allowed the English to take Quebec and drive the French out of Canada. Except for right there… " Curtis was pointing to two small islands on the map off the south coast of the island of Newfoundland.

"Great Miquelon, and Langley, or Little Miquelon, it's hard to read," said Malcolm.

"St. Pierre and Miquelon today, the last bit of France in North America," said Curtis. Then he added, "And *really* France, too, like Bordeaux, not a colony. Cook named or renamed places when he made that map. Most of his names were accepted, and we still use them today. There still are some French names, but you wouldn't believe how they're pronounced here."

"So the French had Newfoundland once?" asked Malcolm.

"And the Dutch briefly, too," said Curtis. "The English took it for good in 1762 by sneaking into Torbay a few kilometres to the north of St. John's. They stormed the French battery on what we now call Signal Hill. It overlooks 'The Narrows', or the entrance to the harbour. I took you up there for a quick look at the monument and tower, remember? Marconi received the first wireless message there from across the Atlantic Ocean."

"I remember, Curtis," said Malcolm. Then he added, "Now, here is some history *you* may not know. Marconi was competing with Tesla to be the first scientist to achieve the 'across the Atlantic Ocean' wireless communication feat."

"Not that guy again!" said Jerome loudly. He had been listening intently to the conversation. Then he added with a laugh, "I thought we left that 'bad boy' back in Labrador!"

Malcolm laughed as well, then said, "Sorry about that, old chap! Yes, our dear old friend, Tesla, built a facility on Long Island, New York in 1900. He called it his 'Wardenclyffe Tower'. He ran out of financing and could not finish it before Marconi received the 'Letter S' message from England in Newfoundland in December, 1901.

"Then Tesla 'changed gears' completely and asked his financier for funds to demonstrate wireless transmission of electrical *power* at Wardenclyffe. I think he managed to raise the tower to almost seventy metres, but that was the end of that project. Lack of funding in the end foiled Tesla. He died a pauper at a ripe old age of 86."

"Skipper Will, I bet you thought your crew were just dumb old Newfoundland 'Townies' and 'Bay Men', not mad scientists, right?" asked Jerome with a laugh.

Will smiled back, and said, "You wouldn't *believe* what we get on about when we're 'crabbing', and we get stuck in fog."

23

While Curtis and his group were starting their second day anchored in fog, Walter was starting his day in the hotel office with his first cup of coffee. When he heard a soft rap, Walter looked up from his desk to see Constable Dan standing in the doorway to the office.

"Walter, can I come in for a second?" asked Constable Dan.

"Of course you can, Dan," said Walter. "Here, have a seat."

Constable Dan then entered the small office, and closed the door behind him. He then sat down on the chair beside Walter's desk.

"Thanks for your help, Walter, the radio-telephone hook-up works just fine," Constable Dan said with a smile. Then he looked sad suddenly, and added, "I just had a long talk with the regional superintendent. He thinks I've been derelict in my duty. He said I should never have let your friends leave Bowhead Arm, and the RCMP may officially reprimand me."

"I can't *believe* it, Dan!" replied Walter angrily. "Wouldn't you have had to *charge* somebody to hold them here? And they're heading for the provincial capital, for crying out loud! You *certainly* have not been neglecting your duty, either. We all would be in a 'world of hurt' around here without you."

"Thanks, Walter, I needed that," said Constable Dan quietly. Then he confided, "You know, I've heard that kind of talk from him before. They're rare people, but there are a few bullies in the RCMP, like I'm sure there are in any large organisation.

"But I suspect nothing will come of it. The *real* reason I'm here is to tell you that your statement and photos have *really* 'stirred up a hornet's nest'.

"And before it 'cratered', it seems some NATO country's spy satellite photographed one of the 'big sparks' flashing into Churchill Falls from about where Weldon Purdy's body was found. The US and the other NATO members have now joined Canada in a state of war-readiness.

"The Canadian government wants to send an investigation team up here right away. But the idea has become a real 'political football'. *Everyone* wants to be involved, the Yanks, the Canadian military, the Department of Public Safety, the Canadian Security Intelligence Service, the Minister of Defence, the *Deputy* Minister of Defence, and *whole bunch* of other political people and agencies.

"The investigation may not be under the direction of the RCMP. But while they're sorting it all out, they want me to find a 'local guide' familiar with the area. I've already told them no one could be better for that job than you. And they have already said 'yes' to my suggestion, as you've already been to the 'crime scene'.

"Well, thanks for that, Constable Dan, I think," said Walter doubtfully. "What do you think that will entail?"

"I have *no* idea, Walter," said Constable Dan bluntly. Then he said, "I've only been on the force for eight years, and I've *never* been involved in anything like this. That might be part of the bigger problem though, no one 'up the ladder' has either, by the sound of it.

"I know they want to do a fly-over in clear weather to get some photos. Then they think they'll come here, to Bowhead Arm, and go in by boat. But all of that is still being discussed."

"Did they ask *your* opinion, Dan?" asked Walter. "I mean, about *who* should be on an investigation team?"

"No, but that doesn't mean we should not offer a suggestion," said Constable Dan. "Why, what are you thinking?"

"Well, I heard Brad and Malcolm talking about it," said Walter. Then he explained, "With the site so busted up, they thought an archaeologist should be involved, or maybe an aviation crash investigator, you know, someone who can systemically 'piece things together' without damaging evidence in the process. They also thought maybe a university professor should be involved, one that knows *all* about the work of Tesla. And maybe some other scientists and engineers too, who might know what the equipment at the site did, or was intended to do."

"I agree with all of that, Walter," said Constable Dan. Then he smiled weakly and said, "So, it's now *our* suggestion. I think I'll forward it a bit higher up, to make sure it doesn't get blocked. That will *ensure* I get that reprimand! Then again, if the higher authorities agree with us… " He trailed off with a bigger smile.

"It's *amazing* the political, petty crap that creeps into any job, isn't it, Dan?" asked Walter.

"I can live without it," said Constable Dan bluntly. Then he stood up and said, "I'll let you know when the plans firm up, Walter. They may tell us who you will be guiding, but don't count on it.

"And, thanks for listening, Walter!"

24

The fog finally lifted just after noon on their fourth day out from Bowhead Arm. It was now the early morning of the sixth day of their journey.

They could now visually confirm with binoculars that an unidentified 'blip' on the radar screen was in fact a fishing boat about eight kilometres away.

"Vessel off Cape Bonavista, do you copy, over?" asked Will White Bear over the radio.

"Copy you five by five, vessel is fishing boat Wilma Williams, who are you, over?" was the clear reply.

Will looked at Curtis and Jerome who were with him in the wheelhouse. They were both nodding, and smiling back at him. Then Jerome put his right thumb up in the air.

Finally, they had made contact with another boat.

"We are fishing vessel Martha's Nieces from Bowhead Arm heading for St. John's, over," said Will over the radio.

There was a ten second pause, and then they heard the reply, "Can you come alongside of us, we have some news for you, over?"

"Okay, will do, over," responded Will.

As they approached the other boat, they could see that it was drifting with the wind and the waves. When they got closer, they could see two teenage boys jigging for cod on the port side, and they could see there was a tall man at the wheel.

Will positioned his boat a comfortable twenty metres away, in a sea that was running about a metre in height.

"I just called to shore, and the RCMP would like to talk to you!" yelled the other skipper, possibly the father of the two boys who were with him in the boat. The skipper appeared to be a man in his forties, and he was wearing a red baseball cap.

"He must have used another channel," whispered Curtis to Will and Jerome.

"They've been asking us to take turns out here looking out for you!" yelled the other skipper. Then he offered, "If you don't know the harbour, I can lead you in! We have enough fish now!"

Curtis and Jerome looked at each other. They both shrugged their shoulders, then nodded their heads at Will.

"Okay, we'll follow you in!" yelled Will to the other skipper.

It took a half hour to reach the harbour entrance. It looked like every boat was in port. When they got right into the harbour, the other skipper pointed at an empty spot on a wharf. An RCMP officer and a civilian man were standing above the empty spot, seemingly waiting for them.

Will's boat did not have a bow thruster to assist him, but he skilfully manoeuvred the boat into the tight space. The man on the wharf took the lines that were passed up to him by Kelvin and Ryan, and tied them off on cleats. "I'm the Harbour Master!" he yelled to them. "Welcome to Bonavista!"

"Can I come aboard?" asked the RCMP officer.

"Yes, sir," said Will without hesitation.

"I'm Constable Rutledge," said the RCMP officer when he had stepped off the wharf ladder on down into the boat. Then he asked, "Is this everyone that left Bowhead Arm?" Everyone was up on deck now.

"Yes, sir," said Will. "I'm the skipper, William Ikkusek." They shook hands.

"Mind if I take a quick look below?" asked the Constable.

"No, sir," said Will. "Mind your head going down."

The constable re-emerged from below after only a minute. Then he asked, "Is everyone all right?"

"Yes, sir, just fine," said Will.

"And you're still heading for St. John's, is that right?" asked the constable.

"Yes, sir," said Will. "I'm going to look in on my Mom in the hospital, and hopefully bring her home. These folks are heading back to their homes."

The constable looked carefully at all of them in turn. He smiled at Ryan and Kelvin. "Are you two all right?"

"Yes, sir, best kind," said Kelvin. Ryan just nodded in reply.

"How long will it take you to get there?" asked the constable, turning back to Will.

"About nine hours if this wind from the north holds up and keeps the fog away, sir," replied Will. "We still have lots of fuel."

"Yes, that's about what they thought in St. John's too," said Constable Rutledge while nodding his head. Then he said, "You won't get there faster by any other means. My orders were to confirm you were all still on board, and if you were seaworthy with no concerns, to send you *immediately* on your way.

"There will be a 'reception party' for you on the dock when you get there. You are to call the St. John's Port Authority on Channel 11. You will find the harbour is being controlled by the Navy and the Coast Guard now. If you follow instructions *exactly*, they say you will be okay."

"What are things like, Constable?" asked Curtis.

The constable took his hat off and smoothed his hair. Then he said, "Well, we still have no power here. Some parts of St. John's apparently have power now, off and on, as far as we know. Some radio stations are broadcasting again, at least some of the time. The phones and cell phones are still out. Gasoline and diesel are restricted to emergency responders, the police and the military. I think a few cabs are allowed to run in St. John's, but they're restricting the number on some kind of a rota basis.

"The Come by Chance refinery is a complete mess. No tankers are coming any time soon from Saint John, New Brunswick or wherever. One of the offshore platforms had a big fire. The others were shut in okay.

"So far, it's quiet and calm everywhere on shore. People are helping each other out. Now, I need to follow my orders, and send you on your way, right now. But I wish you the very best of luck!" He then shook everyone's hand, and went up the wharf ladder.

The harbour master took off the lines and handed them back down to Kelvin and Ryan. "No charge this time, folks!" he yelled. "Come back in happier times, b'ys!"

They all waved goodbye, and Will manoeuvred the boat out of the harbour.

25

While Curtis and his group were departing from Bonavista Harbour aboard the *Martha's Nieces*, Walter was standing outside the front door of his hotel. There were some Canadian Army soldiers in uniform milling around, and Walter wondered what was happening.

Everyone watched as a heavily-armoured, tracked-vehicle then pulled into Walter's hotel parking lot. Walter recognised it as an 'APC' or Armoured Personnel Carrier. It stopped abruptly, right at the front entrance.

A burly, middle-aged, dark-haired man with a handlebar moustache was standing up in the APC, talking into the microphone of a lightweight headset. When the man noticed Walter standing on the hotel doorstep, he took his headset off and came down off the vehicle.

"We will be making this hotel our command centre, Mr. Cartwright," said the man with a voice of confident authority. He was wearing a perfectly-fitting, camouflage suit with no insignia. "We will need *all* of the rooms."

"Okay," said Walter eying the man carefully in front of him. "You seem to know me, but I don't know you. The room rates are on the wall inside, Mister...?" He trailed off with an inquiring look on his face.

"You will call me the 'Deputy Incident Commander'," said the man brusquely. "None of the incident command staff members will tell you their *real* names or who they work for, so do not ask them those things. And we will be using the restaurant, the bar and everything else in the hotel," continued the Deputy Incident Commander sternly. Then he growled, "You will keep everyone else, and I mean *everyone* else, away. If this is a problem for you, soldiers will step in and enforce these guidelines."

"Okay," said Walter. "The prices are on the menu, and on every table in the bar. Just let me know what you need."

"I'm sure you will keep *good track* of everything and give us a *concise and accurate* bill when we leave," said the Deputy Incident Commander forcefully. Then he added, "I will need an itemised invoice of everything as well for my own records, of course."

"I'm sure I will kick you all the *hell* out of my hotel if I run out of cash and supplies, and can't keep the place running," said Walter with a bit of anger in his voice.

The man smiled smugly. Then he said, "*We* will help you keep the place running, Mr. Cartwright. Now, is the wooden 'helipad' out back of the hotel *operational*, say for a Bell 427? It looks a bit *suspect*."

"It's sound as *hell*," said Walter. He was really starting to get 'pissed off'. Then he added, "You'll have to get your fuel somewhere else though."

"That is all being arranged," snapped the Deputy Incident Commander. Then he said loudly, "Now, some of my people will talk to you this afternoon at thirteen hundred hours. They will also take your fingerprints to help with our forensic work. Then you will go with some people by helicopter to show them the site where you found the two burned corpses.

"And we need you to sign this 'oath of secrecy' document, *right now*." He was holding an official looking document, and thrust it at Walter.

Without looking at the document, Walter said, "Can I ask a stupid question, sir? What if I don't sign it, or obey it, or let you take my fingerprints?"

"Then we will *arrest* you immediately, Mr. Cartwright," said the Deputy Incident Commander with a confident smile.

"I think I can find a pen inside," said Walter. "What colour would you like me to use?"

26

Walter and his small staff had mostly just watched as the Bowhead Arm Hotel was converted before their eyes into an 'incident command centre'. Walter told everyone who asked that he didn't know what the 'foreign' visitors were up to either, or how long they might be staying. That was basically true.

As Walter expected, the local people were no trouble at all for himself, or for the mysterious visitors. The unprecedented sight of military vehicles and armed, uniformed people in the village was enough for them to want to keep their distance.

Just before one o'clock in the afternoon, Walter went looking for his 'interview'. He guessed it would occur in the largest room in his hotel, where most of the 'visitors' seemed to be congregating.

Walter knocked on the closed door to his bar. It was opened from within by an armed guard. He could see three men and a woman were seated behind one of the long tables in the hall he used for poker and bingo nights. The four people behind the table were all facing him.

They were dressed casually, but in the latest expensive golfing attire, not 'Labrador casual' attire. The rest of the large room was barricaded off. He could hear voices on the other side of the three-metre high freestanding barricade.

"Come in, Mr. Cartwright," said the woman at the table. Walter did not miss the irony that he was being invited into his own bar. Then the lady suggested pleasantly, "Why don't you take a seat, Walter."

She was a rather large, middle-aged, red-headed woman with a stern face and no make-up. She was sitting on the extreme right side of the table facing him. The man at the extreme left end of the table was small in stature, in his twenties, and had longish brown hair, and a goatee beard. The two men seated behind the middle of the table could have been twins. They were both in their thirties, muscularly-built, with very short military haircuts and clean-shaven faces.

The soldierly-looking guy who had let Walter enter the room was wearing a camouflage jumpsuit without insignia, and a smart-looking black-leather holster. He stood at ease at the door while Walter took his seat. The only chair available was a hard wooden chair facing the middle of the long table.

"We have a few questions for you now, if you don't mind?" asked the woman. The slight young man at the other end of the table was preparing to take notes. The woman picked up a remote control handset, and then aimed it at a video camera with a microphone. It was placed on a tripod in the corner of the room. Walter could see a red light appear on the camera.

Walter made no response. "All right, that's great," said the man in the middle on Walter's left side. Then he said, "Now, we've re-read your statement, Walter, and our questions are mostly for *clarity*. Firstly, how long have you known Mr. Weldon Purdy?"

"Well, I don't really know him," said Walter slowly. Then he said, "I've known *of* him all of my life. I've only talked to him directly a couple of times."

"Well, then, tell us as best you can what *kind* of a man he was," said the right-hand man in the middle. Then he said soothingly, "Take your time, Walter, and relax. There's a water bottle on the floor beside your chair. Help yourself whenever you want."

"Well, his family settled near a Moravian mission on English Bay," said Walter. Then he added calmly, "They had a house there, that his grandparents and parents both lived in. It's gone now. The church is still there, though. People collect money sometimes in the village here to try to preserve it.

"Both his grandfather and father were fur trappers, and they fished too, in the summers. I used to see Weldon sometimes with his father when I was on a snowmobile trip back in the country. But mostly they kept to themselves.

"People around here stopped seeing Weldon when he grew up. His father told a fishing guide that he ran away. I'm not sure if the police ever looked into it. Anyway, Weldon just showed up again about eight years later, apparently with a wife. I never saw her, but some guides said they did. Both of his parents were dead, and the houses around the mission were all abandoned by then.

"He built a cabin on the Owl River estuary, on family-owned land. I stopped in once for a visit, but he met me on the beach carrying a shotgun. He told me to 'go away and never come back'.

"Often at night, when we were on the Owl River salmon fishing, we would hear him going up or down the river. Curtis Furlong and Jerome Efford saw him doing that a few times, late at dusk or just before sunrise. He would 'run The Chute' even at night.

"Some guides told us that he had another place up the river. An old guide named Sid Lambton said Weldon shot at him once when he went up there for a look. Some guides claimed they saw him with a boy a few times, and talked about him as his son." As Walter was talking, both the young man and the red-haired woman were jotting notes furiously. He wondered why they were doing that if a video camera was recording everything. Then he figured they had to back up everything somehow.

"You must know a *lot* more about him than that," said the left-hand man in the middle. Then he snarled, "You went up there *illegally* with a handgun! Maybe you were going up there to settle a grudge? Or maybe you were going to *rob* him? It's time you came clean with us!"

"Now, let's not get carried away," said the right-hand man in the middle, reprovingly. "Walter was doing great. Now, anything else you can tell us, Walter?"

Walter suddenly realised with disgust that they were using the 'good guy, bad guy' ploy on him.

"Look, I had heard enough reasons over the years to be afraid of Weldon," Walter replied angrily. Then he added, "And, like we said in the statement, we thought he may have been a 'techno-terrorist' of some sort. Taking the gun along with us just seemed to be the sensible thing to do." He shrugged because he had no idea where this was going.

"To *shoot* him first, and ask questions *later* perhaps?" said the left-hand man in the middle. Walter silently decided to label him the 'Demon'.

"Now, let's not get carried away again," lectured the right-hand man in the middle. Walter silently labelled him the 'The Angel'. Then the 'Angel' added quietly, "After all, Mr. Cartwright has not been charged with anything, *yet.*"

The Demon then looked at some photographs that were in front of him, which he then passed to the Angel. Then the Demon said, "We asked the fishery and ice patrol folks to make a flight over the site in a twin-engine Beechcraft turboprop. They gave us these photographs, and a video recording. *Some* aspects of the site appear to line up with what you said in your statement, however it is a *lot* bigger in extent. How can one account for that discrepancy?"

"Well, it was foggy, and we had to get back by dark," said Walter. Then he added, "And none of us were used to looking at dead bodies. We were all a bit rattled. I guess we may not have looked around as much as we could have, in hindsight."

"How could *one man* have built such things, and kept it all secret?" asked the Demon. Then he growled, "Surely he must have had *accomplices*?" There was real venom in his voice now.

"I don't know," said Walter bluntly. Then he explained, "It is an isolated location, and there is a snowmobile trail nearby, and that connects with many other trails that can take one just about anywhere in Labrador.

"I'm not aware of *anyone* being a friend of Weldon. He went out of his way to avoid contact with people. He mostly succeeded in that. And frankly, I'm completely *fed-up* with the way you're talking to me."

As Walter had been talking, the sound of thumping rotor blades, and the whine of jet turbines, had been steadily increasing in volume. Obviously a helicopter was now landing just outside the back of the hotel. Everyone in the room could now see the machine through a small window, hovering over the helipad in a cloud of dust.

"Well, saved by the 'Bell' it seems, pun intended," said the Demon with a frown. "Well, you better go get ready to be a *guide* now, Mr. Cartwright."

"We'll talk to you some more when you get back, Walter," said the Angel with a smile. "We have made a nice, friendly start."

"Sure thing, *friends*," said Walter sarcastically. "But you can read me my *rights* first, next time we talk."

Then Walter jumped up, walked quickly out through the door of the 'interview' room, then done a hallway and out through the back door of the hotel. He walked right into the downdraft from the helicopter. He put his fingers in his ears, and watched the helicopter blades wind down and stop.

Seven passengers then got out of the helicopter. They were dressed casually, again in 'posh' golfing attire. Walter recognised one of the passengers as the Deputy Incident Commander and walked over to him.

"Hello, Mr. Cartwright," said the 'DIC' with a smile. Then he said happily, "We just got a full load of fuel at the airport. We're about to look at the site from the air, and we're hoping you could come with us to keep us from 'getting lost', ha-ha, and to tell us what we're looking at there. What do you say?"

"I'll go with you, as long as you call off your 'hounds'," replied Walter angrily. "They just gave me a 'grilling', and treated me like a suspect."

"Please give me a minute, Walter, and I'll look into that just now," said the DIC quietly. Then he turned smartly on his heel and went into the hotel, while the other passengers remained by the helideck.

A tall, older, distinguished-looking gentleman with a kind face and a friendly smile walked over to Walter and offered his hand. "I'm the Incident Commander, Walter," he said. Walter shook his hand. Then the 'IC' said, "Can I make some introductions?"

"Sure thing," said Walter pleasantly. He shook hands as each introduction took place.

"This person is our Operations Section Leader, or 'OSL'" said the IC. The man was fit-looking, swarthy, and in his forties. He had a grim, determined look on his face.

"Here's our Logistics Section Leader, or 'LSL'." He was a rather stout, jovial-looking man with a ruddy complexion.

"And this person is our Planning Section Leader, or 'PSL'." She was a classy-looking, mature lady with perfect make-up. Walter later found out that she had a French-Canadian accent.

"This person is a technical adviser in the Planning Section." She was a petite and pretty young woman, and looked a bit shy.

"And this man has joined us from Ottawa." Walter had seen him before. He was a tall, muscular, middle-aged man with a permanent smile and high cheekbones. He looked perfectly natural in golfing clothes. Walter recognised him as the Federal Minister of Defence.

"You probably don't remember me, do you, Walter?" asked the technical expert in a soft voice after the handshake introductions were completed. Then she said, "I stayed in your hotel off and on about ten years ago. I was doing research, and digging for Paleo-Eskimo artefacts."

"I *do* remember you, sorry," said Walter. "How are you… ?" He was about to add 'Margaret', but thought better of it.

"Just fine," she said quietly as she turned her eyes away. He remembered she really was a shy person.

Then the DIC came out of the hotel. He walked right over to Walter, and said, "Sorry about that, Mr. Cartwright. I sorted them out in there. That won't happen again. You're *definitely* not a suspect. We just got off to a rough start, that's all, and we're sorry about that.

"Look, we could *really* use your help. Will you come along with us, and be our guide?"

"Okay, sir," said Walter with a smile. He suspected what had just occurred had been carefully orchestrated. But maybe he should have expected that. These people were clearly suspicious of everyone right now, and Walter thought they must be under immense pressure to get results quickly.

Everyone climbed into the helicopter, buckled up, and put on their earmuff headsets. Then the pilot wound up the engine for take-off.

As they climbed upwards and moved towards English Bay, they could see the village of Bowhead Arm below them.

"Still about four hundred people living here?" asked the minister.

"About that, yes, sir," answered Walter.

It was a clear, sunny day. There was no activity in the harbour. There was one small powerboat heading out into English Bay.

"You can see the radar dome now, over to the left, on top of that high ridge," said the minister.

About ten minutes into the flight, Margaret said, "That's an old Moravian mission, down to our right."

"Weldon Purdy grew up there," said Walter. That got everyone looking intently out of the windows.

After another twenty minutes, the pilot said, "We're coming up on the mouth of the river now."

"That's Weldon Purdy's place there on the left," said Walter.

"There's nowhere to land there," said the pilot.

"That's okay," said the DIC. "I don't think we'll be asking you to land anywhere today."

When they flew over The Chute, the pilot said, "Wow."

"Roger that!" said the IC.

"We're coming up on the Owl River Salmon Club, to our left," said Walter. They could see the main lodge and the six cabins. Walter knew Rob and Diane were waving at them from the front deck of the lodge. Walter also thought the deck appeared to have been completely rebuilt.

"Any chance we could make some use of that facility, Walter?" asked the LSL.

"Well, it's owned by my friend, Curtis Furlong, and managed by my son, Dwayne," said Walter. Then he added, "It looks like the salmon fishing season is going to be a complete 'write-off' this year, so I can't see why Curtis and Dwayne would say 'no' to you."

"Where could you land a helicopter here?" asked the LSL.

"When rich guests say they want to come here 'by chopper', Dwayne cuts down the alder bushes in the spot now down to our left, across the little brook and upstream from the lodge."

"Mr. Cartwright, the place we're going to is about fifteen kilometres from here, right?" asked the pilot.

"Yes, sir," replied Walter. "Just follow the river."

The pilot slowed their forward speed a bit. They could see nothing of interest until they approached the falls.

"We're coming up to the site now, up on the ridge to the right," said Walter suddenly. "You can see Weldon's boat down on the bank now, and his hover plane, and the spot where the young man's corpse is located."

"It doesn't stand out much, does it?" said the DIC looking out his window at the site. "You might almost miss it if you didn't look right at it."

The pilot slowed the helicopter to a near hover as they moved up the ridge at about fifty metres above the treetops. He followed the trail to the clearings. He went up the slope at a forty-five degree angle to the direction of travel to allow the OSL in the front left seat to take some photographs. The pilot was obviously very skilled.

"You can see one tower still standing over there, to our left," said the PSL. Then she added with excitement, "And we can see the wreckage of three more towers that have collapsed. They form the corners of what looks like a perfect square, with about three hundred metres on each side."

"Is that the main building below us now, Walter, where you found the adult male body?" asked the DIC.

"Yes, sir," replied Walter.

"This matches your description very well, Walter," said the IC with his right thumb up in the air.

"Seen enough?" asked the pilot.

"There is nowhere to land safely here, is there?" asked the LSL.

"I wouldn't try it anywhere that I can see," said the pilot.

"Do you think you could help us locate and build a good helipad up here, Walter?" asked the LSL.

"Yes, sir," said Walter. "It would be a 'piece of cake' with the right crew. I know some guys who do that sort of stuff all of the time. *They* could come in by boat, but it would be quicker if a chopper could sling-load in their camping gear, the building materials and their tools. That way, I bet they could have it all finished in a couple of days."

"That all sounds fine, Walter, thanks," said the LSL.

"Minister, have you seen enough?" asked the IC. When he saw the minister nod back at him, the IC said, "All right then, take us home now, James."

The IC did not seem to know he had called the 'mystery man' from Ottawa 'Minister'.

When they were back over the river again, heading downstream, Walter looked at the DIC sitting beside him, and asked quietly, "That's not the pilot's real name, is it, sir?"

"No it isn't, Walter," said the DIC with a wry smile.

27

Walter was scanning the hotel business ledger in his office.

They had all returned to the hotel in the helicopter a few hours before, except for the Minister of Defence. He had left them at the airport. He had immediately climbed aboard a Twin Otter turboprop airplane to travel to an undeclared destination.

"Walter, can I bug you for a minute?" asked the Logistics Section Leader while standing politely just outside his office door. They were *all* calling him 'Walter' now, not 'Mr. Cartwright'.

"Sure, please come in and have a seat, sir," said Walter. Then he apologised, "Sorry about the clutter. I'm trying to sort out some unpaid bills."

"No sweat," said the LSL as he sat down. He left the door of the office open. There was nobody in the hotel lobby. Then he said, "Walter, I haven't got much time, so I'll have to be blunt. I'm hoping you'll join my team. I know you could really help us out. How does a thousand bucks a day plus expenses sound?"

Walter sat at his desk thinking for a few moments.

"Okay, how about twelve hundred a day?" asked the LSL.

Walter laughed. "No, I'm not 'hard negotiating' with you! Sorry! I'm just trying to figure out how I could keep this place running while I helped you out."

"Well, if you needed to put someone to work doing that for you, we'll cover those costs, too," said the LSL.

"Glad to join your team, then, sir!" said Walter with a smile while offering his hand.

The LSL shook his hand firmly, and said, "Okay then, I'll go back to the section leader meeting right now, and run the twelve hundred bucks a day number by the Finance Leader. I don't think there will be a problem.

"Oh, and Walter, the 'top brass' said they would like to bring you in at the end of our meeting, before we finish for the day. Would that be okay with you?"

"Okay, just come and get me, sir," said Walter. "I'll be right here, under this pile of paper."

Later in the afternoon, Walter was talking with Phyllis in his office when a soldier in uniform arrived to escort him into the 'section leader meeting'. The soldier was carrying an automatic rifle.

The soldier knocked on the door of the hotel bar. Another soldier with an automatic handgun opened the door, and Walter entered the room.

Walter noted that all of the incident response leaders were sitting around a long table in the room. He also saw a few unfamiliar faces at the table. He was pleased the four people who had 'interviewed' him earlier in the day were seemingly not invited to the meeting. And they must have taken their video recorder with them.

"Here, Walter, have a seat," said the Deputy Incident Commander. Walter was being offered a seat at their table. He figured this might be some king of a milestone with respect to his status.

"Walter, we are about to review our current situation and point-forward plan, and we would like to capture your ideas," asked the DIC. "Okay?"

"I'm 'all ears', sir," said Walter.

"Okay, that's great," said the DIC. He paused to take a long drink of water. Walter figured the meeting had already been going a long time. Then the DIC said, "Special forces people are establishing security perimeters as we speak. Ground access will be restricted at gateposts on the river, at the airport and at

271

the road into town from the highway. Activity around these areas will be monitored by 'unseen eyes'. Those will be 'human' eyes until we can get drones in the air.

"We want to immediately build a helicopter landing pad at the site, and we'd like your help with that, Walter. Then we want to build an equipment staging area at the site. With no roads, we'll have to haul stuff in by helicopter from the airport here, with sling-loads if required. There will be a lot of stuff carefully hauled out too, for forensic study and reassembly at the airport. We are building a big temporary building at the airport.

"There will be the need for a *lot* of logistical coordination, and a lot of local sourcing in our supply chain. We think you can greatly help us with that effort, Walter. Okay so far?"

Walter nodded, and the DIC continued. "Okay, great. There will be a few people staying on site full-time. We would like to make use of the salmon lodge, so we would like you to help us set that up too, Walter. We don't know how long all of this will go on. But maybe count on a month minimum, but more likely two months. You see, we're looking for some fast answers about what actually happened."

The DIC paused and looked at the IC. The IC cleared his throat for speaking, then said, "We'll now tell you a little, Walter, about the 'big picture', and we'll hold you to your 'oath of secrecy'.

"The solar storm was the worst on record. There are now two magnetic 'North' poles and two 'South' poles. A compass will point to the nearest 'North' pole. If you happen to know which 'North' is which, a compass can be *sort of* useful again.

"Every satellite was destroyed. So, we have no GPS, satellite phones, spy satellites, research satellites, or any other kind of satellite. The astronauts in the space station are dead, unfortunately. Go ahead, Walter, take a drink of water now. We know this is bad stuff."

Walter poured a glass of water for himself from a jug on the table and took a long drink. His head was reeling. Brad and Malcolm had made some shrewd guesses.

When Walter looked up the table, the OIC said, "All the media are allowed to cover are local power outages, and local news. *Everything* is being blamed on the solar storm. The 'Emergency Planning Order' is still in effect in Canada; that replaced the old 'War Measures Act'.

The US is at 'DEFCON 4'. They are considering going to 'DEFCON 3'. When there are no serious threats to worry about, they are at 'DEFCON 5'. If they ever reach to push the button to launch ICBM's in anger, that will be 'DEFCON 1'.

"North Korea and Iran are making a lot of threatening noises about being attacked by a secret weapon without warning. So far, they have not done anything stupid.

"Power, telephone and cell phones are still out in most places. The electrical devices in many internal combustion, diesel and jet engines were damaged. So were a lot of other electronic devices.

"The storm was bad enough, but something happened at Churchill Falls and Muskrat Falls to make it worse."

The IC paused to take a sip of water. Then he said, "Before it stopped working, a 'friendly' satellite saw a huge electrical discharge hitting Churchill Falls. The experts say the electrical discharge came from the investigation site. Their conclusion is backed up by 'infrasound triangulation'. Three 'CTBT' or 'Comprehensive (nuclear) Test Ban Treaty' monitoring stations heard the ultra-low frequency 'sonic booms' caused by the ten electrical discharges.

"Huge power surges were sent down the high-tension cables from the two big Labrador hydroelectric power plants before they were destroyed. It will take *months* to replace key devices in the electrical power distribution infrastructure."

"If all that wasn't bad enough, a number of devastating earthquakes occurred right after the ground started shaking here. 'Seismograph triangulation' shows 'resonant excitation energy' came from the investigation site, and experts say the shaking was clearly man-made."

The IC paused again to gather his thoughts. Then he said, "So, this is being treated as an act of terrorism, right up there with '9/11'. Weldon Purdy is the number one suspect. The US is taking the lead on finding out more about him, especially if he could be part of a global terror-organisation like al-Qaeda, or if he was working for a foreign government. He may have spent some time in the US.

"*Our* mission is to try to figure out what he built at the site, and how he did what we think he did. With those questions answered, some very smart people may be able to figure out how to defend against another similar attack. That is, if there are more guys like Weldon out there. Okay, that's the end of my spiel."

"Are you a little more interested now in helping us, Walter?" asked the DIC quietly.

"I'll work for free," replied Walter with passion.

"No, a deal's a deal," said the DIC.

The IC then stood up, which seemed to signal that the meeting was over.

So the DIC asked, "Now, could you open the bar for us, Walter?" And perhaps join us for a cocktail before dinner?"

Walter nodded.

Then the DIC said, "That's great, Walter. And what *is* for dinner?"

"Char", said Walter. Then he started laughing. When the DIC gave him a puzzled look, Walter added, "Sorry, private joke, sir. I'll tell you it about over a drink."

"I bet it's about 'well-done Purdy'?" asked the DIC. "We may have had a similar conversation."

"Sounds like it for sure," said Walter with a laugh. "Come on, follow me! And what will you have, sir?"

28

There had been no more fog, and the day-long trip from Bonavista was uneventful.

The sun was now setting. They could see a naval frigate in the distance, cruising off of Cape Spear.

"St. John's Port Authority, this is fishing boat Martha's Nieces, do you copy, over?" said Will over the radio.

"This is the Harbour Commander, what is your location, over?" was the reply.

"Harbour Commander, Martha's Nieces is passing the entrance to Quidi Vidi harbour, over," said Will.

"Martha's Nieces, proceed to The Narrows, and wait there for your escort, over," said the Harbour Commander.

"Harbour Commander, Martha's Nieces will comply with your order, over," said Will.

When they approached the entrance to The Narrows, they could see their escort would be a 'fast rescue boat' with a huge spotlight. It circled them twice, working the spotlight over them continuously. Then they heard through a megaphone, "Follow us, and do *exactly* what we tell you to do." When the spotlight was pointed ahead and away from their eyes, they could see four men in the boat. One man was standing at a central console, piloting the boat. The other three men were also standing. They were wearing black suits. They all had one hand on an assault rifle and one hand on the metal tubular superstructure of the rigidised inflatable boat

As they passed Fort Amherst on their left, Curtis said, "That looks like a working gun set up in an old World War Two gun emplacement."

When they were almost through The Narrows, they could see a naval mine sweeper holding station in the middle of the harbour. The escort boat circled them again, and the megaphone voice said, "Head for the floating docks, and tie up there."

Will said, "There are no floating docks. They took them out years ago. No wait, they must have put them back in, right where they used to be."

As Will was lining up on the only open berth at the two docks, the men could see some soldiers with automatic weapons. They were standing at ease at the top of the ramp that led down to the docks.

Kelvin and Curtis hopped off first and tied up the bow and stern lines. Will stepped off next and tied up the two spring lines. Then he adjusted the bow and stern lines before climbing back on the boat to turn off the diesel engine.

A 'RNC' or Royal Newfoundland Constabulary officer, and a 'Mountie' or Royal Canadian Mounted Police officer, then came down the ramp towards them.

"Good evening, men," said the RCMP officer pleasantly. "You fellows are all to come with us. We have some cars waiting nearby. You can put your stuff in a pickup truck we brought with us. We'll give you a hand."

"Can we try to reach our wives, officers?" asked Curtis.

"We have contacted them, and they know we want to talk to you first," said the RNC officer. "We'll take you home later."

"Oh, I have something for you," said Curtis. He reached into the small duffle bag he had placed on the dock when he first stepped off the boat. Then he pulled out a thick envelope. "It's from your colleague in Bowhead Arm, Labrador," said Curtis as he handed the envelope to the RCMP officer.

The officer looked at the addressing on the envelope, and said, "Yes, thanks. I'll pass this up the line. Now, let's get started on your baggage."

29

The RCMP and RNC officers who had accompanied the men to the RCMP headquarters building in St. John's never introduced themselves and would not engage in small talk.

There were no streetlights anywhere, and it had rained recently, which made it even harder to see. The buildings were all dark, but they had seen candles burning in a few house windows.

They were met just inside the front door of the multi-storey headquarters building by a burly sergeant. The RCMP sergeant was a serious, professional-looking man, near retirement age. But he smiled at them when they were all assembled in front of him. He checked everyone's name off on a document he had with him on a clip board. Then he introduced himself as Sergeant Prescott.

"Don't worry about your gear, guys, we'll look after it for you while you're upstairs," said Sergeant Prescott. Then he said, "Now, if you'll just follow me, we'll get you started so we can *all* get through this a quickly as possible."

Sergeant Prescott led them up two flights of darkened stairs and then down a dark hallway. Only the emergency lighting was on in the building.

"Okay, guys, here we are," said Sergeant Prescott as he opened a door. He then held the door open, and motioned for them to enter the room. The room seemed to be a brightly lit waiting area, with a wooden table and some wooden chairs.

Then Sergeant Prescott said, "Just relax now, fellows. There's some water, juice and pop in the fridge. You can make coffee and tea over on the counter. Help yourselves to whatever you want. The interviewers are just about ready. They'll handle it from here."

"Thank you, Sergeant," said Curtis, as the sergeant left through the door they had just passed through. They could hear him in the hallway, locking the door from outside.

Curtis suddenly looked far from relaxed.

Brad had just made a cup of instant coffee when the other door to the room opened. A young man in a sharp-looking suit and tie walked in, and said, "Okay, we'd like to start with Mr. Walsh." Brad raised his hand.

Then the man in the suit said, "That's you? Okay. Hi, I'm Ed." He shook Brad's hand, and said, "Bring your coffee with you, Brad, that's all right."

Brad followed Ed into the adjoining room. Ed closed the door behind them, and then sat down beside another man and two women. They were seated at a long table facing a solitary chair with a small side table. They were all dressed in business attire. There was a bubble-eye in the ceiling. Brad was sure they were recording everything.

"You can take a seat right there if you like, Mr. Walsh," said Ed, pointing at the chair facing the table.

Brad sat down on the hard wooden chair, and put his coffee cup on the little table beside him. The coffee was too hot to drink yet anyway.

"Okay, Brad?" said one of the women. Brad nodded, so she said, "I'm Sarah. And this is Jim, and this is Elizabeth. You've already met Ed. We would like to ask you a few questions. It should not take too long. Then we will ask you to wait in another area down the hallway."

Sarah was a smart-looking brunette. Brad though she might have a great figure, but it was mostly hidden by the table. Elizabeth was a grey-haired, older lady with a plain but friendly face. Ed was a young man who looked like an advertising executive from the 1960s. He was even wearing a long skinny tie like they used to wear back then. Jim was a stout, middle-aged man with a bit of a beer belly. He looked uncomfortable in the wrinkled sports jacket he was wearing. The jacket did not fit him very well.

Brad had been a bit nervous, but he could see these were probably just 'normal' people, doing their jobs.

"First off, you're a professional engineer, and a Canadian citizen?" asked Sarah.

"Yes, I work in the oil industry, here in St. John's," said Brad. Then he said, "I did mechanical engineering at Western University in London, Ontario. I've worked mostly in drilling and production. I'm single, divorced. Maybe that goes with working overseas and offshore a lot."

"We've been reading your statement pretty carefully," said Elizabeth. "How did you make the 'Tesla connection'?"

"Well, if you remember, we did use words like, 'in our opinion' throughout the statement," Brad began slowly. Then he said, "The 'Tesla connection', as you call it, is just a theory.

"When Kelvin Furlong and I found the adult body in what we called the 'main building', we noticed a lot of documents and books in the wreckage. We didn't touch any of them, but we took a few photographs. I saw that a lot were about Tesla, or looked to be made by him, copies perhaps. Some were very old documents, and some were newer-looking schematics and sketches.

"I have read a little about Tesla over the years. I've also talked a lot about him with Malcolm Smallbridge, who's outside in the waiting area. He knows more about him, but he would be the first to say he is not an expert either.

"Malcolm thought the long distance electrical discharge, if that's what happened, was something Tesla wanted to do. And the rhythmic earth-shaking was something he apparently did once, at least in one of his labs."

"And you recognised a device you called a 'Tesla Coil'?" asked Elizabeth.

"Yes, in the wreckage," said Brad. Then he explained, "A high school friend of mine made a very small one for fun. That's how I recognised it. It took him a long time to build it, as the wire has to be wound around the supporting tube with great precision. The spacing between the loops of wire is apparently critical for the device to work properly."

"What was your overall impression, Brad, of the site?" asked Sarah. "And what stood out to you?"

Brad thought for a moment before answering. Then he said bluntly, "Well, it looked like 'amateur hour'!

"I mean, there was "shelf item stuff" that had been hobbled together, and modified. There was a lot of heavier equipment there, some well over a hundred kilograms in mass. There were electric motors, transformers, capacitors, coils, switches, insulators, and cables of all sorts.

"Some devices clearly looked handmade, but carefully made, with great skill. Not much attention had been paid to making anything 'pleasing to the eye', so to speak.

"A lot of the timber looked to have been rough-sawn, you know, not like the stuff you get from a commercial mill.

"There were cables that had clearly been laid intentionally on the ground. Other wires and cables had been supported by poles. Some of the poles looked wobbly. They might not have made it through a good wind storm.

"There were mechanical devices too, like slider-crank mechanisms, connecting rods, springs, *et cetera*.

"The trees were very close to all of the buildings. The buildings were really just shacks made of unpainted wood. They had all been knocked down, and singed and blackened by fire to some degree.

"And overall, I think the builder or builders were trying to make everything very hard to see from above."

"You said, 'builder or builders', Brad," said Jim. "Do you think *one person* could really have built what you saw on his or her own?"

Brad paused for a minute to think. Then he said, "I've been asking myself that question a lot. And I talked to Walter Cartwright and Malcolm about it, too. The person would have to be physically strong, very determined, multiskilled, resourceful and cunning, especially if he or she had to steal the stuff. We think one person with all of those attributes could have done it, yes. But maybe with a helper from time to time to move the heavier or awkward stuff? And maybe it *had* to be only one person, to keep it all secret?"

"You've known Walter Cartwright a long time, according to your joint statement," said Sarah. Then she asked, "Is he a good guy? Do you think he could help us with our investigation?"

"Walter is the 'salt of the earth'," said Brad emphatically. Then he said, "He's very experienced in the wilds, and a decent, honest man. And he knows how to get things done in Labrador, you know, very well-connected. I think he could *really* help you with your investigation."

"Last question, Brad," said Jim while looking in turn at his colleagues. "Anything of note with the bodies you saw? Or something that might help us with identification?"

"We thought one was a very young man or a teenager," said Brad. Then he added, "And the other was a man in his fifties, probably. The young man was dressed shabbily in light summer clothes, and he was wearing weird-looking wooden shoes that looked hand-carved, you know, like the traditional Dutch clog?

"The man was wearing motorcycle leather, and the same kind of wooden shoes. He was also wearing hockey gloves and a welder's mask, so again, pretty weird stuff. They were both burned up pretty badly, including their faces. And animals had been picking at the young body." Brad reached for his coffee and a much needed drink. Then he added, "I think we captured most of that in the statement. Sorry, I might be re-telling something."

"That's okay, Brad," said Ed. "You guys put a lot of good detail in your statement. We all thank you for that. Now, I'll show you down the hall to the other room where you can finish your coffee, or make another cup if that one has gone cold. We may call you in again after we talk to Malcolm. And we might call you again later on, during the investigation, if that's all right?"

"If there's anything I can do to help, please call me anytime," said Brad.

"Okay, that's great," said Sarah. She handed Ed a one page document to hand in turn to Brad. Then she said, "We are going to ask you all to sign an 'oath of secrecy' before we drive you home later tonight. You can read it over while we talk to your friends.

"We'll be getting your fingerprints too, since you were at the site, and probably touched a few things, even if you don't *remember* doing so."

Brad just nodded in reply. He was relieved the interview was over, and he felt tired suddenly from all the accumulated stress he had experienced. He stood up and then left the room with Ed.

30

The men were sitting in the 'second' waiting area after their interviews. Only Curtis, Malcolm and Brad were missing from the group.

It seemed most of the interviews had only lasted ten minutes or so.

"They just asked me how I was doing after seeing a dead body," said Ryan. He looked sleepy and was drinking his second can of ginger ale. Then he added, "And they asked me what Walter Cartwright is like."

"Me too," said Kelvin. He was munching on some cookies. Then he said, "And they said they will be fingerprinting me, Ryan and Brad so they can identify, 'other people of interest'."

"They asked me and Fred about Walter too," said Jerome. Then he added, "Also, about when we've seen Weldon Purdy, and what he was doing at those times. I told them I could really 'use a smoke', but they said enjoying a cigarette will have to wait until we're outside."

"They asked me how I managed to get hooked up with you guys," said Will. He sounded a bit angry. He added, "And how we got here, and what I heard you guys say in the boat. I doubt I would have agreed to take you guys if I had known *all this* was going to happen." When, he saw the hurt look on their faces, he added. "Sorry, I don't really mean that. I think I'm just tired and grumpy. You *did* help cover most of the cost of getting us here. And I'll have enough money to take my mom home when she's up to it."

Brad came back into the waiting room. He was looking at his ink-stained fingers.

"They just looked at my passport and asked me how I was going to get back to Norway," said Odvar who was sitting away from the group and looking sad. Then he said, "That was easy, because I don't know."

"You guys need to carefully read those papers they gave you to sign," said Brad, looking at the bubble-eye on the ceiling. Then he explained "We are not supposed to talk about anything that happened today, or on the river. Who's in there now?"

"Either Malcolm or Curtis," Fred said, looking up and seeing the bubble-eye for the first time. Then he said quietly, "We don't know."

31

Curtis and Malcolm were sitting close together in the waiting area. Curtis was having his second cup of coffee, and Malcolm was sipping bottled water. The interviewer named Ed had asked both of them to briefly write down their business details and work histories on some paper he provided, 'to expedite the proceedings'. Then Ed had taken what they had written into the next room when it was Fred's turn for an interview. Ed also had taken Malcolm's passport, and his permit to work in the United States.

Every few minutes Malcolm would stand up, walk around and stretch a muscle or two.

"Are you nervous, Malcolm?" asked Curtis.

"Maybe just a *bit* apprehensive," replied Malcolm. Then he admitted, "I'm not very patient in a queue, especially when I don't know what I'm waiting for."

"Well, I wouldn't worry too much about that, Malcolm," said Curtis. Then he said, "It looks like this is a 'fact-finding mission', and the interviews are not taking more than ten minutes each. The order of who they called into their room is interesting though. I can see why Brad went first, followed by Kelvin then Ryan, as they toured the site where the dead bodies were, and signed a joint statement with Walter. Why they've left you and me to the end is a bit puzzling though."

"Yes," said Malcolm, "And I wonder who they'll want next."

Just then, the door opened, and Ed walked in. "We're ready for you now, Mr. Smallbridge," said Ed with a smile.

"Well, we didn't have to wait very long for the answer," said Curtis. "See you on the other side, Malcolm!"

"You'll obviously be last, Mr. Furlong, but not least," said Ed. "It shouldn't be much longer now."

"No sweat," said Curtis. He was actually starting to sweat a bit.

Ed followed Malcolm into the next room, closing the door behind him. Malcolm took the seat that Ed offered him, and the four interviewers introduced themselves using their first names.

"So, how do you know so much about solar flares and Nikola Tesla, Mr. Smallbridge?" asked Elizabeth.

"Well, I'm not an expert or anything on those subjects," replied Malcolm with an edge of nervousness in his voice. Then he said, "But I've read about Tesla over the years. I seem to have a bit of a 'photographic memory'. Some people have thought me a 'bit of a snob' with my 'wealth of trivial facts'.

"But I just remember things very well. And I like all things pertaining to science. So does Brad. We put our 'heads together' a few times. We know we've been doing some amateur speculating, but we also don't want that to get in the way of what you are doing. We mostly have tried to make observations very carefully for others, the real experts, to analyse further."

"Here's your passport and work permit back," said Ed. Malcolm got up to take hold of the documents from Ed, and then he sat down again.

"How are you planning to get home to Houston?" asked Ed.

"I don't know," said Malcolm. "I have a return airplane ticket."

"That probably won't work," said Jim, shaking his head with concern. Then he said, "You should talk to a good travel agent, but they're struggling with most or all of the communication links down.

"Some 'short-hop' commercial flights are available, on a 'priority-passenger only' basis. But international or cross-ocean commercial flights have not resumed yet." He paused to consider other options. Then he said, "Some trains are running on the mainland, but no buses are working here yet.

"Rail service was terminated in Newfoundland in the late-sixties after the Trans-Canada Highway was completed.

"All types of fuel are being rationed until the refining and distribution systems are restored. Transport trucks and freight trains have 'first dibs', after the military, police and emergency responders, of course. One ferry is working across the Cabot Strait. It waits until enough trucks show up to completely fill it. And it works things a lot slower now, with no GPS to help."

"After we talked to Odvar, we found out some cruise ships are temporarily converting to transatlantic 'liners', you know, like the Queen Mary," interjected Ed. Then he said, "We've heard talk of these liners stopping in New York and Halifax, but not in St. John's yet. You might want to tell your friend about that."

"I will," said Malcolm. "Thanks."

Malcolm suddenly realised this was not going to be some sort of inquisition about his technical knowledge. He took a slow breath, and smiled at each interviewer in turn.

"We haven't heard much about Houston," said Sarah while leaning forward to scan the faces of her colleagues. Then she said, "That's probably a *good* thing. All cities are struggling to get the power back on as a priority, and to maintain law and order. That probably means lock-downs are occurring, and restrictions of many sorts."

"Yes, that sounds logical, thanks," said Malcolm in a subdued manner. Then he said quietly, "One finds it hard to stay scientific and objective about all of these things with no idea about how one's wife and son are faring."

The four interviewers then all stood up to shake his hand. Sarah and Elizabeth both added hugs when they saw Malcolm's eyes were welling-up. His repressed feelings· had finally surfaced.

32

When Ed opened the door and walked in to the waiting room, Curtis was standing up, and looking at the travel poster on the wall for the seventh time.

"We are ready for you now, Mr. Furlong," said Ed, formally. The he said curtly, "Please follow me."

Ed motioned for Curtis to sit down on the chair opposite the panel of interviewers. Ed closed the door, and joined his colleagues at the long table. They were all busy reading documents, with their heads down.

"They are just reviewing the citation for the restricted weapon transportation violation, Mr. Furlong," said Ed. He was studying Curtis' face carefully. He noted Curtis' eyes were now fully dilated.

"Oh, by the way, Mr. Furlong, this is Sarah beside me, then Jim, and then Elizabeth," said Ed without taking his eyes off of Curtis. None of the other interviewers looked up during Ed's cursory introduction.

After a few minutes, Jim and Sarah pulled their chairs closer together to face the wall behind them, and had a conversation in whispers for another few minutes.

Jim and Sarah repositioned their chairs, and all four interviewers finally turned their eyes towards Curtis.

"Constable Lukianow seems to think you should just be warned for a restricted weapon transportation violation, and leave it at that, Mr. Furlong," said Sarah. "What do you think about that?"

"I think I really 'screwed-up'," said Curtis nervously. Then he said, "You don't need a handgun to fend off bears, although they're handier than a shotgun. And Walter could have taken a shotgun with him to check up on Weldon Purdy, I suppose."

Sarah nodded her head, and then she looked at Jim.

"The constable seems to be very impressed with you, and your party," said Jim bluntly.

"We were," Curtis started to say. He paused to clear his throat. Then he said, "We were impressed with him too. He's doing a lot of good for the people up there. He's keeping the peace, and they have all pulled behind him. I think that shows he's very capable, and has earned a lot of respect."

"The Force thinks very highly of him too," said Jim. Curtis smiled when he heard that.

"Your sons have been through a lot," said Elizabeth. "They seem to be holding up well."

"They have impressed the *hell* out of me," said Curtis with a broader smile. "I'm really proud of them. I'm sure their mother will be, too."

"We know you're anxious to get home," said Ed. "We have just a few more matters to address with you.

"The investigation team may need to make use of your salmon lodge to some extent. Can some of our folks talk to you about that, say tomorrow, or the next day?"

"Sure thing," said Curtis.

"Walter Cartwright, in the joint statement, noted you saw and heard Weldon Purdy going up and down the river a few times, and at night," said Jim. Then he said, "Walter also related the time when Weldon scared you, you know, when you offered him a beer? That's not much to go on. Do you have any suggestions about where we should start looking for more information about him?"

"Well, our guides said he went away for years and came back," said Curtis with a shrug. Then he said, "It might be really useful to know where he went, and what he did there. His 'building programme' probably started when he came back."

"Thanks, Curtis," said Sarah. "We'll ask you now to sign an oath to keep all of this to ourselves. And then we'll take you all home. You're going to find things *very different* in St. John's. We hope it works out for you and your family. Times are tough right now."

"I think Will wants to go back to his boat," said Curtis, looking at each interviewer in turn. Then he said, "He's going to try to get up to the hospital to see his mother tomorrow morning, or rather *this* morning." Curtis looked at a clock on the wall. It was just after one o'clock in the morning.

"We'll get Will back to his boat, straight away," said Jim with a smile.

33

Barrington Place in St. John's was a quiet cul-de-sac in the city's east end. Curtis and Susan had lived there for years, renovating the wooden house when it deteriorated through normal wear and tear, or when styles changed.

When Susan opened her eyes, it wasn't because of street noise. She saw that it was quite bright in their bedroom, but that was normal for early summer in St. John's. Then she realised Curtis had suddenly rolled out of bed.

"You're not getting up now, are you?" she asked with surprise. She looked at the bedside wind-up alarm clock. It indicated seven o'clock.

"You know me," said Curtis. "A couple of hours of solid sleep, then I thrash around thinking about things."

"Well, I thought I knew you," said Susan with a sly smile, lying back on the pillow.

Their reunion had been intense and passionate. They were both relieved that Curtis had made it home safely. It had been like when the kids had been small and close by, and they didn't want them to hear. They had told each other 'Shish, be quiet!' a lot.

Curtis laughed, then he said, "Well, it's *great* to be home, and with you again." He leaned over to kiss her on the nose. Then he said, "We haven't eaten since well before we reached the harbour. I'll start putting a breakfast together. I don't imagine the others will get up for a while."

Kelvin and Ryan had both 'partially' moved away from home. Where they lived depended upon the status of frequently turbulent relations with girlfriends. Last night, both sons had decided to stay at the Barrington Place house. Odvar and Malcolm, of course, had nowhere else to go. They had welcomed Curtis' offer to move in for a while.

When the police dropped them off at the house, Susan had lit some candles, and they had a round of beers. Then they enjoyed some Scotch whisky with many toasts to each other, and to Susan. And then Susan had escorted each of them by flashlight to a bed where they could 'crash out'.

"I'll give you a hand, Curtis," said Susan, jumping up and throwing the covers to the side. Then she warned, "It's a bit like camping now. It will give us a chance to talk for a while. You can take a shower, but it will be a *cool* one. They're rotating the power in St. John's, two hours in the morning, and four hours overnight for us here. But at least we have *some* power now. It should come on again shortly."

When they reached the kitchen, Curtis tried the light switch, and was surprised that it worked. Then he asked Susan, "So, what can we make for breakfast?"

"Well, we've got boxed milk and juice, and butter and eggs in one of the coolers," said Susan. Then she said, "I've been making ice in the freezer when the power is on. We've got pancake mix, and bologna which we could fry up. And 'we fishermen wives' all got together two nights ago, to bake some bread. It'll be a bit stale now, but it should toast up all right.

"I've been making 'cowboy coffee' using the barbecue on the deck when the power has been off. But we can use the drip coffee maker right now, of course. There's a 'boil water order' in effect. The city's filtration and chlorination station is not working, but there *is* water pressure, as you know from the shower you just had."

"That sounds pretty good, actually," said Curtis. He started pulling bowls and pans out of cupboards. Then he asked, "So, what's happening with the food supply in town?"

"Well, some stores are still open, but the prices are 'sky-high', and the shelves are almost empty," said Susan sadly. Then she said, "Some supermarkets have become 'food banks'.

"At least twenty per cent of the people in St. John's were at or near the poverty line before all of this happened. A *lot* of people are in a *really* bad way." Her voice cracked a few times when she was talking.

Curtis stopped what he was doing to give her a big hug.

Then Susan said, "On the plus side, the chicken farms and the dairies are still working. Some churches have organised buses to take people blueberry picking. I went with your sisters and your mother one day. Your oldest sister thought we should pretend to be Catholic when we saw where our bus came from!" Susan and Curtis laughed together.

"But that didn't matter, of course," Susan continued. Then she said, "We knew half the people on the bus, and we were welcomed. Your family is doing okay. Your mother gets bounced around between them, they all want to take care of her."

Susan moved about the kitchen, setting the table. As she was working, she said, "They're letting some fishermen go out on the ocean, and they've got volunteers to help with salting and drying. That just about became a 'lost art', as you know. Most of the salt fish goes to the food banks. They're letting some people take a moose, but not within the city boundary. We are allowed to keep a quarter, but the rest has to go to the food banks, where most of it gets bottled. There is bottled seal meat in the food banks, too. We've been asked to cut up and plant potatoes rather than eat them. Most people are doing that. Every packaged vegetable seed in town has been planted, too."

"Is there any talk of a container ship, or a tanker?" asked Curtis.

"Yes to both," said Susan. Then she said, "A tanker is supposed to arrive next week, with diesel and aviation gas. They say they'll start running city buses after it unloads, which will really help. I used up the gasoline in the garage in our portable generator before the power came back on. The big propane tank under the deck is probably still almost full. I haven't been using the fireplace, just the barbecue. They're not even *talking* about the Come by Chance refinery, it must be really 'messed up'.

"The stuff in the freezer is all gone. I used some of the food myself, and shared the rest with family and friends. A container ship is supposed to arrive after the tanker. But it will take a *long* while to get the stores stocked up again. Things are really depleted."

"So, is our truck still working?" asked Curtis.

"Yes, the truck works, and I drove it until it got low on gas, or diesel rather," said Susan.

Curtis had the bologna cut up into slices, and it was starting to sizzle in a frying pan. Susan had the pancake mix stirred up in a big bowl.

"Probably best to scramble the eggs?" asked Curtis.

"Yes," said Susan. "We better get everyone up though before we start that."

"What about money, how's that working?" asked Curtis.

"Well, you can usually get as much as you want in cash now from your own bank," said Susan. Then she added, "And people are accepting cheques again. Electronic banking and the ATM machines are not working yet, though."

Curtis started making pancakes in another frying pan, and Susan started making toast. Ryan suddenly came through the door that led to the basement stairs. He rubbed his eyes, and said, "What are you folks at?"

"Making *your* breakfast, of course," said Curtis with mock anger. Then he laughed, and asked, "Ryan, do you think you could wake the others for us? It won't take long now, and the power will go off some time soon."

"No sweat," said Ryan, and went off to wake the others.

"How are your brother, Matt, and his family coping?" asked Curtis. Susan's relatives lived in a community on Trinity Bay. Both of her parents were dead. Her brother was a federal fisheries officer.

"Best kind," said Susan happily. Then she said, "Matt was driving around yesterday morning in a Fisheries truck. He stopped by for a cup of coffee. He told me was he going up on a patrol plane this morning. He said he would drop by again this afternoon on his way home.

"He said he was on a flight last week that flew over the lodge for some reason, but he didn't see anybody. Maybe you had already left?" Ryan had walked back into the room and heard what she just asked.

"Probably," said Curtis while looking directly at Ryan. "We didn't see or hear any airplane."

"That was really nice of the police to give you a lift here from the dock," said Susan. Then she said, "It was also good of them to bring over the message you sent to a Ham radio operator."

"Yes, it was," said Curtis. Then he added, "They met us at the dock, and asked us what it was like up in Labrador, and what we had seen on the trip back. And they could see we had no ride." Susan seemed content with his short answer. Ryan had 'clued in', and he said nothing.

"Do you think your brother, Matt, could drive us to a travel agent in town before he heads home?" asked Curtis. Then he explained, "I really want to give Odvar and Malcolm some hope, you know, that they can get out of here soon."

"I don't think that will be a problem," said Susan. Then she said, "That's kind of the way people have been getting around anyway, bumming rides from people fortunate enough to have a working vehicle with fuel in it. The government is 'turning a blind eye' to the practice when their employees help other people out."

"The other thing I should do with Kelvin today is try to figure out if we can brew and bottle beer down at the plant, with only six hours of power a day," said Curtis. Then he laughed and said, "Hey, maybe they'll give us more power if we tell them we're performing an 'essential public service'?"

"Doubtful," said Susan slowly with a straight face, then a laugh.

34

Dwayne Cartwright had just started cleaning his jet-boat on the beach below the Owl River salmon lodge. The boat didn't really need to be cleaned, but it was a nice morning, and there was not much else to do.

When he heard the helicopter approaching from down river, he climbed out of his boat and started wading in his tall rubber boots along the edge of the beach. It was actually easier to stay in the water than scramble over the slippery boulders and scraggy brush. He looked up to see the helicopter descending for a trial pass over the little clearing he had just made for a temporary helipad.

The helicopter was red and white, but it was not marked otherwise. When Dwayne reached the little brook, he crossed it easily. The water level was way down, and he knew which route to take to stay on firm, gravel bottom.

The helicopter was on final approach as Dwayne was forcing his way through thick alder bushes beside his 'helipad'. He averted his eyes to avoid all the dirt and debris the helicopter downdraft was stirring up.

Dwayne was surprised when he saw his father was in the helicopter. Besides the pilot, there were two other men in the machine. Dwayne waited until the rotors had fully stopped before approaching the front left door where his father was sitting.

Walter and Dwayne worked together to open the door. "We just thought we would drop by, Dwayne, how are you?" asked Walter with a big grin.

"Just fine, Dad," said Dwayne. "How are you?"

"Good too," said Walter, as he stepped out of the helicopter. Then he said, "I'm going to be working with these guys for a while." He turned to look at the two men in the back seats. The two men just smiled back. "They would like to have a look around, if that's okay?" asked Walter. "Maybe we could go up to the lodge, and talk for a while?"

"Sure, Dad," said Dwayne. "Diane can make us some fresh coffee."

The pilot stepped out of the helicopter through his front right-side door. Then he slid open the door to the back seats. He helped the two men get out of the helicopter. One man was in some kind of uniform without badges. The other man was dressed in casual clothes, and was wearing a light jacket. Neither man was wearing rubber boots.

Walter always wore his rubber boots, and he stashed moccasins wherever he thought he might want to take them off.

When Dwayne recognised the situation, he said, "We'll have to pole ourselves across the brook in a camp-boat. If you follow me, I'll take you to the boat. It's on the bank of the river below the rapids."

"I'll stay here with my 'osprey'," said the pilot with a grin. "I brought my own lunch."

The path to the camp-boat went by Rob, who was standing up to his knees in the river at the bottom of some fast water. He was wearing some old, patched-up hip waders, and fumbling around with a fly-rod.

"I didn't know you were a salmon fisherman, Rob," said Walter pleasantly. "How are you?"

"I'm just *fine*, Mr. Cartwright!" said Rob happily. Rob smiled and nodded at the two strangers who were with Dwayne and Walter. Then he said to the two men, "Hello there, it's a fine morning, isn't it?" The two visitors just smiled and nodded back at him.

"I know nothing about salmon fishing, Mr. Cartwright," Rob continued. "But the river is suddenly *full* of sea-run trout, and they 'come savage for a fly', as the guides say, no matter if it's actually a *salmon* fly tossed at them by an *amateur*!" Rob opened a basket on the bank behind him, and they could see half-a-dozen fair-sized trout inside.

"Okay, we'll leave you to it, then," said Walter with a laugh. "Have fun!"

When they got to the camp-boat, Dwayne and his father waded into the quiet water and pushed it off the sand beach over to a rock ledge. Then Dwayne said to the two guests, "You guys can step into the boat from this rock. Please step into the centre of the boat so we don't flip it, and then sit together in the middle."

When the two men were seated, Walter and Dwayne swung their legs into the boat and stood up. They grabbed some oars, and used them to push the five metre long aluminium boat towards the beach below the lodge. There was no motor on the boat, as the water was too shallow to use one.

When they had the boat pulled up on the beach, they helped the two visitors to step out so they could keep their shoes dry.

"Would it be all right if we had a look around the place ourselves?" asked the man with the uniform, while pulling a small digital camera from his pocket.

"No sweat," said Dwayne. "Have at it."

Dwayne and his father then went off on their own. They went up on the refurbished deck and sat down. Diane brought them each a cup of fresh coffee. After a few sips of coffee, Walter said, "I might have some paying guests for you, Dwayne. Maybe a *lot* of guests."

"That would be great, Dad!" said Dwayne. Then he said, "I think Rob and Diane would like to hear that. I told them I was going to wait two more weeks to see if anyone would be coming this year. Curtis will be glad, too."

"These *guests* will probably want to stay for a couple of *months*, so you'll have to stay open longer than you ever have before," said Walter quietly. Then he added cryptically, "And they won't need guides because they won't be fishing. And you won't be able to have any other guests here while they're here."

"Are they involved in the investigation?" asked Dwayne.

Walter just nodded.

"Okay, so no more questions about that, I get it," said Dwayne. Then he smiled, and asked, "So, how's Mom?"

"Oh, she's *really* busy," said Walter. Then he added, "She's running the hotel, with some extra part-time help. And she's keeping the restaurant going, too. Your Rachelle is helping her out, when the baby is sleeping. The place is completely filled up, and under very tight security." He paused for a moment, then added, "I think that's what you should get ready for here, too."

"Okay, then I'll need some more help to run the lodge," said Dwayne. He sat silently for a while, clearly thinking about all of the issues he was suddenly facing.

Walter let Dwayne have a minute to absorb all of the new information, then he said, "The two guys with me will want to talk to Rob and Diane now. They'll also want to talk to anyone you want to bring in from town."

"I understand, Dad," replied Dwayne quietly.

Walter was staring hard at the river. He suddenly looked sad, so Dwayne asked, "What's wrong, Dad?"

"Maybe it's the same with every disaster, I don't know," Walter said slowly. Then he said, "A few lucky people actually come out ahead, somehow." He met Dwayne's gaze, and added, "I'm feeling *guilty as hell*, Dwayne. The village is still a complete mess, and a lot of people are really struggling."

Dwayne squeezed his father's left forearm with his hand, and said "Well, you've had your share of hardship too. I remember when the hotel burned down."

Walter smiled, then said, "Yes, and we rebuilt it, didn't we? That took years of hard work after years of hard work. But here we are! Well-equipped and 'Johnny on the Spot' to help some rich people with some very important work to do."

35

The next morning, the incident response section leaders met again for their daily meeting. It was held as usual in a cordoned-off section of the big hall and bar in Walter Cartwright's hotel.

"Can we have an update now on the progress made by your peripheral team?" asked the Deputy Incident Commander.

"Okay, we have some more about Mr. Weldon Purdy," said the Operations Section Leader. He stood up and looked at some handwritten notes. Then he said, "Let's see, he was recruited by the US Army in New Orleans, as an 'out of work eighteen-year-old'. He had crossed the border as a 'tourist' at Houlton, Maine. He didn't have a driver's licence at the time, so we don't know how he did that, but maybe he was riding a Greyhound bus. The recruiter thinks he remembers from his notes that Weldon had some money, and sort of looked the part of a tourist. A 'scraggly, beat-up' looking one though." The group chuckled.

Then the OSL said, "You do not need to be an American citizen to join the US Army. He had a Canadian birth certificate, was physically fit and he had no criminal record. He put 'None' on the application form for both 'Parents Names' and for 'Religion'.

"He quickly qualified as a 'sharpshooter', saw combat duty, and was a '*really* good sniper'. His sergeants described him as a 'loner', and, 'not leadership material'. So he stayed a private, but never complained about that, at least not officially."

The OSL took a big gulp of ice water before continuing. It was a warm, sunny morning outside, and the hotel was not air conditioned. He wiped his brow with some paper towel, then he said, "But after four years, he applied for a Rangers special forces unit. They took a harder look at him. He put 'Druid' for 'Religion' on the application form this time. So, either he had some form of weird revelation in the 'regular' army, or he had developed a strange sense of humour. He scored very highly on aptitude tests, 'off the chart' was the comment from one examiner. But they failed him on the psychological and behavioural tests. The 'loner' thing again, and, 'clearly anti-social, perhaps dangerously so.'"

The OSL stopped to look at the faces around the table. He was pleased to see everyone was clearly paying close attention. Then he said, "Then the Central Intelligence Agency approached him. They would not tell us why they did so, or how they found out about him. He spent *four years* with them. He worked in 'Central America'. The Agency said he had a girlfriend when he was in the US, but he never married her, according to their records."

The OSL put his notes back on the table, stretched his back muscles, and then he said, "After four years, he asked to leave the CIA. They released him, 'in good standing'. They don't seem willing to say more about him, other than they have found no connection to a terrorist organisation, 'yet'."

"I'll press a few buttons, and see if they'll 'cough up' some more information about him," said the Incident Commander.

The OSL nodded, then continued. "Twenty-eight years ago, he crossed back into Canada at Sarnia, Ontario in a car with Tennessee plates. He had a Canadian passport, issued in Washington, D.C., and a Tennessee driver's licence. There is no evidence that he brought a woman back with him. Of course, she could have been hiding in the trunk, or something. We have nothing right now to help us figure out who his wife or girlfriend was, or is. There are *lots* of missing women in the US and Canada, unfortunately. He put Newfoundland plates on the car three months later. He never crossed the border again. And he never filed taxes in Canada, but he filed twice in the US. His declared US income was just what the US Army paid him as a Private."

"Anything back from the autopsy?" asked the DIC.

"Just preliminary, they're doing more analyses," said the OSL. Then he said, "Probable cause of death was 'electrocution'. The body was badly burned, even melted a bit. He had no tattoos or other distinguishing marks. He was filthy, lice-ridden, with poor hygiene, bad teeth and no dental work. Probable age was early to mid-fifties, that matches up. There was no ID on him, not even a wallet. They took DNA and forensic samples.

"The other body was a male, probable age late teens. Again no ID on the body. There were no tattoos or other distinguishing marks. He had the same poor hygiene as Weldon. Preliminary DNA analyses, 'strongly suggests a father-son relationship'. Probable cause of death also was 'electrocution'. He was malnourished and had numerous vitamin deficiencies. If he was Weldon's son, there is no birth certificate to support that. He may not have been born in a hospital."

"Okay, so, loner, anti-social, trained killer, tax evader, mostly outside of 'the system' and 'under everyone's radar'," summarised the DIC. Then he said, "He was a very scary dude. What else?"

"Well, we should add, 'mechanical genius' and 'master thief' for sure," said the OSL. Then he explained, "His home-made 'hover plane' is brilliant, and an original design. A lot of the documents at the site were library books that he 'forgot to return'. He wrote a lot of notes in them, which might prove to be useful for us. He *definitely* had an obsession for Nikola Tesla. He also had books and documents that have been reported stolen from universities and private collections."

"There was no document titled, 'How and Why I Did the Dastardly Act', unfortunately. There was no suicide note. There were a lot of scribbled notes with calculations and sketches on them. A lot of the electrical stuff was definitely stolen from Muskrat Falls, and other electric utility installations and warehouses in the province. He didn't bother to scrape off or paint over serial numbers and labels. That probably means he either did not expect to get caught, or he figured he would do his 'dirty deed' before he got caught."

"I can add to that a bit," interjected the Planning Section Leader, while standing up.

"Okay, we are about to get to Planning," said the DIC. He was mildly annoyed at the PSL. He liked to be in total control of the meetings he chaired. Then he asked, "Is there anything else we need to know right now from Operations?"

"Well, we've just started poking around his house too, you know, the place down near the estuary of the river," said the OSL. Then he added, "We secured it immediately of course, and so far it looks to be untouched by thieves or anyone else. I think we'll be able to update everyone about what we find there in our next meeting."

"Okay," said the DIC. "Let's hear from planning now."

The PSL had remained standing. She looked a bit anxious and impatient. She said, "We wondered how he moved the heavier stolen stuff around. It's clear that he disassembled things, presumably to make them easier to move. He either unfastened bolts and screws, or cut things up with a hack saw or a welding torch. Then he put things back together again, sometimes differently to create another kind of device.

"Some of the things at the site are very elaborate. We have *no idea* yet what some of the devices he made did. Some are obviously induction coils, transformers, capacitors, resistors, switches, breakers, *et cetera*, electrical devices of all kinds. And there are solid state and tube amplifiers, and circuit boards, electronic stuff. And there are mechanical devices of all kinds, too.

"We don't understand how it all worked together as a system, or independently for that matter. If there are control systems, they are original designs."

She stopped to look directly at the DIC, then said, "We're going to try modelling it as a system with computers after we have it fully mapped out. The forensic experts are *really* helping us with the site mapping effort. But we may actually have to work with physically-reconstructed equipment and mock-ups.

"I'll close with this today, this is not going to be easy to sort out, and it will take us some time."

36

Curtis was sitting with Susan's brother, Matthew, in the front seat of a 'Fisheries and Oceans Canada' pickup truck. It was parked outside a travel agent on Water Street in downtown St. John's. Odvar and Malcolm had been inside the travel office for twenty minutes.

Curtis and Matt had been talking about family and friends. They were both being careful about what they were saying.

"So, are they keeping you busy, Matt?" asked Curtis.

"Yes, they are," replied Matt tentatively. "But we're mostly assisting with coastal patrol now. I can't talk much about it."

"I understand," said Curtis while nodding slowly.

"I told Susan we flew up the Owl River," said Matt. "I probably shouldn't have done that."

"She told me," said Curtis. "I think just to say you hadn't seen us."

"How did you guys get on?" asked Matt. He was looking straight ahead through the windshield.

"I can't talk about that either," said Curtis. "They made us swear an oath. I probably shouldn't even have said that."

"There's a lot of this kind of secrecy on the go," said Matt.

They both sat in silence for a minute. There were very few people on the sidewalks, and only the occasional truck moving along the street.

"We had to leave the company van up there," said Curtis. Then he added, "I don't think anyone will be asking about it for a while yet. The trip back by boat went pretty smoothly. We didn't see many ships on the ocean."

"Yes, it's still that way," said Matt.

"How are things around Trinity Bay?" asked Curtis.

"Well, fishing for food, and sealing for food, are wide open," said Matt. Then he explained, "The cod fish have come back, and there has been no shortage of seals since the Europeans stopped buying fur coats. No one is abusing the relaxation of regulations.

"It's kind of like the unofficial moose system during hunting season. A lot of people are unable to go fishing or sealing, but others do it for them, and gladly. We're letting them do all that of course. If whales were still common in the bay, we would let them go after them too. It would be a hell of a lot worse if we didn't.

"But people are mostly keeping their spirits up. You knew my nephew has always been into sea trout fishing in the bay, didn't you? Well, he's an even *bigger* hit now with his friends. They supply the gas and some lunch, and he's the 'tour boat Captain'. They take a rifle with them too, in case they see a seal. They might have to start rowing him around in a dory soon," Matt laughed, but then was serious again. He said, "Some people are already doing that. But they're not trolling for sea trout."

"Here they come," said Curtis, as Malcolm and Odvar came out of the travel office. They climbed into the back section of the 'crew cab' truck. They were both smiling. Matt started the truck and pulled away from the kerb.

"How did you get on?" asked Curtis, turning around to look at his foreign guests.

"Well, a really friendly lady thinks she can help us both," said Odvar. Then he said, "She thinks the best thing for me will be a bus ride to Halifax, then get on a converted liner to Hamburg. Then, either take a ship or an airplane to Bergen, depending upon what the situation is like when I get across the ocean."

"She thinks the best thing for me is to get on the same bus with Odvar to Halifax," said Malcolm. Then he said, "She's working on booking short-hop planes for me starting in Halifax. There might be more bus rides as well needed to get me to Houston.

"The bus to Halifax is the most uncertain part. A tanker with diesel is supposed to be here in a week's time. They hope to start another ferry working across the Cabot Strait in three days' time."

"Well, you know you're more than welcome to keep staying with us as long as you need to," said Curtis. "And I kind of got you into this mess, after all."

"No, you didn't, Curtis," said Malcolm forcefully. Then he said, "*No one* saw this coming. And after all, I *did* experience some salmon fishing!"

"And I've got a *hundred* more interesting stories to tell people now!" added Odvar with a laugh. Then he remembered his 'oath of secrecy', but decided not to correct himself with Matthew in the truck.

"Where to now, gents?" asked Matt.

"Oh, sorry, Matt!" said Curtis. "Could you drop us all off at the brewery? Kelvin thinks he has a way to get us home from there later."

"You've got it," said Matt happily. He turned the truck to go up a steep hill away from the harbour.

37

While Matt was driving Curtis, Malcolm and Odvar around St. John's, Walter was piloting one of the salmon lodge boats. He was escorting the Logistics Section Leader to Weldon's house. It was on a high ridge, downstream from The Chute, and only accessible by a trail that ran down to the Owl River estuary.

Walter decided to approach Weldon's old landing area by working his way upstream. He figured he would have better control of the boat that way in the fast ebb tide current.

"Okay, please stand up in the bow now sir, and step out when we nudge up on the beach," said Walter as they were approaching a narrow gap between two huge boulders.

When the bow eased into soft sand, the LSL stepped out cautiously. An armed guard suddenly appeared out of the woods near the landing area. Walter stopped the engine and pulled the propeller out of the water. Then he walked forward and stepped off the boat at the bow. The guard helped them drag the boat further up on to the beach. Then Walter threw a grapple into some boulders and tied the anchor-line off to the bow-cleat.

"I'll go and fetch the Operations Section Leader," said the guard. Then he said, "Please stay here until I come back with him. Some other guys you can't see are keeping a lookout."

The mosquitoes were pretty bad at Weldon's old place. Walter and the LSL both sprayed some 'fly dope' on their exposed skin. The spruce forest here was thick, and it ran right down to the water.

After five minutes, they could see their guard and the OSL walking down a broad path towards them. "Thanks for coming, guys," said the OSL in greeting. Then he said pleasantly, "I'd like to hear what you both think of some things we have found here."

It was a hot, sunny day. It felt hotter on the trail because they could no longer feel the breeze. The mosquitoes got thicker as they climbed upwards and further into the forest.

"The breaking news is we just found a grave behind the house," said the OSL, while swatting mosquitoes off his arms and neck. Then he said, "'Forensic' has that all taped off."

Further along, the OSL pointed up at a strange-looking black box on a tree branch overhanging the trail, and said, "That's a homemade, electric-eye motion sensor that he installed. There are ten more around the perimeter of his Crown lease. The electric-eyes are all tied into a bell alarm in his workshop. There are trip wires in a few places too, not for setting off land mines, thank God, just for triggering the central alarm."

"This is just like the path up to the other investigation site," said Walter. "Look at all this *crap*, it's another junk yard!"

The OSL stopped at a small clearing on the right side of the trail. "Have a look at this thing," he said.

After crawling around for a careful look, Walter said, "It looks like he put four high-performance snowmobiles together. The four treads would work independently, allowing the rig to work over rough terrain. But it looks like everything was controlled using just one of the machines, so that's where he must have sat. I've never seen anything like this before, it's ingenious as hell! Judging by the hitch on it, and that big sled over there, I'd say he used it for pulling heavy loads in the winter."

"So, how much could he pull with it, do you think?" asked the OSL.

"Well, it would put out about three hundred horsepower," said Walter. Then he said, "Maybe it could do as well as a pickup truck on a dirt road? I would guess it could move a tonne of mass or more, depending upon the snowpack, and the condition of the trail. The river freezes over every winter, and the snow doesn't melt until spring. So, with care, he could have hauled heavy things from here up to the other place."

"There's something like it near the workshop, only with 'quad ATVs' linked together to pull a wagon or skid," said the OSL. Then he said, "There are *twenty-one individual* snowmobiles here as well. Some of them some work, but most are abandoned in the surrounding woods. And there are *eleven* individual ATVs, some of those are old, three-wheeled jobs. We counted *thirty-three* outboard motors, and *eight* aluminium boats. It's the same deal with those. A few are in working order, while the others are broken and have been stripped for parts, or worn out completely and abandoned in the woods."

They continued walking up the steep path. They could see a large clearing up ahead.

When they reached the top of the hillcrest, the OSL said, "Here we are at the homestead, finally. The house is not much to look at, is it?"

The house had obviously started out small, but additions had clearly been made over many years, both upwards and outwards. Nothing matched; the siding, shingles, windows and doors were all different, and nothing had been painted.

"But the workshop and warehouses are something else entirely," said the OSL. He started pointing at places around them. He said, "That's a water tank, and an electric pump. The water tank has an electric heat-tracing wire in it to keep it from freezing up in the winter. He dug a well nearby, by hand. He buried plastic pipe about two metres deep to move water around his place. He must have used a jack hammer in places where the rock is exposed. There is a sawmill in that building over there, with air-drying racks and a huge wood or sawdust stove. He could make rough lumber for construction in there, including beams. There is some lumber drying in the racks."

They walked further along.

"That's a pile of firewood obviously, a very large pile," said the OSL while pointing. Then he said, "He used that chainsaw and axe, at least for some of the pile. There are about *thirty* old chainsaws in the woods around here too.

"That's where animals were skinned, and furs were put on racks for curing, as you can see. *That* is obviously an outhouse, with two abandoned ones beside it. There are no toilets, and no hot water plumbing. So, not a lot of effort was put into providing 'creature comforts'."

The OSL stopped to wipe his brow with the back of his right wrist. He was wearing a long-sleeved shirt, presumably to dissuade the ravenous biting insects from a free lunch. Then he pointed and said, "That's an incinerator, but it's been modified pretty ingeniously to eliminate smoke. There are a lot of moose and caribou bones by the incinerator, and other animal skeletons. It looks like people have been here for a long time, judging by the volume of material that has been burnt-up or 'pooped-out'." As they walked further along, the LSL stumbled on an old stump; the ground was pretty rough.

"That's a generator shack," continued the OSL. Then he explained, "The AC generator is 100 KVA, and diesel-powered. It is bigger than he needed, even if he ran everything here at once. It's also not working. It looks to have been damaged by the 'electrical storm'. That's a diesel tank. That's a gasoline tank. There are smaller tanks on sleds and wagons around those bigger tanks, presumably for 'collection' operations."

They continued walking along. "Okay, now it gets more interesting," said the OSL. "This is one of three 'warehouses'. Have a look inside this one." The men walked over to a large dilapidated shack on their left.

It was dark inside the shack, but there was a flashlight standing upright on the floor just inside the door. The OSL turned on the flashlight and panned it around. Inside the wooden structure was a separate cage made of welded re-bar and steel mesh, with a metal door, and a stout latch and padlock. The OSL said, "This shed is full of boxed up generators, electric motors, electrical parts for two-stroke and four-stroke engines, light bulbs, batteries, the list goes on and on. Not 'mad scientist' stuff. Rather, electrical stuff one would need for living here year round, for a long time. We are still checking police records, but we've already found a lot of stolen stuff. The cage is very stoutly grounded. Our experts say it is a 'Faraday Cage', a kind of electrical shield. Now, what does that suggest?"

"That old Weldon wanted to protect some valuable equipment and spares from a solar storm, or his own electrical storm, and maybe shaking ground to some degree," said Walter. Then he added, "And he thought there would be a tomorrow, and he could 'hit the ground running again' while everyone else was struggling."

"That's what we think, too," said the OSL. "And maybe something went wrong, and his plans were ruined?"

"I bet my son and Curtis Furlong would like to have a look inside here," said Walter. "Some of this may have come from the Owl River Salmon Lodge."

"Yes, I bet they would like to poke around in here," said the OSL shaking his head slowly. "But that's not going to happen, it's all evidence now."

They went back outside. "Those are the other two 'warehouses'," said the OSL pointing them out. Then he said, "There are a lot of canned and sealed dry-food containers in them, including flour and beans. And homemade bottled food too, mostly meats like salmon, caribou and moose. There are also bottles of seal meat and seal blubber, presumably to prevent scurvy. He poured a concrete floor in both shacks. It would be difficult for rats and other animals to get into them. He lined the inside of the wooden shacks with sheet metal. There are also cans of cooking oil inside, and jugs and jugs of motor oil and two-stroke engine mix-oil."

They continued walking along. "And this *monstrosity* is a 'mother' of a workshop," said the OSL. He motioned them to follow him over to a large barn-shaped building. He said, "We've got our own portable generator running to light it up and blow some air around inside. It's hotter than *hell* in there. He must have worked a lot with the windows and doors opened in the summer. He did not install air-conditioning, or electric heat for that matter, anywhere. There are a few small air-blowers around some of the machines inside. There is a large wood stove in there, and smaller ones in the house, and in the warehouses, all homemade. 'Forensic' is working inside this building now, so I can't take you in there, but have a peek inside the door."

The door was propped open. They could see groups of people working in teams inside. They were wearing full-body suits with attached hoods, rubber gloves, boots and masks.

"The building is fifty metres long and ten metres wide," said the OSL. Then he said, "This is by far the best made building on the site, even though it looks like a 'crappy' old barn from the outside. He installed a reinforced-concrete floor in a few places. He has used homemade steel girders within a wooden frame, either bolted or welded together. There is a *full* machine shop in there, including a metal lathe and a milling machine. There are overhead hand-operated cranes and pulleys. There is a welding shop. There is a sheet metal shop. There is an electronics bench with multi-meters and oscilloscopes, and even an antique tube-tester. There is a big, handmade double garage door on the other side." They continued walking along the right side of the big building. Walter and the LSL were trying to look through greasy windows while the OSL was talking.

"That's a stolen satellite dish," said the OSL pointing at the roof. Then he said, "He was stealing satellite service for television. It looks like he basically lived in the workshop building, at least recently. There is a cot inside. There is a kitchen of sorts, with a sink, an old electric stove with an oven, a freezer and a refrigerator. There is an old cathode-ray television and an old multi-band tube radio. He put up an antenna as you can see for the radio." The OSL stopped walking and looked hard at Walter then the LSL.

"There are no telephones of any kind here, or at the other investigation site," the OSL continued slowly. "There are no calculating machines, or personal computers at either place. He did not access the internet. We found three old-fashioned slide rules, two here, and one at the other site. There is an old optical survey transit here, and some long tape-measures. There were no GPS devices found anywhere. There were no CB radios found anywhere."

The OSL seemed to have finally run out of things to say.

"So, what's in the house?" asked Walter.

"It looks like someone was using a bed in one of the bedrooms," said the OSL while starting to walk again. Then he exclaimed, "But it's a horrible mess! There is thick dust and dirt everywhere. There are mice in it. A porcupine is living underneath it. It sounds like the animal is eating away at the floor! There was a lot of paper garbage but no food garbage inside. We've gone through all of the paper in the house and the workshop. We haven't found any documents like those that were found at the other place." The OSL motioned for them to follow him back towards the house.

"We did not find a bible or any other religious books, anywhere," continued the OSL. "There were no household appliances inside the house. There is a wash tub with a hand-wringer in a back porch, and a clothesline at the back door. We found men's and boy's clothing inside, all well-worn or worn-out. We did not find a still, or evidence that he drank, or smoked, or used drugs. There was an unopened beer bottle in the workshop on a high shelf, the type Curtis Furlong makes. There was no pornography found anywhere. There were no pictures on any wall. There is no coffee or tea in his stores."

The OSL stopped walking and looked hard again at Walter and then the LSL.

"So, our conclusion is, the guy lived like a well-behaved monk! I would say 'like a Mennonite' if we had found religious books, and if he had not been using electrical and fuel-powered machinery."

Walter looked up to the sky, and said, "The cleared area would not look 'out of sorts' from above, unless you flew right over and hovered in a helicopter. The big workshop building is certainly out of place though. I must admit I've flown up and down the river many times and don't remember seeing it. And you know, all of these buildings are invisible from the river."

"The big building may be a fairly recent addition," said the OSL. "Or maybe it replaced something less elaborate? We're checking to see if we can find recent and past, aerial and satellite photographs."

"It's all *damned* impressive," said the LSL. "Especially considering how *isolated* this place is, and what he had to work with."

They walked over to a large tent with screen windows. There was a portable chemical outhouse beside the tent. The OSL said, "Walter, in this tent you'll find some coffee and cookies, some bottled water, and a place to sit down. Help yourself to the 'john', too. I want to talk to the LSL for a while, in private.

"As you can well imagine, investigating this place as well as the other one up river has added a *lot* to our logistical headaches."

38

The men were all standing around a blazing firepit out behind Jerome's house. In typical Newfoundland fashion, the men and women had split into separate groups at the start of the dinner party. The power was out again. The women were bouncing between the back deck and the kitchen, telling tales and getting the bulk of the upcoming dinner together. The ladies had lit dozens of candles in the kitchen and set up four 'Coleman' lanterns around the deck.

The men were 'planking' a salmon, and having a few drinks. Jerome's son had caught the salmon on the Gander River while taking a work break with his construction crew buddies. A highway bridge across the Gander River had been damaged by an earthquake, and Jerome's son was working with many others to fix it.

Curtis and Jerome had split the salmon open like a butterfly, and 'wired' it to a board. They had wrapped snare wire around nails placed at the edges of the double fillet to hold it in place on a piece of plywood. The skin-side was facing the board, and the board was propped up nearly vertical at the edge of the firepit. The flesh of the fish was facing the fire.

"We usually like to do this on the river one evening, especially with first-time guests along," said Jerome. Then he laughed, and added, "A few things got in the way of that this year, though!" They all laughed with Jerome.

"We're cooking it with radiant heat, but we're also getting a nice 'hot-smoke' for flavour," explained Curtis to Malcolm and Odvar. "The native people used to do it this way. But I don't believe they used snare wire and nails!"

"You can see it starting to get nicely brown, and it smells *great*!" said Malcolm licking his lips. "This will definitely be a first for me."

"So, are you all set?" asked Fred.

"Yes," replied Malcolm. "The bus for Halifax is leaving tomorrow, and we've both got tickets."

"Well, we hope you come back again soon, and have a happier time with us," said Fred while sipping his beer.

"Malcolm and I have been talking about that with Curtis, and that is something we would like to do," said Odvar. "If there is enough space, I would like to bring my daughter with me next time. And Malcolm would like to bring his son along."

"It may not have been *happy* all of the time, but it was never *boring*!" said Malcolm with a laugh. "And we have made some new friends." He raised his glass in recognition.

"Can we toast to friendship, then?" asked Odvar.

"To friendship!" they all said as they touched their glasses and beer bottles together.

Each man stood looking into the fire for a while, with his own thoughts. It was a fine, clear, cool evening, with no wind. They were wearing sweaters or light jackets, and the warmth of the fire felt good.

"I know we agreed we wouldn't talk about the things that happened up there," said Curtis quietly. Then he said, "But it's probably safe to do that here for a moment. I got a nice call from Constable Lukianow today. Matt arranged for the call to come into a government office in St. John's. Dan sounded in pretty good spirits, and they're getting along okay in the village. He passed the phone over to Walter. Walter said everyone in his family was doing fine, and that he was helping with the investigation. He said the investigation team is using the hotel, and they would like to use the salmon lodge too, paying twice the normal rate. I told him 'no problem with that', as long as Dwayne agrees, and they don't trash the place."

"There's still nothing in the news about the investigation," said Brad quietly, looking around as if someone else could be listening. "And there has been nothing in the news about any possible link between what happened there, and the earthquakes and major electrical damage."

"You've got to wonder how long they can keep doing that," said Jerome. "Or *why* they're doing it, I suppose?"

"I think they're primarily worried about other terrorists getting ideas, you know, to stage a 'copycat' attack," said Malcolm. "That is, if the man up there acted alone."

"Walter said they haven't figured out yet what Weldon did exactly," said Curtis. "That was probably more than he *should* have said. Constable Dan took the phone back from him right after he said it."

"I don't think they can keep the 'Emergency Planning Order' in full effect much longer," said Brad. Then he said, "That is, unless they declare war on someone. Okay, we've never had a solar storm as bad as this one, and they can keep pointing at the storm to explain the electrical and communication catastrophe. But the coincidental major earthquakes at the same time, come on! I bet some smart journalists are just *itching* to start speculating about a 'cover-up'."

The men all nodded in agreement and quietly sipped their drinks.

39

When Malcolm and Odvar were saying their 'final goodbyes' at the bus station, the incident section leaders were having their daily meeting in Walter's hotel.

"So, is anything back yet from the autopsy of the corpse we found at the homestead?" asked the Deputy Incident Commander.

"Just preliminary results have come back so far," said the Operations Section Leader. Then he said, "It was a woman, early forties, died of disease, probably tuberculosis. The grave was marked by an upward pointing arrow made of small logs. The historical experts tell me that was an old European pagan tradition. It looks like the arrow marker was replaced periodically. Maybe Weldon really was a Druid?

"The grave was shallow. The corpse was just laid on exposed rock, and then buried under a mound. Animals might have been able to disturb it, but they didn't. No coffin was used, just a bed sheet. She was probably buried nine or ten years ago. Preliminary DNA work indicates she was probably the young man's mother. More work might lead to positive identification, and a name. Then again, it may not."

"Anything else?" asked the DIC.

"'Forensic' and 'Survey' have finished most of their onsite work," said the OSL. "But I don't want to steal Planning's 'thunder'."

The Planning Section Leader was clearly eager to say something. She was fidgeting, and half out of her seat.

"Okay, over to you now, Planning," said the DIC.

"We've been building computer models in parallel with the onsite investigation work and the physical reconstruction work occurring in the tent at the airport!" said the PSL with excitement in her voice after she jumped to her feet. Then she said loudly, "Our computer models show he may *indeed* have been able to do what we strongly suspect he did!

"His work had *many* original elements! It looks like he used both electrical and mechanical resonance to trigger the earthquakes. This guy would have been welcomed in *any* university if he had chosen a different path!

"It's just too bad, in so many ways," she said sadly.

40

The president of the United States and his chief of staff were sitting on comfortable, leather armchairs in the Oval Office of the White House. The chief of staff had a tidy-looking leather file holder open on his lap.

"The Canadian prime minister is formally asking for more information about the prime suspect's CIA involvement, Mr. President," said the Chief of Staff.

"No, we have to say 'no' to that," said the president. "Maybe we should tell him it is a matter of national security?"

"All right, Mr. President," said the chief of staff. He stopped for a moment for a drink of ice water from a crystal glass. Then he said, "And now, here is what we have all been waiting for. The investigation team now believe they have found the 'smoking gun' so to speak. They believe there is now sufficient information to link the prime suspect, a Mister..." He stopped to look more carefully at his notes.

After a few moments, the chief of staff said, "Sorry, the prime suspect is a native-born Canadian man, named Weldon Purdy. They now think he *caused* the earthquake disasters, and the massive electrical discharges that wiped out the Labrador hydroelectric facilities and made things a *lot* worse throughout our Northeast and Midwest."

"Really!" said the president. "He *caused* all of that! And what do *our* people think about that, I mean the ones we have on their investigation team?"

"They are agreeing with the Canadian hypothesis, Mr. President," said the chief of staff.

The chief of staff waited politely for the president to internalise the stunning news he had just heard.

When the president looked ready again, the chief of staff said, "The Canadian prime minister also intends to wind down or 'lessen' their Emergency Planning Order. They have sort of been at the equivalent of our DEFCON 3 defence readiness up there, except without having to worry about 'nukes' like we have to. He wants to issue a press statement when he relaxes their defence readiness level. The Canadians are willing to issue a press statement *jointly* with us, Mister President."

"And what does your staff think about that?" asked the president.

"They agree, Mr. President," said the chief of staff. "We want to be out ahead of the press on this one."

"Then, what should we say?" asked the president.

"We think we should say we are treating this like the Oklahoma City bombing," said the chief of staff. Then he added, "You know something like, we suspect a terrible act of *domestic* terrorism has occurred in parallel with an unprecedented natural disaster. And we are broadening the investigation in coordination with our friends to the north."

"Okay, I can see the analogy with Oklahoma City," said the president. Then he said, "Only this guy didn't just turn fertiliser into a truck bomb. He brought us to our *knees*, and severely damaged our economy. Recovery will take years! And he killed and hurt *hundreds* of people."

"That's right, Mr. President," said the chief of staff. Then he said, "And *domestic* terrorism may be the worst kind of terrorism. It comes from within. It is the hardest to detect. And it could be the hardest to prevent.

"Also, we might not want to leave the CIA 'off the hook' as you indicated earlier. We do not have a clear profile of the one suspect, and he *worked for the CIA once*."

"So, is this an 'oh shit' moment?" asked the president anxiously. "We may have *trained* this guy? We may not be able to see this *coming again*? And we may not be able to find a way to *defend* against it?"

"It very well could be, Mr. President."

"Oh, *shit*."